OATH OF ALLEGIANCE

Peter J Foot

UPFRONT PUBLISHING
LEICESTERSHIRE

First Published 2002 by
MINERVA PRESS

Second Edition 2002 by
UPFRONT PUBLISHING
Leicestershire

OATH OF ALLEGIANCE

*This book is dedicated to all Royal Marines
past present and future*

Glossary

AW	Amphibious Warfare
BEM	British Empire Medal
BMH	British Military Hospital
CBE	Commander of (the Order of) the British Empire
CO	Commanding Officer
CPO	Chief Petty Officer
DCM	Distinguished Conduct Medal
DSO	Distinguished Service Order
DSC	Distinguished Service Cross
DZ	Dropping Zone
EOKA	Greek Cypriot Terrorist Group seeking union with Greece
FN	Belgium Rifle
GOC	General Officer Commanding
HMS	Her Majesties Ship
ITCRM	Infantry Training Centre Royal Marines
KOYLI	Kings Own Yorkshire Light Infantry
LC2	Landing Craft Second Class (A Qualification)
LCA	Landing Craft Assault
LCM	Landing Craft Mechanised
LCT	Landing Craft Tank
LST	Landing Ship Tank
LVT	Landing Vehicle Tracked
MO	Medical Officer
NAAFI	Navy Army Air Forces Institute
NCO	Non Commissioned Officer
PT	Physical Training
PTIs	Physical Training Instructors
QMS	Quarter Master Sergeant
RASC	Royal Army Service Corps
RM	Royal Marine

RMET1	Royal Marine Education Test One
RMTC	Royal Marine Training Centre
RSM	Regimental Sergeant Major
SBA	Sick Bay Attendant
SBS	Special Boat Squadron
SO	Senior Officer
SLR	Self Loading Rifle
TS	Transmitting Station
USS	United States Ship
WRN	Wren

The Hostile Shore

The USS *Ross* moved to a position within six miles of the North Korean coast and about fifty miles south of the Chinese border. The raiding party of thirty Royal Marines had mustered on the main deck and begun a careful check of their weapons and equipment. The two assault craft, which would take the marines ashore, were lowered to deck level, a quiet word of command and the marines embarked in the craft, fifteen in each plus ten cwt of high explosive which had been loaded earlier.

This was to be the marines' last raid; they had taken part in three operations over the last month, they had blown up two road and one railway bridge, but their task was completed and they were being replaced by a full Royal Marine Commando Unit which had just arrived in Japan and would be operational in the next few days. It would have a strength of three hundred and would be designated as 41 Commando Royal Marines.

The marines in the raiding party would then return to their respective commando units in Malaya where they were engaged in a relentless struggle to defeat the communist terrorists in what was described as the undeclared war.

Now within three miles of the coast, the USS *Ross* reduced its speed just sufficient to maintain steerage-way, and lowered the assault craft into the water and as their shackles were slipped they moved away from the mother ship and headed for the Korean coast.

Twenty minutes later the assault craft grounded on the beach and the marines quickly ran up to the top of the beach and formed a defensive position on the sand ridge, five marines moved off to scout the route to the railway tunnel about four hundred yards away, the marines on the beach began to offload the explosives from the assault craft, when this was completed the two craft returned to the *Ross*. As the aerial photographs had shown, at the top of the beach was a twenty-foot sand ridge then a

7

salt marsh about a hundred yards in width then another high sand ridge beyond that. Three hundred yards away was the railway line and tunnel, the only way across the salt marsh was a track made up of railway sleepers used by local farmers to move seaweed from the beach to use on their fields.

It took the marines an hour to move the explosives from the beach to the railway tunnel and then another hour to place the charges into position halfway along the tunnel length. The first indications of the approaching dawn were evident in the eastern sky. Marine Peter Rhodes looked down from his position on the railway embankment as his fellow marines made the final preparations to blow up the tunnel. Rhodes knew they were running late, the plan had been to withdraw before first light but they were about an hour behind their planned withdrawal.

In the briefing Captain Rogers had said that with a North Korean battalion ten miles to the north if they did not complete the operation in quick time a safe withdrawal would be hard to achieve. Rhodes looked along the sights of his Bren gun at the ridge about three hundred yards away. If the Koreans came, that is where they would first appear.

Sergeant Smith crawled up alongside him and said, 'CO says fuses are set for fifteen minutes. We are falling back now, cover us for another five minutes then follow us back to the beach.' Rhodes nodded his head. Smith left.

'It looks as if we are in the shit, Bob,' said Rhodes as he turned and looked at his No. 2 on the Bren.

'Not the first time is it, but it makes you feel important,' said Bob Jones, smiling.

Rhodes pointed towards the ridge. A line of figures had appeared. He pulled the Bren into his shoulder and fired three bursts. The figures went to ground, but then more appeared. Rhodes finished off the rest of the magazine in three- and five-round bursts.

'Time to go, Pete,' said Jones, and together they slid down the embankment and moved off quickly towards the beach. The Koreans had opened fire but most of their rounds were high. Rhodes and Jones crossed the salt marsh by the sleepered track and took up a firing position on the sand ridge. Suddenly the earth shook as the charges in the tunnel blew. It was spectacular. The hillside slid down and covered the whole of the railway track.

Captain Rogers had split the raiding party into two groups for the withdrawal. Group One was to embark in the first assault craft, with Group Two covering their withdrawal. Rhodes and Jones were in Group Two.

The Koreans had recovered from the shock of the tunnel explosion and were now attempting to rush the salt-marsh track, but Group Two had far too much firepower to allow that.

It was evident to Rhodes that for the second group to get off the beach safely someone would have to stay behind and cover their withdrawal. Captain Rogers moved up alongside them.

'Right you two, leave the Bren with me and get into the assault craft.'

Jones slid down the sand ridge with the others and ran to the waiting assault craft.

'It makes more sense if I stay, sir; anyway, whose the better shot?' said Rhodes, looking at Rogers and smiling.

Rogers turned to him and with a look of relief said, 'I won't let this be forgotten,' and then he was gone.

Rhodes checked his pack. There were six full magazines left plus one on the gun. The Koreans made another rush. Rhodes fired the rest of the magazine and they ducked back behind the ridge, leaving two of their number behind. He glanced back towards the beach and the last craft was about a hundred yards out to sea. Rhodes fired another couple of bursts. He felt strangely calm; almost detached. He would be the third Rhodes to die in the corps. His grandfather had been a corporal and had been killed at Zeebrugge in 1918 and his father, a sergeant, had been killed at Salerno in 1943.

He was coming under quite heavy fire now, just three magazines left. When he got to the last he would fire just single shots. Suddenly Rhodes's world exploded. He was thrown into the air. Something smashed into the side of his head and a great shadow passed over him.

It's the angel of death, he thought, but why all the fucking noise? Another massive explosion rent the air. Another shadow passed over him, there was a shape to it. It was a plane. He began to refocus and marshal his scattered senses. They were planes! He watched as another made its run in from the sea. Its machine guns poured a torrent of fire into the Korean position. The ridge opposite was a smoking mass. Another plane roared over. They were Sea Furies, three to be exact. He looked back out to sea and one of the assault craft was almost back on the beach. They had come back for him.

He gathered up the Bren and the empty magazines and staggered back to the beach. His legs seemed to be going in a different direction to the way he was moving. His head was pounding and blood was running down the side of his face. He took off his green beret.

I don't want to get blood on that, he thought.

Someone was shouting at him and welcome hands dragged him into the assault craft. His fellow marines were talking to him and Bob Jones was trying to tie a field dressing around his head. Rhodes just sat there looking into space, nothing seemed very important any more. He vaguely remembered being helped aboard the USS *Ross* and sitting on a bunk in the sickbay. The American doctor stitching the cut on the side of his head examined his eyes and then his ears. Two sickbay attendants undressed him, washed him down and put a white shirt on him. The doctor gave him an injection and for the second time that day the world of Peter Rhodes slipped away and he fell into a deep, dark, but very comfortable pit.

Rhodes emerged from his deeply sedated world in the early hours of the next morning. He took stock of his surroundings. He was still in the sickbay and was in a cool clean comfortable bunk. His headache had gone and he felt fine, but very thirsty. His movement attracted the attention of the duty sickbay attendant who put on a low light and came over to him.

'How do you feel, son? Would you like something to drink?'

Rhodes asked for something cold. He was given a large glass of chilled fresh orange juice. It was wonderful.

'Go back to sleep now, it's only three o'clock in the morning,' said the SBA. Rhodes complied and quickly slipped back into a deep sleep.

At seven he awoke and was given a breakfast of melon cubes followed by a large steak and two fried eggs. He was being spoiled rotten. He was allowed to dress in hospital shirt and slacks and have a wash and shave. He was seen by the ship's doctor, who told him he was quite happy with his condition and that he could return to the marines' quarters in time for lunch. However, he added that there were some people who wanted to see him. To his surprise the captain of the USS *Ross*, Commander Reinhart, was the first to visit. He was so friendly. He sat on Rhodes's bunk and spoke to him like a father. He told him how proud he and the ship's company were of the operations the Royal Marines had completed while they were on the *Ross*.

The captain explained that when he had learned of a marine still ashore covering the withdrawal of the others, he contacted Naval Air Command who were able to divert the flight of Sea Furies from HMS *Theseus*. They had been lucky, as the aircraft were only available because their original targets were covered in low cloud. He also told him that the *Ross* was now going back to Japan, to the port of Sasebo, and that the marines were leaving the ship and flying back to Singapore via Hong Kong.

As he stood to leave, Commander Reinhart smiled at Rhodes and said, 'I have endorsed Captain Rogers's report on the last raid and in particular the part you played, I'm glad to have met you, son.'

When he left, Captain Rogers and Sergeant Smith came in and they confirmed what the commander had said about flying back to Singapore and added that the marines were to have two days rest and recreation in Sasebo.

'That means two days and nights of drinking and shagging your lugs off,' said Smith.

'Only the single men of course,' said Captain Rogers with a grin.

Later that day, Rhodes returned to the marines' quarters where he was greeted with good-natured shouts of, 'You skiving bastard! We had to clean your Bren and all your equipment. Welcome back, Pete, glad you are in one piece.'

The next day the marines left the USS *Ross*. There was a certain sadness in their departure. When they had first arrived, the ship's company had seemed a little distant. It was, for many of the crew, the first contact they'd had with a British unit. However, after the first operation they had warmed to the marines and this had progressed to a genuine friendship. It therefore came as no surprise to the marines, as they left their mess deck for the last time, that the route to the gangway was lined by the ship's company who shook everyone by the hand. At the head of the gangway Commander Reinhart had a personal word with every marine as they disembarked. On the jetty the marines formed up in three ranks facing the ship. Captain Rogers called the marines up to attention then turned and saluted the USS *Ross* and its company. There was a cheer from the crew as the gesture was appreciated. The marines then turned to the right and marched smartly to the waiting transport which would take them to the holding camp prior to their flight back to Singapore.

The transit camp was administered by the US Army and the marines were welcomed by an American senior NCO who showed them to their accommodation. This comprised of two wooden huts, which were clean and comfortable. He told them where the mess hall, showers and toilets were, then told them what time the bus went into Sasebo for as he said, 'Drinks and Pussy.'

The marines quickly settled into their new surroundings and made their way to the mess hall. The food was great. Steak, chicken or huge pork chops, potatoes (creamed, roasted or fried), peas, beans, cabbage and onions, with apple pie and three flavours of ice cream as a sweet filled the menu, supplemented by fruit juice, milk, tea or coffee. After they had eaten, the marines cleaned themselves up for the liberty run into Sasebo.

They were each issued with a packet of 'French letters' and told that the best place for a good time was The Green Parrot, a nightclub, brothel and bar combined and, what was most important, was inspected daily by the camp medical officer, who, they were told, 'Fucks there too.'

When they arrived in Sasebo they found their way to the Pleasure Palace. It was quite large, the first floor being used as a bar and dance floor, while upstairs were the rooms for personal entertainment. As the evening wore on, more girls arrived, much beer was drunk and the dance floor became a mass of tightly packed male and female bodies. Rhodes and Jones had already selected their partners for the evening, they were both very attractive girls who spoke quite good English. The girl with Rhodes said her name was Mai Ling and she came from a fishing village ten miles from Sasebo. Her hand had been busy under the table stroking the top of Rhodes's leg, the effect of which was soon quite obvious to them both.

She looked at Rhodes and said, 'You big boy, Peter, really big boy.' She then said something to the other girl in Japanese. They both laughed. Rhodes thought of a comment his uncle had made when he told him he was going to join the corps.

His uncle had said, 'You are six foot tall, built like a brick shithouse, and hung like a dockyard donkey, what else would you join except the marines?'

Rhodes took Mai Ling onto the dance floor. She only came up to his chest but fitted her body to him like a tight glove.

When the dance finished she pressed his hand and said, 'Shall we go upstairs now?'

Rhodes nodded and they made their way up. At the top sat an old woman, who in return for some yen gave them a key for room thirty. It was clean and consisted simply of a bed with a white sheet draped across it. Mai Ling kissed him and then removed her clothes; Rhodes followed her example and pulled her to him. They lay on the bed and explored each other's bodies. His cock fascinated her. He had been circumcised when he was a baby and this was the first one she had seen without a foreskin. As their passion reached the limits of control he got on top of her and as she spread her legs he entered her gently at first and then in response to her body thrusting up to him he pushed himself fully into her. She gasped and their bodies danced up and down on the bed. One final massive thrust and he shuddered as they came to a climax together.

They lay there for a few minutes; then Rhodes kissed her gently on the lips.

She said, 'You nice boy, Peter, you see me again?' Rhodes nodded and they got dressed and went downstairs.

It was time to get the bus back to the camp. Rhodes kissed Mai

Ling goodbye. It seemed that the rest of the marines were saying goodbye to their partners. They made their way back to the bus pick-up point. The bus soon came along and in no time at all they were back at the camp.

Sergeant Smith was waiting for them. 'Bad news, lads. The flight's been advanced. We fly back to Singapore tomorrow. Parade for departure at 0900 hours.'

They left for the American Air Force base at about 0930 hours the next morning. It was a two-hour journey and some of the marines slept during the coach trip while others talked quietly to one another. On arrival at the airfield the large variety of military aircraft became a talking point. There were fighters, bombers and large transport aircraft scattered around the place with some deployed for action while others were being serviced. This gave the place a strange mixture of urgency and lassitude.

They were taken to the departure building, given coffee, and told they would embark in about an hour's time. Some quite senior American officers gave the marines some curious glances, two took the trouble to come over and talk to them, the marines stood up as the officers approached.

'Sit down, boys, sit down,' the senior officer said. 'Tell us where you have been, and where you are going.'

For the next half hour they answered all the Americans' questions; the two officers were clearly impressed and said so. The conversation had not been forgotten, for when the marines boarded their aircraft there was no segregation of ranks, Rhodes found himself sitting next to an American Lieutenant Colonel in the Army Air Force; the officer put Rhodes completely at ease and the flight to Hong Kong passed quite quickly. Rhodes had learned a lot about bombing missions and the American officer asked what raiding behind the enemy lines was like. At Hong Kong the American officers left the plane, about ten British officers boarded in their place but occupied seats away from the marines. The flight to Singapore was going to be quite a long one. Rhodes, now with an empty seat next to him, slept for a while, then he began to review in his mind his life since the death of his father, a sergeant in the Royal Marine Commandos at Salerno, in 1943.

The Early Days

He was eleven years old when his father was killed. He remembered coming home from school and finding his mother crying in the kitchen. June, her friend from work, was with her.

His mother said, 'It's your father Peter, he's been reported killed in action in Italy.'

Rhodes remembered putting his arm around his mother and holding her tight; tears ran down his face but he said nothing. June said she would come round again that evening and had left them to their grief.

After a time, things returned to as they had been before his father's death. To a schoolboy in 1943, wartime was exciting. German aircraft still made bombing raids on Chatham dockyard, which was about a mile from where they lived and although the raids were not as frequent as they had been earlier in the conflict, his mother and their neighbour June continued to work in the canteen at Chatham railway station, taking the threat from stray bombs in their stride.

Out of school Rhodes led a very active life, one minute riding his bike to the scene of a crashed aircraft, German or British, the next beginning to learn about girls in the air raid shelter behind the school. Rhodes's best friend was Jack Marks, and after school he would persuade the Dane sisters to visit the shelter with them. They would then play a game of 'dare' starting with them both kissing the two girls. This then became a game of 'You show me yours, and I'll show you mine'. The fact that Rhodes had been circumcised and Jack Marks had not, led to both girls deciding that Rhodes had a bigger one because of the circumcision.

'It lets it grow better,' the girls said.

The boys were then allowed a brief look at the girls 'things' but were not allowed to touch. However, as time went on the girls allowed the boys to touch them but little else. One day Rhodes was alone with Jill Dane when she confided that her elder brother made her play with his 'thing' until she made it 'sick'. Would he like her to do it to him?

Rhodes said, 'Yes, please.' So she did and after some gentle tugs and sharper pulls, it 'spat' some three feet onto the wall of the shelter. Jill was most impressed, but said his 'thing' was too big to push into a girl's 'thing' as it would most likely kill her.

A year after his father's death, Rhodes suffered another hammer blow when an army lorry hit his mother coming home from work in the dark and killed her instantly. Rhodes was devastated. June took him to live with her, and with her kindness life slowly came back to normal. The only direct relative Rhodes had left was his late father's brother. Uncle Bill had a farm at Wouldham about ten miles from Chatham where he lived and worked with his wife, Marie, and son, Mark, who was about the same age as Rhodes. It was agreed he would live with June, but spend the school holidays on the farm, and when he left school he would go there to live and work until he decided what he was going to do with his life.

Rhodes was happy living with June. She was a widow who had married when she was twenty, but her husband, a sailor, had been killed when his ship, HMS *Hood*, was sunk in the early part of the war. She told Rhodes that she and her husband had wanted children but the doctors had told them both that an illness she had as a child would prevent her becoming pregnant. As June was only twenty-five, Rhodes saw her as a sister rather than a foster mother.

The school holidays on his uncle's farm were great fun. He got on well with Mark and his relationship with his Uncle Bill and his Aunt Marie became very close as they treated him like a second son. Rhodes was growing into a big lad; almost six feet tall and well built. His uncle who had been a promising boxer before an incident had left him with a permanent limp, taught the two boys how to box. Rhodes enjoyed boxing more than Mark but it did not affect their friendship. Their lessons took place most evenings for about half an hour.

Aunt Marie was French, and had met Bill Rhodes when he had taken some animals from his then employer to the Brittany area to sell. Marie's father had a large farm near Coutances, and had bought the animals from Bill. In due course he and Marie had married and as a wedding present the wealthy farmer had bought them a small farm in Wouldham in Kent. Both the marriage and the farm had prospered. Aunt Marie never let her love for her country or its language die, every weekend from breakfast time to bedtime on Saturday and Sunday they only spoke in French. Rhodes had no idea what they were talking about but he slowly made progress and began to make himself understood, though his accent made them howl with laughter.

When the holidays were over he returned to live with June, he only had a year left at school now and he had already decided that when he was seventeen he would join the Royal Marines and become the third generation of Rhodeses to serve in the corps. When he told June of his plans, she told him not to make up his mind too soon and not to tell Uncle Bill until nearer the time as he may have plans for him and Mark to run the farm. Rhodes took her advice and kept his plans to himself. He still enjoyed school, was a useful footballer and cricketer and knew some French, which impressed the girls no end.

One of the school bullies, who was even bigger than Rhodes, singled him out one day and called him a 'Frog bastard'. Using the boxing skills his uncle had taught him, Rhodes gave the bully a straight left and a right cross, leaving his would-be assailant sitting on the ground with a bloody nose. As a result, his stock with the girls was never higher, and his ultimate reward came when one of the older girls let him go all the way. She had even provided the 'French letter'. This time the reference to his aunt's homeland seemed most appropriate given what was about to be delivered. In fact it was very satisfying for them both and in spite of Jill Dane's 'life-threatening' fears no damage was done from the coming together.

After this and several similar encounters Rhodes felt very confident with himself and life was good. There was also a change in his feelings towards June. He was becoming sexually attracted to her, but was careful to hide his growing interest from her. Nonetheless, he took a great deal of trouble to watch her when she washed or combed her hair, or straightened her skirt or stockings. Little did he know but she was also becoming aware of him. The months went by and his fourteenth birthday was only a week away, as his birthday was in April, it had been decided that he would leave school when they broke up for the summer holidays.

June and his Uncle Bill thought this was the best time to make a permanent move to live on the farm, though he could always spend a weekend at June's if he wanted to. Rhodes was still very attracted to June and took every opportunity to get close to her, to smell her scent and brush close to her. His birthday came and went, June had bought him a shirt and tie, and when he had tried them on she straightened his tie for him, it was as close to him as she had ever been, and he put his arms around her and kissed her full on the lips.

She tried to pull away but he held her close and she sighed and returned his kiss. That night after he had heard her go to bed he went to her room and got into bed with her; she put her arms out to him and he fell into them. He had never experienced sex like this. June had lived like a nun since her husband had been killed and all the pent-up sexual frustrations that had built up inside her were released that night. Rhodes was stunned by her response but delighted, and felt he was truly in love.

The next morning after another passionate encounter, June told him that what they had done was wrong. Rhodes would not accept this and said it was the result of two people being in love. Over the next week Rhodes began to understand what she had meant. They still made love as often as they could, Rhodes thought it was wonderful, June had taught him so much, and his lovemaking skills progressed in leaps and bounds.

He left school when they broke up for the summer holidays, the war had been over for a year, and things were getting back to normal again. June helped him pack his case for the move to his uncle's farm. She kissed him goodbye and after he had told her he would come back to see her in a fortnight, he left and before turning the corner at the end of the street he looked back. She was still standing in the doorway. He waved and blew her a kiss. She did the same. I'm a man now, thought Rhodes, as he made his way to the bus stop and waited for the bus to Wouldham.

He enjoyed life on the farm, he was strong and a hard worker.

He got on well with his aunt and uncle and had a good friend in their son Mark. He saw June from time to time and their lovemaking was always good, but there were two land girls still working on the farm. One of them made it quite clear to Rhodes she was available and he made love to her a couple of times a week in the hayloft.

The weekend French progressed well and they no longer laughed at his accent. His aunt took the trouble to improve his grammar and Mark and he would often use French in their conversations during the week trying to outdo one another. This delighted Aunt Marie but his Uncle Bill wasn't too pleased, saying, 'You live in England, you know.'

Rhodes was now almost seventeen, he was dreading telling his aunt and uncle of his intention to join the Royal Marines, but strangely enough they seemed to know. When he eventually broke the news they confessed that they had always suspected that he might follow in the footsteps of his father and grandfather; that he would follow his destiny. All the same, the news was not what they wanted to hear. Mark was the most upset, which was understandable as they were almost like brothers.

Rhodes went to the Royal Marine recruiting office a week after his seventeenth birthday and filled in the application forms. Where it said father's name and occupation Rhodes wrote, Robert Rhodes, sergeant, Royal Marines, killed in action Salerno 1943, and later in the forms where it asked about other relatives who are serving or have served in the Royal Marines, Rhodes wrote, grandfather, Albert Rhodes, corporal, Royal Marines, killed in action Zeebrugge 1918. Two weeks later he had a letter from the Admiralty telling him to report to the Royal Marine recruiting office in the Chatham High Street, to be enrolled and commence his training.

He left the farm a day before. The farewells from his aunt, uncle and cousin were tearful. As he left they said, 'Remember, Peter, there is always a home for you here.'

He spent the night at June's. It was a passionate farewell. She said he should make the most of it and he did. The next day she kissed him goodbye on the doorstep in her dressing gown.

She said, 'I don't care what the neighbours think, I'm proud of you.'

He walked off; at the end of the street he turned, waved and blew her a kiss, and she did the same.

Deal

He reported to the Royal Marine recruiting sergeant who checked his papers and then told him that he was taking him to the RM Barracks to be sworn in. Once there, he was taken to see the officer in charge of recruiting. He was a major and, as he looked through Rhodes's application forms, he asked him about his father and grandfather. Naturally, he was pleased that Rhodes had decided to follow in their footsteps.

'The Royal Marines are a family,' he said, 'and I am delighted to welcome you into it.' Then he handed a bible to Rhodes, told him to take it in his left hand and read what was printed on the card in front of him.

The officer warned, 'You are now going to take a solemn oath which is binding till the day you die.'

Without hesitation, Rhodes read as instructed, 'I, Peter James Rhodes, swear by Almighty God that I will be faithful and bear true allegiance to His Majesty King George the Sixth, his heirs and successors, and that I will, as in duty bound, honestly and faithfully defend His Majesty, his heirs and successors, in person, crown, and dignity against all enemies, and will observe and obey all orders of His Majesty, his heirs and successors, and of the generals and officers set over me, so help me God.'

Rhodes was well aware of the enormity of the oath he had just taken, and that he was bound to it for all time. The major shook Rhodes by the hand and said, 'Go and enjoy your new career. I feel you will be a credit to your father.'

Rhodes thanked him, and the recruiting sergeant was instructed to escort him back up the town to the office. When they had returned Rhodes was given a sealed envelope and a travel warrant for the train journey to the Royal Marine Depot at Deal.

'Best of luck, son. There is a train to Dover in about fifteen minutes.'

Thirty minutes later, Rhodes was on the train, rushing

through the Kent countryside, bound for the Royal Marine Depot at Deal.

At Dover he changed platforms for the Deal train. Already on the platform were about twenty other young men, all about Rhodes's age and all looking warily at one another. Nobody spoke. The train arrived and they all piled in. The fifteen-minute journey was completed in total silence. On arrival they stood on the platform and then one of their number said, 'I was told to wait outside the station until transport arrives to take us to the barracks.'

The barrier of silence was broken. Yes, they all agreed, that's what they had been told. They all picked up their cases and went outside the station to await the promised transport; after about ten minutes, a Royal Marine arrived on a bike.

'You lot for barracks?' he asked. There was a collective nod. 'Then follow me,' he said, and rode off down the road. It became obvious that the word 'transport' was all part of marine humour. They all trotted off after the marine who thoughtfully waited at each road turning before riding off again. Twenty minutes later they arrived at the gates of East Barracks. The marine pointed to a sergeant standing by a doorway. 'That's who you want,' he said, and then rode off. The sergeant waved them to him.

'Welcome to the Royal Marines. I expect you are hungry after your journey. Come inside and get some food.'

They put their cases down outside the mess hall and went inside and lined up in front of the serving counter. They were all given two large soused mackerel and a large helping of peas and mashed potatoes.

'Enjoy,' said the sergeant.

One innocent among them said he did not like fish. There was a stunned silence.

'Eat it,' said the sergeant. The innocent complied.

The cook then said, 'Treacle pudding to follow, and hot sweet tea.' In anticipation they all began to talk.

'Shut up,' said the sergeant, 'and eat.'

After the meal the sergeant told them they were going to get their hair cut, after which he would show them where they would sleep that night. He then took them to the barber shop where two very senior marines were the barbers. They went about their task with enthusiasm; hair flew everywhere.

One of the waiting recruits muttered, 'Fuck shit, they are butchers, fucking butchers.' To which one of the barbers said, 'I heard that, you're next.' He was and after they had finished him his head was devoid of hair. Mouths were kept firmly shut after that and there were no more complaints.

Rhodes had very short hair to start with and suffered no more than a few token snips. After they had been sheared they were taken to a large barrack room where there were already some recruits waiting. In total they were now thirty-nine.

'You are the 553 squad,' said the sergeant. 'You will commence your training tomorrow and it will last for a year, sixteen weeks here, eight weeks at Portsmouth (including two weeks' sea training), sixteen weeks at the Infantry training centre at Lympstone in Devon and eight weeks at the Royal Marine Commando School at Bickleigh, just outside Plymouth. You will then pass for duty. Tomorrow you will meet your squad instructor and be allocated to your barrack rooms and start drawing your kit. Tonight you will not try and leave the barracks. You can get some cocoa and a bun at eight tonight. Lights out is at ten, that's 2200 hours. Reveille is at 0600 hours, breakfast is at 0645 hours. You will be in this room at 0745 hours to meet your instructor. Good luck.'

When the sergeant had gone they all started talking. All the beds had some clean bedding on and Rhodes selected one near the window and made up his bed. The others started to do the same. Later that night they went to the dining hall and had their cocoa and a bun. Soon after that they started to get ready for bed. It was obvious that for some it was their first time away from home as they were embarrassed to undress in front of strangers. When the lights were put out at 2200 hours, there were a few muttered goodnights and after about thirty minutes the barrack room concerto started, a couple of coughs, a sneeze, two loud farts and a sob, life in the marines had begun.

Rhodes managed quite a decent night's sleep and when reveille sounded at 0600 hours was amongst the first out of bed. It was then a frantic rush to wash, shave, make up their beds and get their breakfast. At 0745 hours they were all back in the barrack room to await the arrival of their squad instructor. The door opened and he came in. He looked like he had stepped out of a recruiting poster. About six feet tall with broad shoulders, he was immaculate, dressed in his uniform blues with two rows of medal ribbons on his chest and his hat seemingly glued to his head, this was the man who would turn them into Royal Marines.

He spoke in a loud clear voice. 'My name is Sergeant Brown. You are the 553 Squad and I am your squad instructor. You will obey without question all of the orders I will give you and in return for your full cooperation I will turn you into Royal Marines and make your parents and loved ones proud of you. Now when I say move you will double outside and fall in three ranks. You will do this in absolute silence. Move.'

The recruits doubled outside and did as they were ordered. All of them felt they had met a god.

The next two weeks flew by. They were allocated to their barrack rooms in M block. The squad was split into three rooms. Rhodes was in a room with seven others. Theirs was the smallest room of the three. Each room contained a trained marine, all with long service and their role was to show the recruits how to clean their kit, press their uniforms, and survive.

They were issued with masses of kit, measured for uniforms and while they waited for these they were dressed in denim fatigues, boots and a blue beret. Sergeant Brown drilled them for hours at a time, broken only by sessions in the gym with the PTIs. They used endless tins of black polish to shine their boots and webbing equipment. Another set of webbing was blancoed white. The occasional lecture by one of the officers broke up the frantic pace of their days. In a surprisingly short time all of their uniforms had been tailored and, using photographs of appropriately clad marines which were pinned to the barrack room wall as a guide, each marine learned how they should be dressed. The squad started to come together.

Sergeant Brown was superb; he had great patience, and in spite of being a strict disciplinarian, he knew a kindly word at times was the best solution to the problem.

They now were fully kitted and beginning to really look like marines. They went to North Barracks each day, for the morning parade and to drill in the huge drill shed. They saw other squads drilling. There were about seven squads, each two weeks ahead of the other in training. One afternoon they saw the senior squad at drill.

Sergeant Brown told them that during the last two weeks of their training each squad becomes the most senior and is then known as the King's Squad. He went on to say that as a mark of their seniority they wear their cap chin-stays down. He allowed 553 to watch them drill. The King's Squad were magnificent with each drill movement crisp and precise. As they marched by with their feet striking the ground as one and disappeared out of the drill shed, Sergeant Brown said, 'And you, the 553, will be better.'

Rhodes had taken to the training like a duck to water and enjoyed every part of it. He was big and strong and with the many sessions of PT was fitter than at any time in his life. On Wednesday afternoons they played games on the sports field, the PTIs deciding what the activity would be. All of the other squads were there and each competed against the other. On this occasion he decided that the 553 would take on the 552 at milling. This was something like boxing only with fewer rules. Each squad lined up in single file, facing each other, and opposite numbers took each other on. Size was irrelevant. When the whistle blew the next in line of each squad jumped into the ring and for one minute tried to knock seven bells of shit out of his opponent.

Rhodes was about four from the front; when he saw that the marine in front of him would fight a massive marine from the other squad, he quickly changed places with his squad mate who gave him a look of gratitude. It was Rhodes's turn to go into the ring. The whistle blew and he jumped in and gave his opponent two crisp punches to the head. To his surprise he was given two hefty punches back. For the rest of the round they stood toe to toe trading punches. The whistle blew, but they carried on. Two of the PTIs jumped into the ring and pulled them apart.

After the milling was over they were called over by the sergeant PTI who asked, 'Is there bad blood between you two?' They both smiled through their bruised lips and replied that they had never met until that day. The sergeant let the other marine go but stopped Rhodes to ask him why he had swapped places with the marine in front of him.

'Because he was too small to fight that big chap,' Rhodes said.

'In war,' said the sergeant, 'in hand-to-hand combat you have no choice but to take on the nearest enemy to you irrespective of size, do you understand?'

'Yes,' said Rhodes. 'I am sorry, Sergeant.'

'Carry on,' said the sergeant, 'and by the way that was a good scrap.'

After they had completed a month's training, they were allowed a weekend pass, from 1200 hours Saturday to 2359 hours Sunday. Rhodes went to Chatham and spent the time with June. She was delighted to see him and told him he looked like a younger edition of his father in his uniform. That night their lovemaking reached new heights. When it was time to go back on Sunday evening she said, 'Next time you must go and see your aunt and uncle.' Rhodes agreed, they kissed goodbye and he made his way back to the station for the train for Deal.

Over the next two weeks most of the squad managed to pass the Royal Marine Education Test 3. Until they had passed this, they could not move on to the next stage of training at Portsmouth. Another test they needed to pass was the swimming requirement, a standard all marines must meet. This consisted of swimming two lengths of the pool in overalls, floating around for ten minutes and finally jumping off the top diving board. This test is intended to represent a warship sinking and the marines on board having the ability to survive it.

The squad was now reduced to thirty-six. One marine had failed the stringent medical examination they had all been subjected to in the first two weeks of training. Another had broken his ankle during a PT session and one had failed to return from his weekend leave. In spite of these setbacks the squad's performance increased in leaps and bounds. All their equipment had reached the standard required. All the brasswork gleamed and you could see your face in the mirror shine of their boots. The webbing of their belts and fighting order had responded to the many tins of black polish, with a shine almost to that of their boots. Their blanched white webbing was also now pristine. The squad now had a great team spirit. They helped each other over any difficulties, engendering an 'esprit de corps' that no Royal Marine unit should be without.

One of the great moments in their training was when the band was on parade. When you marched behind the band you grew two inches and your collective heels striking the ground sounded like thunder. It was an inspiring and an unforgettable experience. They had been told Royal Marine bands were the finest in the world and in their minds there was now no doubting this.

There was a two-week break in the training for summer leave. Rhodes spent the first two and the last two days with June. The rest of the time he spent on the farm. Uncle Bill and Aunt Marie were delighted to see him, as was Mark. He helped with the work and began to realise just how strong and fit he had become. His French came back to him very quickly and he enjoyed the heavy work and the fresh air.

Mark confided in him that the two local girls who had re-placed the departing land girls had introduced him to the pleasures of the flesh.

'You mean,' said Rhodes, 'that you are shagging them?'

Mark nodded and confided that he bought the French letters in the village chemist's. The time went quickly and it was soon time to go to June's for the last two days of his leave. Bill, Marie and Mark were sorry to see him go.

'Remember, Peter,' said his Aunt Marie, 'there is a home for you here whenever you need it.'

Rhodes sadly said his goodbyes and left. June was pleased to see him and they made the most of his last two days' leave.

Back at the barracks their training progressed. All of the squad had now passed their education and swimming tests and had become familiar with their rifles in terms of arms drill. They were taken to Kingsdown rifle range, a few miles from Deal, to fire them. They each fired ten rounds just to see what it was like. They were all surprised how loud a discharged round was and how much the rifle kicked.

'When you get down to the ITCRM you will fire hundreds of rounds on the range there,' said the instructor. 'It will become second nature to you and you won't notice the noise or the recoil.'

They were now in the last two weeks of their training. They were now the 'King's Squad' and they wore their chinstraps down. When they marched by and noticed the other squads watching them, they realised they had reached their peak. Their drill and marching were superb. The final accolade came as they marched past the RSM.

After a dress rehearsal for their passing out parade, they heard him say, 'One of your best squads, I think, Sergeant Brown. Well done.'

On the day of their passing out they were all very nervous. Rhodes had asked Bill, Marie, Mark and June to come, as the rest of the squad had invited their parents. The day was bright and sunny, and Sergeant Brown, with all of his medals on display, formed them up a hundred yards short of South Barracks Gate and behind the band. They would do their passing out drill programme in front of the officers' mess on what was known as the Small Parade Ground.

Sergeant Brown stood them at ease and said, 'You will remember this day for the rest of your lives; you are the best squad I have ever had, now go and show your guests just how good you are.'

He then called them up to attention, the barrack clock's hands moved to ten o'clock, and they heard the drum major say, 'Band ready.'

Sergeant Brown called out in a loud voice, '553 King's Squad, by the right quick march,' and with the band playing and the clock striking ten, the squad marched on to the parade ground. The whole display, including the inspection, took about thirty minutes. None of the squad took any notice of the large number watching. Their concentration was on the drill and they surpassed themselves. Their final movement on the move – fixing bayonets on the march – was one of the longest sequences in a drill movement and it was done to perfection. At last it was over. Sergeant Brown reported to the inspecting officer, an army general, that their display was completed and asked for permission to march off.

The general said, 'A superb display, Sergeant, in the finest tradition of the Royal Marines, please carry on.' Sergeant Brown saluted and with the band playing 'A Life on the Ocean Wave' they marched off to tremendous applause. They halted by the sergeants' mess in South Barracks where tea and coffee were laid on for the marines and their guests.

As the marines mingled with their guests, tears and compliments flowed in equal amounts. Rhodes was warmly embraced by June and Marie, while Uncle Bill and Mark shook his hand. They all were amazed by the display they had just witnessed.

'Your mum and dad would have been so proud,' said his uncle. 'Just as we are.'

The hour allowed for their guests quickly passed. That night they would hold their squad supper and the next day they would start a weekend's leave. On the Monday they would travel to Portsmouth and Eastney Barracks to start the next phase in their training. Rhodes's and the other marines' guests left to cries of 'See you tomorrow.'

At the squad supper, the guest of honour was of course Sergeant Brown and his wife. It was a great success, everyone felt at ease and the genuine affection they felt for their instructor was obvious to all. Rhodes was nominated by his squad mates to propose the loyal toast and give a speech of thanks. When he stood up to do this, one of his squad mates called out, 'Make sure it's in English.'

Rhodes spoke for ten minutes, stating how much they owed their instructor, thanking him for his patience and good humour.

He finished by saying, 'Wherever our careers take us, we will never forget you.'

Sergeant Brown was clearly moved by the warmth of their feelings, and so was his wife. He rose to his feet and thanked them for a wonderful evening which his wife and he would remember for a long time. They gave him three cheers and two verses of 'A Life on the Ocean Wave' with words of their making but suitable for a lady to hear. The evening concluded with the presentation of some flowers for his wife and a framed copy of their squad photograph, which they had all signed.

The next day they went home for the weekend. Rhodes spent

one day with June and one day on the farm with his aunt and uncle. When the squad returned to Deal Barracks on the Sunday evening they all started to make a start to pack for their transfer to Portsmouth the next day. In the morning they placed their kitbags on a lorry for transfer to the station. They then fell in on the parade ground behind the band and marched to the station. It was a great feeling. Sergeant Brown was still with them, and would stay with them until they went on to ITCRM in eight weeks' time.

Sea and Shells

They changed trains at Dover and in London, each time they had a reserved carriage. On arrival at Portsmouth Harbour station they could see many large warships in the harbour. Sergeant Brown pointed out two huge battleships to them. 'That is the *King George V* in front and the *Duke of York* behind.'

A lorry and a bus then took them to Eastney Barracks and they were directed to a large barrack room big enough for the whole squad. They were told that the next day they would go aboard HMS *Royalist*, a cruiser in Portsmouth harbour for two weeks' sea training. They were given a list of kit to take with them. The remainder of their kit would stay in their barrack room, which would be locked until their return.

The next morning they were taken to the dockyard to begin their sea training.

Sergeant Brown left them at the jetty, saying, 'I will be here a week on Friday to take you back to Eastney Barracks.'

As he left, a large motorboat pulled into the jetty and a marine sergeant ordered them to get aboard with their kit. When they arrived at the *Royalist* they realised how big it was and it was only a cruiser. They passed all of their kit up the gangway and were told as they got to the top to face the stern and salute, something they would be required to do every time they boarded a ship. They were then taken down below to their mess decks. Two adjoining messes with eighteen men to each. It was very cramped, not a bit like a barrack room.

For training purposes they split into four groups, each of which had a marine sergeant. The group Rhodes was in had a sergeant named Evans as its instructor. He seemed friendly enough and told them that when on board ship it was not necessary to shout orders in a loud voice as it was a cramped environment and shouting would cause confusion with other groups.

31

They were told how the messing system worked. A rota was drawn up so that each day two marines from each mess would be responsible for collecting the food from the galley and keeping the mess deck clean. The marines were then taken to the stores and issued with their bedding and hammock canvas, they were then shown how to make up their hammocks, how to sling them and how to get in and out of them. The sergeant then told them that when in their hammocks at night they would be so close together they would have no secrets from one another.

After being shown how to lash up and stow their hammocks, they went through the procedure a couple of times and satisfied their instructors that they had some idea how to do it. It was now time for dinner and the marines detailed for the task went and collected the food from the galley after which they all tucked in.

Once lunch was over, they were told to fall in on the top deck. They were issued with a training programme for the two weeks they would be on board the *Royalist*. This included boat pulling, learning all the knots in use in the navy, splicing rope and wire, performing all the duties of a Royal Marine on board ship and how to scrub floors properly. They were then told to go and put on their swimming trunks. A climbing net was then hung over the side of the ship and with a safety boat slowly circled the ship, they were then told to jump over the side, swim up to the bow of the ship and climb back on board via the climbing net. The marines did this, some finding it easier than others thanks to the time spent in the swimming baths at Deal.

After they had showered and changed, they were given a tour of the ship. It was a maze of passages, hatches and ladders. They were shown inside one of the gun turrets and told that once they had completed their gunnery course they would be able to operate the guns with complete confidence. They were then told to secure for the day, so they went back to their mess decks and completed their unpacking.

That night, after the officer of the watch had inspected their mess, a custom known as Evening Rounds, they attempted to put up, or sling, their hammocks. It was hilarious. The hammocks were either too low or too high. Attempts to get into the hammock resulted in getting in one side and falling out the other, but after many attempts they began to get it right and by lights out they were all safely aboard. They soon realised that any movement in the hammock resulted in the whole row swaying, but in due course everyone managed to get some sleep.

The next day they had a full programme to contend with, but they enjoyed learning the various skills a marine on board a ship was required to know. The boat pulling was physically the most demanding, the oars weighed a ton (or so it seemed), and rowing the boat in harmony with them all pulling together was at the start a shambles. The instructor in Rhodes's group suggested that he had seen Wrens do better. This had the required effect and the boat seemed to fly through the water.

Learning to tie knots had a more practical use to the marines. Their instructor told them that once they started their cliff climbing at the commando school the ability to tie a bowline knot became a matter of life and death.

The days flew by, but at the weekend there was no leave. Saturday and Sunday were working days. On the Sunday they were required to parade in their best blues for 'Divisions' and when the ship's captain inspected them.

Towards the end of week two they had their tests in boat work, knots and splicing, as well as general seamanship. They had all achieved the required standard and on Friday afternoon they were told to pack their kit. Their instructors had a final word, wished them good luck and they were taken by motorboat to the dockyard jetty where, awaiting them, was Sergeant Brown.

The transport took them back to Eastney Barracks. When they had unloaded all their kit, Sergeant Brown fell them in and said, 'You all look very sloppy, we must put that right with about an hour's drill.' This he did. He was back in charge. They spent the weekend settling in, pressing their uniforms, doing their washing and cleaning their kit as on the Monday they would commence the gunnery course.

They had a copy of the six-week gunnery course programme pinned on the barrack room notice board. Each day they fell in on the main parade with Sergeant Brown as their marker and after they were inspected they marched off with all the other squads to the Gunnery School. The last period in the morning was usually drill with Sergeant Brown. The last period in the afternoon was PT in the gym.

Their first morning was spent going round the school finding out where everything was. Their instructor was Sergeant Lewis who told them that before they had finished the course they would be able to operate a six-inch gun, a bofors gun, a multiple Pom Pom, an oerlikon and a five-point-two-five anti-aircraft gun. On top of which they would also know how to set fuses and be able by sight and feel to recognise the different types of shells in current use. There would be practical, written and oral tests in the last week of the course and anyone failing these tests would be 'back squaded'. That threat was enough to ensure that there would be no slacking.

The squad was split into three groups of twelve and Rhodes had been placed in Sergeant Lewis's group. In the afternoon they had their first session on the six-inch gun which took six men to operate. Each was given a number and on the command 'Change' moved up one. Number one became number two and number six became number one and so on. This was done to ensure that the team could perform all of the duties on the gun. The titles of loader, trainer, layer, breech operator, ammunition supply and communications number became part of the squad's night-time dreams or perhaps nightmares.

Sergeant Lewis had a simple but effective method of getting the best out of them. They were each allowed to make one mistake per session. More than one and he would say, 'You are inattentive;' and, 'Double round the block with this six-inch shell.' Judging by the numbers of marines running around the block it was a common but effective punishment.

Rhodes, as did most of the marines, wrote home once a week. In his case it was two letters home as he wrote to June as well as Uncle Bill and Aunt Marie. He had had one weekend at June's since he had started the gunnery course so the next one must be at the farm.

Each day their knowledge of gunnery improved and there were fewer mistakes being made. In week three they did live firing of the bofors and oerlikon guns, aiming at a sleeve target towed by an aircraft.

'If you hit that plane,' said Sergeant Lewis, 'you will all go back to week one at Deal.'

Needless to say, the plane remained undamaged, but they did have hits on the target. Sergeant Lewis reminded them that the target plane was only doing about 200 miles per hour, an attack by a modern fighter or bomber would be between 400 and 600 miles per hour.

In week five the squad spent a day at sea on HMS *Zest*. She had one six-inch gun mounted in an open turret. They were split into groups of six and each group fired one shell in the direction of the Atlantic. The naval petty officer in charge swore continuously. At what, no one was quite sure. They were all deafened by the gunfire and decided they preferred to fire their rifles. The petty officer had by then had stopped swearing and he said they had done okay and was pleased they hadn't been seasick.

Week six came. They had read and re-read their notes and gunnery manuals until lights out and then asked one another questions, such as, 'What action do you take in the event of a misfire?'

'Run,' somebody answered.

'No, inform the TS, and wait the appropriate time before opening the breech,' came a more informed response.

'Is that right?' several asked.

'Sounds all right,' the majority decided.

This went on for an hour or so. Then they slept, having nightmares about starting week one again at Deal.

On the day of their tests, and by way of a change, the first period was in the gym, so with a cold shower to follow it wasn't a bad way to start the day. The written tests took the rest of the morning and in the afternoon the practical and oral were taken. After it was over, they were all asking each other how they had answered this question and that question, but of course it was too late to change anything now.

The next day they assembled in the large lecture room to hear their fate. The commandant of the school came in followed by their instructors. He gazed at a pile of papers in front of him.

'I am disappointed,' he said. A collective shudder went through the squad. He went on, 'That I won't see your smiling faces any more after today.'

The relief on their faces was obvious.

'The marks you have obtained reflect well on you and your instructors. I wish you well at the Infantry Training Centre Royal Marines. Good luck.'

They stood as he left. Their instructors had a final word and then they were handed over to Sergeant Brown who told them, 'You can go home for the weekend, collect your railway warrants from the company office. Be back here by 2359 hours on Sunday. On Monday you go to ITCRM.'

Rhodes spent most of the weekend at the farm, but managed Friday night at June's. As usual she had been delighted to see him and their physical relationship was still satisfying to them both. His aunt and uncle always gave him a warm welcome and were delighted with the progress his squad had made. Since the passing out parade at Deal they felt a pride in seeing them all do well. He saw June again on the Sunday afternoon but had to catch the early evening train back to Portsmouth as he had his kit to pack for the journey to ITCRM the next day.

On the Monday it was hectic. All of their kit had to be in the drill shed at 0900 hours and they had to scrub out their barrack room, leave it clean and tidy and pass the inspection of Sergeant Brown. They were now aware that this was their last day with him. He would take them to Exeter station and there hand them over to their instructors from ITCRM.

Khaki Marines

The train journey to Exeter took about two hours. They unloaded their kit on the platform and Sergeant Brown fell them in, called them up to attention, and wished them well. He then ordered them to 'About turn'. In front of them stood their new instructors, a sergeant and four corporals.

'You are now Charlie Six Platoon. My name is Sergeant Ford,' said the lead instructor. 'Your corporals are Corporals Flynn, Woods, Hill and Archer. For the next sixteen weeks you will work as hard for us as you have for Sergeant Brown.'

He then stood them at ease and then easy. They looked around. Sergeant Brown had gone.

About ten minutes later a four-carriage train came in and they were told to put their kit aboard and get in. Twenty minutes later the train arrived at Woodbury Road station where they were told to collect their kit and fall in on the platform. A lorry was waiting outside the station. They placed their kit aboard, and it then drove off up the hill and into the distance. They were then ordered to fall in and were marched off in the direction of the lorry. Fifteen minutes later they marched through the gates of the Royal Marines Infantry Training Centre.

The next two hours were the usual hectic moving in routine. They were shown their accommodation and found they were in two adjacent single-storey brick buildings. They were very clean and brightly painted. Once they had placed their kit on their beds, they were split into four groups and were given a tour of the camp, a corporal being in charge of each group. The centre was well spread out and built on a gentle slope above the River Exe. It took an hour to show them where everything was. The assault course was most impressive, consisting of about ten various obstacles about twenty yards apart. Higher up the slope was a large oak tree. Almost at the top was a small platform and a rope stretched from above the platform about a hundred yards to the bottom of the slope.

On completion of the tour they were issued with additional kit, their highly polished boots would only be worn on parade. They were issued with two pairs of boots (which were not new but they were clean and had been dubbined), a complete set of webbing, belt pouches, a large and small pack, gaiters and rifle sling, to be scrubbed once a week, and two denim suits.

The last period of the day was spent in the lecture theatre where they met their platoon officer, a Captain Ward. He told them what they would be doing over the next few weeks, telling them that there would be a greater emphasis on the physical side of training as well as weapon training. There would be a two-week range course to turn them into near marksman and competent Bren gunners.

He finished by saying, 'Your instructors are here to help you through this course, they will not carry you. They will encourage and advise, but the effort must come from you, nothing less than total commitment will be acceptable, you have been warned.' They were then given their training programme for the next two weeks and dismissed for the day.

The next day, their first two periods were on the assault course. Dressed in PE kit they first walked the course with the PTIs who showed them the right and the wrong way to complete each obstacle. The rope slide, or death slide as it was called, caused a few hearts to flutter as the PTI with his wrists through a rope sling jumped off the platform and slid at great pace down the long rope, his progress being halted by a rope brake and a landing zone of mud and water. The advice they were given to achieve a good landing was to start running just before they hit the rope brake.

They were then taken back to the start of the assault course and lined up six abreast. As the first six cleared the first obstacle the next six started and so on. On completion of the first run they were all breathing hard; now to the death slide instructed the PTIs. They followed one another up the rope ladder leading to the high platform, there was only room for one of them plus a PTI who made sure the rope sling was over the rope and both wrists. 'Away you go,' he said, and the first man jumped into space. On completion, they were told they were pretty useless, and must do better. They then did the assault course and death slide again. They were exhausted, but slightly better, agreed the PTIs. 'Now double away and get a shower.'

For the rest of that day they seemed to be running from one class to the next.

'You will get used to it,' said Sergeant Ford, 'after about a month.' He would be proved right.

Over the following weeks life was pretty hectic for the platoon as they learnt how to fire a Bren gun, and strip it down and reassemble it blindfolded. They were now doing the assault course in 'small arms order' with improving times. A marine from another platoon broke his leg on the death slide, proving the old adage, 'That it's perfectly safe, until you forget it's dangerous.' They spent two weeks on Straight Point rifle range, which was the other side of Exmouth. They zeroed in their rifles and learned to shoot properly ranging from 200 yards progressively back to 600 yards. Poor scores to start with, but improving all the time, it was impressed on them all the time that progress meant improvement. Halfway through the course they had two weeks' Christmas leave. Captain Ward and Sergeant Ford warned them to be prepared to work twice as hard when they returned.

Rhodes spent his leave mostly on the farm with his aunt and uncle. He saw June two or three times over the two weeks. Their encounters were always passionate and satisfying. The weekends were still given over to speaking French, which was good fun and his aunt was pleased with the way he had progressed. She told him he would always sound like an Englishman speaking a second language, but also an Englishman who enjoyed speaking French and French people would like that.

His Uncle Bill had not been blind to his relationship with June and in his direct way had said, 'You are poking her, aren't you? Just remember she's twelve years older than you and the attraction won't last for ever.'

Rhodes was annoyed and was about to explode, but he saw what his uncle was getting at and merely said, 'We know that, Uncle Bill, we are both being sensible about it.'

On the last morning of his leave he said his goodbyes to them all at the farm and spent the last two hours before his train left in June's bed. It was as exciting as always and their naked bodies stayed fused together for longer than normal. June saw him off at the station and waved to him until the train moved out of sight. She sensed that their relationship was about to change.

When the marines arrived back at ITCRM they saw that the programme had them down for an a.m. and p.m. with the PTIs. The next day they were chased all over the place in their PE kit, a five-mile run, a ten-minute break, then over the assault course and down the death slide. After 'stand easy', another five-mile run, a shower, then lunch.

After lunch they did it all again. On the completion of the day's programme the PTIs said, 'Well, that's the Christmas leave out of the system.'

It certainly was. The days and weeks that followed were at the same pace and Sergeant Ford told them to get used to it. 'When you go to the Commando School it will be harder than this.'

They were in their last two weeks at ITCRM now, but they had all qualified on the range as either First Class Shot or Marksman on the rifle or Bren gun and had thrown live thirty-six grenades to the accepted standard. They had practised field craft till they had dropped. They had two periods of drill a week, which they enjoyed and had not let the high standard they had reached at Deal slip.

The next two days and nights were spent on Dalditch, a large field training area ten miles from the camp where they had to dig slit trenches which they would spend the night in and repel an enemy attack which would take place any time between 2200 hours and 0600 hours. They were given 'blank' ammunition to defend themselves.

During the night it rained hard and the slit trenches had at least six inches of water in them. At 0300 hours two large explosions on the right flank of their positions jolted any thoughts of sleep from their minds. Two more explosions to their front and rear convinced them the attack had begun. Somebody fired their rifle and then they were all joining in, their imaginations were providing targets all over the place.

Sergeant Ford resolved the situation with a bellowed, 'Cease Firing! Only fire if you clearly see a target. You are like a bunch of girls on their first date, get a grip!'

The remainder of the night passed quietly and coldly. At first light their instructors took them for a ten-minute run to warm them up. They cleaned their rifles and had their breakfast, which had been brought out from the main camp in hay boxes. They then moved to another part of the training area and on the way were split into four sections of nine in preparation for practising field craft formations, extended line, files, arrowhead and 'fire and movement'.

On arrival at their new positions they dug slit trenches again, and constructed shelters for themselves out of their waterproof groundsheets. After their evening meal, they were placed three to a slit trench. On a rota system two could rest in the shelters and one alert in the slit trench. At 0100 hours they were attacked on both flanks, explosions and machine gun fire seemed to pour over them. They could see shadows or figures moving from the right flank. They engaged the targets as they appeared. The enemy then broke off the attack and it all went quiet. Twenty minutes later and another attack came in, this time from the rear. After about five minutes this broke off and the rest of the night passed without further incident.

The next day they returned to ITCRM, tired and cold. After a shower and breakfast they were given a free period to clean their rifles and kit. After this they went to the lecture theatre where they were shown a training film on field craft and night attacks. On completion of the film Sergeant Ford went over the last two days with them.

'It wasn't all bad,' he said, 'just most of it!'

He outlined their mistakes and indicated how they could have done better. He explained that at night an enemy has only one advantage and that is surprise. Prepare for that and you can repel the attack and make it too costly for him to try again.

The last week arrived. On the Monday they did the final run over the assault course and death slide. This was to be in full fighting order with rifles. If they did not complete the course in the required time they would do it again in the afternoon.

Halfway along the course, two marines at the rear failed to climb the high wall. They tried again but they had lost their momentum. Rhodes and Pearce, who were in front of them, climbed back on the wall and pulled them over. They all completed the assault course and the death slide and they all sat down getting their breath back while they awaited the verdict of the instructors. They did not have to wait long.

The sergeant PTI glanced again at his notes and said, 'Too slow. We saw what happened and that showed a good team spirit, but you will have to go again. Now or after lunch?'

They looked at one another. There was agreement they would do it now. So they were marched back to the start of the assault course and allowed to take a ten-minute break after which they lined up again for the start. The whistle blew and they were off. This time there were no mistakes. They all completed the course and waited their turn on the death slide after which it was all over.

A smiling PTI said, 'Well done, that was one of the fastest times this year, a good team effort.'

They were marched to the lecture theatre to see a film on First Aid, followed by one on venereal disease, after which they all agreed never to have sex again, at least, not until the next time.

The rest of the week passed quickly. On the Thursday evening they were all pressing their uniforms and cleaning their brasses and white webbing ready for their passing for duty parade the next day. They were all wondering if their squad would be awarded a King's Badge. If so, who would win it? They thought of three possibles: Rhodes, Pearce and Walters; most favoured Rhodes or Pearce. The next day, they formed up behind the Royal Marine Band just off the main parade. Captain Ward and Sergeant Ford marched them on, both resplendent in their dress blues and medals and they were halted in front of the VIP, a Royal Marine major general. They presented arms after which he inspected them, having a word with each of them in turn. After the inspection, the commanding officer of ITCRM, Lieutenant Colonel Harrington, DSO RM, spoke to them and told them they had done well in all aspects of their training and they were a credit to all the instructors who had got them this far.

He then said, 'In 1918 His Majesty King George V visited the

Royal Marine Barracks at Deal and saw the passing out parade of the senior recruit squad. He was so impressed that he decreed that the senior recruit squad in the last two weeks of training would be known as the 'King's Squad' and that the best recruit in the squad would be awarded the King's Badge, which he would wear for the rest of his service in the corps. I am delighted to tell you that one of your number has been awarded this honour. Marine Recruit Peter James Rhodes, please step forward.'

In a daze Rhodes marched to the front, was ordered to ground arms and march to the waiting general, who pinned the King's Badge to Rhodes's upper arm and said, 'I am delighted to make this award; from what I have been told you a worthy winner. They tell me your father and grandfather served and died in the corps. They will be proud of you today. Good luck. I am sure you will have a fine career.'

He then shook Rhodes's hand. Rhodes saluted, turned about and rejoined the squad. They then marched off the parade with the band playing, 'A Life on the Ocean Waves'. That night they had a squad supper in the mess hall. Captain Ward, Sergeant Ford and the other instructors were all invited and it was a fine evening. Each had two bottles of beer, compliments of the NAAFI and the next day they were off to the Commando School.

Quest for the Green Beret

The next day, with all their kit packed, they were taken to the station, escorted by Sergeant Ford who would stay with them all the way to Bickleigh. They changed trains at Exeter and again at Plymouth. At Yelverton station a lorry was waiting to take their kit to Bickleigh Camp; they would march there. It took about thirty minutes to march to the camp. At the entrance to the camp was a large sign that read: 'Royal Marine Commando School'. They were met inside by their new instructors, a sergeant and two corporals.

The sergeant said, 'My name is Sergeant Hawkins, your two corporals are Corporals Wicks and Carter. While under instruction you will double everywhere. You may think you are fit, but in the next two days you will find you are not fit enough, but you will be. The only thing you will clean here are your teeth. I will now show you the camp and draw some extra kit. Right turn, double march!'

The next two hours were spent showing the squad where everything was and drawing kit. Each marine was presented with one pair of cliff climbing boots with pointed studs, a combat smock with a press stud gusset, a khaki wool hat and an extra pair of denims, plus a set of scrubbed webbing fighting order. They were taken to their huts; brick-built affairs that accommodated eighteen. They were told to change into PE kit and then they were doubled out of the camp back gate, down a hill and into a wood that had a fast running river running through it.

'This is Bickleigh Vale assault course,' said Sergeant Hawkins. 'You will spend many happy hours here.'

They looked around and noticed that about twenty feet up were rope walkways strung between the trees, sometimes a single rope, sometimes a double rope side by side. There were also two ropes, one three feet above the other that crossed the river at two places. This arrangement went on for about a hundred yards. On the other side of the river was a high rocky feature, about a hundred feet high, at the top of which they could just make out a platform. A rope stretched down over the trees and ran down to the ground crossing the river in the process. The landing point was a muddy pit. Clearly many hundreds of feet had landed there. This was the famous Commando School death slide.

Sergeant Hawkins looked at his watch. 'We have just got time for a demonstration on how to do a "regain" while doing a cat crawl across the river on a single rope. Corporal Carter will oblige.'

A 'regain' was a method of getting back onto the rope in the event of a slip.

Carter climbed the rope ladder into the tree and positioned himself on the rope hands forward, head and chest centred over the rope, one leg hanging down and the other leg bent at the knee. His foot was draped over the rope. He then pulled himself along hand over hand, his hanging leg acting as a balance. When he reached the centre of the river he swung off the rope hanging by his hands, simulating the slip. He then made his body sway back and forth, the momentum gained enabling him to swing his leg back over the rope. He then swung the other leg over and his body was once more fully back in position. He draped his bent leg over the rope and returned to crossing the river.

'There you are,' said Sergeant Hawkins. 'Nothing to it and if you fall off you'll only get wet.'

Corporal Carter re-crossed the river, this time hand over hand. As he climbed down from the tree the squad looked at him with respect. Here was somebody who 'could do'. They were then doubled back up the hill to the camp where Sergeant Hawkins halted them outside their huts.

'You can now secure for the day. Get yourselves and your kit sorted out. The eight-week programme is on your hut notice board. Next to each session is a code letter, this tells you what you are to be dressed in and an explanation of the code is on the side of your programme. Goodnight and dismiss.'

The first thing the squad noticed was the food, which great and plentiful. When they went to the serving counter the cook sergeant, who was supervising the serving of their meals, said, 'If you want more you can have it if we've got it. You are growing boys and you will need plenty of our good food to keep up your energy levels, so dig in.' They did.

They were now the junior squad again, but they knew quite a few of the marines in the other squads and had plenty of questions for them about what lay ahead. The next day started with a run over the scramble course, a four-mile run over the hills, down across a river, back through the hills and then home to the camp. They would do this every morning. Dress for the first week's run was PE kit, followed by denims and boots for weeks two and three, small arms order for weeks four and five and finally, full fighting order for the remaining weeks.

They had their first instruction in unarmed combat. This taught them how to overcome an enemy sentry, using their hands or a knife, where to hit someone, where to aim your blow or kick. This led to some spirited encounters in the huts at night, with many a bloody nose to show who won or lost.

The days flew by and they had their first encounter with the assault, or Tarzan, course. This presented them with a problem where queues built up at various points on the course. These occurred at the different rope stages. Half of them fell into the river at their first attempts at the 'regain', but as the days went by they improved and solved the bottlenecks by mixing up the quickest and the slowest, thus evening things out.

They went onto Dartmoor for some live firing which involved using two-inch mortars, a Piat anti-tank gun, their rifles and Bren guns. They had their first experience of being fired at. As they crawled along a ditch, an instructor fired over their heads from about a hundred yards away. They had lectures on mines, explosives, trip flares, then went out and used them. They used all types of grenades and were taught how to fuse them and how to make booby traps with them. They did night exercises where they ambushed each other.

They split into sections to do the Tarzan course and death slide dressed in small-arms order. Most of the time they did the regain and stayed dry. At weekends they went into Plymouth and had a few drinks at the Navy Club until their money ran out.

Rhodes wrote to June and his aunt and uncle once a week, and had letters in return. June's letters were always scented, and the other marines in the hut demanded a sniff.

The tailors' shop had sewn the King's Badge on all of his uniforms. It was in gold on his best blues, in red on his blue battledress and second blues, and in khaki on his khaki battledress. The badge showed the letters 'G R' with a 'V' in the centre.

As the weeks went by, they could feel how fit they were. They were now doing the scramble and Tarzan course in full fighting order and their times were hardly affected by the additional weight. However, their instructors were always pushing them to do better, but just the same the squad could sense they were pleased with the group progress. There was already a lot of talk of what their future would be when they finished their training. The speculation was soon ended when Sergeant Hawkins told them they would be going into Commando Holding Company at Plymouth Barracks to await a draft to the Far East to the 3rd Commando Brigade Royal Marines at present in Hong Kong.

It was now week seven, and they spent the whole week in Plymouth Sound. Half the time they were engaged in cliff climbing, the other half landing on the rocky shore line from small raiding craft. Jumping from a raiding craft, which is being buffeted by the wind tide and a moderate sea was not easy, but at least their boots with the spiked studs gave them some purchase on the wet rocks. However, falling in the sea in the first period of the day gave them a real incentive to get it right the next time.

The cliff-climbing lessons were exciting and the ability to tie a bowline around themselves in all conditions and positions showed the value of the sea training they had had on the *Royalist*. One of their instructors, Corporal Wicks, was a brilliant climber. He could climb the sheerest rock face, come down and show them the best foot and hand holds so they could better attempt what he had so easily achieved. Most of the time he climbed to the top of the cliff with a rope coiled around his body. When he got to the top he would secure the rope to metal pegs, which were already in place, and then they would climb the cliff using the rope. Not more than ten were allowed on the rope at any time. At the top they would abseil down one at a time, their safety feature being the rope itself. At the top they held the rope in their left hand, passed it between their legs and over the crook of their right arm. It was only the thick material of their combat smocks that stopped them getting rope burns at the bend of the arm, as this was the point at which pressure was applied to slow the rate of descent as they jumped out and down the cliff in eight to ten foot bounds.

As the week progressed they became more and more confident in cliff climbing and landing from the raiding craft. By midday Friday Sergeant Hawkins was satisfied with their performance and they returned to Bickleigh Camp. Corporal Wicks now was called 'Everest Wicks', not to his face of course. Once again the squad admired and were grateful for the quality of their instructors.

It was now week eight, the final week. On Monday morning they ran over the scramble course for the last time in groups of three. All of the groups achieved the required time and one group set a new course record that was recorded on a large notice board outside the training office where it would stay until it was bettered. The rest of Monday was spent revising types of grenade, how to identify them in the dark and how to prepare demolition charges.

On Tuesday they did the nine-mile speed march wearing full fighting order. This involved the squad doubling for one hundred yards, marching for one hundred yards, then doubling again and so on. At the end of the nine miles they were given ten live rounds and told to fire five rounds rapid then five rounds in their own time. At the end of the shoot the targets were examined and hits counted, they had achieved ninety-two per cent. They were told that this was acceptable, but that the record was ninety-eight per cent. Oh well, they thought, we did okay.

The next day was the final run over the Tarzan course and death slide. They were told if any one fell in doing the regain, that person would have to start again and his finishing time would be the final squad time. This piece of news caused them all to focus their minds on the task in hand; then they were off.

The next fifteen minutes passed in a blur of concentrated effort. As each finished the death slide, they lay on the ground getting their breath back and counting each squad member as they finished. Once they were all home the question in all their minds was, What was our time?

The instructor kept them waiting, then said, 'You have achieved the third best time recorded. Well done, and no one got wet.' They all breathed a collective sigh of relief – another hurdle cleared.

The next day was the thirty-mile trek across Dartmoor in full fighting order. They were started in groups of three, ten minutes apart and each group had a map and a compass. There was one instruction that had to be followed, no matter what happened each group must stay together. There were five checkpoints en route and each group had to check in at each point. The group Rhodes was in were the fifth to start and they made good progress, catching up with the group in front of them by the time they reached checkpoint two where they stopped for a pint of hot sweet tea and a ten-minute break.

It was a hard slog and by the halfway point they were all feeling the pace. They caught up with another group to find that one of the marines in that group had pulled a muscle. They decided to go on as a group of six, taking it in turns to carry parts of the injured marine's equipment. After they had passed the last checkpoint, pretending all was well, it was obvious he would have to be carried most of the way home. Rhodes and another marine took it in turns to carry him. With two hundred yards to go he was given his kit back and, supported by the other two in his group, managed to double up the hill into the camp, closely followed by the group Rhodes was in. They had made it, but they were exhausted.

The next day was the last day, they were all stiff and had blisters on their feet, but after treatment in the medical centre all were pronounced fit, even the marine with the pulled muscle. At 1100 hours they were paraded outside the training office and marched to the lecture theatre where the camp commandant, Lieutenant Colonel Whitehead, DSC Royal Marines, addressed them. He told them that they had now completed the last stage of their training and they were no longer recruits but were now Marines 2nd Class. However, what was most important to them was that now they were entitled to wear the famous Green Beret of the Royal Marine Commandos. He finished by wishing them good luck in the future and added that they would be transferred to Commando Holding Company in RM Barracks Plymouth the next day.

That evening the squad met in The Roborough Arms to have a farewell drink with their instructors. It was a good evening, everyone was at ease and Sergeant Hawkins and Corporals Wicks and Carter had them in fits with stories of their overseas adventures. The evening ended with a few marine songs, 'Five and Twenty Virgins Came Down from Inverness' and 'The Prick of Steel'. The landlord at this stage asked them to leave, but the locals insisted on just one more verse, so they sang 'The village undertaker dressed up in a shroud swinging on a chandelier and pissing on the crowd'.

'That's it,' said the landlord, 'out.' So ended the evening.

The next day they were taken to Stonehouse Barracks and were put in one large barrack room. The sergeant major of the holding company told them to paint the bottom of their large kitbags black and a panel one foot square on their small kitbag black also. He told them where they could find the paint and then went on to say that on Monday they would draw their tropical uniforms from stores, have their injections for overseas service and, with luck, commence fourteen days' embarkation leave on the Wednesday. On Monday they had their injections, drew their tropical kit and painted in white using a set of stencils, '30978 Hong Kong', on the black squares they had previously painted on their kitbags. The next day they were told to paint over 'Hong Kong', but no reason was given. They then all had a medical to ensure they were fit for drafting and later that day they were told to paint 'Malaya' in place of Hong Kong. There was great excitement at this as they knew this meant active service. The next day they all went on leave.

Rhodes spent the first two days of his leave with June. She was delighted to see him. She looked at the King's Badge on the left arm of his uniform and he told her the history of the badge as she told him how proud of him she was and how proud his parents would have been. That night their lovemaking reached new heights. June was a passionate woman and Rhodes was able to satisfy her for his body was at a peak of fitness. He told her he would be going to Malaya for two and a half years. She was stunned by this and burst into tears. Rhodes had to spend the rest of the night consoling her.

When he went to the farm they were all pleased to see him and admired the King's Badge on his uniform. When he told them he would be going to Malaya and for how long, they remarked that this seemed such a long time, but knew how exciting it would be. Rhodes enjoyed his leave but was secretly longing to get back to barracks and start the great adventure. With two days left he said his goodbyes to them all on the farm. Aunt Marie was quite tearful as she kissed him and told him not to forget to practise his French. Uncle Bill gave him a big hug then turned away visibly upset. Rhodes shook hands with Mark and then he left.

The last two days with June were special. Both sensed their lives were about to change and they made the most of the remaining time. When he left she was tearful and gave him a long embrace. As he walked away from the house he turned and looked back. She was not there. Rhodes sensed their relationship had now changed for ever.

Back at Stonehouse Barracks they were given more information about their draft to Malaya. They were told to hand in their rifles to the armoury, what kit to pack in their small kitbags and what to pack in their large kitbags. They attached labels to their kitbags with their name, number and '3rd Commando Brigade Royal Marines Malaya' clearly showing. The sergeant major told them they would be leaving for Southampton Docks the next day. They would have to parade at 0830 hours on the Main Parade and march behind the band to the railway station. There would be sixty of them going, their entire squad plus marines from another squad, which had been ahead of them in training.

The next day was fine and bright and at 0845 hours they marched out of the barracks with the band ahead of them. As they marched down Union Street large crowds of people applauded them as they passed by. It was a proud moment for them all. Finally, they reached the station and were reunited with their kitbags, which had been brought to the station ahead of them and were already on the train. They took their seats in the reserved carriage and then the train moved out of the station. They were on their way.

The Empire Fowey

The journey to Southampton took about two hours. When they arrived in the docks they could see several large ships alongside the jetty and wondered which one was theirs. They were told to collect their small kitbags and move to embarkation point one, where the sergeant in charge marched them to the first gangway. The troopship seemed huge. As they made the ascent they could see the name of the ship, the *Empire Fowey*, proudly proclaimed against the grey superstructure. Once on board a seaman was told to take them to F2 troop deck. He led them through a maze of passages and down stairways on to their troop deck. They were invited to select a bunk each and put their kitbag on it. There were just enough bunks, or 'standees' as the navy called them, to meet their needs. They were told that once they reached the Med they could, if they wished, sleep on the upper deck as it would get very hot and stuffy down on the troop deck.

They were now free to have a look round. They were not allowed to go ashore but could explore the areas that were open to them. Signs saying 'Out of Bounds to Troops' would soon show them where they could or could not go. It soon became apparent how segregated the ship was. They were not allowed in areas reserved for officers, married families, unaccompanied civilian females and female members of the armed forces.

The upper deck provided an ideal vantage point to watch the other servicemen boarding and being constantly shouted at by their NCOs. It was chaotic. The troop could not believe what they were seeing. This was their first contact with the army and air force and it was a shock.

Their sergeant, who was watching with them, gazed at the shambles down on the dockside and observed, 'Not quite like us, are they? But remember most of these poor chaps are national servicemen and they have had only a few weeks' training.'

By 1700 hours all of the troops were on board. They had been told they would be sailing at 1800 hours and that there were a total of eight hundred personnel embarked. While they waited, they took the opportunity to visit the dining hall and had their evening meal. It was an acceptable serving of fish and chips and as they finished their meal someone shouted out that the ship was moving away from the jetty. This was the signal for them to dash up on deck and, sure enough, they were moving away from the jetty. With the aid of two tugs the ship was eased out into Southampton Water and they were soon moving out into the English Channel. They were on their way.

By 0600 hours the next morning they were in the Bay of Biscay and sea was rough. Most of the marines went to the mess hall for breakfast. One or two army lads came in but did not stay long when they saw it was kidneys on fried bread for breakfast.

Sergeant Saunders gave them a briefing after breakfast, telling them that the ship's RSM wanted ten marines to cover the two gangways from the troop deck to the unaccompanied female quarters. This was one deck up and there were to be five marines assigned to each gangway, maintaining a watch of two hours on duty and eight hours off. Rhodes and nine others quickly volunteered. Ten others were required to serve the meals out in the mess hall. He added that the RSM wanted the marines for this task for two reasons, they were clean and they could handle bad weather. The remaining forty marines would be split between cleaning their troop deck, and preparing and cleaning vegetables in the galley. Sergeant Saunders added that the RSM had given them the pick of the jobs because he knew they could be relied upon.

He went on to tell them about the *Empire Fowey*. She was of 16,000 tons with a speed of between fourteen and eighteen knots according to sea conditions. The captain was of course in charge of the ship, but the army had a permanent staff on board consisting of a Lieutenant Colonel who was in charge of all service personnel. To assist him he had a captain as adjutant and an RSM responsible for discipline. The ship had been built by the Germans in 1935 as a cruise ship known as the *Potsdam*. During the war she had been earmarked for conversion to an aircraft carrier but the war ended before this could be carried out. At the end of the war the British Government had seized her as a war prize and since that time she had been used as a troopship.

Sergeant Saunders then went on to tell them that at 0600 hours every morning, unless they were on their assigned duties, they would do twenty minutes PT. He told them that the ship would be calling in at Gibraltar, Malta, Port Said, Aden and Colombo and as a treat he would endeavour to take them for a forty-five-minute run at all of these ports.

'I don't want to see you getting sloppy,' he said.

It was pleasant on the ship. The marines got on well with the rest of the troops. Most of the soldiers had come to terms with national service, but they were treated poorly by their NCOs, and they resented this. At the first port of call, Gibraltar, Sergeant Saunders obtained permission, and took them for a run around the dockyard, which took about thirty minutes to complete. They then had fifteen minutes' foot drill before going back on board ship. The ship only stayed in Gibraltar for six hours, enough time to load fresh produce and water, before it sailed on for Malta.

They were now dressed in their tropical kit, consisting of khaki drill shirt and shorts. They were also getting a suntan. They had plenty of time to themselves and each afternoon the ship hove-to for thirty minutes and gangway lowered so that those who wanted to could have a swim. All of the marines who were free of duty took advantage of this, but the other embarked troops just watched.

Rhodes was enjoying his sentry duty as the women invariably came over and spoke to both him and his fellow sentry on the other gangway. One woman was attracting more attention than the others as she had a habit of standing next to the railings overlooking the marines' deck. The troops below had a good view of the outline of her body as the breeze pressed her thin dress to her. Now and again a slightly stronger gust would lift her dress and expose the tops of her legs. The troops, as an expression of their gratitude, referred to her as Mrs Fuck. Her real name was Joyce Lang, and she was on her way to Singapore to join her husband, who was a chief petty officer at HMS *Terror*, a shore base on the island.

Malta came and went, but provided another opportunity for a run, which took them from the ship down to the Marsa and back, a round trip of about three miles.

The next stop was Port Said and this would be the first opportunity for a run ashore in the social sense. Port Said was a dirty, dusty place and they had been warned to stick to the main road and avoid the back streets. Arab boys who wanted to sell them dirty pictures which were not really dirty at all, except for the sweaty finger marks, constantly pestered them. The alternative to the pictures was the offer of, 'You fuck my sister, she virgin, only sixteen.' There were no takers.

Sergeant Saunders, who was with them, said, 'A camel would be a safer bet and more affectionate.' It was assumed he was not talking from personal experience.

That night at midnight the ship started its passage through the Suez Canal. Searchlights were rigged in the bow to enable the pilot to see the banks. Rhodes was on duty from 0200 hours until 0400 hours and to his surprise, shortly after he started his watch, Joyce Lang appeared saying how romantic it all was and how the tropics made people do strange things. Rhodes asked her what she meant.

'This,' she said and kissed him full on the lips. He kissed her back and she responded by pressing her body to his while he put his hands on her bottom and pulled her even closer. She moved her hand down to his cock, their hands fumbled to open the buttons on the front of his trousers. At last they succeeded and his swollen member sprang clear and stood rigidly to attention. Rhodes lifted the front of her dress and discovered to his delight that she was not wearing any panties. He turned her round and put her back up against the outside of the cabin bulkhead. She guided him into her and gasped as he finally thrust his way fully home. The next few minutes were full of gasps and grunts as they both lost any control they may have had over their bodies. They both reached a climax within seconds of one another. A calm gradually came over them and their breathing slowly returned to normal as they rearranged their clothing.

Joyce looked at Rhodes and said, 'I can't believe we just did that, but I'm not sorry, are you?'

Rhodes smiled, 'I feel a bit guilty, but I'll never forget what happened. Ever.'

She kissed him, 'I'll see you tomorrow,' she said, and went to her cabin.

Rhodes watched her go. He looked at his watch. It was 0245 hours. The encounter had lasted about twenty minutes.

Christ, he thought, suppose we had been caught.

The *Empire Fowey* left the Suez Canal at about lunchtime and moved into the Red Sea; as a result most of the troops were sleeping on the upper deck, which made it too risky for Joyce and Rhodes to continue their relationship, but she did manage to pass him a note. It simply read, 'See you ashore in Colombo.'

It was very hot and there was not a breath of wind. Rhodes had come back on watch at midday. At about 1300 hours he felt a light touch of a cool hand on his arm. It was Joyce. She did not speak as she passed by him.

Later that afternoon the ship stopped and they had thirty minutes of swimming. When Rhodes walked back up the gangway he looked up and saw her watching him. Sergeant Saunders tried to keep the marines occupied, but it was so hot that any activity had to take place first thing in the morning or in the early evening. They moved out of the Red Sea and anchored in Aden harbour, but there was no chance to go ashore. A water tanker came out to the ship and, when it had transferred its load, they sailed out into the Gulf of Aden and then into the Indian Ocean. When the ship arrived at Colombo, they were told they could have shore leave from 1700 hours to 2300 hours. The ship would sail for Singapore at midnight. Rhodes waited until he saw Joyce Lang leave the ship then he followed her. She was waiting for him on the corner of the main street.

She grabbed his arm, and led him down a side street, saying, 'According to my Colombo street guide there are some small hotels down here.' About another hundred yards on were two small hotels, one of which was called The Paradise.

'This one will do,' she said. As they went in a small man got up from his seat and Joyce asked if he had a room they could rest in for a couple of hours, adding that they would require two iced beers to be brought to the room. He nodded, and led them to a room on the second floor. It was clean and a large fan spun overhead to cool the occupants. He left, but was soon back with the beer. They each took a long drink; then it was a race to see who could get their clothes off first. They embraced and fell onto the bed together. Joyce took hold of his cock, kissed it and took it in her mouth. Rhodes pulled away from her and kissed her lips, then moved down to her firm breasts. His mouth lingered on her nipples, then moved slowly down her stomach, his journey ending between her legs. Twice in the next two hours they made love. Then it was time to go. On the way out they paid the little man, he smiled and gave a little bow. The couple made their way back to the ship, but at the dock gates Joyce walked on ahead. Two marines caught up with Rhodes and, noticing Joyce Lang ahead, one was prompted to say, 'I'd like to fuck the arse off that.' Rhodes and the other marine agreed, indeed they would.

The *Empire Fowey* made good progress through the Indian Ocean and Rhodes managed one more encounter with Joyce before the ship reached Singapore. They said their goodbyes as the ship left the Straits of Malacca. She gave him an address of a friend in Singapore where he could write. 'She will only give the letter to me,' said Joyce. 'I trust her completely.'

Early the next morning the ship slowly made its way through the mass of little islands that mark the approaches to Singapore. By 0900 hours the ship was alongside the jetty and the marines were making they way ashore. Rhodes looked back to the ship where he could see a hand waving to him. He lifted his hand in response, but it did not go unnoticed by Sergeant Saunders who looked at Rhodes and whispered enviously, 'You're a dirty lucky bastard, Rhodes, a perfect example of a standing prick having no conscience.'

They collected all their kitbags, which were loaded onto a lorry. The marines followed on separately. At the dock gates was an armoury. All of the marines were issued with brand new No 5 Jungle Rifles and a bandolier of fifty rounds. Sergeant Saunders obtained some rags and gave the marines fifteen minutes to clean the rifles to an operational standard. They then boarded a waiting train, occupying a complete carriage to themselves. Other servicemen boarded the train and after a thirty-minute wait it started to move. An army major came into their carriage and spoke to Sergeant Saunders then moved on up the train. Sergeant Saunders told them to charge the magazines of their rifles with ten rounds, but not to put a round up the spout, 'We don't want any accidents.'

As the train crossed the causeway into Malaya, a sentry was posted at the front and rear of the carriage. They had been told that the terrorists often took a shot at trains as they passed close to the jungle's edge. They looked out of the windows, all they could see was a mass of vegetation and so many shades of green, from a dark, almost black shade, to a lighter green that was almost a shade of yellow.

The train never seemed to go very fast, twenty miles per hour seemed to be its limit. They were later told that the reason for the slow speed was safety. In front of the engine were two flatbed carriages piled three feet high with sandbags. If the track in front of the train was blown up the flatbeds would absorb the main shock and the driver could bring the train to a controlled halt.

Early in the afternoon, the train suddenly came to a halt. Sergeant Saunders ordered the marines to stand-to and they took up firing positions at the windows. On one side of the train was a rubber plantation, on the other thick jungle. The army major came through their carriage and nodded his approval when he saw they had taken up defensive positions. He spoke to Sergeant Saunders for a few minutes and they both laughed as the officer turned and moved on down the train. Saunders then told them that there was a train ahead that had broken down and it was being towed away.

At 1600 hours two railway attendants brought them some tea and a cheese sandwich each. Sergeant Saunders told them that they would be getting off the train at Ipoh. The expected time of arrival was about midday the next day. All of the marines took a turn at sentry duty, just one hour at a time.

It soon got dark and it began to rain hard. It was still very warm and even the slightest exertion made them sweat. The carriage had just two lights, both in the ceiling that gave just enough light for them to see one another. At 2000 hours a meal was brought to them consisting of a Curry Something and plenty of rice to go with it. Thankfully, it tasted better than it looked. As the night went on they all managed to get some sleep. Rhodes thought of Joyce Lang, She would be in bed with her husband now and I expect he is making up for the months they had been apart, the bastard!

The next morning they all managed a wash in the small toilet at the end of the carriage. Breakfast was a pint of tea, two hard-boiled eggs and a bread roll. Afterwards there was a patient queue for the toilet. At 0930 hours they arrived at Kuala Lumpur where most of the army personnel left the train. Their NCOs were shouting at them, which didn't seem to help a lot, as they all appeared to remain completely bewildered.

Soon the train was on the move again and at 1130 hours they arrived at Ipoh. There were five lorries waiting for them and their kitbags were quickly loaded. They climbed into the remaining three lorries and were soon on their way to Brigade HQ. On arrival, a sergeant major told them they would be allocated to their commando units the next day and would then go to their troop locations. They were allocated their tents and they settled in. It was a large camp surrounded by barbed wire and they were told to keep their weapons with them at all times. They found the showers and enjoyed the chance to wash the dirt and sweat from the train journey off themselves.

The next morning they paraded outside the sergeant major's office. He called out their names and told them what commando unit and troop they were joining.

'Rhodes, A-Troop 42 Commando.'

Rhodes was pleased to hear Sergeant Saunders receive the same message. They were then instructed to collect their kit and move to various pick-up points in the camp where they would be collected by their troop transport. Rhodes and Saunders waited with a few others in the shade of a palm tree for about an hour before an open top lorry arrived.

'Are you for A-Troop 42?' the driver asked. They replied, 'Yes,' and with their kit they climbed aboard. It took about fifteen minutes to reach A-Troop's location, which was about a mile past a small village called Tambun. The camp was at the side of the road and consisted of six tents to the left of the large house with another six tents to the right. They offloaded their kit onto the drive and followed the driver's directions to the sergeant major's office. His door was open and the sergeant major was sitting behind his desk. He stood up and they observed that he was massive and covered in thick black hair.

He said, 'I'm QMS Higgins, welcome to A-Troop.' He did not smile as he said this. In the same tone he told Sergeant Saunders that the sergeants' mess was on the ground floor of the house and there was a small room there for him. After Sergeant Saunders had left, Higgins looked at Rhodes.

'You will be in D sub-section. Report to Corporal Green, he will put you right.'

Rhodes left the office and went to the tent indicated. He found Corporal Green and was given the one vacant bed in the six-man tent. Corporal Green told him that most of his kit was going to be sent back to the UK and gave him a list of kit to keep, saying, 'Put the rest in your large kitbag, label it with your name and number and put it in the troop store. Ours is there. It goes down to Singapore tomorrow.'

Over the next two days Rhodes got to know the rest of his sub-section. There were two corporals and ten marines, twelve in all. They were one half of one section, the other being C sub-section. The total strength of No. 1 Section was twenty-six consisting of twenty marines, four corporals, one sergeant and an officer. No. 2 Section occupied the six tents on the other side of the house and consisted of three sub sections, E, F and G. Their total strength was thirty-eight, thirty marines, six corporals, one sergeant and one officer. The rest of A-Troop consisted of the sergeant major, a sergeant QM, two signallers, two cooks, a naval sickbay attendant, three drivers and in command, Captain Baker, Royal Marines. So the total strength of A-Troop 42 Commando Royal Marines was about seventy-five in all.

Considering A-Troop had only been in their camp a week, it was well organised. Workers from the Public Works Department were already constructing a wash place, toilets and a shower. The priority for A-Troop's CO was getting to know their area. Over the next few days the sub-sections were dispatched to cover different points, the tin mines, rubber plantations and the small villages. The huge area of jungle they were responsible for stretched to the Pahang border. The area the whole commando brigade was responsible for was about the size of Wales, with 40 Commando to the north, 42 Commando in the centre and 45 Commando to the south.

In A-Troop's area were a number of huge limestone features called gunongs. Some were almost a thousand feet in height and honeycombed with caves and passages. During the Japanese occupation the resistance fighters used them to good effect and now the communist terrorists were doing the same. Captain Baker decided that the first operation the troop would mount was a search of one of these gunongs, in particular Gunong Rapat. At 0400 hours the troop were driven to a point half a mile from the gunong. In darkness, the troop, in single file, moved to within a hundred yards of the feature before they spread out in a line five yards apart and waited for daylight.

When daylight came they moved in. D sub was on the right flank and all of the marines had cocked their weapons with the safety catches applied. As the light improved and they got close to the gunong they could see it was almost entirely covered with vegetation. The plan was for one section to move to the right and search and for the other to work their way to the left and do the same. They took it in turns to search, one sub-section covering the other. After about an hour they were drenched in sweat, so they all drank from their water bottles and took a ten-minute break.

At 1600 hours the troop commander called the search off. All they had discovered was some human bones, an Aussie hat and a few rounds of ammunition. These were all found in a small cave ten feet above the ground, a sad reminder that an Australian battalion had fought a rearguard action here during the invasion. The bones were left where they had been found and the local war graves people would be informed. The troop returned to their camp, now aware of the huge task confronting them over the next two years.

In the next two weeks all of the sub-sections got a taste of jungle bashing, going out for three days at a time. It was on the return from one of these patrols that Rhodes was told the troop commander wanted to see him.

'I'm going to lend you out for about six weeks along with Marine Jones from E sub. You leave this evening for Singapore, best of luck,' and he was dismissed. The sergeant major gave him instructions on what to take with him. When Rhodes asked the sergeant major where he was going, a strange expression came over Higgins's face, a twist of one corner of his mouth with his eye on that side moving upwards. Rhodes realised he was smiling.

'Korea, that's where you're going,' he said.

Back to Malaya

Rhodes was suddenly aware that somebody was talking to him. It was the American flight attendant.

'Put your seatbelt on, we are about to land in Singapore.'

He was back where it had all started, in Malaya.

During the next two hours they collected their rifles and ammunition from the airbase armoury where they had left them six weeks before, grabbed a meal and were taken to catch the train to Ipoh.

Bob Jones had become a good friend over the last six weeks and knew of his involvement with Joyce Lang, so when he said, 'What a pity we are not staying over in Singapore, you could have looked up your friends,' Rhodes shared a knowing smile with his friend. Before they had gone to Korea he had written to the address she had given him and she had replied with a very affectionate letter saying how much she missed him. Strangely enough June's letters were in a similar vein – how complicated life could be.

The journey up to Ipoh took about the same time as before and when they arrived they were whisked to Brigade HQ where Captain Rogers and Sergeant Smith said goodbye to them all. With the farewells out of the way they started to be picked up by their own troop drivers to go their separate ways.

Back at A-Troop the sergeant major was waiting for them. 'The whole troop's out on a seven-day bash, so I want you two on guard tonight. There are only six of us left in camp, so I'm pleased to see you.'

Rhodes and Jones made their way to their respective tents where Rhodes found on his bed letters from his Aunt Marie, June and Joyce Lang. He lay down and spent the next half hour reading them.

Three days later the troop returned from their seven-day patrol. Rhodes went to pick them up, acting as escort on one of the lorries. All of the marines looked exhausted and they smelt awful. It was a sour smell, with a strong influence of shit, they were all to realise later that this was the smell of the jungle. Several of the marines had mild cases of dysentery, caused by drinking water straight from the rivers and not using their water purification tablets. It was a sharp and painful lesson and they wouldn't make that mistake again.

They had also experienced their first air drop. It had been taken on a ridge some five hundred feet above the river level and, as it had been raining hard, the dropping zone was at times hidden by low cloud. The pilot of the Dakota, an Australian, enquired over the radio, 'Where the fuck are you?' Despite the smoke flares he could not see them. The drop was finally made by them telling him, 'Drop now, drop now!' And the supplies crashed through the trees, their parachutes only just checking their descent. A tactical lesson was also learnt. If the terrorists were not aware of their presence, after the air drop they certainly would be. The marines of A-Troop quickly absorbed these lessons.

The most effective patrol strength was a sub-section, or even half a sub-section, just six marines. This size of patrol gave them speed and the ability to deploy quickly in the event of a contact with terrorists in thick jungle.

Over the next two months A-Troop patrolled their area constantly, keeping one sub-section in camp, the other four subsections were out on patrols of different durations, and locations. The last thing they wanted was to have two patrols clashing in the thick jungle. This had happened with an army patrol to the south of their area, with tragic results.

Rhodes was now in the scout group of his section, he liked being in front and though it was hard work cutting a path through the jungle, he knew that if there were a contact the scout group would be in the firefight first. D sub-section was organised in the same way as the other sub-sections in the troop, a scout group, consisting of a No. 1 and a No. 2 scout, both with Sten guns, a rifle group of six men, all with No. 5 Jungle Rifles and fifty rounds of ammunition. The sub-section commander, Corporal Green carried a Sten gun and positioned himself normally to the rear of the scout group. Behind the rifle group came the Bren

Group, No. 1 on the Bren and his No. 2 who carried a rifle. The 2 IC of the section was Corporal Holt, who carried a Sten gun. All of the patrol carried two 36 grenades or one 36 and one 80 (smoke) grenade, so even if the sub-section split into two their firepower was still considerable.

Acting on information from the police, D sub-section spent three days and nights in ambush on the pipeline a mile north of a small village called Juang. It rained all the time. The nights were cold and the days hot. At night mosquitoes kept up a relentless attack on any uncovered parts of their bodies.

On the forth morning as they were about to move from their position, two figures appeared out of the misty rain walking along the pipeline. They were terrorists and both were carrying M1 American carbines. As they drew level with the marines, Corporal Green said, 'Fire.' The two figures were hurled off the pipeline by the hail of bullets, after which the marines stopped firing. Corporal Green sent Corporal Holt and Rhodes back along the pipeline in the direction in which the terrorists had appeared while the rest of the patrol made their way down to where the figures had fallen.

When Rhodes and Corporal Holt returned the patrol had posted a sentry further up the pipeline. The two bodies had been hit repeatedly and had died instantly. To their surprise one was a woman. They tied the bodies to bamboo poles and carried them back along the pipeline. As they returned through Juang, a village made up of just four wooden huts that housed the pipeline workers, they found that the occupants had disappeared. Obviously, memories of the Japanese occupation and the reprisals that went with it were still fresh in their minds.

It took three hours to make their way back along the pipeline. At the point where it went underground there was a tin mine called French Tekka Tin. Corporal Green sent the two scout-group marines ahead while he told Rhodes to ring the camp and arrange transport and to tell them they had two presents for Sunray (the troop commander). When Rhodes arrived at the tin mine he went to the manager's house, where he was invited in. Rhodes used the phone and passed on the message to the sergeant major who said he would send the transport straight away. The manager gave Rhodes and the other marine a cold beer.

The man's wife appeared, her nose twitched and she said to her husband in French, 'They stink like pigs, get them out of the house.'

Before her husband could reply Rhodes said in French, 'My apologies, Madame, but you insult the pig, we smell far worse than that.'

Her mouth fell open in surprise, but then to her credit, she burst out laughing and embraced both the marines. In English she said, 'I am ashamed, please forgive me, you boys risk your lives to protect us.'

At that moment the rest of the patrol came into sight, carrying the bodies of the two terrorists. When they left the tin mine the section were in possession of a crate of Carlsberg, a gift from the manager and his wife.

When they arrived back at A-Troop, marines from some of the other sections still in camp came over to examine the bodies. The fact that one was a young Chinese girl surprised them. The troop commander, Captain Baker, came over and congratulated them and within an hour two red stars had been painted on the 'A-Troop 42 Commando Royal Marines' sign that was at the entrance to their camp.

Later that night as Rhodes lay on his bed he thought of what they had done that day. They had taken two lives, yet he felt nothing. It was the first time he had seen anyone who had died violently as a result of his actions and that of his fellow marines. He thought of the Korean troops he had shot on that last raid, but somehow because he had not seen their bodies they did not count.

About two hours after the patrol had returned, the police had arrived at the camp to collect the bodies. All terrorists killed or captured had to be handed over to the police so that they could be identified from police records. The treatment of the bodies by the young Malay policemen did not go down to well with the marines and an attempt by one of the police to push his stave between the legs of the dead girl provoked an angry response. The police sergeant in charge struck the constable across the face and they quickly left the camp.

About a week later, Captain Baker met the manager of the French Tekka Tin Mine and his wife at a social function at the Ipoh Club. They told him that shots were being fired at their compound and several had hit the roof of their house. The compound had a permanent guard of four young Malay police-men who had been terrified and wanted to leave, so the manager was asking for help. Captain Baker asked where the shots were coming from and was told that the source was Gunong Rapat which was about four hundred yards away. He said he would put six of his men in the compound for two days, they would deal with the problem. Paul and Helen Dupré were grateful and Mrs Dupré asked if one of the marines could be the one who speaks French so well. Captain Baker was not aware that any of his marines could speak French but he merely said that he would try.

Later that evening when he was back in the camp he asked the sergeant major, 'Who speaks French in the troop?'

The sergeant major laughed and said, 'Half of them can't even speak English, sir!'

'Well, somebody does,' said Baker, 'find out who.'

The next day the sergeant major saw all the corporals who were in camp and asked them if any of their marines could speak French. They all laughed, but Corporal Green said, 'It could be young Rhodes in my sub-section.'

'Send him over to my office,' said the sergeant major.

When Corporal Green got back to the tent he told Rhodes, 'Hairy Henry wants to see you, straight away.'

Rhodes reported to the sergeant major who asked, 'Do you speak French?'

'Yes, sergeant major,' said Rhodes.

'Shit, another clever sod. Okay, go back to your tent,' said the sergeant major who then informed the troop commander.

The next day Corporal Green was briefed about the problem at the tin mine.

'Take half of your sub-section including Rhodes and take the two-inch mortar and ten rounds of HE. That should solve the problem,' said Captain Baker.

When the patrol reached the tin mine the next day they were given an outbuilding to sleep in. They then checked the compound for any obstructions that would compromise the firing of the mortar. A cooked meal was brought over to them from the house with a bottle of beer each.

Later, as it got dark, they set up the mortar and the Bren gun. At about 2100 hours a shot was fired from the direction of the gunong. They heard it hit the roof of the house, but did not see the muzzle flash. Another shot and the flash was spotted. Corporal Green ordered the mortar to fire high angle slightly above forty-five degrees. They fired two bombs, which landed slightly to the left of their target. A correction was made and the next two bombs appeared to be spot on. They fired four more bombs, while using the Bren to fire a magazine below and above the point of the mortar bomb's impact.

The noise of the explosions echoed around the hills. The Duprés were most impressed. No more shots came in their direction that night and the next morning they made their way across to the gunong and climbed up the gully from where the shots had come. It was a stiff climb and their jungle greens were black with sweat. They came across evidence of the mortar bombs' impact, shredded bushes and fragmented rock and then some bloodstains, a green hat, a small pack containing dried fish, rice and some papers. They followed the bloodstains; just a few spots here and there, up to the top of the gully and down the other side. They then lost the trail completely. They spent another hour searching before returning the way they had come.

On return to the tin mine compound they showed the Duprés what they had found and told them about the trail of blood. They were delighted. Corporal Green told them that it was clearly just one person doing the firing and it was unlikely he would do that again.

They rang the camp and were told to stay out there that night and that they would be picked up the next day at 1000 hours. The Duprés sent them over another meal that evening, then they brought them some beer. Paul and Helen Dupré sat and talked to the marines with Rhodes and Helen Dupré speaking in French. She corrected some of his grammar, but told him that his accent was that of a person from Brittany. Rhodes told her that his aunt came from there and as she had taught him he had picked up the accent from her. They spent a pleasant evening together and when they left the next day the marines had made some good friends.

Conditions in the camp had improved, their tents now had a paving slab floor and they had a one-bulb electric light to replace the oil lamps. A local contractor had installed three Chinese women to provide a laundry service. The marines were disappointed that laundry was the limit of their services. Despite that, they were all Fat and Fifty the old adage, 'Any Port In A Storm' came to the marines' minds. The same contractor had also arranged for two elderly Indian men to provide a snack service, so that at any time the marines could buy a mug of tea or a chip or egg banjo. The tent at the end of one section's lines was well used in the evenings and the two Indian men were referred to as Old John and Young John despite the fact that both were over sixty.

Toilet facilities had also improved. A corrugated iron-covered wash place and shower meant they could enjoy these facilities under cover. The sit down toilets, ten in number, were partitioned, but open at the front. The boxes had a large bucket in which to evacuate. These were emptied each day by a local farmer who had a habit of pulling out the bucket without checking whether or not it was in use. A shout of 'Fucking hold on a minute' usually allowed time to complete the job at hand.

The troop commander tried to allow the marines a 'run ashore' in Ipoh once a week, but their operational commitments did not always allow this. However, when it became possible, leave would be from 1400 hours to 2300 hours. Their rifles and ammunition were required for the journey, but were deposited at the military police armoury on the edge of Ipoh Town. There was an uneasy truce between the marines and the MPs, who in the main decided to ignore one another. There were two cinemas in Ipoh, the Odeon and the Ruby, both of which had air conditioning. There were several restaurants, the Broadway being the most popular with the marines. There were also two open-air dance halls, one called the Celestial and the other the Happy World, where some of the ticket dance girls provided other services, as did the many small hotels where rooms were provided on a short-term basis. There was also a brothel behind the Ruby Cinema where, on entry, you were required to leave your shoes on the stairs before going to see what was available upstairs. Some of the marines found that their shoes had disappeared when they came back down. They would then choose a pair which fitted and depart.

The army ran a medical centre near by and if you took advantage of their prophylactic service you were given a chit with your name and number on it plus the date. If in due course you developed a venereal infection, production of the chit gave you immunity from prosecution. This state of affairs, however, did not last long and an infection rendered the unfortunate to be charged with 'whilst on active service did render himself unfit for duty'. This carried an award of stoppage of pay and stoppage of leave, a harsh penalty for a moment of weakness.

The marines were not too impressed with the quality of the rations they took out on patrol with them. Each twenty-four-hour pack contained a tin of corned beef, or a tin of Irish stew, or a tin of herrings in tomato sauce and a container made of tin which had inside packets of tea, sugar, powdered milk, nuts, boiled sweets, curry powder, rice, raisins, matches and five sheets of toilet paper. There was also provided some solid fuel tablets and a small metal stand. These rations were adequate, but when re-supplied by air the marines would find that a complete three-day drop contained nothing but herrings in tomato sauce.

The brigade commander took this up with the divisional commander, who said, 'But those rations have been discontinued, they were left over from the war and have been replaced by the new-style ration packs.'

He promised he would look into why the marines were being supplied with old rations and added that if someone was pursuing a dumping policy on your men, heads would roll. The marines never found out if heads did roll, but the rations provided from that day on were superb.

Two main rivers ran through the marines' area, the Sungei Kinta and the Sungei Raia. Both were a starting point for many patrols who found that a swift start could be made into the dense jungle by following the tracks alongside the river banks, made by either wood cutters or wild pig.

D sub were dispatched up the Kinta valley on a three-day patrol. Rhodes following Corporal Green's instructions, kept as close to the river as he could as the heat was stifling. Soon all of the patrol were drenched in sweat. It was important to keep from dehydrating, so it was necessary to refill their water bottles from the river once every hour. On each occasion one marine would descend the riverbank and fill the bottles as they were passed to him while the rest of the patrol would spread themselves out along the riverbank and provide cover for him.

Corporal Green had decided that they would 'basha-up' at 1600 hours on a ridge just above the river, but on the other side. Rhodes and then Martin, who made up the scout group, were told to look for a place to cross the river. They found a reasonable crossing point and, with the rest of the patrol covering them, Rhodes and Martin made their way across, keeping at least five yards apart. The water was up to their waists and running quite fast, but within ten minutes all of the patrol were across.

The maps in use in Malaya at that time were not completely accurate, but Corporal Green was an experienced NCO and with a lot of wartime patrols in Burma behind him, he had the knack of getting where he wanted. Just before 1600 hours, they were at a point where the ground rose away from the river to their right. They climbed up about thirty feet and were on Greens Ridge, a site was selected for the four bashas and while the others started to make camp for the night Corporal Green, Rhodes and Martin did a recce to make sure it was a safe site.

Tall trees along the ridgeline had ensured a clear track and thick undergrowth to each side made any approach from the sides impossible to make without detection. The bashas consisted of three ground sheets joined together by their press-studs. Using a rough frame cut from the mass of small trees around them it was simple to construct a lean-to shelter to accommodate three people, which would mean a fairly comfortable night.

The first marine to be on sentry was posted a few yards down the track and he would do a two-hour watch. After an hour another marine would join him. So at night two would be on watch, but there would be a change every hour, so as to have one marine with his eyes already night adjusted and familiar with the natural noises around him. All of the patrol did a watch.

The routine after the bashas were built was to clean weapons, make a meal from their rations and strip off to remove any leeches that had climbed aboard during the day. It was not unusual to have at least a dozen of these creatures attached to various parts of the body, but they were easily removed by applying a hot cigarette end to them. Their blood-gorged bodies would drop off without leaving the head stuck in the flesh, which would otherwise cause an infection. Most marines dreaded the thought of a leech going down the eye of their penis. When they asked Corporal Green how they should deal with this, he said, 'Get one of your mates to suck it out.' Looking at the shock on their faces, he added, 'That's how you find out who your friends really are.'

As soon as it was dark the mosquitoes attacked and despite the application of repellent, it was relentless. Even the frequent torrential downpours failed to stop their assault. In spite of this most of the marines managed some sleep but the stand-to, at first light, was not always welcome.

After breakfast they removed the evidence of their stay and continued their patrol along the ridge. Just before noon, Rhodes and Martin stopped the patrol and told Corporal Green that a track had crossed on to the ridge. Clearly visible was the outline of several footprints made by some persons wearing basketball boots – favourite footwear of terrorists. Green quietly passed the information on to the rest of the patrol and they continued along the track. About an hour later, the track of the terrorists left the ridge to the right and they continued to follow it down the slope. It then crossed a small stream and here the trail was clearly in more frequent use. The marines were now in a high state of readiness.

As he climbed the slope out of the stream Rhodes could see a clearing ahead and what appeared to be the top of some attap-covered huts. At that moment a burst of automatic fire ripped through the foliage above their heads. Rhodes, Martin and Green charged forward spreading out and firing their Stens from the hip in the direction of the huts. When they reached the centre of the camp it was deserted. The rest of the patrol arrived and spread themselves out, taking up a defensive position.

The camp consisted of four huts. Some rice was cooking over a small fire, enough for perhaps four persons. Only one of the huts appeared to be in use and a shirt, trousers and blanket had been left in the rapid escape from the camp. Corporal Green, Rhodes and Martin followed the terrorists' route, leaving the rest of the patrol to make a careful search of the camp and the huts. The trail split into several different directions, so it was pointless to follow and they returned to the camp. Under the floor of one of the huts was a store of rice, about twenty-eight pounds in weight, and a gallon can of paraffin with a large bag of dried fish. Nothing else was found. Corporal Green got on the radio to A-Troop's camp to inform them of what had happened. They were told to ambush the camp that night and the next day destroy the food and the camp and make their way back to their patrol start point.

The night passed without incident, apart from the rain and mosquitoes, and the marines greeted the dawn with relief. They burnt the huts and the food, mixing the rice and paraffin together and then throwing the mixture on the burning huts. Satisfied that nothing of value was left, the patrol made their way back to the river and retraced their footsteps, this time on the opposite bank. At about 1600 hours they arrived back at the patrol start point and awaited the transport to take them back to camp. They did not have long to wait and by 1700 hours they were back in camp. It took them another hour to clean their weapons, unload, clean and reload their magazines, remove the detonators and clean their grenades. Then they attended to themselves, having a good scrub in the showers. Into clean clothes and with a meal inside them, life was pretty good.

Rhodes had some mail, as did the others and he spent the next hour reading his letters. The main news was from June, who told him she had met a lovely man. He worked at the station and, though he was five years older than her, she thought they had a future together and she added that she was sure he would understand. Rhodes was not too surprised, he had been away from England now for just over six months, and it would be another two years before he would return. He decided he would write and tell her how pleased he was for her and wish them all the best. There was also a letter from Joyce Lang. She said she would love to see him again and if he ever came down to Singapore to let her know and she would arrange for them to have some time together. His aunt and uncle were both well. Mark was doing most of the running of the farm and enjoying the responsibility. His aunt said she was pleased he had met a family who were French. She closed by reminding him to take his Palludrine each day; she didn't want him to catch malaria. Rhodes wrote his replies and put them in the mailbox, then he turned in and slept a dreamless sleep.

The next day all the other sub-sections went out on patrols in different parts of the area and for varying lengths of times, E and F subs for seven days, G sub for three days and C sub just for the day. Rhodes's section, being the only ones in camp, were the guard section. The troop commander had gone into HQ in the armoured scout car and on his return Rhodes was standing guard at the camp entrance. The troop commander, on seeing Rhodes, poked his head out of the scout car and said, 'Rhodes, troop office in five minutes, get yourself a relief.'

Christ, thought Rhodes, Joyce's husband has found out and has made a complaint. He got himself relieved and presented himself in the troop office as instructed. The sergeant major was looking at him in a very strange way, a sort of 'puzzled and pity' look. Rhodes's heart sank. He was in deep shit.

Captain Baker said, 'Do you remember Captain Rogers in Korea?'

Rhodes said, 'Yes I do, sir.'

'Well,' said Baker, 'he's been awarded the Distinguished Service Cross.'

Rhodes smiled and said, 'I couldn't be more pleased, sir.'

'And you,' continued Baker, 'have been awarded the Distinguished Conduct Medal. I am delighted for you. From what I understand it is richly deserved, well done.' He then got to his feet and shook Rhodes by the hand.

The sergeant major, not to be outdone, added his own congratulations and, with that strange twisted look that passed for a smile, patted him on the shoulder.

Rhodes went back to his tent with his head in the clouds, but was quickly brought back to earth by a shout from the camp entrance; his relief wanted relieving.

Two days later, D sub were sent to the Ampang police post for a week. The six Malay policemen were refusing to stay in the post overnight. The reason, they were told, was that the Chinese and Malay workers in the nearby tin mine had seen some armed men emerging from the jungle some hundred yards away and were taking a lot of interest in the police post. The whole sub-section, plus Lieutenant Pope, moved into the post, which was situated on a hillock some fifty feet high. The area around the base was ringed by barbed wire and there were some electric lights on posts to illuminate the perimeter and the area outside it. The post was constructed of wood with a tin sheet roof and it had a five-foot-tall defensive wall around it. The outer and inner walls were constructed of railway sleepers with the two-foot gap between filled with sand.

The marines were not impressed with the attitude of the police and they all thought that the place could have withstood a tank attack. The police were pleased to see them and the marines had soon made good friends with them. At 1700 hours the police were picked up, night fell and the marines made themselves comfortable. Two marines would be on guard, while the rest slept. At midnight all the lights went out and the marines stood to. Nothing happened and they stood down.

The next morning the police returned and Lieutenant Pope and Corporal Green decided they would split the sub-section in two and scout the area to look for tracks between the fort and the jungle edge. They spent most of the day searching the area, but they found nothing. The mystery of the lights going out was solved. The power was provided by the tin mine generator and at midnight it was always turned off.

Late that afternoon the police departed as usual and at midnight, when the lights went out, Lieutenant Pope took half the sub-section and moved out into open ground between the jungle edge and the police post. As they moved the moon appeared from behind the clouds and the marines were suddenly bathed in the light of the full moon. They froze instantly as they could see just a few yards in front of them what appeared to be a body. As the moon was partly obscured by some drifting cloud they moved forward to examine the suspected body. It was a large sack. On examination it was found to contain two bags of rice and some clothing. Lieutenant Pope quietly briefed the marines. They would pull back ten yards from the sack and with their backs to the police post lay in waiting. The hours passed. It had been mainly dry, just one heavy downpour that lasted a few minutes. The sky began to lighten. Then, as happens in the tropics, it was suddenly daylight.

The small patrol did one last sweep of the area, picked up the sack and returned to the police post. A more thorough search of the sack's contents revealed nothing new. Clearly it had been deposited by someone from the nearby tin mine. As the workers lived in a communal house, or kongsi, who would admit to being responsible? When the police arrived at the post they were informed of developments. A police inspector came out from Ipoh and the workers at the tin mine were questioned. They admitted providing the rice and clothing, but said they had been threatened by two armed men, who said they would be killed if they did not provide the food and clothing. The inspector told Lieutenant Pope that it was a common occurrence and that the tin mine workers could not be blamed. No doubt the terrorists had observed from a distance what had happened. D sub-section stayed at the police post for the rest of the week before returning to their troop location.

On his return, Rhodes was called to the troop stores. Sergeant Hayes, who was the troop quartermaster, had obtained some DCM ribbon. In fact he had done better than that, he produced a bar with four ribbons on it, the DCM was first followed by the ribbons of the General Service Medal (for service in Malaya), the Korean Medal and the United Nations Medal (Korean Service). Rhodes thanked him.

Hayes said, 'Don't thank me, it was the sergeant major's idea. He said he would send me out on patrol in the jungle, if I didn't produce the goods.'

When Rhodes returned to his tent, the rest of the section took the mickey in a good-natured way, saying he had more medals than John Wayne. The next day Rhodes went to see the sergeant major. He thanked him and showed him the medal ribbons.

QMS Higgins gave Rhodes his strange smile and said, 'Keep it to yourself, son, I don't want these bastards thinking I'm a soft touch.'

After one day in camp, the whole of one section went out on a seven-day patrol. It was the height of the monsoon season and it rained almost all the time. After three days they took an air drop. Some of the five parachutes missed the DZ and drifted down the valley. It took them the rest of the day to recover the supplies; thankfully the rum had survived the heavy landing. One of the perks of having an air drop was that each man on the patrol was given a tin of fifty cigarettes for free and enough rum to give each person a tot every evening. A water bottle top provided a generous and consistent measure.

They found two terrorist camps; one was clearly disused, but the other showed signs of recent occupation. They destroyed both camps when nothing was found. They returned to the pick-up point in the afternoon of the seventh day. Their clothing was rotting on their bodies. The humid conditions and the constant rain was too much for the shirts and trousers to stand. Foot rot was endemic and nobody escaped. Suggestions for a cure were varied, urinating on your own feet or somebody else providing the urine. The best cure available, but only back in camp, was a bowl of water containing permanganate of potash – at least your feet came out with a nice tan.

In the next few weeks, E and F sub-sections had two contacts with terrorists. They had one marine wounded, but killed two of the enemy. The wounded marine had been lucky in that the bullet had passed through the fleshy part of his right buttock. It was not a serious wound, but quite painful and offers to kiss it better were not appreciated. He was taken to BMH Taiping, where he spent two weeks until the wound had closed, and then a week in the Cameron Highlands at the army rest centre. When he returned to A-Troop, he had a week excused patrols, then went back to jungle bashing. He resisted all of the requests to see his scar, merely commenting that with all the fuss the nurses made of him, being shot in the arse was no bad thing.

Over the next few months several of the marines and two of the corporals returned to the UK. Two and a half years was the length of a marine's tour overseas and then replacements were sent out. They were now at their most effective in terms of jungle craft. They had been helped by the policy of providing four Iban trackers to each troop. The Ibans were from the Dyak tribes of Borneo and were still classed as headhunters. They were very small men, all under five feet in height, but very muscular and strong. They became great friends with the marines and willingly passed on their tracking knowledge. In camp they were given their own tent, but out on patrol they shared bashas with the marines. Whoever shared with those Ibans was guaranteed a dry night.

Their tracking skills were legend; they would look at a muddy track and say, 'Five men, two hours ago, moving quick.' As the marines' tracking skills improved so did the Ibans' English. Being taught English by a group of Royal Marines was probably not the best way to learn and the word 'fucking' initiated all of the Ibans' sentences. A visit to A-Troop by the wife of the CO of 42 Commando was a perfect example.

She, 'How do like it here in A-Troop?'

Iban, 'Fucking good.'

She, to the troop commander, 'They are very small.'

Iban interrupting, 'Me fucking big.'

She, moving away, 'Yes, I'm sure you are.'

When she had left the camp, Captain Baker went to the Ibans' tent and asked, 'Did you enjoy talking to the colonel's wife?'

'Yes,' said the Iban. 'She got fucking big tits.'

A Lincoln Strike

The whole of the troop were involved in one particular operation, assisted by Y-Troop, the object of which was to search a large hilly feature in A-Troop's area called Hill 1066. Y-Troop were to provide a defensive perimeter, into which A-Troop would drive any terrorists as they swept over the hill. A key component of the operation was a flight of three Lincoln bombers, who would drop high-explosive bombs ahead of A-Troop's sweep.

Y-Troop moved into position the night before the operation. The other troops moved to their start line at 0400 hours and at 0600 hours, just as it was getting light, the drone of the approaching Lincolns was heard.

A-Troop's start line was the Sungei Rai, where they were in an extended line on the west side. They lay on their backs watching as the Lincoln Bombers came closer. When they were about three hundred yards from them, the marines could see that the bomb doors were open. To their surprise and concern the leading aircraft released its bombs. It was like a giant sack of potatoes being emptied.

Corporal Green, who was next to Rhodes, said, 'Fuck shit! Get right down, he's let them go early.' As the aircraft passed overhead, the other two released their bombs. The bombs from the first aircraft passed over the marines' heads and the first two struck the ground less than a hundred yards from where the marines were laying. Rhodes was sure the earth lifted a foot in the air as the bombs exploded, the noise was deafening. Then in a manic creeping wall of destruction the rest of the bombs devoured the western side of Hill 1066.

The marines rose to their feet as they were signalled to advance with the shock waves still reverberating around them, and waded the river; it was less than two feet deep. They swept forward and upwards through the torn and mangled ground at intervals of five paces to give the troop a wider front. For most of the marines it was the first time they had seen the effect of a bombing strike. All of the NCOs had fought in the last war, as had the troop commander, so it was not a novel experience for them. However, most of the marines had gone through the wartime air raids but this was different. As they made their way up the hill, they were all of the opinion nothing could have survived this as most of the smaller trees had been reduced to matchwood. The lower ground-hugging foliage had been obliterated, while the large trees had remained standing but were now leafless.

Onwards and upwards they went. About a hundred feet from the crest was the first evidence of a terrorist presence. It was the remains of a large basha, big enough to sleep at least a dozen men and it had sustained severe blast damage as the very last bomb had struck the ground only eighty yards from it. They looked in its shattered remains for any bodies. They found nothing. Clearly the terrorists had not been at home when the bombs had struck. A careful search produced a couple of empty sacks and some old torn clothing. They moved to the crest of the hill. Y-Troop, meanwhile, were being kept informed of the position of the advancing marines. Keeping as straight a line as possible, they made their way down the reverse slope. A challenge was heard to their front, which prompted the quick cries of A-Troop and a dangerous situation was averted.

After a short break they retraced their footsteps. This time Y-Troop took the left flank and A-Troop the right and both troops went back over the hill in a long extended line. Again nothing was found, but the operation was considered a success and an example of what air co-operation could produce.

On the way back to their camp all of the marines bored one another with tales of how close the bombs had been. One bright spark suggested he could see the lettering on one of the bombs.

'I can't see how,' said one of his mates, 'your head was so far down in the ground you'd have to have eyes in your arse.'

When they arrived back at camp and after all the weapons had been cleaned, they were all, except for the duty sub-section, given permission to go into Ipoh.

'Transport will leave in thirty minutes. Be at the pick-up point at 2300 hours,' said the sergeant major. 'No excuses will be accepted.'

Rhodes and his mate Bob Jones made the most of the time, big eats, a visit to the cinema, thirty minutes of pleasure with Ida Tan and her sister and three bottles of Tiger beer.

'You know,' said Bob Jones, 'life can't get much better than this.'

Rhodes agreed; then he thought of Joyce Lang. 'Perhaps just a bit,' he said.

A Long Walk

Three days later, the whole troop, less those on the sick list, went out on a three-week patrol. Captain Baker, when he briefed them, stated that he wanted to penetrate as far into their area as they could. For the first time the marines took the larger Bergan rucksacks instead of their normal packs. Each marine carried six days' rations and laden as they were this was not going to be easy.

The plan was to take an air drop on the seventh day and at that site make a base camp. From there they could send out sub-sections for one-, two- or three-day patrols, trying to ensure each sub-section a rest period in the base camp after their exertions.

It was Malaya's dry period, which lasted normally about a month, in between its regular two monsoon seasons. The first two days of the patrol were hell, the going was appalling, thick jungle, steep slopes and deep fast-flowing rivers. At last the Bergans were getting lighter; they were only carrying four days' rations now. Some of the marines had taken the decision to consume extra rations in the first two days in order to reduce their loads, accepting that they would have reduced rations as well, but it was their choice.

They had three signalmen with them. These marines had the added burden of a 68 Set. While crossing a river one of the signalman lost his footing on the slippery rocks and was carried sixty yards downstream. As he was dragged beneath the surface he slipped off the wireless set he was carrying and was pulled from the water. The wireless was recovered but it had taken a battering and was later found to be unserviceable.

At about noon on the seventh day, they reached the site of what was to be their base camp. It was a good site, on a flattish ridge just above a large stream. The air drop took place two hours later. It was a large drop, nine days' rations for sixty men. For the next couple of hours the marines gathered in all of the parachutes and stacked their contents in the centre of the camp. The sections then constructed their shelters as darkness was only an hour or so away. The troop commander and the sergeant major had already allocated the position of the sections, all facing outwards in an all-around defensive shield. They just had time to prepare and eat a meal when darkness fell. It was a surprise to find how cool the night was and it was almost mosquito free. After a good night's sleep and breakfast, all of the sub-sections were allocated tasks to bring the base camp up to the troop commander's liking. D and C subs were sent out in opposite directions to do a circular sweep around the camp, to a distance of about one hundred yards, to make sure there were no nasty surprises close by. The other sub-sections dug latrine pits and gash pits, so as to keep the camp tidy and clean. When these tasks were completed the marines were given the rest of the day to improve their bashas and, section by section, to have a good wash in the stream below their watering point.

Over the next week, the marines patrolled large areas to the north, east and south. Two camps were found. One quite old and the other had been in more recent use. Both were destroyed. The deprivations inflicted by the jungle conditions on the patrols had resulted in several cases of diarrhoea and four of the marines had been badly stung by hornets, but in the main the troop remained quite healthy.

One of the troop commander's biggest worries was about what could be done if any of his men were wounded or taken seriously ill. At this time in Malaya the use of helicopters was considered too risky, even for emergency evacuations. The base camp concept had been a good idea; with each section given a rest day on return from a three-day patrol, the marines managed to remain fit and healthy.

On the fourteenth day of the patrol, C sub-section, patrolling to the north, had a contact with a group of five terrorists. In the ensuing firefight, two of the terrorists were shot dead and at least one other was wounded. It took the section another day to return to the camp, carrying the two bodies with them. The rest of the troop were already preparing for the return march and, having taken another air drop, had sufficient food for the march back. The Ibans with C sub had wanted to cut off the heads of the two terrorists, suggesting that two heads were easier to carry than two bodies. The marines thought this was very sensible; however, Captain Baker was not convinced that this was an acceptable practice, so the march out began on the sixteenth day carrying the bodies.

On day eighteen Captain Baker told the Ibans to cut off the two heads; he had realised that to carry the bodies any further was pointless, the stench was awful and in the difficult terrain was likely to cause one or more of the marines to sustain injury. Strangely, the Ibans were not too keen to remove the heads now, it was all to do with the treatment of an enemy and the release of his spirit. Eventually, the deed was done, the marines were surprised how hard it was to cut off the heads, the bodies were buried in very shallow graves and the heads carried back in some parachute silk. On the twenty-second day, they finally made it back to the pick-up point. As darkness fell they arrived back at Tambun camp, as one marine put it, 'Totally fucked.'

Penang, Pearl Set in a Silver Sea

There was minimal activity over the next few days. Rhodes had about nine letters to reply to. June had decided to marry her new man friend and said they would both be pleased to see him when he returned to England. His aunt and uncle were both well and were so proud of him being awarded the DCM. The news had even been in the *Kent Messenger*. Rhodes wondered why June had not mentioned it. Too involved in her coming marriage, he thought, anyway it didn't matter. There were two letters from Joyce. One started, 'My Hero'.

She's heard, thought Rhodes. Both letters were full of love and longing and seemed to suggest she could be persuaded to leave her husband if he wanted her to. Rhodes decided it was time to cool that particular friendship, but how?

They had two runs into Ipoh. Rhodes spent two hours with the lovely Ida Tan. She didn't charge him full price, but she wanted to take a photo of his thing.

'Make other girls jealous,' she said.

Captain Baker sent for him the next day. There was to be a medal presentation in Brigade HQ and he was required to attend. That afternoon Rhodes and Captain Baker went into HQ and, to Rhodes's delight, Captain Rogers and Sergeant Smith were there. They had a long chat before the ceremony. The GOC Malaya presented the medals, on behalf of His Majesty King George VI. Captain Rogers received the DSC, then Rhodes the DCM and Sergeant Smith was Mentioned in Dispatches. The GOC had a chat with them all. He was very nice and insisted they all had a drink together; after about an hour they all went their separate ways. On the journey back to A-Troop, Captain Baker told Rhodes that the bringing back of heads was causing concern and he said, 'It's under review.' They both laughed.

The campaign medals for the marines began to arrive at the camp. For serving in the Malayan Emergency Service men and women received the General Service Medal with a bar on it with the word 'Malaya'. To qualify for this medal the person had to have been in Malaya for twenty-four hours. People serving in Singapore did not qualify. The marines were aware of the abuse of the medal system where servicemen from Singapore would travel up to Ipoh by train and return straight away. As this would take slightly longer than twenty-four hours they were then entitled to the medal. All servicemen engaged in the conflict considered this an insult to themselves and to their comrades who had lost their lives in fighting the terrorists, but little was done to correct this. Along with his General Service Medal, Rhodes also received his Korean and United Nations Medals.

Not bad, he thought, and I have only been out here for twelve months. Just two years in the Royal Marines and I'm wearing four medals.

Since the three-week patrol, the marines had not been out for longer than three days. In a tactical sense three days was the most effective patrol time. These and the patrols of shorter duration allowed them to cover their area more efficiently. The subject of the removal of heads from dead terrorists was still being debated. The police wished to see the bodies of all enemy killed. They had extensive photographic records of active communists and wished to be able to eliminate them from these records. In jungle conditions cameras were almost useless. The damp and at times poor light did not inspire confidence in this method of obtaining a good likeness. So a compromise was agreed, but not promulgated, a fudge to be proud of and in the best traditions of Whitehall.

After twelve months abroad, all marines were entitled to seven days' local leave. The sergeant major informed Rhodes that he and Jones were the next to go. There was a choice, Singapore, living in HMS *Terror*, the shore base there, with permission to come and go as they pleased or Sandycroft leave centre in Penang. Rhodes thought of Joyce Lang and the delights of her body, then of her husband.

'Penang, please, sergeant major,' said Rhodes.

'Well, that's a surprise,' said QMS Higgins. 'With all those scented letters coming from Singapore, I'd pencilled you in for

HMS *Terror*. Still never mind, the choice is yours.'

Rhodes thanked him again and left the office with the strange sound that went for laughter coming from Hairy Henry.

The following Monday Rhodes and Jones were taken into HQ to join up with marines from the other troops to go by lorry to Penang. There were only eight of them, the popular choice being Singapore. Four hours later, they arrived at the ferry. The crossing took twenty minutes and within thirty minutes they were at the gates of Sandycroft leave centre. They were told to report to the military police post just inside the gate. They looked at one another in disgust. MPs were about as popular as smallpox. Inside the post sat an MP sergeant. On his desk was a nameplate: Sergeant D Jones RMP. He looked a miserable sod. He looked at them.

'I don't like marines,' he said, 'they cause trouble. Just watch your step or your feet won't touch.'

Bob Jones looked at him and said, 'My name is Jones, Sergeant, I wonder if we are related and incidentally, where can we all get treatment for our jungle sores?'

This was too much for the sergeant, who said, 'Don't get sarky with me, son. Label up your rifles and leave them and your ammunition in the armoury next door. You'll be given a receipt.'

Over the next hour they had a good look round the camp. It was well laid out and very clean and the beach was only yards from the dining room. The accommodation itself was good. They were in four-men huts and had crisp white sheets, but no mosquito nets. There were female service personnel in the camp and they shared all the facilities except sleeping accommodation, which was fenced off. They changed into their civvies and went down to dinner. The food was very good with a choice of starter, three choices of the main course and three choices of pudding.

That evening Rhodes and Jones stayed in the camp. There was dancing every night and a well-stocked bar. After a few drinks they both asked some of the girls if they would like to dance. Rhodes had several partners during the evening. They were all quite nice. They asked him what regiment he was in and when he said 42 Commando Royal Marines they seemed quite impressed. All the guests had arrived that day and by 2300 hours most had gone to bed. Rhodes had the best night's sleep since he had arrived in Malaya.

At 0700 hours they were awakened by the rattle of teacups as Malay mess boys brought their morning tea. After breakfast they went down to the beach to swim and sunbathe. The day passed pleasantly and that evening Rhodes and Jones went into George-town where the two main attractions were The City Lights cabaret and The Imperial Dance Hall. They both had decided not to 'indulge in the flesh' as they had only a limited amount of money and they had the rest of the week to go. Also Bob Jones had suggested they might get lucky with one or two of the servicewomen.

'Why pay for something when you might get it for free?' they both agreed.

Georgetown was awash with servicemen as there was a substantial army garrison on Penang Island. The MPs were kept busy, as fights broke out among the service personal. The marines kept well clear, no point in spending your leave in some army guardroom. The cause of the problem soon became clear, a battalion of a Scottish regiment had a private war going on with two companies from the KOYLIs who were in Penang for retraining. The cause of the conflict was obscure and mostly trivial. It turned out that the KOYLIs had dared occupy one side of the City Light cabaret, which the Jocks considered theirs.

After a few beers Rhodes and Jones decided to go to the cinema. They saw *Rommel, Desert Fox* and they thought James Mason was great as Rommel. They both wondered where they could buy a leather greatcoat just like Rommel's.

The next day they joined a coach trip from the leave centre to Penang Hill, but only about a dozen had taken advantage of this free trip. Seven of the party were women and one of the girls was particularly stunning. She looked like Doris Day's younger sister, short blonde hair, blue eyes, a nice tan and a figure that brought a rush of saliva to Rhodes's mouth. He turned to Bob Jones, 'I've just fallen in love, Bob, isn't she gorgeous?' Jones thought she was all right, but preferred the one sitting next to her, the one with the dark hair.

When they arrived at the base of Penang Hill they had a ten-minute wait for the cable car. Rhodes took advantage of this to get as close to her as he could. She surprised him by turning around.

She smiled at him and said, 'They say it's ten degrees cooler at the top.' Rhodes was lost for words.

He thought, I'm standing here with my mouth open, looking like the village idiot. He struggled for something to say and all he could manage was, 'I think you're lovely.'

She smiled, her eyes full of mischief. 'Thank you,' she said, 'and so are you.'

Laughing, she grabbed the dark-haired girl's arm and they made their way on to the cable car. Rhodes, Jones and the rest of the party followed on. Halfway up they had to change to the second stage vehicle, it clattered on up the very steep slope, it went through some low cloud and broke through into some brilliant sunshine. At last they had reached the top, the views were spectacular, they were two and a half thousand feet above sea level, and it really was cooler at the top.

Rhodes was unable to make any further contact with the girl; she always seemed to be moving away just as he got close enough to talk to her. They finished the trip and returned to Sandycroft. As they made their way back to their hut, Jones said, 'Well, you certainly fucked that up, Pete, where did all the Rhodes charm go?'

'I'm sorry,' said Rhodes, 'she completely knocked me off my feet.'

'Well,' said Jones, 'perhaps she and her friend will be at the dance tonight.'

After dinner that evening they had a couple of beers and then went into the dance hall. It was crowded and it seemed that the entire leave centre were there. Rhodes and Jones spotted the two girls over in the corner and they lost no time in asking them for a dance. To their delight both girls agreed but the dark-haired one grabbed Rhodes and Jones was grabbed by Doris Day's sister. In spite of this, they enjoyed dancing with the girls and they swapped partners at the start of the next dance. Doris Day's sister was called Julie Grey and the dark-haired one was Jane Fellows. Rhodes and Jones were soon completely at ease with the two girls and the evening was a great success. They agreed to meet the next day and go swimming. As Rhodes and Jones went back to their hut they felt they had made progress and both slept well that night.

After breakfast the next day, they made their way along the beach together. They found a quiet spot and spent the day swimming and talking. The two girls both were wearing one-piece costumes and Rhodes was worried that so much desirable flesh being so close to hand would cause him to show his appreciation. The girls told them they were both nurses from the British Military Hospital at Taiping and the two marines told them what unit they were from. It was time to go and they agreed to meet in the dining hall for dinner.

As they made their way back along the beach, Julie said to Rhodes, 'I'm sorry for teasing you on Penang Hill. I really was flattered by your comment.'

Rhodes said, 'It's me who should apologise, but thank goodness we got over that dodgy start.' He squeezed her hand and she returned the pressure.

After they had their evening meal together they made for the dance hall. It turned into a special evening. They danced a lot together and Rhodes could feel Julie's body getting ever closer. She had noticed that she was arousing him and decided they would sit the next dance out and have a drink. Jane and Bob were experiencing the same problem, so they to decided to join them. Rhodes went over to the bar and as he waited he heard raised voices coming from the direction of their table. A large man was making a fuss over something and had clearly been drinking. From the comments being made the dispute involved both of the girls.

When Rhodes arrived on the scene he was just in time to hear the man say to Julie, 'You've been giving me the eye all week, now it's time to come across, we can start with a dance.' With that he tried to pull her to her feet.

Rhodes knocked his hand away. 'I suggest you leave, while you can still walk,' he said.

'Oh,' said the man, 'a fucking tough guy.'

At that moment two MPs came in and grabbed hold of the drunk, saying, 'Not you again, Fraser. We will take you back to your hut and you can sleep it off.'

With that they took him away, but Julie was quite upset.

'I have never seen him before today and I wouldn't lead him on anyway,' she said.

They sat talking together for another fifteen minutes after which Jane Fellows suggested that they go for a walk along the road to the village. Julie said she wanted to get her shawl from her room.

'Won't be a minute,' she said, and left.

After a couple of minutes they decided to go and meet her, but as they walked along the path they heard someone cry out, it was obviously a female. Rhodes ran in the direction of the sound and saw a couple struggling by the side of the path. She cried out again and he heard her dress rip. In two more strides he was at grips with the figure who was trying to pull her to the ground. He swung the man round. It was the drunk from the dance hall. The woman was Julie. Rhodes swung a punch that struck the man squarely on the nose and there was a satisfying sound of crunching bone and blood spread across his face. Another two punches and the man went down. Rhodes drew back his foot ready to kick him in the balls, but checked himself; he had done enough damage.

There seemed to be a lot of people now on the scene. The matron from the girls' quarters had her arm round Julie and was leading her away.

Jane Fellows said, 'Leave her now, Peter, we will see you to-morrow.'

Rhodes and Bob Jones made their way back to their hut.

'What a way to end what should have been a perfect day,' said Rhodes. 'I do hope Julie's okay.' They chatted for a while, and then went to bed.

The next morning they sat on their beds drinking their early morning tea when the door opened and in came two MPs.

'Who is Rhodes?' they asked.

'I am,' said Rhodes.

'We want you up at the police post at 0900 hours. You are being charged with assaulting Sergeant Fraser. He is in hospital.'

Bob Jones said, 'Best place for that bastard.'

The two MPs left and Rhodes and Jones got dressed into their uniforms and made their way to the police post. They went in and the MP sergeant named Jones looked up.

'I knew you marines would be trouble. You, Marine Rhodes, will be charged with committing gross personal violence against Sergeant Fraser of the RASC. What have you got to say for yourself?'

Rhodes looked at him and said, 'Is Fraser being charged with attempted rape?'

Sergeant Jones looked at him, 'I know nothing about an attempted rape, explain.' So Rhodes did.

When he had finished Sergeant Jones told them to go back to their room. He would send for them when he had completed his enquiries.

A couple of hours later Rhodes was told to report to the police post. Bob Jones came with him, but waited outside. Rhodes knocked on the door and was told to enter. Seated at the desk was the provost marshal, a major behind whom stood Sergeant Jones and the matron from the girls' quarters. Rhodes saluted and gave his full name and number.

Returning his salute, the major said, 'The circumstances of the incident have been investigated. Sergeant Fraser is being charged with, one, indecent assault, two, being drunk and three, bringing disgrace on His Majesty's uniform. When he is fit to leave hospital, he will be remanded by his commanding officer pending trial by court martial. Sergeant Jones will read the statement you have made. You will then sign it and you may then continue with your leave. Read his statement, Sergeant Jones.'

Jones then read the statement. 'I was walking back to my quarters from the dance hall. It was about 2300 hours when I heard a woman cry out. In the moonlight I could see two people struggling. The woman cried out again, "Please leave me be, you are hurting me." I ran over to them and tried to pull the man away from the woman. I had to strike him to make him let her go. He fell to the ground and struck the side of his head on the concrete path. Other people came and the man was escorted away. The woman was helped away by the matron of the female quarters. Signed Marine P J Rhodes, DCM, Royal Marines.'

Rhodes signed the statement.

The major looked at him and said, 'I doubt if you wish to add to that.'

Rhodes said, 'No, thank you sir.'

The major went on, 'A badly broken nose and a fractured cheekbone will heal, but getting his stripes back will take a very long time. Now go and enjoy the rest of your leave.'

Rhodes saluted and left. Outside Bob Jones was waiting.

'How did it go?' he asked.

'Fine,' said Rhodes. 'That MP sergeant is okay, they are not all bastards.'

'No,' said Jones, 'just most of them.'

Later that day they were sunbathing on the beach when Jane Fellows came up to them.

'Julie's okay,' she said. 'Matron made a fuss of her and gave her a sedative. She has been sleeping most of the day, but we will all go out tonight. Is that okay?'

Rhodes and Jones looked at one another. Indeed it was.

They all met up in the dining room at 1900 hours. Julie looked a little pale, but smiled when Rhodes and Bob Jones stood up as the girls reached their table. They talked about everything, except the previous night's trauma. As the evening progressed it became obvious that Julie had recovered her confidence.

After dinner they went dancing, Rhodes held Julie close, but not too close. She smiled and said, 'I'm not a piece of fragile china, Peter. I won't break.'

Rhodes pulled her closer and really began to enjoy the even??ing. Bob and Jane had their own agenda and after a passionate embrace decided to go for a walk. Rhodes satisfied himself with the dancing and at about 2300 hours, after Jane and Bob had been gone about an hour, Julie suggested that they go and find them.

'We don't want to interrupt anything,' said Rhodes.

'Have no fears on that score, I know my Jane,' said Julie. About a hundred yards down the beach, they heard the sound of laughter. Homing in on the sound, they found Jane and Bob sitting on a fallen tree trunk.

'This girl has just told me a series of disgusting stories that have made me blush,' said Bob. 'These nurses have no shame.'

'But they are all true,' said Jane interrupting. 'How about a couple from you, Peter?'

Rhodes declined, but offered to give them three cleaner verses of 'Five and Twenty Virgins'. After he had finished, both girls cried 'More, we want more,' so he followed up with 'Eskimo Nell'.

It was now almost 0100 hours.

'Time for bed I think,' said Rhodes. 'Remember, tomorrow is our last day.'

They all made their way to the gate of the girls' compound. Rhodes kissed Julie. She kissed him back. He could see Jane and Bob were doing the same. Julie and Jane reluctantly broke away and went through the gate into their cabin. On the way back to their own quarters Rhodes asked his friend, 'Did you?'

Jones looked at him and said, 'No, I did not and do you know, Pete, it wasn't important. I must be in love!' They both laughed.

The next morning, after breakfast, they went into Georgetown. The girls got some picture postcards to send to friends and relatives. The marines did the same. They had a snack and some cold drinks and then returned to Sandycroft. That afternoon they went to the beach to swim and sunbathe. The day was passing so quickly and after dinner they danced and had a few drinks.

They decided to go for a walk along the beach for the last time and after a passionate embrace, Julie said, 'I want to, Peter, but I won't. Jane and I have strong feelings on girls who give in too easily, it gives all of us a bad name.'

Strangely Rhodes wasn't disappointed and he was sure his friend was having a similar experience. Before they parted they agreed to see each other in the morning. The marines were leaving at 0900 hours, the girls an hour later.

After breakfast the marines took their kitbags up to the police post and waited for their lorry. At a quarter to the hour Julie and Jane arrived. It was the first time they had seen the marines in uniform. They exchanged addresses and, as they had a final embrace, Julie ran her finger along the medal ribbons on Rhodes's shirt.

'We will meet again, Peter, I know we will.' She gave him a final kiss and walked away. She didn't look back. Rhodes and Jones watched the two girls until they were out of sight.

When their lorry arrived, they put their kit on board and then went into the police post to collect their rifles and ammunition. Sergeant Jones, the MP, came out just as they were about to get into the lorry.

'Had a good leave?' he asked. They both agreed they had.

'Well, look after yourselves,' he said.

As the lorry pulled away, he lifted his hand and they returned the gesture. The lorry turned the corner and he was out of sight.

'Well, what about that then?' said Rhodes. 'I told you they are not all bastards.'

Jones reluctantly agreed.

Farewell at Batu Gajah

They arrived back at A-Troop in the late afternoon, but there was a sombre air about the place. Two marines from G sub had been killed. Corporal Thomas and Marine Hicks had both been shot dead in a clash with a terrorist group. Four terrorists had also been killed, but the marines could not accept their colleagues' deaths as a fair trade. The funerals would take place the next day. Rhodes and Jones both asked to be in the guard of honour. The next morning Sergeant Saunders drilled them for an hour in firing volleys. At noon the whole troop, less six to guard the camp, were taken by lorry to Batu Gajah military cemetery.

The guard was marched to the gravesides, while the rest of the troop marched ahead and behind the two coffins, which were covered with the Union Jack. Rhodes could see Paul and Helen Dupré and other members of the Planters' Association, a strong contingent of the Malay police, and of course the commanding officer of 42 Commando Royal Marines who stood next to Captain Baker. The chaplain led the burial service and, as the coffins were lowered into the graves, the guard presented arms and the marine bugler sounded the last post. The guard then fired three volleys and the bugler sounded reveille, while the rest of the troop then paid their respects by filing past the two graves, pausing to salute as they did so. Lieutenant Colonel Mason, DSO Royal Marines, the commanding officer 42 Commando, and the troop commander, Captain Baker, were the last of the marines to pay their respects. The Malay police followed on, followed finally by the Planters' Association.

On completion of the service, the marines made their way back to their transport. Rhodes saw Paul and Helen Dupré coming towards them and he went to meet them. Paul shook his hand while Helen embraced him and greeted him in French. They stood there chatting for a few minutes before it was time to go. As the marines left he could see the Duprés talking to 42's CO and Captain Baker. The return journey was completed almost in silence, most of the marines lost in their thoughts.

It is marine tradition that the property of colleagues killed in action are auctioned off. The money raised is then sent to their relatives. But first, the sergeant major and the section sergeant go through the dead marine's letters, photographs, etc., and any item that could give offence to the relatives is destroyed. The remainder are sent on to his family. The auction then takes place. Civilian clothing, shirts, socks, pants, vests, trousers and shoes are sold to the highest bidder. The object is to send this money home to the deceased's loved ones with a letter of condolence from the troop commander. Rhodes paid ten dollars for a pair of pale blue trousers, on which Joe Hicks had appeared to have been sick on his last trip into Ipoh. He also paid one dollar for a dirty pair of socks with a large hole in the toe. When the auction was over, two hundred dollars had been raised on behalf of each marine. It was also traditional that the items purchased were then burnt in a farewell salute of smoke and fire. Rhodes was not sorry to see his purchases go up in smoke. The other marines felt the same.

Rhodes caught up on his mail. June was now happily married, but Aunt Marie was worried about Uncle Bill's chest. Mark was courting the daughter of the headmaster of the village school and Joyce Lang was pregnant. She said her husband was delighted and perhaps they should cease their correspondence. Thank Christ for that, thought Rhodes, June and Joyce off my back in one go! It then struck him how strange it was that most of the women in his life had names beginning with J. He then applied himself and wrote letters to them all. He wrote last of all to Julie, as he wanted to say everything in words that he had failed to say to her face on that last day at Sandycroft. It was a letter that came easy to him, because he meant every word.

Rockets Galore, Fire and Water

The troop continued to saturate their area with patrol activity. No. 1 Section did a sweep up a large gully in the Gunong Rapat cluster, but not before two Brigand fighter bombers had fired a dozen rockets in two passes at the target. In the follow-up, the remains of a ten-man camp were found, no bodies or food. It looked as if it had not been used for some time. It was decided that D sub-section should spend the night in the gully, just in case any terrorists had remained hidden during the air strike. It was an uncomfortable night as it rained heavily and the mosquitoes were voracious. Dawn could not come soon enough, and they all made up their minds not to repeat the feat of trying to sleep on a steep wet slippery slope.

During the next few months, Rhodes had several letters from Julie. They made plans to spend their next leave together, which was ten months away. Jane and Bob were planning to do the same. It surprised Rhodes that he did not seem to feel the heat now as he once did. Corporal Green told him it had been the same in Burma, 'All of a sudden, you get used to it.'

Julie had told him that the nurses in Taiping Hospital could tell who had been in Malaya the longest by how fast the fans in their rooms had been set.

D sub were sent on a three-day patrol up past the village of Juang. Rhodes felt uneasy, something was wrong. When they stopped for a breather, he told Corporal Green, who had also noticed how quiet it was.

'We will bring the Bren group up just behind us and spread out a bit more,' said Green.

At about 1600 hours Corporal Green decided to stop for the night. They quietly made camp, had a meal and settled down for the night. At about 0200 hours there was a most tremendous storm. The campsite was about ten feet above a stream and they could tell that its volume of water had increased dramatically. The torrential rain had made their bashas almost useless. Suddenly they could hear a thunderous roar.

Corporal Green shouted, 'Grab hold of something, there's a wall of water coming down the stream.'

The marines got hold of their weapons and tried to secure themselves to the nearest small tree. Then it was upon them.

Rhodes felt a great weight of water hit him. It seemed icy cold as he clung desperately to the base of a tree while somebody was hanging on to his belt. Then the wall of water was past.

He was covered in leaves, twigs and mud, water drained from his clothing.

Christ, he thought, where are the others?

It was too dark to see much of his changed surroundings, who had clung on to his belt? He called out his friend's names, silence.

Then a few feet away a voice said, 'Bloody hell, I just thought I was having a nightmare, where are the others?'

To Rhodes's relief, he heard Corporal Green calling out as well. At least three of them were safe! Within five minutes another five of the section had appeared from downstream of the camp. Corporal Green had a torch that he switched on and they started to gather what remained of their ponchos and the rest of their belongings. The first priority was to find their weapons and ammunition. Fortunately, most of them had managed to hold on to these while the majority of their kit was found jammed in a stand of bamboo along with some torn ponchos, but where were the other four marines?

As soon as it was light, Corporal Green took Rhodes and two others to search for the missing marines, leaving the other four to sort out the mess that had been their camp. They followed the stream for about fifty yards. It was now just a gentle flow. They found another poncho stuck in some branches, some ten feet off the ground, also two packs and a pair of trousers. Moving further downstream, they found some more clothing and one jungle boot, they then heard voices. They listened, only a marine could swear like that. They now heard several other voices. They called out, 'D sub, D sub.'

A reply came, 'Over fucking here.'

They made their way to the voices and were relieved to find

them. Two had their jungle boots on, but little else, one was completely dressed and the remaining marine was stark naked except for one jungle boot.

They were all delighted to be together again. It would not be marine-like to show emotion, but they all came close to it. They made their way back to the camp, collecting on the way further bits and pieces of kit. When they reached the camp, the other marines had made some tea which they shared with those just returned. They each had a mouthful and felt almost back to normal. The naked marine with one jungle boot asked Corporal Green for some of the recovered clothing.

'I'm thinking about it,' said Green, 'but I must say I find you dangerously attractive as you are.'

After a further search most of their kit was recovered. Now they all had their clothes on and luckily all of their important equipment.

Corporal Green decided to follow the ridge that ran parallel to the stream and after about an hour, they found some tracks. Having no Iban with them, they decided for themselves that they were made by at least ten people, but the tracks were blurred by the sliding that had taken place on the undulating terrain. They followed the track for another hour before Rhodes called Corporal Green to the front. Now on the flat he pointed out some distinct, but very small footprints, bare feet. In fact, it could now be clearly seen that all the prints were made by bare feet.

Green looked at Rhodes. 'I think they're Sakai, probably got washed out last night. For Christ's sake don't shoot them.'

Rhodes nodded and they moved on. About a hundred yards further Green's suspicions were confirmed. There were fifteen in total, five children of various ages and they looked in a bad way. Normally, the Sakai would avoid contact with anyone. They were the original aborigines of Malaya and were left in peace even by the terrorists. The marines had a few sweets left in their rations and they gave these to the children who grabbed them and ran to their parents, but the adults wanted nothing to do with the marines. Corporal Green said they should give them one tin of meat from their rations; twelve tins were put in a pile, with a tin opener on top. The marines then moved on past them, after sixty yards they looked back, the Sakai had gone and so had the tins.

The next day they made their way back down the pipeline and eventually arrived at the French Tekka Tin Mine at about 1600 hours. The Duprés were pleased to see them and Helen insisted on working on Rhodes's French, much to the amusement of the rest of the patrol. They were given plenty of hot sweet tea. They told the Duprés about the flash flood and the naked marine. Helen Dupré said she would have liked to have seen that. 'Which one of them was it?'

Mick Benson blushed. They all pointed their fingers at him and said, 'Him.'

The transport arrived from A-Troop and they said their good-byes and left. On arrival at camp the marines cleaned their weapons and equipment, while Corporal Green reported the events of the patrol to the troop commander. They all showered, then had their various cuts and bruises treated by the camp medical orderly. After a hot meal they lay on their beds and read their mail. Life was good.

Taiping Reunion

The next day D sub were duty section, so it was a day in camp. Corporal Green told Rhodes to act as escort to Captain Baker, who was being driven by jeep to BMH Taiping. Rhodes couldn't believe his luck. His pleasure was so obvious that Captain Baker asked him if he was okay.

'Yes, thank you, sir, I'm fine, I have a friend at the hospital, that's all.'

Baker looked at him, 'A nurse, I suppose?'

Rhodes nodded and thought, Best not to say too much.

The jeep took about ninety minutes to reach Taiping and Rhodes wondered if Julie would be free to see him. Captain Baker said he would be about two hours; he would be visiting a friend who was a captain in 40 Commando who had been wounded a week ago, but was now on the mend.

Rhodes went to the reception desk and asked where he could find Nurse Julie Grey. He was informed that she was on ward six and was escorted there by one of the orderlies. Julie saw him as he came through the door to the ward. She smiled and waved and the ward sister told them to use the nurses' rest room, but to behave themselves. Once in the rest room, they embraced. Julie told Rhodes how much she had missed him. He couldn't take his eyes off her. She looked stunning.

The door opened and a formidable female figure walked in.

'Nurse Grey, what are you doing off the ward?' she asked.

Julie stood up. 'This is my boyfriend, Matron, the Royal Marine I told you about. We met in Penang.'

The matron looked at Rhodes, then smiled. 'Oh yes, your knight in shining armour, so you are the rescuer of maidens in distress?'

Rhodes felt embarrassed. 'Yes, Matron,' he managed to say. She was a bit like Hairy Henry, but not so hairy.

'Well, young man, you and Julie can have one hour, take him

to the canteen and buy him a cold drink.'

The hour passed quickly and Rhodes walked Julie back to the ward. She told him her ward treated all the gunshot wound cases. Some of the patients were in a bad way, but most would recover and return to duty. The more serious cases were sent back to the UK. Rhodes gave Julie a prolonged kiss and then he made his way back to the jeep. He stood talking to the driver until Captain Baker returned; to his surprise Matron was with him.

'Just been hearing about your exploits in Penang, Rhodes, glad to hear you upheld the honour of the corps,' said Captain Baker. They all got into the jeep.

'Take care,' said Matron, and she waved as they drove away.

Death in the Afternoon

Two days later, the troop did an operation with a police jungle squad that involved doing a sweep through a rubber plantation. Parts of the rubber had become overgrown and provided a perfect place to leave food and clothing for the terrorists. After four hours they had found nothing and it was decided to return to camp. Soon after they had arrived back, they were all busy cleaning their weapons when a jeep raced into the camp with a police lieutenant on board. Something was up! The policeman remained in the camp for about an hour. Lieutenant Pope was in deep conversation with him right up to the point that the jeep pulled away.

About an hour later Corporal Green was sent for. When he returned Rhodes was told to report to the troop commander. Captain Baker told Rhodes that information had been obtained that several terrorists were meeting at the junction of two streams at the point where they joined the Sungei Rai. The information was considered accurate and the plan was to insert two or three of the troop, under the cover of darkness, and ambush the terrorists. Rhodes said he knew the place. He explained that there was an old tree trunk that had been washed down stream in a storm and over the months it had silted up to form a ten-foot-high mound. It was now covered in vegetation.

Rhodes finished by saying, 'There would only be cover for a couple of men.'

'Good,' said Captain Baker, 'Lieutenant Pope and yourself will be inserted there tomorrow morning at 0400 hours. Lieutenant Pope will now brief you.'

For the next hour they talked over the plan. It was decided that they would both carry the newly issued Owen gun which was an Australian weapon with a higher cyclic rate of fire than the Sten, two hand grips, magazine on the top giving a gravity feed, a 9 mm calibre, and above all it was accurate. Rhodes could confirm this as he had been carrying one for the last month. They decided to take two water bottles each, as they would be there for about nine hours. In addition, they would each carry two 36 grenades and five magazines each for their Owen guns.

All of one section were briefed. The plan was for both sections to go by lorry to the French Tekka Tin Mine at 0200 hours. The lorry would not have a cover on so D sub would remain clearly visible, while C sub would keep out of sight by laying flat on the floor of the lorry. On arrival at the tin mine, D sub would make their way up the trail to Juang, while C sub would remain at the tin mine out of sight. When D sub crossed the junction of the two streams, it would still be dark. Lieutenant Pope and Rhodes would then break away from the patrol and make their way to the mound and climb onto it from the rear, so as to leave no tracks. D sub would continue up the track to Juang and would wait there until it was daylight before returning to the tin mine the same way they had come. Instead of getting into the lorry, D sub would hide in one of the mine outbuildings. C sub would then stand up in the lorry and make themselves visible as it left the mine. When the lorry reached the main road it would be driven under some trees and would wait there for further instructions.

At 0200 hours the next morning the patrol left the camp as planned. When they reached the junction of the two streams, Lieutenant Pope and Rhodes slipped away and made their way round the back of the mound and moved into the scrub on the top. D sub continued on up the track to Juang where they stayed until it was light. They then made their way back. As they re-crossed the stream junction, Corporal Green took a quick glance at the mound; he couldn't see Pope or Rhodes. At the tin mine D sub moved into one of the out buildings. The lorry then left with C sub standing up. Hopefully, the deception had worked. D sub kept their weapons to hand. When the trap was sprung it would still take them thirty minutes to get back to Lieutenant Pope and Rhodes's position.

As the sun rose it began to get very warm and although the mound provided some cover, it did not have a mature canopy of trees to provide shelter from the direct rays of the sun. Lieutenant Pope and Rhodes had made themselves as comfortable as they could. They were in a sitting position. If and when the terrorists came, to get an effective shot they would have to change to either kneeling or even standing. As the morning progressed they were glad they had decided on taking two bottles of water each. Rhodes was more than halfway through his first bottle and Lieutenant Pope had drunk slightly more. They were sat about a yard apart and when the time came to engage the enemy they would try and increase their spacing, but they did not have a lot of room to manoeuvre. They both tried to flex their limbs and they changed from sitting to kneeling, trying to make their movements as slow as possible, so as not to attract attention.

Just before noon two figures appeared from the direction of Juang. They were dressed in light green clothing and they were both carrying M1 carbines. Lieutenant Pope indicated not to fire. The two sat on the side of the track opposite the marines and then two more appeared from the same direction. They had No. 5 Jungle Rifles. Lieutenant Pope gave the signal to prepare to fire. Out of the corner of his eye, Rhodes noticed four more terrorists coming to the edge of the stream from the opposite direction. They crossed over and joined the others. The four newcomers had a variety of weapons, one Sten, two No. 4 rifles, and a Bren.

Lieutenant Pope whispered, 'You start from the right, I'll work from the left, get the Bren gunner first or we're fucked.'

They both opened fire together. Rhodes put a three-round burst across the chest of the Bren gunner, then two more bursts accounted for the one next to him. As he fired to take out his third terrorist, the two marines were raked by return fire.

Rhodes felt an almighty blow high up on his left leg; it was as if he had been struck by a stick wielded by a giant, but although thrown off balance, he continued to fire. He changed magazines. He had to stand now as his leg was numb, but he fired the rest of the magazine and his four targets were down. Changing magazines again he glanced towards Lieutenant Pope who was slipping slowly to the ground with his shirt front covered in blood. More shots came Rhodes way and a bullet slashed across his upper left arm. He fired two more bursts where he thought the shots had come from.

Grenades. The thought sprang to his mind. He pulled out the pin and lobbed the grenade high into the air in the direction of the remaining terrorists. He dropped to the ground, a shaft of pain screamed through his body. The grenade exploded, he lobbed another, another satisfying blast of sound, then silence.

Back at the tin mine, D sub sprang to their feet at the sound of firing and started to jog up the trail towards the ambush position. The volume of firing worried Corporal Green, his experienced ear telling him that more than two terrorists were being ambushed. He could also detect gunshots different to the sound of Owen guns. Paul Dupré was also concerned, so he drove his old jeep up the trail after the marines. As he caught up, six managed to jump aboard his jeep. The marines clung on for dear life, as the jeep slid from one side of the trail to the other, it hit a leaning tree and one of the marines was knocked off. He got to his feet and continued after his disappearing colleagues. C sub had also heard the firing and as they raced back to the tin mine in their lorry, they heard the two explosions from the grenades. They looked at one another, that amount of firepower wasn't in the script.

After he had thrown the two grenades, Rhodes had moved across to Lieutenant Pope who was now barely conscious after being hit in the right side of his chest. Rhodes could see the entry wound, pink frothy blood was oozing from it. He put his hand round to Pope's side and there was the exit wound. He knew he must check on the terrorists, they could be all dead or about to attack them.

Rhodes quickly tied a field dressing round his leg as tight as he could and slid down the back of the mound and round to the front. As he moved into the open he could see five bodies, another lay half in the stream. Where were the other two? There was movement to his right. He fired a burst, then another and the movement stopped. He moved over to the body. He could have saved his ammunition as the man was minus his leg from the knee down. A few yards further on was the eighth terrorist, a woman, with a massive wound in her chest and no signs of life.

He returned to where he had left Lieutenant Pope and used the officer's own dressing to cover the entry wound.

Pope opened his eyes, 'We okay?' he gasped.

'We are fine,' said Rhodes. 'Surrounded by dead terrorists, but fine.'

At that moment he could hear the sound of an approaching vehicle. Help had arrived. Rhodes's leg was now giving him considerable pain and he could only crawl towards his rescuers.

He called out, 'We are over here.'

Within minutes Rhodes and Lieutenant Pope were in Paul Dupré's jeep and with two marines to hold them as still as possible Dupré drove very carefully back to the tin mine.

At the tin mine, Helen Dupré tended their wounds and using torn sheets she bandaged them making them as comfortable as possible.

'Oh, Peter,' she said, 'you both could have been killed, what a waste that would have been.'

At that moment a military ambulance arrived and with it 42 Commando's medical officer, Surgeon Lieutenant Monk.

He quickly checked them over and said, 'I'll give you boys something for the pain and then you are off to Taiping.'

At the ambush site, Corporal Green had made a complete search of the area. The eight bodies were laid out with their weapons to one side while in their packs he found some documents and a couple of maps which had some interesting marks on.

What a day, he thought, and what a result.

Captain Baker arrived with a senior police officer, who when he saw the dead terrorists and the maps, said, 'This is the best we could have hoped for, it's a major success.'

The tin mine was soon awash with senior police and marine officers. Lieutenant Colonel Mason, CO of 42 Commando, had arrived and was in deep conversation with Captain Baker; he wanted to know the condition of his two wounded marines. Captain Baker, who had earlier talked to Surgeon Lieutenant Monk, was able to assure him that their wounds were serious but not life threatening.

Corporal Green, with the aid of C sub and the Duprés' jeep, had moved all the bodies, their weapons and packs, to one of the out buildings at the tin mine. The Duprés had allowed their house to be used by the officers to decide what action was to be taken in the light of this major success. Lieutenant Colonel Mason told the Duprés how grateful he was for their assistance and the prompt help they had given to his wounded marines.

Helen said, 'Colonel, they are our friends. The boys in A-Troop are like family to us, they protect us, and when they are in trouble we help.'

Colonel Mason turned to Captain Baker and said, 'I think in the circumstances you should base a sub-section here for the next week. The last thing we want is some retaliatory act by the terrorists against our good friends here.'

Captain Baker agreed, 'I'll leave Corporal Green and D sub here, we will get some rations sent out from the troop straight away.'

BMH Taiping

The ambulance was now within ten miles of BMH Taiping. Rhodes was half awake and half asleep, he seemed to be floating, the bumps and lurching of the vehicle as it went too fast on some rougher parts of the road did not affect him at all. He could see that Lieutenant Pope had been placed in a semi-sitting position. Rhodes assumed it was to make breathing easier. He had no pain, just numbness in his leg and arm, and the bonus was that he would see Julie. He dreamed he was at the base of Penang Hill and Julie was saying, 'They say it's ten degrees cooler at the top.' He wanted to answer her but his tongue had swollen so much that it filled his mouth.

What an idiot, he thought, and slipped back into a dreamless sleep.

At the hospital they had been warned that two gunshot cases were on their way. In the reception ward Julie, Jane and two other nurses were preparing to receive the new patients. The ambulance came up to the ward and the male orderlies carried the two stretchers in. Jane Fellows recognised Rhodes straight away. Julie was attending Lieutenant Pope. They quickly removed the marines' clothing and as they checked their identity tags, Julie called out, 'Lieutenant David Pope, Royal Marines.' Jane called out, 'Marine Peter Rhodes, Royal Marines.' Julie turned with a look of horror on her face and then went back to preparing her patient for surgery. When both were ready, they were wheeled to the doors of the operating theatre, where the theatre nurses took over.

Rhodes was climbing out of a deep hole, he could see a bright light, and it was getting nearer. He was now almost at the top and it felt so much cooler. At least ten degrees cooler, yes, ten degrees cooler. A hand was on his shoulder and was gently shaking him.

A voice said, 'Wake up, Peter, wake up, Peter Rhodes, some-one wants to see you.' He opened his eyes. It was Doris Day's younger sister. It was Julie.

As the day went on Rhodes slipped completely free of the last dregs of the anaesthetic. The ward nurses gave him lots of cold drinks and then, at lunchtime, he was fed some scrambled eggs and some ice cream. Julie came into the ward. She leaned over and kissed him.

Someone in the next bed said, 'Hey, what about me?'

Julie turned to him and said, 'He's my boyfriend,' and then to Rhodes, 'I was so shocked when Jane called out your name, all of that bloodstained clothing. I thought you were dying.'

Rhodes interrupted her, 'How is David Pope?'

'He's going to be fine,' she said and went on, 'the bullet must have struck him at an angle. It broke a rib then went out of the side of his chest and a piece of the rib punctured his lung, but he's on the mend, and so are you.'

They were then disturbed by Matron. 'Nurse Grey, there are some officers in reception to see Marine Rhodes. Please go and collect them, then go back to your ward. You can see him again later.' Matron smiled at Rhodes, and left.

Lieutenant Colonel Mason and Captain Baker talked to Rhodes for an hour and he told them what had happened, the complete sequence of events from start to finish. They asked him at what stage he had been wounded and when Lieutenant Pope had been hit. They seemed satisfied with his answers. They then told him a signal had been received from the GOC Malaya, congratulating the troop on their major success. It would also be headlined in tomorrow's *Straits Times*. They then left to see Lieutenant Pope and Rhodes asked them to pass on his best wishes.

That evening, after he had had his evening meal, the soldier in the next bed, a corporal in the Green Howards, said, 'I get run over, no bastard comes near me, you get shot, and you get visited by more brass than I've seen in months.'

Rhodes smiled and said, 'If any more come, I'll point them in your direction.'

At that moment Julie arrived with Jane Fellows.

The corporal cried out, 'Jesus Christ,' and turned over and read his book.

Julie told Rhodes that in a couple of days he would be moved to her ward as the ward he was in was for post-ops. They stayed chatting until 2200 hours, and then left him to get a good night's sleep.

The next day, he was given a copy of the *Straits Times* and the front page carried the full story of the ambush without naming names. The headline read, 'Two Marines Ambush Eight Terrorists' followed by a sub-headline, 'Marines Kill Eight Terrorists, Five Miles From Ipoh'. It went on to say, 'Among the dead were two senior platoon commanders from the Tapah area, both marines from 42 Commando were wounded in the vicious and prolonged exchange of fire, but are expected to make a full recovery. The general officer commanding all security forces in Malaya states this is a major coup and a huge blow to terrorist morale.'

Rhodes read some more, and then put the paper down as he cast his mind back to the ambush. He was surprised how little he could now remember.

His reverie was interrupted by the voice of the corporal in the next bed, 'Can I have a look at the paper? I want to check the UK football results.'

Rhodes passed the paper over and thought, Someone's got his priorities right.

A few hours later, Rhodes was visited by the Duprés. Helen kissed him and conversed with him in French. The corporal in the next bed just lay there with his mouth open. Paul confused things further by speaking in English.

Julie arrived during their visit and Rhodes introduced her to the Duprés as his girlfriend.

Helen turned to Rhodes and said in French, 'You are a lucky boy, Peter, she is beautiful.'

Rhodes said, 'I know, I can't understand what she sees in me.'

Helen thought to herself, I can.

After an hour the Duprés left, but Julie stayed for a few more minutes before she left to go on duty.

When everyone had gone, the corporal in the next bed said, 'Where did you learn to speak French?'

Rhodes said, 'All marines speak French, it's part of our

training.'

'Bloody hell,' said the corporal, 'do you get paid extra?' Rhodes nodded.

The next morning, Rhodes was moved into Julie's ward and the nurses told him Julie was on duty at 1400 hours. They changed the dressings on his leg and his arm and thought the doctor should take a look at his leg as it was inflamed and when he was examined the surgeon decided to increase his antibiotics. Later that evening Rhodes developed a high temperature and he was drenched in sweat.

Julie called in the ward doctor who said, 'If he's no better in the morning, we may have to open up his leg again.'

Rhodes drifted into a dream-filled sleep. When he awoke, he felt much better and his temperature was back to normal, so the nurses decided to give him a bed bath to freshen him up. To his embarrassment, as the nurse washed his groin area he developed a massive erection.

The nurse pretended not to notice and said, 'Are you Julie Grey's boyfriend?'

Rhodes nodded. The nurse said to herself, Lucky Julie.

Later that day Rhodes had the pleasant surprise of a visit from Lieutenant Pope, who was brought to the ward in a wheelchair. He told Rhodes he was making a good recovery and for an hour they discussed the ambush and the wonderful treatment they were getting at the hospital.

Before he left, he told Rhodes, 'You realise, we are part of corps history now, being involved in that ambush was a great career move.' They both laughed.

At that moment Julie arrived on the ward and Rhodes introduced her to Lieutenant Pope, who tried to chat her up.

Julie resolved the situation quickly. 'Peter Rhodes is my boyfriend, Mr Pope, and I never go out with more than one marine at a time.'

As David Pope's nurse came to take him back to the ward he smiled and said, 'You are a lucky sod, Peter Rhodes, see you in a couple of days.'

Later that evening as Julie went off duty, she gave him a kiss and said, 'I hear you are feeling a bit frisky. We shall have to do something about that, won't we?' She then left with Rhodes thinking to himself, Wow, am I on a promise.

The next morning the ward had a visit from Matron.

She came over to Rhodes and said, 'Open wide, Peter Rhodes.' She then poured two spoonfuls of a white liquid down his throat.

'That should do the trick,' she said, 'I can't have you knocking my nurses' eyes out with your "uncontrollable".'

So much for being on a promise, thought Rhodes.

He had several letters to answer and spent the rest of the morning writing to them all on the farm. Julie took him out into the grounds that afternoon. It was very pleasant, the flowerbeds were full of heavily scented flowers and they sat in the shade and talked.

Rhodes thought to himself, Life doesn't get much better than this.

As they went back to the ward Rhodes said, 'I had a visit from Matron this morning.'

'Did you?' said Julie, a picture of innocence.

'Yes,' said Rhodes, 'I'm glad she gave me that stuff, I was beginning to find her very attractive.'

Both Rhodes and David Pope were making excellent progress. They had been in Taiping four weeks now and both could walk unaided. They were told that next week they would be transferred to the Cameron Highlands Rest Centre. Rhodes was getting restless and as much as he liked being near Julie, he wanted to get back to the troop.

Captain Baker and the sergeant major had visited and told Rhodes that the Planters' Association had sent the troop eight cases of Carlsberg, one case for each terrorist killed and the normal remuneration.

The sergeant major with his strange smile, added, 'Of course, it's all gone now, but we drunk to your health.'

Captain Baker added, 'When you are back in the troop I'm sure the sergeant major will buy you a drink.' Judging by the expression on the sergeant major's face Rhodes thought that would be unlikely.

The Cameron Highlands

The following Monday, Lieutenant Pope and Rhodes were discharged to the Cameron Highlands Rest Centre. Julie and the other nurses were sorry to see them leave; even Matron gave Rhodes a squeeze.

Julie gave him a long embrace. 'Perhaps we can arrange a weekend together, Peter, we need some time alone.'

Rhodes agreed, 'The sooner the better.' He kissed her hand and waved as his lorry drove away.

It took three hours to drive to the Cameron Highlands and as the lorry climbed up into the hills they noticed how fresh the air felt. When they arrived, the accommodation was hospital-like and there were six of them to a ward. The ward sister told them they would be seen the next morning by the chief medical officer, who would decide on any treatment to restore them fit for active duty. Lieutenant Pope was placed in the officers' ward, but he told Rhodes he would see him the next day. They had become quite friendly, despite the difference in rank.

When Rhodes was seen by the medical officer the next day he was given a through going over. His leg was bent, pulled and stretched. He was made to squat then stand upright several times.

'I expect that bloody hurts, young man,' said the MO.

'It's a bit stiff, sir,' said Rhodes.

'I'm going to put you on a course of exercise and massage, plus an hour's swimming every day. You are a very fit boy, but you have become a bit soft due to your time in bed. I'll see you again in a week.'

As Rhodes made to leave, the doctor added, 'Read about your little exploit, well done.'

Over the next few days he was put through the mill, the best part was the massage. The nurse insisted he just wore a towel around his waist. Her hands and some oil really eased the ache the extra exercise had caused. The sliding of her hands to the top of his leg led to the inevitable result, she raised an eyebrow, then the towel.

'Well,' she said, 'not much wrong there.'

A few days later, after the evening meal, he was sitting in the grounds and it was just getting dark. The nurse who had been doing the massage came over and sat down beside him.

'You need a bit of company,' she said, and kissed him.

He kissed her back. 'I'm engaged,' said Rhodes.

'Don't worry, so am I,' said the nurse.

His hand slid under her dress while she undid the buttons on his trousers. His pride and joy sprang out.

'Christ!' she said. 'It's my birthday.'

She skilfully slid a French letter over his penis and then she was sitting astride him, lowering herself until she had fully taken him in. The next ten minutes were a frantic sexual dance; gasping and groaning, they both sought and found relief from their frustrations.

When it was over, he felt guilty. What if Julie found out?

Rachael, the nurse, solved all. 'I needed that as much as you did, it's our secret. Consider it part of the treatment,' she said.

After two weeks, the medical officer said he could return to duty. Rachael had twice given him extra 'treatment'. She was engaged to a sergeant in the Scots Guards and they were to be married at Christmas. As he left she waved him goodbye, smiling a special farewell. David Pope was staying an extra week, but Rhodes was glad to getting back to the troop.

Return to Duty

He was deposited in 42 Commando Headquarters. Surgeon Lieutenant Monk asked him if he felt fit for duty and Rhodes told him he couldn't wait to get back to A-Troop, so later that day he was dropped at the entrance to the camp. Even the sergeant major seemed pleased to see him and that night as Rhodes lay on his bed he felt he was back where he really belonged.

Within two days Rhodes was back on patrol with D sub, taking part in a three-day incursion up the Kinta Valley. It was as though he had not been away, but he was glad when he could rest at the end of the first day; perhaps Rachael had over done the treatment. Day two of the patrol was accompanied by torrential rain. The track they were following up the side of a steep slope became very slippery and the Bren gunner slipped as he tried to negotiate the incline. As he swung round he caught his number two with a sickening blow to the face with the butt of the Bren. The injury caused Corporal Green to basha for the night. The marine who had caught the full force of the swinging Bren had broken his nose. However, his discomfort was somewhat compensated by comments from his fellow marines, who suggested he looked really rugged. The next day they completed their patrol by swinging round and returning to their start point, another triumph of Corporal Green's navigation.

That night they heard that the high commissioner to Malaya had been assassinated, but luckily his wife had escaped the ambush and was unhurt. The immediate reaction from Whitehall resulted in the number of anti-terrorist operations being dramatically increased. As a result, the next day the whole troop was sent out on three-day patrols to the various points of their area. They had been told that air strikes were available and they were to submit their targets and wait and see what priority they would be given. After the assassination revenge was in the air.

A-Troop called in two air strikes and both were accepted. Two flights of Brigands fired their maximum complement of sixteen rockets. Very impressive, lots of noise, hundreds of square yards of jungle shredded and not a terrorist to be seen. Rhodes by now was back to his full fitness and enjoyed the pure physical challenge of jungle patrolling. Corporal Green told Rhodes he had applied to join the Malay police as a lieutenant as his time in the marines was nearly up. He had a lot of leave due to him because after the war ended he had stayed out in the Far East with the commando brigade rather than go home. Rhodes was appalled to think the corps were to lose such a first class NCO, but what could he do?

When they arrived back in camp, Rhodes went to see the sergeant major and he told him what Corporal Green was planning. To his surprise Hairy Henry was sympathetic and said, 'Leave it with me, lad, I'll do what I can.'

A week later Captain Baker sent for Green and told him he was being sent on a senior NCOs' course and that promotion to sergeant would follow completion of the course; he could then stay in A-Troop if he so wished. Green was delighted and asked if he could extend his service in the Royal Marines from twelve years to twenty-two and pension. Captain Baker told him he would be pleased to arrange this. All of the section was pleased with the outcome, Corporal Holt would become section commander and in due course they would get another NCO posted in as a replacement.

The following Monday, Corporal Green left for his four-week SNCOs' course, while the next day, D sub went out on a seven-day patrol carrying the full seven days rations with them in Bergan rucksacks. After a three-day trek, they came across the biggest terrorist camp they had seen, eight bashas in good condition, no sign of life, food supplies or clothing, but the camp had a capacity for between forty and fifty men. After contact with troop HQ they were told to lay up in ambush for two days and nights and then return to their pick-up point after destroying the camp. The marines were not overly impressed as it meant they would be out of rations for the return journey.

They took up a position on the higher ground on one side of the camp and waited. The first day and night passed without incident. On the second day at about 1500 hours they heard voices, but no one appeared. Thirty minutes later two figures were observed on the edge of the camp. Corporal Holt had ordered that he would initiate the ambush and no one should fire before him. He anticipated more than the two. The figures melted back into the jungle. Fifteen minutes later they were back and this time Corporal Holt opened fire, followed by the rest of the sub-section. It was all over within five seconds, one fell to the ground, and the other staggered a few yards before he too fell. Nobody moved for five minutes, then Corporal Holt, Rhodes and two others moved forward, the other marines providing cover. Both of the terrorists were dead, only one was armed, it was an early pattern Sten gun, and he had been carrying four magazines.

It was now almost dark; they dragged the bodies into one of the bashas, and then went back to their ambush position. They were well aware that after the burst of firing it was highly unlikely that any other terrorists had stayed in the area, but they had no choice but to see the night out. To add to their discomfort it then began to rain, it poured down for the rest of the night. When morning came they were wet, cold and hungry and after they had eaten, trying to conserve their depleted rations, they had the task of removing the heads.

As they had no Ibans with them, they had to cut the heads off themselves. The grisly task was at last completed. The heads were wrapped in some of their spare clothing and carried on a couple of sticks. They burnt the camp, leaving nothing standing. The two headless bodies were buried in very shallow graves and the patrol made its way through the jungle avoiding the route they had come in by.

The next day at about 1600 hours they reached their pick-up point and they were hungry and exhausted. The remainder of their food they had shared out for breakfast that morning. Two hours later they were back in camp. After the debriefing they cleaned their weapons, showered and had a hot meal. The police came out the next day and collected the heads and the Sten. Later they were told only one of the heads had been identified, the other must have been a new recruit to the cause.

Rhodes had some letters, two from Julie and one from his

aunt and uncle. Julie and Jane wanted to arrange to meet with Bob Jones and himself in Ipoh. Matron was prepared to give permission if Bob and he could make it. The sergeant major told them they could have the one evening till 2300 hours as normal on the Saturday, providing they were not required for patrols and he said, 'If you go over my head on this I'll never forgive you.' He did, however, allow them to use the phone in the troop office. Rhodes rang Taiping, spoke to Julie and it was arranged for the next Saturday. Luck was on their side, they went out twice during the week and on Friday they were duty section, so barring emergencies Saturday was clear.

Transport was laid on to take the marines into Ipoh at 1100 hours, giving them almost twelve hours of liberty. At 1000 hours Rhodes was on his way back to his tent from the shower when he heard the sergeant major call out his name.

'Rhodes, phone call, in the troop office.'

He knew straight away something was wrong. He picked up the phone and said, 'Peter Rhodes.'

A familiar voice said, 'Matron here, I am sorry to tell you Julie Grey's father has been taken seriously ill and as she is the only child her mother has requested she be sent home. She is flying back to the UK tonight. She says she will write to you as soon as she can. Jane Fellows is helping her pack, so their trip to Ipoh is off. I am so sorry.'

Rhodes asked her to pass on his love and best wishes and ended the call. He told Bob Jones and as a result Jones said he would stay in camp and save his money.

French Leave

When the transport left for Ipoh, Rhodes was on board. He had decided to have a few drinks and go to the cinema; *Colorado Territory* was on at the Ruby. On arrival in Ipoh, he left the other marines as he wanted to be on his own, he wasn't good company. He went to the Broadway Café and ordered a bottle of Tiger beer, found a table in the corner and noticed that the place was almost deserted. A second bottle of Tiger was in front of him.

Fuck it, he thought, sod the cinema, I'll just get pissed.

He was surprised to see a familiar figure standing in front of him. It was Helen Dupré. As usual, she greeted him in French, but his reply was curt and lacked his usual good manners.

'And what,' she asked, 'has spoilt your day?'

For the next ten minutes he explained everything, his frustration and disappointment were obvious. Helen listened quietly to his outburst, then as he finished his tirade, she said, 'Buy me a drink, Peter, I'll have a Carlsberg.'

Helen was good company and they saw off three beers together.

She then said, 'Paul doesn't pick me up until tomorrow morning. I have a room at the Celestial. I do this once a month, do a bit of shopping, visit a couple of female friends, it makes a break from the tin mine. Let's have a meal, go to the cinema, have a dance and a few drinks, then it will be time for you to catch your lorry back to camp.'

Rhodes felt much better. He apologised for his bad manners and said, 'I had almost forgotten what a good friend you are, Helen.'

They ordered a meal, a mild curried chicken and rice, and two more beers. When they had finished, they made their way to the Ruby cinema and for two hours enjoyed the air-conditioning with Joel McCrea killing every outlaw in sight within *Colorado Territory*. Rhodes was also aware of the closeness of Helen Dupré. Was it his imagination or was the pressure of her leg against his deliberate rather than accidental? When it happened the second time, he returned the gesture and was rewarded by her hand finding his and holding it against the top of her thigh.

Rhodes was sorry when the film ended. When they made their way outside it was almost dark. Helen suggested she needed her shawl before they went dancing, it would only take a few minutes to collect it from her room at the hotel. He was going to wait outside, but she would not hear of it and he followed her upstairs to her room. As soon as she had shut the door it was obvious that she did not have dancing on her mind.

She turned to Rhodes and said, 'Peter, what we both need is a good fuck, it will do us both good.'

With that she embraced him, her lips finding his, her tongue probing the inside of his mouth. He sucked her tongue, his hand sliding under her dress, seeking and finding the soft silky flesh at the top of her stocking. He moved further up her leg and ran his finger over the gusset of her panties. Helen gasped and placed her hand over his erect penis that was fighting to get out of his trousers. They managed to free themselves of their clothes and fell onto the bed both naked. Helen's mouth and hands were everywhere. Rhodes was only just in control of himself, but managed to put on a French letter that had been intended for Julie. The thought of her brought some semblance of control back to him. He was kissing Helen's breasts, running his tongue around her erect nipples; they were like firm black grapes. He left a trail of kisses down to the tops of her legs.

He was about to move his lips between her legs, when she cried, 'Now, Peter, now!'

He moved his body and thrust himself fully home. She gasped as he almost drove the air from her body. Then he moved slowly in and out of her, each re-entry making her sigh with pleasure as they harmonised a rhythm, which grew mutually quicker, then frantically out of control as they both climaxed with a second of each other.

They lay there in silence for a few minutes as their breathing slowly returned to normal.

Helen was the first to speak, 'God, Peter, that was wonderful. I had forgotten how good sex was. I must be honest, I have wanted you from the first day I saw you, all smelly using our telephone at the mine that day.'

Rhodes leaned across and kissed her. 'You did not sound that way to me, I thought you were a right bitch, who deserved to have her bottom smacked.'

Helen laughed and said, 'You will never have a better chance than now.' She turned onto her stomach and waggled her firm buttocks at him. Rhodes playfully gave her a few light smacks.

Helen quickly turned over again, saying, 'I think we will stop that. You look as if you are beginning to enjoy it too much.'

They lay there for a while and just talked. Rhodes looked at his watch. It was 2130 hours.

'I think,' he said, 'that I am about ready for another love struggle.'

Helen smiled. 'Well,' she said, 'I'm not planning to go any-where for a while.'

The second bout of lovemaking was a much more controlled effort than the first. The frantic haste of the previous encounter was replaced by a measured progress as they both sought to give each other maximum pleasure. The climax, when it came, was deeply satisfying to them both. When they regained their control Helen told Rhodes that nothing had changed.

'I love Paul, you love Julie. Tonight has not altered that. We needed this and now we carry on as before.'

Rhodes was relieved. As much as he liked Helen, Julie was his future. They were both nineteen, Helen was thirty, a lovely woman in her prime but married to a husband ten years her senior, but who adored her.

It was time to make his way to the liberty pick-up point, one last kiss, he squeezed Helen's hand and left.

When Rhodes arrived at the lorry most of the marines were already there waiting. As he stood talking to the two vehicle escorts one of the marines threw up over the side of the truck, depositing six bottles of Tiger and a chicken curry over the gleaming green paintwork.

'Oh, for fuck's sake!' cried the driver, not placated by two of the marines attempting to wash the mess away with jets of high pressure urine. At last all were accounted for and the lorry made its way first to the armoury to collect the marines' rifles and fifty rounds and then up the road to their camp. On arrival they were met by the sergeant major, whose very presence insured they went quietly to their tents like mice.

The next week flew by with most of the sub-sections involved in some patrol activity. D sub spent the week in a cave a hundred feet up the side of a gunong. Corporal Holt, who was a trained Class One cliff climber, climbed up to the cave at 0400 hours taking with him a long rope. When this was secured the rest of the section climbed up and joined him. The rope was then pulled up and for most of the week they spent the day looking for any terrorist movement from their high lookout post. They took it in turns to come down at night to collect water and to ambush the pipeline, returning to the cave before it got light. The week passed without incident and D sub returned to camp on the Friday afternoon.

Among Rhodes's mail was a letter from Julie. Her father had died the day after she had returned home. At least she had been able to be with him when he died. Both she and her mother were distraught. The letter was brief, but she said she would write again in a few days. Rhodes wrote to her straight away and told her how desperately sorry he was for her loss, how much he loved her and how important it was to give her mother all the support she could. His other letter was from Aunt Marie. She and Uncle Bill were fine and she wrote how he was glad he was fit and well again and that they were so proud of him; he had made the front page in one of the national dailies. She also told him Mark was now engaged to the headmaster's daughter and they hoped Rhodes would be home for the wedding.

Lieutenant Pope was now back from hospital and fit for duty. He told Rhodes that they had both been nominated for bravery awards. The CO had said it was just a formality and they would hear something shortly. He also said he had met a nurse called Rachael at the Cameron Highlands who wished to be remembered to him. Rhodes asked him if she had given him a massage.

'No such luck,' said Pope. 'The nurse who attended to me was like Bert Assarati's mother.'

Rhodes told him what had happened to Julie and the death of her father. Pope asked to be remembered to her and to offer his sympathy when Rhodes next wrote.

The Kroh Forest

The next day there was a briefing for all the NCOs. Something was up. They did not have long to wait as the whole troop was moving out of area to take part in a large operation. This was to be conducted along with the Gordon Highlanders, at a place called the Chikus Forest, between Tapah and Bidor. The camp was to be left in charge of C/Sergeant Hayes and six marines, who at the time were excused patrols. The next day they left for Tapah. It took two hours to get there and another hour to get to their base camp, a disused tin mine half a mile from the main road. They had attached to them a police lieutenant who was familiar with the area. They had one of their camp cooks with them, so the rations were compo, not individual ration packs. The marines liked this because on return from patrol they did not have to cook their own meals. The troop was housed in an old long tin shed which was almost rain-proof. They were all engaged in getting to know their new area of operations. It was a different terrain to what they were used to, quite flat, swampy in parts and large areas were old tin mine workings which had become over grown. D sub spent the day making their way through the old tin tailings, but they found nothing to suggest any terrorist activity.

As they were making their way back to the base camp, they heard a burst of firing. It came from their left and was at least a mile away. Over the radio they heard E sub explaining they had bumped into three suspected terrorists who did not appear to be armed, but had run when challenged. They had fired over their heads to persuade them to stop, but they had kept running, and had been lost in the undergrowth.

Back at the base camp, the police liaison officer expressed his opinion that the suspects had been Min Yuen, or messengers, not armed, but used by the terrorists to bring food or messages to pre-arranged pick-up points. That night D and C subs were put out in ambush positions on the maze of tracks that covered the old mine workings. The only movement they noticed were a noisy group of wild pigs which, on scenting the marines, dashed squealing into the undergrowth. D sub decided that the pigs had homed in on one of Marine Benson's farts, his stomach being in turmoil due to the rich compo rations. As soon as it was light the marines made their way back to the base camp and spent the rest of the day catching up on their sleep, while E, F and G subs searched other parts of the area.

After a week, with little to show for their efforts, A-Troop moved deeper into the area allocated to them and they made their base in another old mine working. This one still had running water, so showering was available. They were on the edge of a particularly unpleasant area called the Kroh Forest, part of the larger Chikus Forest. This was largely swamp, with masses of dead or dying vegetation. D sub were sent with three days' rations to explore this area which the police lieutenant said nobody had ever patrolled since the emergency had started. Rhodes and the rest of D sub were not overjoyed by the prospect, but Captain Baker thought it was worth a look-see.

'See what you can stir up,' he said.

After several hours of wading through swamp, sometimes just a few inches deep, then almost up to their waists, the marines could understand the reluctance of other units to enter this particular area. At 1600 hours they found a place to basha for the night – it was about the only dry piece of ground they had seen all day. That night it rained heavily and within minutes they were laying in two inches of water. The mosquitoes then joined in to make the night one they would prefer to forget. In the morning they made the usual radio call. The information they obtained was not what they had expected. King George VI had died the previous day, 6 February 1952.

They were now Queen's Marines instead of King's Marines; Rhodes remembered his oath of allegiance. His heirs and successors, so nothing had really changed. All that day they made their way through the stinking swamp. At last, just before it was time to look for a decent campsite, the ground started to rise and they found themselves out of the swamp and on the edge of an old and neglected rubber plantation. They found a tin shed with just about enough of a roof on to make a decent shelter. In the past it would have been used by the plantation manager to store the latex sheets. There was only just enough time left to make a quick meal and a mug of tea before night fell. They spent a good night with just a few mosquitoes for company.

In the morning they followed the edge of the rubber plantation, which brought them to within a mile of A-Troop's camp. By 1400 hours, as they approached the camp, a 15 cwt lorry was just leaving. On the back lay two bodies and on the seating sat a pale-looking marine with a bloodstained field dressing on his upper arm. Rhodes could see it was Bob Jones. A quick wave from Jones with his good arm and the lorry sped away. When they reported in, they found out that the two terrorists had been ambushed as they were collecting supplies from a food dump that E sub had found the previous day. Over the next week A-Troop found another two food dumps, but had no luck with the subsequent ambushes. They were then invited into the Gordons' camp, at Tapah, for a shower and a decent meal, followed by a decent night's sleep. The following day they went back to their own area, and the delights of Tambun camp.

Medals and a Move

The next day Rhodes managed to fiddle his way as escort to Taiping to see Bob Jones. He found him in good spirits; sitting on his bed was Jane Fellows. Jones put on a good act, for Rhodes's benefit, of the wounded hero bravely fighting the pain. They spent a couple of hours chatting before it was time to leave. Jane shared with Rhodes the bad news that Matron had given her. Julie would not be coming back. As her mother was living in Petersfield, Hampshire, Julie would be posted to the BMH at Aldershot.

Saddened by the news, Rhodes consoled himself with the thought, That's not too far from Eastney and I only have ten months left to do of this commission. This raised his spirits.

As the jeep made its way back to Tambun, Rhodes was beginning to give some serious thought to the future. When he returned to the UK he would try to get on a junior NCOs' course. Being a holder of the King's Badge, this would give him additional seniority. Normally, a marine is considered for promotion when he has four years' experience.

When the jeep arrived back at Tambun, Rhodes was told to report to the troop office. When he went in, Captain Baker, Lieutenant Pope and the sergeant major were sitting talking.

'Where the hell have you been, Rhodes?' asked Captain Baker. 'This beer is getting warm. Sit yourself down. I've just had a signal from HQ. It reads, "Congratulations on the award of the Military Cross to Lieutenant David Pope and the Military Medal to Marine Peter Rhodes. Arrangements re. the presentation of awards to follow."'

Everyone in the room was shaking hands, the beer was poured and Lieutenant Pope and Rhodes were toasted, first by Captain Baker, then by the sergeant major. What impressed Rhodes most was how genuinely pleased the troop commander and the sergeant major were and when Captain Baker said, 'The awards are yours, but the pleasure is ours,' it just about summed it up.

There was a letter from Julie on Rhodes's bed. It confirmed what Jane Fellows had told him, she was being posted to BMH Aldershot and things were settling down at home. Her father's will had solved a lot of problems for her mother. The house was now paid for and other insurances left her mother financially secure. She told Rhodes that her father and mother had both worked at the same school. Her father had been headmaster and her mother intended to carry on teaching. She hoped to see him just as soon as he could return to England and then they could discuss their future.

Rhodes wrote off straight away, giving her all the news, but he did not mention his medal; in the circumstances it didn't seem right.

It was now April and Bob Jones was back in the troop. There were rumours floating about that they were being moved to another part of Malaya. As with most rumours, there was an element of truth in this one. Only 42 Commando was being moved down to Selangor, the state to the south of Perak. Over the next two weeks most of their stores were made ready for the move, while the marines continued to patrol their area. Rhodes had managed a Saturday evening with Helen Dupré in Ipoh, very satisfying for them both. She knew all about the move and thought this would be their last time together. She was right and, after many farewells from all the friends they had made, 42 Commando moved south in the last week of April.

A-Troop were based in the corner of an existing army camp, at a place called Wardiburn, eight miles outside of Kuala Lumpur. The marines were not too keen to share a base with the army, but after a week things were pretty harmonious, much to everyone's surprise. A classic solution had been reached; each side just ignored each other. Within a week, the troop were out patrolling and getting to know their new area. It was confirmed that the commando brigade was moving to the Middle East, Malta to be precise. 42 Commando would be the last to leave, at the end of June, having completed their two-year spell of duty.

Rhodes and Jones both applied and were given a week's leave in Singapore and Jane Fellows would be there. Rhodes and Jones stayed in accommodation in the shore base HMS *Terror*, while Jane had a room at a nurses' rest home. They had a good week together. Rhodes gave Bob and Jane as much space as they wanted and everyone seemed happy. One day, as Rhodes was leaving the base, he walked straight into Joyce Lang.

She smiled and said, 'Sorry, can't stop, I have a friend looking after my baby. He's called Peter.' And she was gone.

Rhodes told Bob of the encounter, who said, 'You are well out of that, mate, keep well clear.'

After a relaxing week they reluctantly returned to duty.

On one patrol, D sub, who were out for three days, found a four-basha camp that had four tracks in and out. That night the section split itself into four groups and lay an ambush at each point. About midnight, a light was seen on a hillock opposite the camp. It flashed three times, and then again. As the three marines nearest could not respond to the signal they fired in the direction of the light. All went quiet after the echoes of the shots had faded. All was then silent for the rest of the night. As soon as it was light they made their way to the area they had fired at. Neither bodies nor bloodstains, but several sacks of rice and a large tin full of water containing a dozen live fish. Before they left the camp, they spread the rice on the floor of the basha and burnt the lot. The fish were released into the nearby stream. A few days later an air strike took place on the area around the campsite, but no follow-up patrol was ordered, so the result of the air strike was not known.

The next week, Lieutenant Pope and Rhodes were presented with their medals by the GOC Malaya. It was a troop parade and among the guests were Helen and Paul Dupré who, to their surprise and A-Troop's delight, were presented with framed commendations in recognition of their assistance on the day of the ambush. Afterwards as Rhodes said goodbye to Helen and Paul, they all thought it would be the last time they would meet and it was an emotional farewell.

In early June 42 Commando moved down to Singapore to await passage to Malta. 40 and 45 Commandos had already arrived in Malta and were housed in St Patrick's and St Andrew's Barracks.

On arrival in Malta 42 Commando would share the same accommodation. In Singapore, A-Troop and the rest of the commando were housed in tents whose condition were appalling. The marines had the feeling they were being punished for their farewell performance at Kuala Lumpur railway station. The GOC Malaya and his wife, as well as other notables, saw the commando leave on the train to Singapore. A military band played some appropriate marches, but unfortunately the march they played just before the train left was one the marines had some special words for. As the music started, five hundred marine voices roared out the refrain:

> We're a shower of bastards,
> Bastards are we,
> We'd rather fuck than fight for liberty…

As the train was frantically waved out of the station, the GOC and his wife smiled bravely as, thankfully, the train withdrew from sight. What the marines did not know was that the GOC and his wife thought that the whole episode was hilarious and was mentioned at many a dinner party as 'The Night the Marines Left Malaya'.

Troopship Dilwara

The time spent in Singapore was put to good use. Each troop was given a trip to the Tiger Brewery, where a good time was had by all, though not all of the marines could remember much about it. They were also given a flight in a Valleta aircraft from RAF Changi, over the jungle, covering in one-minute ground which on foot had taken several days. The swimming pool at the shore base HMS *Terror* was also a popular venue. Rhodes kept a look out for Joyce Lang, but there was no sign of her, perhaps just as well, he thought.

At the end of a week spent enjoying the Singapore fleshpots, they packed their kit and were taken to the docks, where they embarked on the troopship *Dilwara*. With about an hour of daylight left, the ship sailed out of Singapore harbour. Most of the marines were on the upper deck as Malaya, which had been their home for two years, slowly faded from view in the gathering darkness. It was very quiet, no shouting, no smart remarks, they were leaving behind thirty-four of their fellow marines, who would never go home. They would rest for all time in the military cemeteries at Batu Gajah and Taiping. The number of terrorists killed by the marines was two hundred and sixty, in fact the number was sure to be far higher than that, as a wounded terrorist had nowhere to escape except further into the jungle and a slow painful death.

Rhodes stood next to Bob Jones. They both had met girls who would become part of their future. Jane Fellows had only two months left to serve in Malaya and Julie of course was already back in England. Rhodes thought of the Duprés and Helen in particular, both good friends, one a lover. Joyce Lang, now with a son called Peter. Was he the result of that night in Colombo? Rachael in the Cameroon Highlands; now that, thought Rhodes, is what I call nursing. Then there was Ida Tan and her sister, who made their trips into Ipoh worthwhile. After a while Bob and he went down below to their troop deck, took a meal and had a couple of beers in the ship's canteen after which it was time for bed.

After clearing the Straits of Mallaca the *Dilwara* ran into some bad weather which got progressively worse as they headed into the Indian Ocean. Over the next three days, the marines stayed below decks until the storm blew itself out. Two days later they docked in Colombo and Rhodes and Jones went ashore. They went to The Paradise Hotel. The same little man bowed as they went in. Rhodes ordered two beers and as they sat drinking a young couple came in and went upstairs.

Rhodes looked at Jones and said, 'This is where Joyce and I came. I shan't forget this place.'

They finished their beers and left. As they looked back at the small hotel, Jones said, 'You really are a soft romantic bastard, Pete, you can't go through life revisiting your prick's greatest moments.' They both laughed and made their way back to the waiting *Dilwara*.

A few days later, in hot sunshine, having briefly called at Aden, they entered the Red Sea. At 1600 hours each day the ship stopped and most of the marines went for a swim. It was a great way of washing away the close hot sweatiness of the troop decks. Somebody on the ship had been given some of the records that one of the marines in A-Troop used to play in his tent. The two great favourites were Doris Day and Buddy Clarke singing together 'Boys Were Made to Take Care of Girls' and Peggy Lee singing 'Through the Long and Sleepless Night I Whisper Your Name'. Those two records along with Jo Stafford's 'Shrimp Boats Are Coming' were played to destruction.

Once through the Suez Canal they had one day in Port Said, still full of smells and dust. The marines arranged for a message for Sergeant Saunders to be piped over the ship's tannoy stating that a camel was at the gangway asking for him. They were glad when the ship sailed that evening, another three days and they would be in Malta.

Rhodes had written to Julie, Helen and Paul Dupré and of course Aunt Marie and Uncle Bill. The free and easy routine the marines had enjoyed on the ship suddenly ended with the introduction of morning and afternoon parades, PT sessions and lectures on their change of role, which would mean they would be performing garrison duties.

They sailed into Grand Harbour at 0700 hours and by 1100 hours the whole of the commando unit were in St Andrew's Barracks, sorting out a mountain of equipment. The two-storey barrack blocks were constructed of Maltese sandstone, they were cool and clean, and each troop had their own block. By 1600 hours all was ship shape, it was as though they had been there for weeks.

Over the next three days they adapted to the barracks routine, guard duties and weapon training. They were all issued with new rifles and spent a day on the range zeroing them in. Rhodes played cricket for the troop against S-Troop, scored forty runs and took three wickets. Major Price, S-Troop commander, was captain of the commando team and invited Rhodes to play for 42 Commando against the Royal Air Force. A partnership of a hundred, with Major Price scoring sixty and Rhodes forty, saw the commando victorious and Rhodes's sporting star in its ascendancy.

Several members of the troop had left for England. Sergeant Major Higgins had gone and was replaced by QMS Ryder, who was on his last commission before retirement. A young marine, who should have known better, made the comment within the sergeant major's hearing, that he looked old enough to have fought in the battle of Omdurman. Two hours later, the young marine was trailing the sergeant major by two circuits of a forty-lap challenge around the parade ground. Nobody had told the young innocent that the sergeant major, up to a year ago, had been the Royal Marines' cross country champion.

A-Troop were detailed for palace guard in the last week of August and Rhodes was selected in the twelve marines for this detail. The guard was mounted outside the guard room opposite the governor's palace, which was on the other side of Kingsway. Lots of people watched as the Royal Marines marched to their guard duty behind their band. It was Rhodes's last duty and he had been told he was going home in seven days.

Many of the marines who had served the full two years in

Malaya were being allowed home three months before the end of their two and a half year commission. Rhodes and Bob Jones were going home with fifty other marines on the aircraft carrier HMS *Vengeance*. On 10 September 1952 they sailed out of Grand Harbour; they all had developed deep tans, something they had failed to do in Malaya due to their constant patrolling. The *Vengeance* was completing its last voyage as an HM ship for she was shortly going to be loaned to the Australian Navy. They called in at Gibraltar, it was a great place for shopping, and Rhodes bought presents for all his loved ones. Julie was to have a silver bracelet inset with precious stones, Aunt Marie a pearl necklace, Uncle Bill a Rolls razor, Mark a gold watch, Julie's mum, who he hoped to meet soon, a silk shawl. He decided after some thought to buy a silk scarf for June as it might be a bit tricky meeting her and her husband.

Home Again

On 18 September, HMS *Vengeance* sailed into Portsmouth Harbour. As they disembarked, Rhodes caught sight of his Uncle Bill and next to him Aunt Marie and there, standing between them, was Julie. The marines were given fifteen minutes with their families before boarding a train for Plymouth. Rhodes gave Julie a long embrace, then fond hugs to his aunt and uncle. Julie had been instantly recognised by his aunt and uncle from Rhodes's description of 'Doris Day's younger sister'.

'She is lovely, Peter,' said his aunt. 'You make a very handsome couple.'

They then hurriedly discussed his leave arrangements. Julie's mother had invited him to stay for his first week, then on to his aunt and uncle's. Rhodes then had to rush to join the other marines as their train left for Plymouth.

When they arrived at Plymouth Station two coaches and a lorry swiftly took them to Stonehouse Barracks. They were experts now in moving in or out of camps, so they quickly were at home in their barrack room. They were told they would be paid at 0900 hours the next morning, then collect travel warrants and start their leave, two days for every month they had been abroad. Rhodes worked out that he would have fifty-four days. The next morning, everything went like clockwork and by 1030 hours they were at the station. Bob Jones was going to his parents' in Finchley, so he caught the London train. The Portsmouth train left ten minutes later. He was on his way.

On arrival at Portsmouth Harbour, he changed to the London train and twenty minutes later was in Petersfield. Julie had given him instructions on how to get to her mother's house. She had said it was a ten-minute walk from the station. Rhodes surprised how large the cottage was, he had imagined a small country cottage, cottage it may be, but small it wasn't.

Julie's mother had seen him approach. She had seen a photograph that Julie had showed her of them all together in Penang, but this boy, or rather man, was far bigger than she had thought. He was dressed in his khaki battledress and Green Beret. She noticed his medal ribbons and his deep tan. Unaware that he was being scrutinised Rhodes spoke to a man who was passing. They both smiled and laughed. Mrs Grey saw at once what had attracted her daughter to this man; women would find him very attractive. Mrs Grey went to the door and opened it just as Rhodes reached the step.

'You must be Peter,' she said. 'Please come in, Julie will be home soon.'

Rhodes shook her hand. 'It is most kind of you to allow me to stay,' he said.

Over the next half hour he was shown where he was to sleep and Mrs Grey made him some tea. They were soon at ease with one another. When Julie arrived home, she noticed how happy her mother looked. All the strain that had shown in her face since the death of Julie's father had now gone. Rhodes gave Julie a long kiss, not too long as he did not want to upset her mother, then held her hand and told her how lovely she looked.

Julie giggled, and said, 'You look lovely too. Doesn't he, Mum?'

Mrs Grey laughed. 'I'll get the meal on,' she said, and went into the kitchen.

That night when it was time for bed, Rhodes noticed that his room was one side of Mrs Grey and Julie's was the other.

Rhodes thought to himself, Her mum likes me, but that doesn't mean she trusts me.

After breakfast Mrs Grey left to go to her school and Julie caught the bus to Aldershot. After today, she had the rest of the week as leave. Rhodes had a wander around the house and garden. It was overgrown in parts and the lawn needed cutting. He spent the rest of the day working, pruning, digging and mowing and by four o'clock, it was transformed. He was just putting the lawn mower away when Mrs Grey came in the gate. She stood looking at the garden that had been her husband's pride and joy. It was immaculate, just has her husband would have liked it. Rhodes had

139

not noticed her arrival. He was wearing a vest and a pair of football shorts. He was very brown, but she could see the scars on his leg and arm.

She spoke. 'You are a guest here, Peter, I don't expect you to do the garden chores, but I must say it looks wonderful, thank you.'

Rhodes smiled. 'I just like to keep busy and I enjoy gardening.'

They went into the cottage and had some coffee while they waited for Julie to come home.

The next day they all walked into Petersfield town centre. Rhodes only had the civilian clothing he had bought in Malaya, in total a couple of shirts, two pairs of trousers, some underwear and a pair of shoes. Julie bought him a long-sleeved sweater.

'Light blue,' she said, 'to match your eyes.'

Rhodes insisted that they were grey. Julie's mother solved the problem by saying, 'They are blue grey.'

As they wandered around the town, they noticed a car whose driver was asking for directions in French, with little success.

'Go on, Peter,' said Julie, 'help him out.'

Rhodes walked over to the driver and greeted him in French. They chatted away for a minute or so, then Rhodes turned to Julie and said, 'He wants to go to see the house of Jane Austen, where do I send him?'

Julie looked at the map the driver had and, with Rhodes translating, directed him. The driver and his wife thanked them both and drove off, waving cheerfully as they did so. Mrs Grey looked at Rhodes with evident admiration.

'Is there anything you're not good at?' she said with a smile.

'I can't spell very well,' he said.

That afternoon Mrs Grey went out to see a friend, telling Rhodes and Julie she would be gone about an hour. As soon as she had left Julie came over to Rhodes and sat on his lap, and they were soon in a passionate embrace. It would have been easy for them both to rush upstairs and make love, they both wanted to. She could feel his penis. It was fully erect and pressing hard against her bottom.

She stood up. 'We need to cool down a bit, let's have a walk in the garden.'

As Rhodes stood up, his cock was standing out like a flagpole.

He said, 'I hope this goes down before your mother comes back, if she sees this I'll be asked to leave and never to return.' They both laughed and went into the garden.

After dinner that evening, Rhodes gave Julie and her mother the presents he had bought for them in Gibraltar. Julie thought the bracelet was wonderful and her mother insisted on wearing the shawl while they drank their coffee in the sun lounge. Only two days were left now of his week with Julie, but she had already asked her mother if he could come again.

Her mother's reply had surprised her when she had said, 'Why not, your father would have been delighted with your choice and so am I.'

The final two days went quickly. There had not been the opportunity of any more intimate moments.

Just as well! thought Rhodes, I can't control it for ever.

When it was time to go to Petersfield station only Julie came with him. Mrs Grey said goodbye to him at the cottage. She gave him a warm embrace and said she would see him again soon. At the station Julie gave him a prolonged kiss, every inch of her body pressed against him, there was an unspoken promise in the gesture. When the train arrived, Rhodes swiftly got into the carriage. As it was leaving there was a last touch of hands and Julie carried on waving until he was out of sight. When Julie arrived back at the cottage, her mother gave her a hug and asked, 'Are you and Peter lovers?'

'Not yet,' Julie replied, 'but we will be.'

Later that evening Rhodes arrived back at the farm. Nothing had changed. His aunt and uncle were delighted to see him.

Mark gave him a big hug and said, 'Wait till you see my girl-friend, she's a corker.'

His old bedroom seemed smaller than he had remembered, but the house still had that lovely comfortable smell about it, fresh cooking and furniture polish. When he had unpacked he gave them their presents and they were delighted. Aunt Marie shed a few tears and insisted on wearing her necklace. He showed his uncle how to use and strop the Rolls razor and Mark wore his new watch to bed.

In the morning Rhodes was up early and worked hard on the farm all day. Later that afternoon, Mark introduced him to his girlfriend. She was dark and very attractive. Her name was Linda, she had a nice personality and Rhodes thought Mark was a lucky bugger. Later that day Mark told him they hadn't done it yet. However, she liked him to touch her breasts and feel between her legs, but that was it so far. Rhodes told him not to be in too much of a hurry, the moment would come, just be patient.

Rhodes spoke to his aunt about whether or not he should go and see June. His aunt told him they had heard that her marriage had not been a success and, yes, he should visit. With some misgivings, he took the bus into Chatham. He had left it until late in the afternoon, as June did not finish work until 1700 hours. He had with him the silk scarf he had bought her in Gibraltar. He only planned to stay for about an hour, perhaps less if her husband was there. He walked up to the front door and the memories of their relationship came flooding back; this could be tricky. He knocked on the door. After about a minute it opened and there stood June.

She cried out, 'Oh, Peter, how lovely to see you, come in.'

Once inside she embraced him warmly. She asked him lots of questions and told him that his exploits in Korea and Malaya had made the local paper. She then told him she would make some tea while he told her about Julie and their plans for the future. June told him how pleased she was for them both. He asked what time her husband finished work because he would like to meet him.

June looked troubled, then she said, 'We split up six months ago, I believe he is living with a woman in Dartford, he transferred there from Chatham.'

After he had been there an hour Rhodes was feeling uncomfortable. June was still a very attractive woman and his previous relationship with her was still vivid in his mind. He decided to give her the silk scarf then leave and go back to the farm. His aunt had suggested he might be asked to stay the night, so she was not expecting him home. He gave June the scarf and she thought it was beautiful. She moved in front of him and put it on in front of the mirror. He was standing behind her.

'I think it looks great,' she said and stepped back.

She was so close he could smell her perfume and he gave a little groan to himself as he felt his penis begin to harden. She moved back until her bottom was brushing his groin. His control snapped when she pushed herself fully back into him. He put his arms round her and kissed her neck. He fondled her breasts through her blouse, it was not enough, he lifted her skirt and pushed her gently forward over the back of the settee. He slid her panties down to her knees and freeing his erect penis slid deeply into her from behind. There followed a few minutes of frantic activity, then as he came he pushed himself as deeply into her as he could, her buttocks rammed tightly into him.

She moved away from him with a sigh.

'I wanted you to do that, Peter,' she said. 'This changes nothing, your Julie will never know about this from me. We have a special relationship and it will end when you want it to.'

Rhodes was just managing to get his thoughts back together. He had needed to have sex and as always with June it had been great.

She said to him, 'Please stay the night. It will most likely be the last time we do this together. I will have such memories to brighten my ageing years.' They both laughed, the strain had gone.

She made a meal for them both and by eleven o'clock they were both naked in June's bed, passionately exploring each other's bodies. At dawn it was time for June to get ready for work.

'Just one more time, Peter. I want something to remember you by,' she said.

Rhodes summoned up what was left of his energy and took her vigorously, their bodies slammed against one another. Then after a frenzied few minutes they reached their relief. Rhodes and June left the house together, she to work and he to the bus stop.

Rhodes had not realised how quickly his leave had gone. He had thrown himself into work on the farm with great energy. Weekends were a joy, he loved to speak French and it was as though he was transferred to another world. He had written twice a week to Julie and was to spend the last week of his leave at the cottage. He had visited June on three occasions and stayed the night once. The visits were a sexual safety valve and enjoyed by them both. Uncle Bill was well aware of what was going on and shared a secret smile with Rhodes whenever Aunt Marie mentioned her name. He had letters from the Duprés, they were both fine. The army company who had relieved the marines were okay, but did not patrol as deeply into the jungle as A-Troop had.

The day before he went down to Julie's, he said goodbye to them all at the farm. Mark had told him he had managed to have his way with Linda and she had made him do it again within the hour; she kept touching him there, whenever she thought no one would notice. A final call at June's, with predictable results, and Rhodes made his way to Petersfield able to resist the lovely Julie, for a couple of days at least. Mrs Grey made him welcome as before, Julie came home about an hour after he had arrived. She looked so good that Rhodes could have eaten her on the spot. After a long embrace she asked him how they all were on the farm. Rhodes passed on his aunt and uncle's love. He told her about Mark and Linda, omitting the sexual progress. They both agreed that an invitation to a wedding seemed in the offing.

Julie told him on the second night of his stay that should he visit her during the night in her bedroom, she would be unlikely to scream for help.

Rhodes gave it some thought. 'We would have to be like mice,' he said, 'with your mother just a few yards away. To her it would sound like an earthquake. I want to, but not here.'

Their chance came unexpectedly. Two days before Rhodes's leave ended, Mrs Grey had to go to an education conference in Eastbourne. They saw her off at the station and made their way back to the cottage hand in hand.

Julie won the race to her bedroom by a short head. She made a pathetic and deliberately weak attempt to push him out of the door.

She cried out, 'Oh please, sir, do not dishonour me,' then burst out laughing. Rhodes quickly removed his clothes.

At the sight of his rampant member Julie gasped and said, 'Christ, have you got a licence for that? I think I've changed my mind.'

However, the speed with which she stripped to her bra and panties gave Rhodes the green light. He gently kissed her, starting with her lips and throat, then moving down to her breasts. He removed her bra; her breasts were delightful, slightly larger than he had thought. Her nipples like little black bullets. His mouth moved downwards, pausing to slip off her panties, he was conscious of Julie's little gasps of pleasure as he kissed her between her legs. She was making little thrusting movements with her hips. He slid a French letter over his penis and positioned himself between her spreading legs, placing his hands under her buttocks. He slowly entered her. She gave a gasp, then a little cry as his cock progressively slid deeper into her, then she was lifting her hips to meet his thrusts, finally taking him entirely in. Their movements, at first slow, began to quicken and then in a final rush of movement they came to a shattering climax.

They lay still and quiet for a few minutes as they began to get their breath back.

Julie was the first to speak. 'You are very filling, Peter, I'm surprised I managed to take all of you.' She laughed. 'Jane saw your pride and joy when you were being undressed in Taiping that time. She said it was a monster and she did not exaggerate, but I think it's lovely.'

Rhodes kissed her. 'I was frightened I might hurt you,' he said, 'I don't think I could have held out much longer. Your mother's conference was a godsend.'

Julie raised herself from the bed and pointed to the used French letter. 'Got anymore of those?' she asked.

'Only two,' Rhodes answered.

'Well, you'd better get dressed and pop down the chemist's before they shut then,' she said. 'But not just yet,' and she pulled him close to her.

The rest of his leave went by in a flash. Mrs Grey returned home two hours before his train left. She noticed how relaxed and happy they both were and knew the reason for their happiness. As the train left the station, Rhodes knew his life had now changed; his future would be with Julie. They were now wedded together in spirit for all time.

He arrived in Plymouth two hours before his leave expired and was almost the last one back. The next day they collected the rest of their kit, which had been left in the drill shed. It had followed them up from Portsmouth when the *Vengeance* had finally unloaded all their baggage. They were left to their own devices for the next day and took the opportunity to give every item of their kit a good clean. It was soon back to the standard of their recruit days.

A Home Fleet Posting

All of the returning marines were paraded the next day and they were told where they were being posted. To his surprise, Rhodes was posted to Eastney Barracks for reassignment. Several others were going with him, including Bob Jones, who had a letter from Jane Fellows to say she was on her way home from Malaya. Two days later they were in Eastney Barracks, or rather in Hutment Camp, which was attached to the barracks. The reason for this posting was soon apparent. They were being transferred to ships of the Home Fleet. They were told that the names of the ships they would be joining would appear on the notice board that afternoon. Rhodes hoped he could stay in the camp for a couple more weeks so that he could visit Julie in Petersfield and renew their close relationship.

The word that the lists were up led to a rush to the notice board. Rhodes looked. There it was. Halfway down the list, Marine P J Rhodes, DCM, MM, RM, to HMS *Theseus*. Bob Jones was being sent to the HMS *Swiftsure* with effect from the next day.

That evening Rhodes wrote to Julie and his aunt and uncle telling them where he was being sent. At least being in the Home Fleet would mean they would stay in England. The next morning, after completing their leaving routine, they were taken to the dockyard to join their ships. Rhodes climbed up the forward gangway of the *Theseus*. The ship looked massive and this was only a light fleet carrier. The corporal of the gangway, a marine, greeted him with a friendly smile.

'Just in time, mate. The port watch started their Christmas leave last week. Next week when they come back we start ours, then on 6 January we sail for the Med.'

It took Rhodes a couple of days to settle in and the sergeant major seemed friendly enough. Rhodes was told that after he had been on board a couple of months he would have to do a six-month stint as corporal of the gangway. He met the captain of marines. His name was Judge and he was a corps cricketer who also played for the navy. He informed Rhodes that he expected a great deal of him.

'Your career has had a remarkable start, two gallantry awards in two years, you have a lot to live up to.'

With only half the marine detachment aboard, there was plenty of room in the mess deck. The following week the other marines returned from their Christmas leave and Rhodes, with the rest of the Starboard Watch, began his.

He spent the first week of his leave on the farm. His aunt and uncle thought it unfair that he was to go abroad again so quickly. Mark and Linda had decided to get married in June.

Just as well, thought Rhodes, they can't keep their hands off one another.

He decided not to see June, he knew what would happen, and anyway he was saving himself for Julie. The week on the farm went by in a flash and he made his way to Petersfield with eager anticipation. Julie was in bed when he arrived, so was her mother, they both had flu. In spite of his disappointment, Rhodes set to and provided a first-class nursing service, but both Julie and her mother turned down the offer of a bed bath. However, his cooking and general care were much appreciated. There was no opportunity for any sexual activity, Julie was not well enough and his leave ended with a kiss and a cuddle.

Off to the Med

On 6 January, HMS *Theseus* sailed out of Portsmouth Harbour. Rhodes was in the ceremonial guard on the flight deck and, with the Bluejacket Band playing, the guard paid respects to the senior flag officer as the ship left. Once they were into the English Channel the ship turned into the wind and flew on two squadrons of Sea Furies, and one squadron of Fireflies. Rhodes was enthralled watching the planes land. As he watched the Sea Furies he remembered how they had saved his life in Korea.

Going through the Bay of Biscay the sea was very rough and the *Theseus*, despite its size, pitched and rolled. It was with some relief that they reached Gibraltar and had two days in port. Rhodes was well into the routine of the ship and though he was not keen on scrubbing, marines did a lot of that, he had fitted in well. The marines on board were a good bunch, a few had been in Malaya, and two had served in Korea. He spoke to one of them about Korea and tried to find out what Sea Fury squadrons had been aboard at that time.

The marine had a think and said, 'Lieutenant Commander Blackwell was on board then, he flies Sea Furies, ask him.'

The last day in Gibraltar was a Sunday. After the ship's company paraded for divisions and, as they were being dismissed, Rhodes had Lieutenant Commander Blackwell pointed out to him. He approached the officer and saluted. The officer returned his salute and asked what Rhodes wanted.

As Rhodes explained Blackwell smiled, 'So it was you we diverted for.'

He called out to another officer and said, 'This is the marine we saved from a fate worse than death, what a coincidence!'

Rhodes told them how grateful he was. The two pilots told him that the third pilot had failed to return from a raid shortly after.

Four days later the *Theseus* entered Malta's Grand Harbour

and formally joined the Mediterranean Fleet. Malta was a good run ashore and Rhodes had a walk along Kingsway as far as the palace to see who was on guard there.

It was the army. Scruffy bastards, thought Rhodes, not a patch on us.

It was the football season in Malta and Rhodes had a couple of games for the marine detachment and on the strength of his performance he was picked to play for the ship's side. He had a good game playing at right half. Their opponents were RAF Luqua and they beat them three–one. The *Theseus* then sailed with the fleet to the Eastern Med. They took part in exercises with the Turkish Navy, the Italians and then the Greeks. The whole fleet then sailed to Istanbul. They had five days there. The Massed Bands of the Royal Marines 'beat retreat' in the Dolia-marche Palace Square. It was magnificent and the Turkish spectators were enthralled.

Coronation and Fleet Review

In April, they were finally allowed to return to the United Kingdom. The Coronation was to take place in June, then shortly afterwards there was to be a fleet review at Spithead.

Rhodes had maintained a frequent exchange of mail with Julie and he had also written weekly to them all at the farm. Once a month he wrote to Helen and Paul in Malaya and in their letters it was obvious that the situation had not improved much.

Mark and Linda were getting married on 6 June and they wanted him and Julie to be there. Rhodes wondered if June would be there, as it could be an awkward meeting. In mid-April, the *Theseus* arrived back into Portsmouth. That night he dashed up to Petersfield to see Julie, but had to be content with a kiss and a cuddle as she was about to leave on night duty just as he arrived.

The *Theseus* was in dry dock for a week, a slight leak from a fuel tank required some welding. Rhodes took every opportunity to see Julie, but his attempts to make love to her always seemed to be foiled by circumstances; she was either about to go on duty or her mother was there, but he still thought love would find a way.

In mid-May, each ship of the Home Fleet was required to send a number of marines into Eastney Barracks to rehearse for 'Route Lining' in London for the Coronation. Rhodes was selected with three others from the *Theseus* and they spent hour after hour drilling on the parade ground. In total, about three hundred marines would line certain sections of the route. They rehearsed marching into position, spacing and standing for long periods, at 'the present', 'at ease' and 'at the slope'. At the end of May they all went up to London for a dress rehearsal and they stayed in one of the London barracks, which was packed with servicemen of all branches. On 2 June, Coronation Day, they moved into their positions at 0730 hours; then the long wait began. Every thirty minutes, the sergeant in charge of each section would stand them 'at ease', then call them up 'to attention', 'two paces forward march', then 'two paces step back, march', then 'stand at ease'; all designed to ease their muscles and keep their concentration.

At last the great event began to unfold. The huge procession began to move past, the Royal Coach, a glimpse of the Queen, as they 'presented arms', then she was gone. They then had to wait for the return procession. It seemed hours before the sound of the bands revived their attention. They again 'presented arms'. Rhodes thought the Queen had looked right at him and smiled, but then so did the hundreds of other marines. Finally, the long procession was past.

The marines then marched forward, turned on command then marched in three ranks behind the procession. They stayed the night in London. It seemed there was a huge party going on everywhere and they all joined in the celebrations and the drink flowed. Rhodes wished Julie had been with him, but she was in Aldershot on duty at the hospital. In the morning they made their way back to Portsmouth and by the evening Rhodes was back on the *Theseus* totally exhausted.

The following weekend, Julie and Rhodes went to Kent for Mark's wedding. It took place in Wouldham Church. Rhodes was best man and the wedding went off without a hitch. Linda's mother and father were very pleasant. June was there and made a fuss of Julie; Rhodes need not have worried, as June had said, it was 'their secret'.

The reception was held in a large marquee at the farm. Rhodes made his best man's speech, the food was superb and the dancing went on until midnight. Mark and Linda left for Paris, to start their honeymoon, at six in the evening. Rhodes had a bet with Julie that Linda would be pregnant by Christmas. When all the guests were gone, all that were left were Aunt Marie, Uncle Bill, Rhodes and Julie. Julie's room was just along the passage from Rhodes and when all was quiet he slipped into her room.

She said, 'You took your time,' and laughed.

He stayed there until it began to get light. They had made love wildly once and once less wildly.

As Rhodes left her bed Julie said, 'You have ruined me, sir, not once but twice,' and added, 'would you care to try again?'

Back at Portsmouth, the harbour was beginning to fill with ships; some were already at Spithead while the *Theseus* was still getting her final coat of paint. Rumours were flying round the ship that after the review they were going back out to the Med. The *Theseus* finished her painting and made her way out to Spithead; the number of ships there was growing by the hour. Each class of warship was in a different line and the *Theseus* was seventh in a line of nine aircraft carriers; ahead of them was the battleship *Vanguard*. There were hundreds of ships of all shapes and sizes, and of all nationalities; it was a magnificent sight. There were three days to go before the review by Her Majesty the Queen.

Julie and her mother took advantage of the occasion and came out to visit the *Theseus*. Hundreds of people were visiting the various ships. Rhodes met Julie and her mother at the head of the gangway.

'Goodness, Peter, it's huge!' said Mrs Grey.

Julie burst out laughing, thinking, Where have I heard that before?

Rhodes gave them a tour of the ship. He took them down on the lift into the hangar deck where a lone Sea Fury stood and beside it was Lieutenant Commander Blackwell.

He called out to Julie, 'Would you like to see in the cockpit?'

Rhodes helped Julie on to the wing, while the pilot explained the controls. When he had finished there was a group of young children queuing to be shown over the aircraft, so Rhodes thanked the officer and took Julie and her mother down to the 'canteen flat' to buy them an ice cream.

He showed them the quarterdeck and his watch position when the ship was at sea, which was life buoy sentry. He explained what it entailed. It was now time for them to leave the ship, so Rhodes escorted them both down to the gangway. He gave both Mrs Grey and Julie a farewell kiss.

As they left the ship he called out, 'Hope to see you Saturday,' and waved until the motorboat was lost from sight.

On 15 June it was sunny, but with a fresh wind. An hour before the Queen was due to start the review of the ships' companies, all the vessels taking part were assembled on deck.

Rhodes was part of the guard of honour. At last they began to hear bugles sounding the 'Alert', bands were playing 'The Royal Salute' and gradually HMS *Surprise*, with Her Majesty on board, slowly sailed down the line of aircraft carriers. As she drew level with HMS *Theseus*, the Royal Marine Guard of Honour presented arms until she had passed. It took two hours for the review to be completed and the Queen sailed back into Portsmouth Harbour. That night all the ships were floodlit and at 2200 hours they all took part in a massive fireworks display. All of the sailors and marines involved realised they would not see a sight like this ever again.

Over the next few days all of the ships departed, the *Theseus* sailed back into Portsmouth Harbour and berthed alongside South Railway Jetty. They had all been informed that they would sail to the Mediterranean on Friday morning and would return in time for Christmas.

Five months away from Julie, thought Rhodes, and this is a home posting! On the Wednesday evening he went up to Petersfield. Mrs Grey was at a teachers' meeting, so he had Julie to himself for a couple of hours. Their lovemaking reached new heights of passion. Afterwards as they lay exhausted on Julie's bed he told her he would be away until Christmas, but when he came home he wanted them to be formally engaged to be married.

Julie smiled and said, 'I thought what we have just done suggested something along those lines.'

Rhodes kissed her breasts, then her lips and said, 'I love you, Julie Grey,' then kissed her again. They dressed and went downstairs and only just in time; ten minutes later Mrs Grey came in the gate.

Sun, Sea and a Shattered Cyprus

HMS *Theseus* sailed out of Portsmouth Harbour at 0900 hours. It was a fine day and, once well out into the channel, they flew on their Sea Furies and Fireflies. When the aircraft were secure they turned south and headed for the Bay of Biscay. The weather all the way to the Med was fine, the bay was unusually benign and the marines took advantage of the good weather to challenge the stokers to a game of deck hockey.

The ball is a rope grommet and the rules are unwritten and minimal, but punching is not permitted, unless a serious foul has been committed. There were many serious fouls. A large stoker struck Rhodes across the shin with his stick. His return blow caused the stoker's eye to swell and a mass brawl developed. The referee was the chaplain.

He restored order by shouting, 'For God's sake, stop!'

The stokers and marines could hardly ignore that and order was restored. The match finished eight–all and honour was satisfied.

When they reached Gibraltar, shore leave was granted. The ship was challenged to a football match, but Rhodes could not play because his shin was still swollen. However, the *Theseus* beat the 1st Destroyer squadron two–nil. Rhodes and the stoker with the swollen eye had a few drinks together to celebrate the victory and peace was restored. On arrival in Malta, they were visited by the commander-in-chief of the Mediterranean Fleet, Lord Louis Mountbatten. Rhodes was in the guard of honour. As he inspected them, the great man paused when he came to Rhodes.

He looked at the medals on Rhodes's chest and said, 'They have a tale to tell, explain.' Rhodes complied.

Mountbatten smiled and said, 'Well done, another chapter to add to the history of the corps.'

The *Theseus* was deployed on various exercises, their aircraft attacking other elements of the Med Fleet and in turn the *Theseus* came under air attack. The Royal Marines anti-aircraft guns were in the Brown Group, which was portside-aft, and any planes attacking the port quarter of the ship were engaged by the Royal Marines. They manned three bofors, two oerlikons, and one multiple Pom Pom. Rhodes was amazed how little time there was to aim and fire before the planes had gone. The day ended in tragedy, one of their Sea Furies crashed into the barrier on landing and spun straight over the ship's side. It sank from view taking the pilot with it.

Later on, in mid-August, they were off the coast of Oran when the ship received a signal to sail for the Greek islands, which had suffered a series of earthquakes. The main part of the Med Fleet were already on the scene, giving medical aid and erecting tents as shelter for the homeless. As the *Theseus* made its way north, the marine detachment made preparations to go ashore. They would take rations with them for two weeks and no weapons were to be carried. They were almost halfway there when they were told to divert to Cyprus, which itself had been hit by several severe earth tremors. They reached the coast of Cyprus a few days later arriving at 0400 hours. By 0700 hours the whole of the Royal Marine detachment was ashore. They made their base camp in a large field just outside the small fishing village of Paphos. The village had suffered substantial damage and the marines spent the morning searching for casualties in the rubble. The mayor informed them that only one person was missing, an old lady who was at least seventy years old. She had been seen last going into the small village church.

Captain Judge RM sent Rhodes and four other marines to search through the rubble of the church. The remainder of the detachment were to erect a large number of ten-man tents that had just arrived, one for each family whose homes had been destroyed. Rhodes and his fellow marines searched until it was almost dark, then just as they were about to give up they heard a tapping that seemed to come from almost beneath their feet. As they frantically moved the rubble to one side, a small voice cried out and there, underneath a church pew, was the old lady. She was clutching a small dog and apart from a cut on her head and being covered in dust, she appeared unhurt, as was the dog. Her son, a local fisherman, stood by as the marines eased his mother gently from under the pew. Once free, the son embraced his mother who chattered away in Greek.

He turned to the marines and said, 'My mother thanks you. God has protected her because she was in his house.'

That night, as the marines finished their meal, there were two more earth tremors and as they lay on their groundsheets in the base camp tent, the earth shook again. In the morning, after an early breakfast, the marines finished putting up tents for the homeless villagers. A lorry then arrived with fifty more tents; these were required in a small hamlet three miles further along the coast. Captain Judge decided to move their base camp there as well. As they were about to leave, the fisherman whose mother they had rescued presented them with a box of freshly caught fish.

He said, 'Not even an earthquake can stop us fishing. We are men. Please accept the fish as a sign of our gratitude.'

The marines moved off, their truck easing its way through the smiling waving villagers.

The small village the marines had been sent to was not on the coast but further inland. They erected a large tent for the local doctor, who was treating some of his patients for broken legs and crush injuries. The houses in this, a smaller village, were of two or more floors. This had caused more severe injuries than the first village, which was all single-floor.

Meanwhile, the *Theseus* had been sent to Port Said to pick up more tents and one of its helicopters arrived with more supplies. It took the more severely injured to the hospital in Famagusta. After three weeks the worst of the homeless had been rehoused and the marines returned to the *Theseus*, pleased with their part in the operation. The ship set sail for Malta, the marines enjoying the chance to shower, have a good meal and read their mail.

Rhodes had five letters, two from Julie, which he read first, two from the farm and one from the Duprés. Julie wanted him home as soon as possible.

'I miss you so much,' she said, 'and there is so much for us to do together.'

Rhodes thought that could mean quite a few things. They were all well on the farm. Mark and Linda were both enjoying married life.

I bet they are! thought Rhodes. Lucky sod.

The Duprés were moving to another tin mine. 'It was a promotion for Paul,' Helen said.

The new mine was between Batu Gajah and Tapah. Rhodes was about to answer his letters when he was told the sergeant major wanted him.

'Got another medal for you, young Rhodes, three Coronation Medals awarded to the detachment and one is for you.'

The awarding of Coronation Medals was a sore point in the services. The widely held view was they all should have been given one. The army, in particular, was upset that the bulk of their allocation went to the guards' regiments.

The *Theseus* arrived back in Malta in mid-September. Anchored astern of her in Grand Harbour was the USS *Wasp*, a slightly larger aircraft carrier. The US Marines on the *Wasp* invited the Royal Marines over to the *Wasp* for a guided tour. Twenty of the marines from the *Theseus* went across, including Rhodes, Captain Judge and the sergeant major. The living conditions on the *Wasp* were far superior to those on the *Theseus*. Rhodes was not surprised after his experience on the USS *Ross*. During the tour Rhodes noticed that on the ship's notice board was a list of all the ship's officers; heading the list was the ship's captain, Captain Reinhart, US Navy.

Rhodes asked one of the US Marine sergeants if it was the same Reinhart who had been on the *Ross*.

'Sure that's the guy, do you know him?' asked the sergeant.

'Yes,' said Rhodes, 'I know him.'

At lunchtime, they were invited to the mess hall. The food was superb and the marines took full advantage and tucked in.

As they were finishing their sweet, strawberry ice cream, the sergeant Rhodes had spoken to said, 'I'm to escort you to the captain's quarters, he wishes to see you.'

Rhodes was escorted along a maze of passages, finally reaching the captain's quarters. An American marine was standing outside the cabin and the sergeant told him that this British marine was the guest of the captain.

The door was opened and Rhodes was ushered in. Captain

Reinhart was sitting at his desk. As soon as he saw Rhodes he got to his feet and, smiling broadly, came towards him with his hand out in greeting, saying, 'It's a pleasure to see you again, son, come and sit down.'

Captain Reinhart insisted that Rhodes told him everything that had happened to him since he left the *Ross*. The conversation went on for an hour and Rhodes was given coffee.

Finally he said, 'I must not take up any more of your time, sir. It has been a great pleasure meeting you again.'

Captain Reinhart phoned the gangway and was told the rest of the marines were just leaving.

'Come on, son, I'll see you off the ship,' he said.

When Rhodes got to the gangway only Captain Judge was left waiting to board their motorboat.

Rhodes turned to Captain Reinhart and said, 'Sir, this is my commanding officer, Captain Judge.'

Reinhart turned to Judge and greeted him warmly. 'I hope you have enjoyed your tour, Captain. Forgive me for delaying you but I heard this young man was aboard my ship, we are shipmates from the Korean War days.'

He then shook Rhodes's hand and wished him well. Rhodes saluted him and made his way down to the waiting boat and his grinning fellow marines. Captain Reinhart spoke briefly to Captain Judge, shook his hand and then as the motorboat moved away from the gangway raised his hand in farewell. All the marines in the boat returned the compliment; it seemed the natural thing to do.

The next day twenty American marines came aboard the *Theseus* to spend the day. As they were shown round the ship the question on all their minds was, Where do you guys live? When it was pointed out to them that the marines mess deck was where they ate, slept and socialised the Americans were appalled. They could not accept the limitations of space and when a marine showed them how to sling a hammock and how to get in and out of it, they fell about laughing. The Royal Marines were concerned that the food their American guests would receive at lunchtime would not be up to the standard of the USS *Wasp*. The cooks on the *Theseus* had prepared a menu of bangers and mash with fried onions and baked beans and for a sweet, jam roly-poly. The Royal Marines' trump card would be a tot of rum for each of the American marines, the plan being to get them half pissed so they would not notice the limitations of the marines' food and comforts. They had arranged with the supply officer to forfeit their next two days' worth of tots so as to give the Americans a double rum ration. A tot of rum is a measure of neat rum mixed with two measures of water; the Americans would be given two tots.

At midday the rum was brought to the mess deck and the Americans given a tot. They were also served their lunch of bangers and mash. The Americans appreciated the rum as American ships are dry or alcohol-free. As the rum began to take effect the Americans tucked into their food with gusto. The second tot completed the transformation. All inhibitions vanished and the Americans thought their British friends were wonderful. At 1500 hours the Americans were returned to their ship and as they staggered up the gangway of the USS *Wasp* under the stern gaze of the ship's police, a firm bond had been established between the marine brothers.

Over the next week the *Theseus* took part in exercises off the coast of Tripoli. American aircraft from the Tripoli air base at Wheelus Field took part and, together with the aircraft from the *Theseus*, attacked the main ships of the Mediterranean Fleet. On completion of the exercises the *Theseus* sailed for Benghazi where the ship's company were given shore leave. A sporting challenge was issued to the ship from the British garrison; a cricket match one day and a football match the next. Rhodes played in both games. Captain Judge RM scored seventy runs. Rhodes batting at number six scored a brisk thirty, including two sixes and three fours. After totalling one hundred and sixty they bowled out the army for ninety-eight, with Judge taking three wickets and Rhodes two good catches in the slips. The football match was a far more physical affair and the army were marginally the better side. Rhodes, playing at right half, clashed several times with the army inside left. The referee spoke to them twice, but good sense prevailed and after a robust encounter the match was drawn.

The *Theseus* returned to Malta where a concert was being

given by the Massed Bands of the Royal Marines in the Hotel Phoenicia. Rhodes and nine other marines from the *Theseus* were detailed to assist with the seating arrangements and act as guides to the invited guests. A naval commander from the C in C staff was responsible for all the evening's activities and his wife was organising the refreshments. The marines quickly took a dislike to the commander, who was immediately dubbed a 'pompous little prick', but his wife was quite attractive and the marines did all she asked of them. The evening came and Rhodes and another marine were detailed to man the main entrance.

The commander fussed around issuing instructions, 'Don't forget to salute and say good evening, sir or madam.'

Rhodes looked at him.

'We know how to perform our duties, sir.'

The commander looked at Rhodes, immaculate in his uniform with his medals gleaming and decided to say nothing.

As the guests arrived the commander fussed and rushed about, issuing pointless instructions to the two marines, which they simply ignored. Almost the last to arrive was the C in C, Lord Louis and Lady Edwina Mountbatten. The commander almost prostrated himself before them, while Rhodes and his fellow marine saluted.

The C in C ignored the commander and said, 'Good evening, Rhodes, should be a good concert,' and walked in.

The commander gave Rhodes a look of pure venom and scampered after the C in C. His wife, who had witnessed the exchange, gave a sigh and said, 'I would keep out of his way after the concert. He can be quite spiteful.'

Rhodes thanked her and said, 'If he tries it on, I'll tell him I will complain to the C in C.'

At the interval in the concert, Mrs Browning, the commander's wife, came up to Rhodes and asked him if he would help her return some wine and spirits to the mess at Manuel Island. She explained that she had a car and that it would not take long. When the concert restarted he helped her load the drinks into the car and she told her husband that she was about to go, but he almost ignored her and said, 'Oh, very well,' and strutted off. They drove to the mess at Manuel Island and returned the drinks. When they got back into the car, she drove along Sliema sea front and stopped at a block of flats.

'Come up for a drink,' she said.

A warning sounded in Rhodes's head. This was an officer's wife. It could be trouble.

'Do you think this is wise, Mrs Browning? Someone may see us and misread the situation,' he said.

'Don't be silly, anyway he will stay the night in the mess, he always does after a function.'

They went up to her flat. When he was inside she poured him a cold beer and then she went into another room. Rhodes took off his tunic and drank some of his beer. Gail Browning came back into the room and sat down beside him. He knew what would happen and it did. She leaned across and kissed him full on the lips, he responded, she forced her tongue into his mouth and her hand dropped to his groin. Her hand freed his penis from the confines of his trousers. It hardened to its full size immediately. She gave a little gasp as her hand measured its length. Rhodes hands were busy too. He had undone all the buttons on the front of her dress. His mouth was busy on her breasts while his hand was between her legs. She had removed her panties when she had left the room earlier. She pulled him to his feet and led him into the bedroom. They both stripped off their clothes and she gave him a French letter from the bedside table. They lay on the bed, his hands and mouth skilfully bringing her to near climax. She leaned over him and took him in her mouth. He pulled her head forward and moved himself back and forward in her mouth. He pulled himself clear and put on the French letter, he spread her legs wide and thrust himself into her. With great gasping thrusts and an equally frantic response he came, she just seconds behind him.

Later she drove him back to the jetty where he could get a boat out to his ship.

'He will never find out from me,' she said.

'Or me,' said Rhodes. 'This is one affair I won't talk about.'

'You are very sweet,' she said, kissing him.

Rhodes got out of the car; she gave him a final wave and drove off. When Rhodes got back aboard the *Theseus* it was after midnight and most of the marines were asleep. In the morning Rhodes had taken up his duties again as corporal of the gangway; his watch finished at noon. When he came down to the mess deck he was told the sergeant major wanted to see him.

'Report to the captain of marines in his cabin at 1500 hours, he's got some news for you,' said the sergeant major.

At 1500 hours Rhodes reported to the OCRM.

'I have two things to discuss with you, Rhodes,' said Captain Judge. 'You have been selected to attend the junior NCOs' course in Plymouth Barracks in April next year. Also the C in C's office have sent a signal to all ships who had men involved in last night's band concert thanking them for their efforts. Commander Browning asked me to thank you for the assistance you gave to his wife in helping her with the return stores, that's about it, you can carry on.'

Rhodes saluted and returned to the mess deck somewhat relieved.

Back Home and a Proposal

Two days later HMS *Theseus* was released from her duties in the Med and sailed for the UK. It was an uneventful trip home. They called in at Gibraltar, where Rhodes and the rest of the crew bought presents. It was early December and Christmas leave would start in a few weeks. Despite the time of year, the weather in the Bay of Biscay was fine. As they cleared the bay and entered the English Channel their three squadrons of aircraft took off and returned to their shore bases. They entered Portsmouth Harbour and berthed at South Railway Jetty. Rhodes was off duty until noon the next day, so he planned to go to Petersfield that evening.

At 1900 hours he was knocking on the door of the cottage; seconds later Julie was in his arms, home at last. Mrs Grey was also pleased to see him. They both said how brown he was and asked if it had been an exciting time. They asked him about the Cyprus earthquakes and how many countries he had visited.

'What was the most exciting moment of the whole trip?' asked Julie.

Rhodes thought of Gail Browning, but said, 'Oh, the earthquakes in Cyprus, without a doubt,' and thought that some things are best forgotten. Before he left that evening Mrs Grey invited him to spend part or all of his Christmas leave at the cottage. Julie walked with him to Petersfield Station. Just outside, he stopped and kissed her.

'Marry me, Julie?' he said.

'Of course, I will,' she replied and he took the engagement ring he had purchased in Gibraltar from his pocket and slipped it on her finger.

'Now,' he said, 'I am committed.'

She kissed him, 'You always were,' she said, 'from that first day we met in Penang I knew we would always be together.'

Back on the *Theseus* Rhodes caught up on his mail, they were all well on the farm. The Duprés had settled in their new location, but the area was not terrorist-free and a nearby rubber plantation had had half of its trees slashed. There was no letter from June. Rhodes decided to leave her off his mailing list, except for Christmas and birthday cards. He thought of Julie. They could get married after he finished the twelve-week NCOs' course, that would be in late July. The weeks went by and soon it was 18 December, when he started his leave. He spent the first five days on the farm and Mark and Linda were still like newly weds, dashing to their room at every opportunity. Linda was responding to the weekend French lessons and they all tried to catch each other out with some obscure word; it was good fun. Rhodes said his goodbyes and went back down to Petersfield. There had been a fall of snow and the cottage looked a perfect Christmas picture.

On Christmas Eve, Rhodes, Julie and her mum went to mid-night mass. It was a perfect way to begin Christmas. As they came back to the cottage Mrs Grey said she had only one regret and that was that her husband had not lived to see Julie and Peter together. That night they avoided the temptation of Rhodes paying Julie a visit; in the circumstances it seemed inappropriate. On Boxing Day afternoon Mrs Grey went to visit a friend, saying she would only be gone a couple of hours. As she disappeared around the corner, there was a frantic race to Julie's bedroom. After twenty minutes of frantic sexual activity, Julie, once she had got her breath back, said, 'You really are disgusting, Peter, if Mum knew what you had just done, she would be horrified.'

Rhodes smiled. 'Are you ready to receive the Flying Scotsman again? It's got a head of steam up.'

Julie nodded and said, 'I like the trains to run on time.'

All too soon Rhodes's leave was up; with much regret he left the Greys and returned to the *Theseus*. When all the ship's company had returned from leave the ship sailed round the coast to Portland Harbour. The Home Fleet were starting a ten-day exercise, but it did not involve any of the *Theseus'* aircraft, so the squadrons stayed at their shore bases. The role of the *Theseus* was to represent a column of ships in a convoy with the other aircraft carriers playing a similar role. The cruisers and destroyers were to provide a protective screen against submarine attack. As they headed out into the Atlantic the weather became quite foul. At

0400 hours the *Theseus* was sunk.

Good, thought the crew, we can now return to Portsmouth. But the admiral in charge thought otherwise. The *Theseus* now became a troopship. Her luck did not change, however, and at 1500 hours she was torpedoed again. She had not been sunk, however, but just disabled and was escorted by a destroyer, HMS *Agincourt*, to seek shelter off the coast of Ireland. Her speed was reduced to five knots due the damage she had sustained. The destroyer circled her at fifteen knots, all to no avail, and they received a signal that they had both now been sunk. With some relief the *Theseus* and the *Agincourt* made their way back into Plymouth; for them the war was over. They remained in Plymouth for the next week. When all the Home Fleet ships were back in port, the commanding officers attended a wash-up of the exercise.

The *Theseus* returned to Portsmouth and after taking on fresh supplies she sailed again for the Med, this time to support an amphibious assault on the North African coast. All of her aircraft flew on once they were in the channel. They called in at Gibraltar and the ship's company had shore leave. Rhodes and the rest of the marine detachment went for a run up to the top of the rock as Captain Judge thought they needed the exercise.

A few days later, Rhodes watched with interest as his old unit, 42 Commando, stormed ashore near Arzeu. He was not fond of being in a ship's detachment and wanted to get back into the commando brigade. At last they were freed to return to the UK and in the last week in February they arrived in Portsmouth. At the first opportunity, Rhodes went up to Petersfield and with Julie's mother they discussed the wedding. It was to be in Petersfield church on 24 July. They made out a list of guests. As well as Julie's relatives, Aunt Marie, Uncle Bill, Mark, Linda and June would all be invited. Rhodes suggested the Isle of Wight for their honeymoon. Julie knew of a nice hotel in Freshwater Bay, so it was all decided.

RMB Stonehouse and the NCO' School

When it was time to leave the *Theseus* and begin his NCOs' course, Rhodes found he was quite sorry to go as he had enjoyed his time on board and had made some good friends.

Captain Judge wished him well. 'I feel sure you are going to have an exceptional career and I wish you every good fortune.'

Rhodes was quite touched and was almost sorry to be leaving. As he left the ship several of the marines helped him with his kit and then a truck took him to the station. Another chapter had started.

It was early afternoon when he arrived in Plymouth and made his way to the Royal Marine barracks at Stonehouse. He reported to the sergeant major of NCO Training Company and was told what barrack room he was in, given his programme and a list of marines attending the course. To his delight he knew many of the marines from his A-Troop days, including Bob Jones. In the barrack room he had the bed next to Bob's. All of the marines in the room were cleaning their kit and, after he had said hello to those he knew, Rhodes unpacked his kit and joined them in cleaning and polishing. That evening he and Bob Jones had a long chat about their girlfriends. Bob asked him if he had done it yet with Julie.

Rhodes said, 'Have you done it with Jane?'

'That's none of your business,' said Bob, and they both laughed.

The next morning they paraded on the main parade and after a rigorous inspection, they were sent to the lecture theatre for the commandant's opening address.

Lieutenant Colonel Mead, MC, RM, stressed the importance of well-led troops and the chain of command. He pointed out it was of little use having a well-thought out plan if the ability did not exist to put the plan into operation. It was down to the enthusiasm of the senior and junior NCOs to make it effective and successful. Lessons of the First World War had not been learnt and it was well into the Second World War before due regard to full briefings was observed. If 42 Commando were to assault an enemy position, they needed to know firstly, why, secondly, how, thirdly, the role of every marine in the operation. It was all pretty straightforward stuff and Rhodes and his fellow marines who had seen active service understood what he was talking about.

Part one of the course lasted six weeks. It dealt with the parade side, good order and discipline, corps history, administration and involved an education test and giving lectures. Each student was to give three lectures, the first of ten minutes, the second of twenty minutes, and the third of thirty minutes. There were forty marines on the course, they were split into four sections of ten and each section had a sergeant as its leader. Rhodes was in section three. On day one, after the CO's lecture, they were taken on the main parade for communication drill. They were spread out on the parade ground, with their sergeant in the centre. He would give a drill order then each student in turn would repeat the order as though he was drilling a squad of marines. This went on for most of the morning, the object being to develop a good word of command. The marines enjoyed this and as the days went on, each would drill the other nine in his section.

The days and weeks flew by and they were allowed every other weekend off. Rhodes and Jones dashed down to Portsmouth to see their girlfriends. Jane was now with Julie at Aldershot Military Hospital. The wedding plans were now finalised and it fitted in with the summer leave period. Guest lists, the reception and church were all arranged.

The final week of the course had arrived and each marine was required to drill the whole group for ten minutes, in a movement of foot drill or arms drill. When Rhodes's turn came he was told to instruct the squad in Fixing Bayonets on the March; luckily he and Bob Jones had practised this in the barrack room the night before. As the day went on Rhodes was pleased with his performance and in comparison with some of the others he had done well. When they finished for the day they were all exhausted as they had worked hard for each other and the instructors were pleased.

The final lectures would take place over a three-day period and the students would have to sit through all forty presentations. After three lectures they had a ten-minute break. These were long days with the final lecture finishing at 1800 hours. The commandant had listened to most of them. Rhodes had chosen the battle of Omdurman as his subject. Lieutenant Colonel Mead stopped him as he was leaving the lecture theatre and asked him why he had not spoken about his DCM or his MM.

Rhodes said, 'I thought it should be a subject that needed researching, sir, talking about my medals would have been the easy way out.'

At the end of the final week of part one, ten marines were told they had failed, but their marks were good enough to be given a second chance in October, if they wished to take part one again. On the following Monday part two of the course began. This was to be all fieldwork, weapon training, live firing, fire and movement, and assaults on various positions. During the six weeks the marines would be given various roles to play, company commander, sergeant major, section officer, sergeant and corporal. They would all get the chance to impress or otherwise. Rhodes was given the task of instructing his section in stripping and priming grenades, a subject he was more than happy to perform. As always, being in the field and living under canvas provided an endless supply of humour. Someone back in camp had been too generous with the chemicals used to keep the water pure in the bowser. As a result everyone got the gallops. After getting fed up with frequently dropping their trousers they soldiered on working on the basis that they all smelt as bad as each other.

The weather for part two was a delight, lots of warm sunshine, and it wasn't until week four that they had any rain. Rhodes was playing the role of company commander, when they were tasked to attack an old China clay works on Dartmoor. His briefing went well and his plan of attack was simple. Four sections moving forward in classic fire and movement to the point of general assault, with section four moving out to the left to provide covering fire in the final assault over the last hundred yards. As they reached their final position for the assault, Rhodes was told his covering section had been wiped out. What was he going to do? He remembered an officer telling them all in a lecture that firm action was seldom wrong, so he said, 'We will attack, sir.'

Deprived of covering fire the marines covered the final hundred yards in record time, they seized their objective and awaited the decision of the adjudicating officer. It was not long in coming.

'You suffered fifty per cent casualties, but you secured the objective, a high price to pay. Was it worth it?' asked the officer.

Rhodes thought about it then said, 'I carried out my instructions, sir. Others would assess the value of the ground gained.'

The officer, a major on attachment from the Suffolk regiment, looked at Rhodes and asked, 'And where did you read that?'

Rhodes said, 'I was researching the battle of Omdurman for my lecture. General Kitchener was alleged to have said it, sir.'

'Well, in that case,' said the major, 'we will count this as your Omdurman.'

The final two weeks passed quickly and towards the end of the last week the candidates were called in one at a time for the final assessment of their performance.

When Rhodes was called, he entered the commandant's office, thinking, Well, I did my best.

He was invited to sit down and then the commandant read out his report.

When they had finished Rhodes thought to himself, Christ, I could not have written it better myself.

For the rest of the day, Rhodes felt he was on cloud nine. The next day they had the final address from the commandant. When he had finished, the sergeant major called out four names, Rhodes was one of them, as was Bob Jones. They were to report to the commandant's office at once.

All four marines were marched in together. The commandant looked at them and said, 'This is a signal from Pay and Records Office Royal Marines, you four have been promoted to corporal as from today. Congratulations, now go to the tailor's shop and get your new rank sewn on all of your uniforms.'

As they were about to leave his office he stopped them and gave to each of them their NCO's whistle and leather strap. With great enthusiasm they took all their uniforms to the tailor's and, after about an hour, left proudly displaying their new badges of rank. Before the course left for summer leave, they were all required to fill in an application form for a specialist course. They had a choice, but were required to list their first, second and third preference. Rhodes listed assault engineer, drill instructor and landing craft in that order. They then were allowed to depart the barracks for summer leave.

Flowers, Vows and Bells

Rhodes and Bob Jones made their way to Petersfield. Both would stay at the cottage prior to the wedding the next day. Julie and her mother greeted them both warmly. All was arranged. Mark would be best man. He, Linda and Rhodes's aunt and uncle would travel down the next morning. June had said she had a bad cold and may not be able to come, but Jane would be there and was as excited as Julie.

The next day was bright and sunny and by midday all the guests had arrived, including June. At 1400 hours Rhodes, in his No. 1 uniform with medals and white gloves, was waiting at the altar. Julie walked up the aisle on the arm of Uncle Bill. She looked stunning. Her wedding dress was peach-coloured satin with matching veil. Rhodes could not take his eyes off her. After the service he had little recollection of what had been said, but Julie was now his and he was hers for all time. The photographs were taken outside the church, the usual groupings, and then the wedding party made their way back to the cottage, which was only a hundred yards away. Rhodes and Julie quietly slipped away to the graveyard behind the church. Here Julie placed her wedding bouquet on her father's grave. They stood there for a few minutes, a tear ran down Julie's face, Rhodes kissed it away.

'He wants you to be happy, it's your day,' he said.

When they were back at the reception, everyone was offering their congratulations. June gave them both a hug and pressed Rhodes's hand. It was a message, an acceptance that everything now had changed. Rhodes spoke to Jane and Bob.

'You two are next,' he said.

Bob said, 'Can't wait, it's Jane who's holding things up.'

'Next week then,' said Jane and they all laughed.

That evening Rhodes and Julie finally got away and made their way to the Isle of Wight and to the hotel in Freshwater Bay. At last alone in their room, they made ready for bed. Julie had put on a black silk nightdress. Rhodes had put on nothing except a smile.

'Look at you,' said Julie. 'For God's sake don't turn round quick, you will knock that lamp off the table, I must say it looks in fine condition, will it last the week?'

Rhodes grabbed her and carried her to the bed. Her nightdress disappeared under the pillow. She was naked. Rhodes kissed and caressed her from head to toe, while Julie grabbed his penis and ran her finger down its length.

'Tonight,' she said, 'you can fill me with babies, lots of babies.'

Rhodes slid his member fully into her and she gasped as he drove it home. Their bodies did a ritual dance, the mattress protesting as they reached a shattering climax for the first, but not the last time that night.

A faint tap on the door woke Rhodes. He glanced over at Julie; her breasts were uncovered.

He slipped the sheet over them and called out, 'Come in.'

The door opened and the landlord's wife entered with their morning tea.

'Did you sleep well, sir?' she asked.

'Yes, thank you,' said Rhodes, 'the bed is very comfortable.'

As the landlady left the room Julie opened her eyes.

'I feel I've been run over by a bus,' she said.

'Have some tea,' said Rhodes. 'It will wake you up.'

Julie sat up in bed, her firm breasts peeping over the sheet.

'And what plans have we for today?' she asked.

Rhodes paused from drinking his tea.

'I was just about to get up and go down for breakfast,' he said, 'but I have just changed my mind.'

He took Julie's cup from her, placed it on the bedside table, then he flicked the sheet back and exposed Julie's naked body. He kissed her nose, her lips, her throat and worked his way down her body. Julie gave a little cry as he moved her legs apart and entered her. The bed and the mattress creaked and groaned as the two bodies moved rapidly up and down, frantically racing to a climax. The landlord, who was passing their room, smiled as he recognised the sounds, and when he got to the kitchen suggested to his wife that, 'The young couple would have a late breakfast.'

Rhodes and Julie went for a walk along the beach later that

morning. It was warm and sunny. They paused by an upturned boat and sat down. Julie turned to Rhodes.

'Will it always be as good as this?' she asked.

Rhodes smiled at his lovely wife.

'Yes,' he said, 'it will get better and better, we are going to have a wonderful married life, full of surprises.'

'I like surprises,' said Julie. 'When is the next surprise due?'

'As soon as we get back to the hotel,' said Rhodes.

The week passed quickly and soon it was time to leave the hotel and catch the ferry back to the mainland. They said their goodbyes to the landlord and his wife. They had become good friends and had been well looked after during their stay.

As Rhodes and Julie got into their taxi, the landlord said to his wife, 'I think that bed wants the screws tightening, it's had a busy week!' They both laughed and waved as Julie and Rhodes drove away.

Mrs Grey warmly embraced them both on their arrival at the cottage.

'I don't have to ask if you both enjoyed your honeymoon, the joy is written over both your faces.'

That night they made love quietly and slowly, each was aware of their partner's likes and dislikes and their lovemaking was improving with each encounter. With a great deal of regret they both had to return to their duties, Julie to the BMH at Aldershot and Rhodes to Stonehouse Barracks at Plymouth. A list was on the notice board of the NCOs' wing. Rhodes scanned the list for his name. There it was, LC2's Course, landing craft, at Eastney Barracks.

Well, thought Rhodes, I'll be near Julie.

Bob Jones was down for the same course and both agreed it could have been a lot worse. They travelled down to Portsmouth two days later and were housed once again in Hutment Camp.

Flat-Bottomed Boats

The landing craft course was quite informal, an almost complete absence of parades, but an awful lot to cram into twelve weeks. They were going to have to learn Morse code, semaphore, pilotage, landing craft handling, how to strip and service a Ford V8 engine, cooling systems and how to do emergency repairs. Rhodes had a great deal of trouble with reading Morse code by sound or light, although he had quickly learnt the code itself. He knew all the combinations of dots and dashes, but just could not read it. His instructor told him not to worry, as it would come to him in due course. The pilotage was great fun, laying up courses and taking three-point fixes in a choppy sea near the Isle of Wight. They learned how to plot true courses, course made good and course to steer. They learnt how to allow for wind and tide, taking turns to steer landing craft onto beaches using a kedge anchor to hold the craft straight against the wind and currents.

The weekends were free, so every Saturday afternoon it was straight up to his lovely Julie at Petersfield. Despite their best efforts she had not become pregnant.

In bed at night Julie told him, 'I want more effort, I don't think you are trying hard enough.'

'Is this hard enough?' said Rhodes with a smile.

'Oh yes,' said Julie, 'quite hard enough, thank you.'

Halfway through the course they were required to complete a top overhaul of a Ford V8 engine, the standard engine in landing craft. They worked in pairs, Rhodes and Bob Jones teaming up together. They were given two days to complete the overhaul. The test of their success would be if the engine restarted after it had been reassembled. The instructor asked them if they had any bits left over. They said, 'No,' and with fingers crossed pressed the start button. Nothing happened.

'Check your battery connections,' said the instructor. They tightened up the connecters and tried again. This time the engine

175

gave a cough and a splutter before breaking into a satisfying roar. After a few adjustments it settled into its normal idling rhythm.

The other landing craft engine they were required to have a working knowledge of was the Hudson Invader, a diesel engine used in the larger LCM, which was used to carry a small number of vehicles.

In week eight they had an interim signals test. Rhodes had, as he had feared, a poor score in reading Morse from the signal lamp, his score being the poorest in the group. His instructors were puzzled. He could recall the Morse alphabet without any trouble; he could read the sound buzzer quite well but not the signal lamp. The standard they were required to reach was not up to the expertise of a Royal Marine signaller, but good enough to send or receive in an emergency.

In week nine they had their navigation tests, a written paper and a practical exercise off the Isle of Wight and they all got good marks. Boat handling was the next practical exam. It was good fun, beaching, retracting from the beach using a kedge anchor, coming alongside with and against the tide, steering the craft with the engines alone and doing a short turn. The last was achieved by turning the wheel to starboard, port engine full ahead and starboard engine full astern, that turned the landing craft 180 degrees in its own length. The next week they had written tests on cooling systems, lubricating oils and systems and types of fire extinguishers.

The whole of week ten was spent landing imaginary troops on Browndown Beach, Gosport. They had six landing craft (assault) and one landing craft (mechanised) to practise on. They took turns to act as coxswains and stokers. It was a poor week weather wise, but they learnt a lot about handling their craft. In week eleven they had their Morse and semaphore tests, when it was Rhodes's turn, he read and sent using the semaphore flags and had a good pass mark. The next day he was first to test on Morse. He scraped by on the buzzer, but failed on the light. All of the course had passed both Morse tests except Rhodes, so he was called into the office of the captain in charge of the course and told he would be given one more chance the next morning.

In the barrack room that evening several of his fellow course members tested him using a torch and after two hours he had improved slightly. The next day came the dreaded test. The course officer stood next to Rhodes as the light began to send its message and at the end he asked, 'Did you get it all, Corporal Rhodes?'

'Most of it, sir,' said Rhodes.

As the officer read what Rhodes had written a hush fell over the other course members. Having finished reading the text he passed it to the instructor who read it again. Rhodes looked anxiously on.

'That's more like it,' said the instructor, 'pass mark is fifty-five per cent, you have sixty per cent. Well done.'

Rhodes gave a sigh of relief.

In the final week they revised the work they had done and by Friday they were all getting anxious about their postings. They went on weekend leave still not aware of their fate. Rhodes and Julie enjoyed a passionate weekend. After one encounter Rhodes put his ear to Julie's tummy.

'I think that last effort did the trick, I can hear some funny noises.'

'That,' said Julie, 'are my insides recovering from your thing's brutal assault.'

The rest of the weekend passed quickly and on the Monday Rhodes and the rest of the course checked the company notice board every hour. At 1500 hours the posting list appeared. Bob Jones was going with three others to HMS *Royal Prince*, a landing craft base on the River Rhine in Germany, while Rhodes and one other were listed for the 2nd Raiding Squadron in Malta. The rest of the course was going to the 1st and 3rd Assault Squadron also in Malta. Rhodes knew that the 1st and 3rd Assault Squadrons were on the LSTs *Reggio* and *Striker*, but the 2nd Raiding Squadron was a shore base near a place called Kalafrana.

By the end of the week the dates of their postings had appeared and they all had a departure date of 18 December. The Malta transfers were by air.

That weekend Julie said, 'I'm not totally sure but I could be pregnant.'

Rhodes was delighted.

'When will we know for sure?' he asked.

'Give it another week,' said Julie, 'then I'll be sure.'

All the next week Rhodes was on tenterhooks and couldn't wait for Friday to come. He played a couple of games of football for Eastney Barracks; both were drawn. As last Friday came and when he arrived at Petersfield Julie met him at the cottage gate.

'We are going to be parents,' she said, her face a picture of delight.

Rhodes tenderly kissed her. Julie had not told her mother and, when together they gave her the news, she burst into tears.

'I am so pleased for you both, you will be wonderful parents.'

The evening was full of excited chatter.

'I think he or she will be born in July about the third week, around about the date of our wedding anniversary. How very respectable,' said Julie.

Several decisions now had to be made. Julie would have to inform the army nursing service that she was pregnant and this would mean she would have to resign. Rhodes and Julie had talked about his posting to Malta. She was determined to go with him which meant the baby would be born in Malta. Mrs Grey agreed that Julie's place was with her husband and though she would love to be in on the birth of her first grandchild, she understood the position. Another surprise was in store when Jane and Bob admitted they had been married the previous weekend. The reason given was a certain tension between their families. Jane's father, a doctor, thought she could do better than marry a Royal Marine. So their action solved the problem.

'A fait accompli,' said Rhodes, 'very sensible.'

On 1 December, Rhodes started his embarkation leave. He and Julie spent the first five days down in Kent on the farm. His aunt and uncle were delighted with the news of Julie's condition, but less pleased that he would be going abroad for another two and a half years. Mark and Linda, contrary to everyone's expectations, were not yet perspective parents. Linda's French had now reached such a standard that she was giving French lessons for beginners at the local school, which delighted Aunt Marie.

Rhodes finished his leave at Petersfield and on his return to barracks completed his leaving routine. He applied for and was granted accompanied status. This meant that Julie would be flown out to join him when he had secured accommodation for them both. On 18 December he travelled to Heathrow Airport for his flight to Malta. The night before he had said his farewells at Petersfield to Julie and her mum. His flight took off at 1400 hours. His plane, a Viking, was very comfortable and only three-quarters full with some wives and children, but mostly Air Force and Royal Marine personnel. They stopped to refuel at Nice Airport, had an hour's delay there and landed at Luqua Airport, Malta, at 2200 hours.

Malta Again and Their First Home

It was midnight before Rhodes and his fellow marines reached Kalafrana. The raiding squadron was housed in a two-storey block where Rhodes had to share a room with another corporal. In the morning, after breakfast, Rhodes was surprised how many of the marines there he knew, some were from recruit training days, others from his time in Malaya. He felt he was among old friends. Later that morning he met the sergeant major and the commanding officer of 2nd Raiding Squadron, they were friendly and helpful. The squadron had five raiding craft (small Dories which could take a maximum of six marines, six LCAs and one LCM). As Christmas was very close the sergeant major asked him if he would cover Christmas Day and Boxing Day as duty NCO.

Rhodes said, 'Of course.'

It meant that the other NCOs could spend all of Christmas with their families. Most of the unit had their wives in Malta with them. They told Rhodes it was a good posting, and accommodation was easy to find.

The sergeant major arranged for Rhodes to see the navy pay officer. His office arranged for the wives to be flown out to join their husbands. He gave Rhodes three forms to fill in and told one of his Wrens to assist Rhodes in their completion. When he wrote on the form Corporal P J Rhodes, DCM, MM, Royal Marines, she was impressed and said with a laugh, 'We don't see that many heroes in this office, if you can find accommodation by 22 December, your wife can fly out on 10 January.'

Rhodes thanked her and left. When he told the sergeant major what the Wren had said about the accommodation, he was given the next day off to find somewhere suitable. The following day he went into Paola. It was a fifteen-minute bus journey from the base and had a regular service to and from Kalafrana. He looked at several flats and then he was directed to some brand new buildings. These were two-storey flats. A portly Maltese man noticed his interest.

'Come and see the insides, they are ready for occupation,' he said.

Rhodes followed the man inside. He was impressed. They were cool and spacious.

'How much are these a month?' he asked.

'Ten pounds, fully furnished and all the furniture will be new,' the owner said.

Rhodes thought about it. With his ration allowance and local overseas allowance he could easily afford that.

'I'll take it,' he said. They shook hands and the deal was done. He was given a rent book.

'You pay a month in advance,' said the man, 'to reserve the property, your pay office will refund that amount.'

Rhodes reluctantly paid the money.

'This flat has no name yet,' said the man. 'What is your wife's name?'

'Julie,' said Rhodes. The man turned to the builder who was watching all this with interest.

'Can you put that on the name stone?' he asked.

'Of course,' said the builder.

As Rhodes walked away from the building, the landlord said, 'My name is Mr Borg, please call me Charlie, let me buy you a cold beer.'

For the next hour they chattered away and when Rhodes told him his wife was pregnant the man was delighted.

'New house, new baby,' he said. 'You will both be very happy here.'

On his return to Kalafrana, he went to see the Wren in the pay office. He showed her the rent book.

'Oh, so you are one of old Charlie Borg's tenants,' she said. 'He has about half the base on his books. He's okay, never had any complaints about him.'

She then told him that the pay officer would complete his application forms now he had a rent book and his wife would be placed on the approved passage list. That evening he went back into Paola and looked again at his new flat. To his surprise the name stone was in place. It looked very impressive, 'Julie', their first home.

By lunchtime on Christmas Eve the base was deserted. Only Rhodes and the five marines of his duty watch were left. The weather was turning quite nasty with heavy rain and an increasing wind. Rhodes phoned the Met Office at the nearby Hal Far Air Station. A storm was approaching from the south, severe gales and heavy rain. All of 2nd Raiding Squadron's craft were secured to mooring buoys in Kalafrana Bay. Rhodes decided to bring the Dory raiding craft into the small inner harbour and double up on the mooring lines of the LCAs and the LCM, which would have to ride out the storm. He took three of his duty watch marines with him out into the bay in one of the raiding craft. It took them two hours to secure all the craft and the conditions out in the bay were by now quite dangerous. When they finally got back onto dry land they were all soaked to the skin. Rhodes sent his marines off to their rooms to shower and get into dry clothes, while he went to the office and entered what he had done in the duty log. Just as he was leaving, a car raced into base car park. It was the CO's. Captain Walters, RM, came running up the steps to the office.

'Get your duty watch together, Corporal, we must get out to the landing craft. We could lose the lot in this storm.'

Rhodes told him what they had done and pointed out that they had brought the smaller craft into the inner harbour. A look of relief spread over Captain Walters' face.

'Thank Christ for that,' he said. 'I had visions of commanding a squadron with no boats. Please, pass on my thanks to the lads for their efforts and a well done to you as well.'

He then sent Rhodes off to get into some dry clothes. 'I'll man the phone until you get back, take your time.'

When Rhodes got back to the office the rest of his marines had returned and they were telling Captain Walters vastly impressive tales of the sea conditions out in the bay.

Marine Jobe, a sombre-looking character, said, 'It was hell, sir, but we did it for you.' The rest of the marines, including Rhodes, put on an act of throwing up at such blatant arse licking. Rhodes escorted his CO back to the car.

'Going out tonight, sir?' he asked.

'Yes,' said Captain Walters, 'my wife and I have been invited to HMS *Phoenicia*. Captain Browning has just been promoted to command the shore base there. I must find out his wife's name as we are taking some flowers over to her.'

Before Rhodes could stop himself he had said, 'Oh, her name's Gail, sir,' then he added hastily, 'When I was on the *Theseus*, I was detailed to help her at a reception after a band concert.'

'Thanks for the info, I'll give her your regards,' said Walters and waved as he drove away.

Oh Christ, thought Rhodes, I must keep away from HMS *Phoenicia*.

The rest of the Christmas passed quietly. The weather improved and with the sun shining, Malta was looking her best. Rhodes had a letter from Julie. She was just waiting for her flight to be confirmed and Jane was getting a transfer to a military hospital in Germany, so she could be with Bob. The sergeant major saw Rhodes on the jetty.

'How's things, got the flat ready?'

Rhodes smiled. 'Just need to get some sheets and pillow slips, Charlie Borgs provided everything else.'

'Go over to the *Phoenicia*, they have a naval families' shop there, all good stuff and half the price you would pay in the shops, you can have this afternoon off,' said the sergeant major. 'And anyway,' he added, 'the CO thinks the sun shines out of your arse, so take advantage while you can.'

With some apprehension, Rhodes visited the families' shop. The sergeant major was right, they had everything and at the right price. He bought four double sheets and four pillow slips. He then noticed some towels and bought four bath size and four large. As he was leaving one of the Wrens called out to him.

'Are you Corporal Rhodes?'

He nodded.

'There is an invitation here for your wife to join the Naval Wives' Club, Mrs Browning dropped it off this morning.'

Rhodes thanked her, took the invitation and left. That night as he was showering, he glanced down to his groin.

One day, he thought, you will really drop me in it.

At last the day of Julie's flight came. He phoned the airport and learned that the time of arrival was 2100 hours. The flat was looking great. Mrs Borg had brought a large bunch of flowers with a nice greeting card for Julie. Rhodes had stocked up with food from the little grocer's just round the corner. The owner and his wife had advised him what he needed; everyone was so helpful. The flat had a brand new refrigerator, powered by paraffin, in fact all the cooking would be down by paraffin cookers. It had electric light in all the rooms. In the main bedroom the bed had a huge white mosquito net over it. Mr Borg had provided a child's cot, which, when in use, would also be encompassed by the net.

At 2000 hours Rhodes got a taxi to the airport. When he arrived he checked to see if the flight was on time. It was. At two minutes before 2100 hours, it landed. Rhodes watched as the plane taxied to the airport building. The passengers disembarked and made their way into the main airport building. Rhodes noticed Julie almost straight away. He called out and waved. She waved back. The woman walking with her said something to her and they both laughed. After they were through the passport check she walked straight into Rhodes's arms. He kissed her and buried his face in her hair, hugging her to him. They kissed again and began to talk about the flight, of how much she had missed him and he her.

After about ten minutes they were called to collect their luggage and then they made their way outside to the waiting taxi. Twenty minutes later they were outside their new flat. Julie was most impressed and when she saw the name stone, she said, 'Perfect, Peter, just perfect.' He showed her round the flat and then sat her down and made them both some tea.

'Would you like something to eat? I've got lots of food in. How about bacon and eggs?'

Julie gave a little sigh. 'I'm not really hungry. We had two meals on the flight out. I just need my bed.'

Rhodes helped her unpack her cases. There was plenty of room in both the wardrobe and the chest of drawers. Julie went into the bathroom and after about ten minutes came out wearing her black silk nightdress. She looked stunning. Rhodes had a wash and cleaned his teeth, but when he went into the bedroom he found Julie asleep, so he put the lights out and got into bed very quietly so as not to disturb her.

He lay there for a few minutes listening to the rhythm of her breathing before settling himself down for sleep. He felt a small warm hand move over his stomach, searching and quickly finding his penis. It leapt to attention, answering the urgent summons. Julie giggled.

'It looks as though it's missed me,' she said.

Rhodes turned onto his side and placed his arm around her.

'I thought you were too tired,' he said.

Her answer was to press her body to him and, finding his lips, her tongue darted in and out of his mouth. Her nightdress suddenly had gone. Rhodes kissed her eyes, nose, mouth and breasts. He moved down to her stomach and paused to greet their child and then on to the tops of her legs. Her legs parted and he reached his goal. She was urging him on.

'Now, Peter, now!' she cried and Rhodes thrust himself deeply into her.

Her legs were up around his waist, her heels beating a rhythm on his back. Two more deep thrusts and he came; she just seconds behind him.

As their breathing slowly returned to normal he kissed her.

'I love you, Julie Rhodes,' he said.

She kissed him back.

'And I you, but will you still love me when our baby swells my tummy and I waddle like a duck?'

'Of course,' he said, 'I was brought up on a farm, and I love ducks.'

They held one another close and each drifted off into a deep contented sleep, at peace with the world.

Rhodes woke first. He quietly slid out of bed and boiled the kettle and made some tea. It was 0730 hours; he sat on the bed next to Julie and watched her slowly awake. He kissed her.

'Have some tea, it will wake you up,' he said.

She drank her tea and then got out of bed.

'I must go to the bathroom,' she said.

When she came back, Rhodes had taken her nightdress from

under the pillow.

'Do you want to put this on?'

'No, it only gets in the way,' she said and sat on his lap, her naked body provoking an immediate and obvious reaction. She raised herself slightly and allowed his swollen member access to her body. A furious few minutes of activity followed and then contented sighs from them both.

'Now I'm ready for breakfast,' she said.

At about midday they walked down the road from their flat and into Paola Square. There was a market there and they looked around the stalls. The meat and fish looked very fresh, as did the vegetables. Rhodes felt a hand on his arm. He looked round. It was Charlie Borg. He introduced Julie to him.

'You never said your wife was so beautiful,' said Charlie and he bent forward and kissed Julie's hand. 'A great pleasure to meet you, Mrs Rhodes. Is the flat to your satisfaction?'

Julie smiled. 'Indeed it is, Mr Borg, we are going to be very happy there.'

They chatted away for a few minutes. Charlie told them the meat and fish were fresh and safe to buy, as were the vegetables.

'But,' he said, 'always give the salad foods a good wash in salt water,' and with a cheery wave he left them.

'What a nice man,' said Julie. 'He will be a good friend.'

They bought some fish and some pork chops and walked back up Arcade Street to their flat. Rhodes gave Julie the note Mrs Browning had left for her.

'It's my membership card for the Navy Wives' Club,' she said, 'and it's signed by Edwina Countess Mountbatten, how nice.'

Two days later Rhodes returned to duty at Kalafrana. He had been put in charge of the five Dory raiding craft. The sergeant major asked how his wife had settled in, then told him that he would be going over to Tripoli for a week with four of the raiding craft.

'We do have to leave Malta for exercises from time to time and we all take a turn, but we are better off than the *Reggio* and *Striker*, they are away for about two weeks a month.'

Rhodes said he understood and was quite willing to play his part. He had seven marines under him as the Dory crews. They spent most of the day cleaning the boats and practising landings on all types of shoreline. Each Dory had a small trolley, which could be placed halfway down the slipway. The Dory could then be steered into the trolley, secured and then pulled out of the water onto the jetty. This method could be used to winch the Dories into the tank decks of LCTS and LSTs.

Rhodes enjoyed his time at Kalafrana, but he would have preferred to be back in the commando brigade. He was talking to Captain Walters one day and asked him if a transfer to the brigade was a possibility.

'Not at the moment,' said Captain Walters, 'but, the future of this raiding squadron is under review and I would be surprised if we are still here in twelve months' time.'

Julie had settled in quickly at their new flat and had made friends with two other wives who had only been in Malta a couple of weeks. The husband of one of the women was in the RAF at Luqua, the other was in the Royal Navy at the Naval Air Station at Halfar.

When Rhodes told Julie he would be going to Tripoli the next week she said, 'Don't worry about me, anyway its only for a few days.'

The night before he left they went to the cinema and saw *Love is a Many Splendoured Thing*. Later in bed they had a passionate encounter and afterwards she kissed him, saying, 'William Holden has nothing on you, my love, and I'm sure you are taller.'

The next morning when Rhodes left, Julie hugged him to her. 'Hurry back, Peter, we will both miss you.'

To the Shores of Tripoli

Later that morning Rhodes and his marines took their Dories out into Kalafrana Bay. They had fitted the trolleys to the Dories. This cut their speed down by half, so they made their way out to the waiting LCT at about four knots. As they approached they could see the ship's name, it was HMS *Bastion*. The ship had its bow doors open and its ramp fully down. Each Dory in turn ran up the ramp, the ship's crew grabbing the bow line and pulling the Dory into the tank deck on its trolley. Once the craft were aboard, the ramp was raised and the bow doors closed and secured. The ship then made its way out of the bay and headed for Tripoli, a hundred miles away. As Rhodes went to report to the ship's captain, a familiar figure walked down the tank deck towards him. It was Sergeant Green, his old sub-section commander from his A-Troop days. They greeted each other warmly. Sergeant Green was now in 40 Commando and he had with him two corporals and seventeen marines. These were the men Rhodes's Dories would be landing.

When Rhodes reported to the ship's captain, a lieutenant commander, he was told that the first landing would be at 0300 hours the next morning and that a full briefing would take place at 1900 hours that evening. Rhodes went to see the petty officer in charge of the tank deck to make sure they knew how to launch and recover the Dory trolleys and after about ten minutes everyone was happy.

Sergeant Green and Rhodes had a long chat that afternoon and after about an hour they were both fully up to date. Green was having a passionate affair with a Wren on the C in C's staff and there had been talk of marriage. Rhodes thought they should take their time and not rush into a marriage they may regret. Later that evening there was a full briefing in the tank deck. They were told that four of their landings would be at night and a landing further along the coast each afternoon. The marines would be withdrawn two hours after each landing and the eight raids were to be on different locations, some onto a rocky coastline, some onto sandy beaches, with different surf conditions. The army units in the Tripoli area would not oppose the landings, but they would try and spot them coming ashore.

The next morning at 0200 hours, the four Dories were launched with their passengers aboard, while the trolleys were released and pulled back aboard by the LCT's crew. They were about a mile off shore as they commenced their run into the beach. They formed line abreast and it took about eight minutes to cover the mile. As the craft grounded on the beach their passengers were out in seconds. The Dories retracted and, in line ahead with Rhodes's craft leading, headed on their back bearing to the waiting LCT. Sergeant Green and his marines quietly made they way inland for about a half a mile and then placed a marker post with a red flag in the ground before making their way back to the beach. Rhodes and his Dories returned on time and collected the marines and within fifteen minutes all were back aboard the LCT for an hour's rest and then breakfast.

That afternoon they repeated the exercise, this time in a rocky cove. Only two Dories could land at a time because of the underwater rocks, so it took a few minutes longer. By the time Rhodes returned to withdraw the marines, conditions were bad and the sea was now quite rough. Only one Dorry at a time could get in to make the pick-up, but at last all were aboard. When they returned to the *Bastion*, the captain was surprised that they had been able to recover the raiding party. The next morning, conditions were even worse with high surf expected, so the LCT launched the Dories a half mile from the coast. Rhodes decided to beach one at a time, using the small kedge anchor to keep the Dory bow straight at the beach. It took twenty minutes to land the marines and Rhodes decided to circle two hundred yards off shore rather than return to the LCT. The pick-up was almost a disaster with one Dory swamped as it tried to beach, only its buoyancy tanks keeping it afloat. The other Dories took the extra passengers and, in addition to its extra load, Rhodes towed the swamped dory back to the LCT. Once aboard the *Bastion*, the marines tipped the swamped Dory on its side and emptied the seawater. After its spark plugs were dried the engine burst into life and the tough little craft was once more ready for action.

Early that evening, the LCT received a severe weather warning and the advice to make for the nearest harbour. The nearest harbour was Tripoli and in conditions that were deteriorating by the minute, HMS *Bastion* reached the safety of Tripoli Harbour in the last minutes of daylight. The storm raged for the next two days and the exercise was cancelled. Some satisfaction was gained by the army reports that only on one occasion had they been spotted and that was when they were withdrawing. The marines kept themselves busy while in the harbour. At the harbour master's request they replaced some of the smaller mooring buoys in the small boats section of the harbour.

Three days after they had been forced to take shelter, with the weather improving, they sailed for Malta. They arrived in Kalafrana Bay at 1800 hours and within the hour all of the marines and the Dories were ashore. The transport that came for the marine commandos also dropped Rhodes off in Paola Square on its way back to St Patrick's barracks. Ten minutes later Rhodes was home and holding Julie in his arms.

Green Berets Meet the White Kepis

As he kissed her she said, 'You smell of the sea and I can taste the salt. Get showering while I prepare a meal.'

They were in bed by 2300 hours and after a few tender kisses they made love, gently at first and then as their passions rose to a frantic pitch the headboard beat out a rhythmic accompaniment as their bodies reached their climax.

Julie was now five months pregnant and she and Rhodes paid a visit to the military hospital at Imtarfa. To their delight the first person they saw was the matron; it was the matron from their days at Taiping.

After lots of hugs and kisses, much to the amazement of the onlooking nurses, Matron said, 'I just knew he would get you pregnant, you poor sweet thing, but at least you resisted him until you were married.'

Julie looked at Rhodes. 'Well almost, Matron, these marines are very persuasive.'

After tea and biscuits in Matron's office, Julie was seen by one of the doctors.

'Everything is fine. About mid-July, I would think. You will have a fine baby and you will have the best of care,' he said.

'She certainly will,' said Matron, giving the doctor a fierce stare.

They managed to get away after about two hours and Matron was invited to visit them in their flat at the weekend. She was delighted.

In April there was a major amphibious exercise in North Africa and the 2nd Raiding Squadron took passage on HMS *Reggio*, where they were to be used as back-up crews for the next three weeks. Rhodes was glad Julie had made some friends. She visited the Navy Wives' Club once a week and saw her neighbours most days. Matron was now a regular visitor and a very good friend.

Apart from the *Reggio*, the other ships were the *Meon*, *Striker*,

Bastion and *Rampart*. Embarked in the ships were 40 Commando Royal Marines. Several destroyers were to join up for the assault on the coast between Arzeu and Oran, but would first collect the 1st Battalion the Seaforth Highlanders from Gibraltar. These troops would follow the marines ashore. The landing would be opposed by the French Foreign Legion, based at Sidi Bel Abbes, who would be in prepared positions along the coast.

The weather was set fair and conditions could not have been better and the landings went like clockwork. As the landing craft began their run onto the beach they received covering fire from the destroyers off shore. As the landing craft beached, the marine commandos stormed ashore. The French legionnaires were further along the coast, so the landing was unopposed. Once the marines were ashore and moving inland, the Highlanders were landed. This took longer than anticipated as the army and landing craft did not get on, chiefly because most of the Highlanders could not swim, so the average soldier was wary of climbing into boats at sea.

That evening the umpires had decided the bridgehead was established and with few casualties. With the marines and the Highlanders holding the bridgehead perimeter, the next morning a squadron of tanks, with some artillery, were landed. Over the next few days all of the vehicles and supplies were safely ashore.

After a week all of the marines and army were withdrawn and, along with tanks and artillery, sailed for Gibraltar, where they spent the next two days. The Highlanders would take no further part, to the relief of most of them. As one of their sergeants said, 'If the fucking ships would stay still for a minute it would be fine, but all that up and down, it's not for me.'

In the middle of week two, they sailed again for the North African Coast, landing this time in a different place. As Sergeant Green had told his troop commander that Rhodes spoke French, he had been attached to their troop as an interpreter. Rhodes was delighted; he felt he was back where he belonged in the brigade.

They landed at 0200 hours and only the troop on their right flank met any opposition. As the day wore on all of the tanks were ashore as was most of the artillery. The exercise went on for two more days, with the marines enlarging the bridgehead and forming a defensive perimeter in depth. When it was completed the English and French umpires discussed casualties and final positions, with Rhodes sitting with Major Rendle, 40 Commando's 2I/C. At times he was asked what the French were saying. In the majority of cases they were objecting to some of the umpiring decisions. Rhodes kept the major informed and the officer was able to raise his own objections in tandem with the French. This prompted the senior French officer to ask for his own interpreter. At last the meeting ended and all participants in the exercise who were ashore were invited to the Legion barracks for a meal.

The barracks at Sidi Bel Abbes were run in a typically French way. The dining hall was used by all ranks and across the end of the room ran a table for the officers. At right angles from each end of their table ran those of the senior NCOs, then the junior NCOs and finally, the legionnaires. They all ate the same food, starting with a thick soup, followed by meat, potatoes and cabbage and a piece of cheese and an apple to finish. Large jugs of red wine were shared between six men. Rhodes, who sat next to Sergeant Green, thought the food was quite good and the wine, though dry, was not bad at all.

Before the marines left the barracks they were given a tour of the museum and the famous 'Hand Holding the Legion's Colours' drew many comments. The curator explained the story. He told them that after a battle that the Legion had lost the colours were so tightly clasped in the dead officer's hand that the enemy had to cut the hand off to secure them. As a mark of respect both the colours and the hand were later returned to the Legion. The marines left for the port of Arzeu later that evening. The French had been good hosts and many new friends had been made.

And Then There Were Three

Two days later the squadron and the marines sailed for Malta. The weather was calm and they made good progress, arriving in Malta at noon on the third day. Rhodes managed to get home by early evening. Julie was by now very obviously pregnant, with just over two months to go. They still made love, but in a very gentle and careful way. Julie found the best way was for her to be on top.

She told Rhodes, 'I feel I'm in control up here and the view's great.'

Matron and Julie were now very good friends and Julie was allowed to call her by her Christian name. It was Mary. For the first time Rhodes found out her surname and on her birthday Julie and Rhodes sent a large bunch of flowers to the hospital addressed to Mary Pendred, Matron, BMH Imtarfa.

On Saturday 23 July, at 0830 hours, Julie gave birth to a son. He was to be called Michael James. Matron insisted on being with Julie throughout and the birth was completed without any problems. When Rhodes arrived at the hospital he was greeted by Matron. After she had hugged and kissed him, she said, 'You have a wonderful baby son, Peter. He is a joy and Julie is just fine.'

When Rhodes saw Julie he was so relieved. She was glowing and looked so calm and relaxed. They sat together and he gently kissed her with his arm around her and their child between them. After about an hour, he told her he had to go to send some cables to England. He kissed Julie and their son goodbye and left to take the bus into Valletta and then to the cable and wireless office at Spinola. He sent two cables, the first to Mrs Grey at Petersfield, the other to Aunt Marie and Uncle Bill at the farm. He told them both what the baby's name would be and he knew Mrs Grey would be pleased as Michael had been her husband's name.

Julie spent a week in hospital and at last Rhodes was allowed to take them both home.

As they left Matron whispered in Rhodes's ear, 'No making

love for three weeks, Peter, I know you will understand.'

Rhodes gave her a hug. 'Of course. I can wait. Thank you for all you have down for us. Come and see us this weekend.' And as the taxi left they both waved to her until she was out of sight.

That evening Mr and Mrs Charlie Borg called, but they only stayed a few minutes. They brought some lovely flowers and a small silver crucifix. Mrs Borg asked them to put it over the baby's cot, saying, 'The priest has blessed it, and God will protect little Michael.'

Rhodes and Julie thanked them and Rhodes pinned the crucifix to the hood of the cot to the Borgs' obvious delight.

Rhodes had been given the rest of the week off by Captain Walters and spent all of his time cooking and cleaning. After a few days Julie spent more time out of bed. She was feeling fine and was looking wonderful. They took the baby out a couple of times a day. Rhodes had bought a pram and took great delight in parading his wife and new baby for all to see.

When Rhodes returned to Kalafrana, Captain Walters sent for him.

'I'm afraid you are to be posted to HMS *Reggio*. They are forming a beach unit and they want you in it. I'm very sorry to lose you and my final report in your record will reflect these feelings.'

Rhodes was upset. What would Julie say? He was told he was to join the *Reggio* on Monday. When he told Julie of his pending move she was quite surprised. She thought his original posting was to last the full two and a half years.

'We will make the best of it,' she said.

On the Monday, he reported to the sergeant major on HMS *Reggio*. He was told that the unit was to be called the Naval Beach Unit, but it would be staffed by Royal Marines. It would consist of one major, one lieutenant, one sergeant, two corporals, six marines and two signallers (one sergeant and one corporal.). All would be based on the *Reggio*, except the major who would be on the headquarters' ship, HMS *Meon*. As there were now eight corporals on the *Reggio*, Rhodes would do one duty NCO every eight days.

The next day the new Beach Unit sat down together and their

role was explained. In any amphibious landing the NBU would land in the second wave of LCAs. Their role was to control and direct the landing of troops tanks and transport, in response to the requirements of the senior officer in charge of the operation. The next week they would be involved with landings on the island of Corsica in cooperation with French troops and 40 Commando Royal Marines.

The following Monday the Amphibious Warfare Squadron (AWS), with 40 Commando embarked, left Grand Harbour for Corsica. Julie had been tearful as Rhodes had said goodbye.

'It should only be for two weeks, then I'll be home,' said Rhodes, thankful that Julie had friends to keep her company.

Four days later they landed on the beaches of Corsica. The Beach Unit made a difference as the follow-up waves of troops and vehicles landed as required and not in some huge disorganised mass on the beach. Rhodes found himself being used more and more in an interpreter's role.

Major Todd, the beach master, told Rhodes, 'Don't trust the French, they say one thing and do something else, they are devious bastards, but they are our Allies, so we must be nice to their faces.'

Rhodes thought this was hilarious, as in his dealings with the French officers he had not found this to be the case. The Beach Unit were a decent bunch and they all got on. Rhodes liked Major Todd and to his surprise the major told him that he had known his father, but had not been with him when he was killed.

After a week in Corsica they sailed for the South of France and anchored off Juan les Pins. Along with the French, they were to do some landings on the beaches there as part of the local Festival of Flowers. The assault engineers of 40 Commando Royal Marines laid lots of gun cotton charges at the waters edge to add some realism to the marines' assault on the beach. The landings went very well and a large audience of the local townsfolk applauded the British and French marines as they stormed ashore. Later the marines were invited to the many functions taking place during the festival and Rhodes and Sergeant Green found themselves at a garden party. Two rather attractive French ladies attached themselves to the two marines.

'We are in here,' said Sergeant Green and they spent a pleasant evening in their company. Rhodes's ability to converse with them in their own language delighted the ladies and when Rhodes made his excuses and left they were disappointed.

Sergeant Green said, 'Don't worry, Pete, I can take of them both.'

When Rhodes saw Sergeant Green the next day, Green said, 'Fuck me, Pete, you don't know what you missed, they were insatiable, but I left them with a smile on their faces.'

When the squadron returned to Malta, they had been away for almost three weeks. Rhodes hurried home to Julie and his son. Little Michael was asleep.

Rhodes cuddled Julie and, as he kissed her, she said, 'It's okay to do again now, Peter, unless you would rather not,' and giggled.

Rhodes made love slowly and gently and when he entered her, slowly thrusting in and out, Julie said, 'I shan't fall to pieces, Peter, give that French letter a real test,' so he did.

Later that night when they went to bed, their lovemaking had returned to its normal frantic pace which satisfied them both.

Michael was now two months old, his first photos were sent to everyone in England, Matron and the Borgs. He was growing fast and Julie and Rhodes were so proud of him.

In September the squadron sailed for Turkey. They docked at Ismir and took on board five hundred Turkish troops. Over the next ten days they landed them in different places along the Turkish coast. The Turks were treated appallingly by their officers and any delay in leaving the landing craft was punished by being hit over the head by the officers' pistol or being kicked and punched. Major Todd raised the matter of the beatings with the Turkish senior officer and was politely told to mind his own business. At last they got rid of the troops, but the toilets, or heads, on the *Reggio* and *Striker* were left in a disgusting state as those allocated to the Turks had been left with shit all over the floors and sides of the toilets, because of course they crouched on top of the toilet because contact between flesh and toilet was considered unclean. It took two days to return the toilets on the LSTs to their normal pristine condition.

The tank decks where the Turks had slept needed several

hosing downs to return it to an acceptable state. The AWS did not return to Malta straight away, but sailed for the Greek islands. There they embarked five companies of Greek troops. Over the next seven days they landed them at different places. The marines enjoyed working with the Greeks, who were quick to learn and well disciplined.

On their return to Malta, HMS *Reggio* went into dry dock for seven days as the bow doors had been damaged when beaching on a rocky shore and were failing to close properly. Rhodes took a few days' leave during which Michael was baptised at the chapel in Imtarfa Hospital. Matron and the friends Julie had made were there, as well as the Borgs. Lots of photos were taken and copies sent to them all at home and to Bob and Jane in Germany.

It was nearly the end of the cricket season in Malta. Rhodes played for the navy against the governor's Eleven which turned out to be a close encounter, with the navy losing by five runs. Rhodes scored thirty runs and took two good catches. After the match he had a sticky five minutes when Julie and Gail Browning were having tea together.

Later that evening Julie said, 'Gail Browning thinks you are the perfect gentleman and should try for a commission, what do you think?'

Rhodes laughed, partly with relief. 'I have no ambitions to be an officer. If I can make sergeant I'll be happy.'

The next day they took Michael into Valleta and after doing some shopping in the NAAFI they had a coffee in Kingsway Square. As they sat there, Gail Browning came by and Julie insisted she had a coffee with them. Gail made a great fuss of baby Michael and said how lucky they were, adding, 'We would love to have children, but my husband wants to wait until we go home.'

Julie left them for a few minutes to change Michael's nappy.

Gail looked at Rhodes and said, 'Don't look so worried, Peter, I would never tell Julie about us. Just let us be friends.' When Julie came back, they were chatting away and the tension had gone. They all had lunch together and shared a bottle of wine.

Cyprus and EOKA

The situation in Cyprus was giving cause for concern. The Greeks wanted union with Greece and the Turks, who formed almost half of the population, wanted things to stay as they were. For some time the tension had been building and a militant Greek Cypriot group called EOKA were beginning to cause trouble. It was decided by the British Government to send 45 Commando Royal Marines to Cyprus to control the situation. The AWS was to transport the marines there and the marines serving with the squadron would land to provide the commando with an extra troop. Rhodes had been told they would be away about a month, but he told Julie he thought it would be longer.

Their last night together was a passionate one and after making love for the second time, Julie said, 'You should go away more often, just imagine what you'll be like when you come back.' In the morning Julie shed a few tears as he left.

'Don't do anything silly, Peter, come home in one piece.'

He kissed Michael and Julie and then left.

Four days after leaving Malta they arrived in Cyprus and within two hours the marines were ashore with their transport. The headquarters of 45 Commando were to be near Kyrenia, with most of its troops out on location. Rhodes and the marines of the AW Troop were based in the hills on the northern coast. It took them a day to set up camp, one large tent and several smaller ones providing the accommodation. The latrine and gash pit were dug and that night thirty of the fifty marines went out and laid three ambush positions. The rules of engagement were quite clear; you did not fire unless fired at.

All of the marines had their rifles and fifty rounds. Rhodes thought it was almost like being back in Malaya, only not quite so dangerous. Rhodes took his nine marines and in the gathering dusk made his way to his designated position. He had carefully briefed his patrol on what they would be doing. Four of his party had served in Malaya; the other five were national service marines. He positioned himself in the centre of the party, his four Malayan veterans, two at each end of the position. It was a warm night and by midnight they had the benefit of a full moon. The hours passed slowly and by dawn it had become quite chilly. Rhodes withdrew his patrol just before daylight and they made their way back to their camp about three miles away. They were on compo rations and one of the marines had volunteered to cook for the troop. If his breakfast was his usual standard they were on to a good thing. After breakfast the twenty marines who remained in camp did a sweep of the area out to a distance of half a mile. The ambush parties tried to get some sleep before the day grew too hot.

There was a small village about a mile from their camp and they were instructed by headquarters to conduct a search there. At 0400 hours the next morning Major Todd led forty marines to the outskirts of the village. He then sent twenty of the marines under a lieutenant and a sergeant to provide a 'stop' line behind the village. At 0500 hours the marines moved into the village. Major Todd had briefed them on how to handle the villagers.

'If they cooperate treat them in a proper manner, if they get awkward then we get awkward.'

Each house was searched, with the villagers seemingly unsurprised by the early visit and all of them being very cooperative. Rhodes and two marines had been instructed to stay close to Major Todd in case any EOKA activists decided to try and take him out, but all was peaceful. After three hours the marines withdrew from the village, disappointed that nothing had been found. Back at the camp Major Todd invited all the NCOs, one sergeant and four corporals, to comment on the operation. When it was Rhodes's turn, he suggested they repeat the exercise, saying, 'They know we are here and would expect to be searched, but they may not be expecting a return visit so quickly.'

Major Todd looked around; they were all nodding their heads. 'Right,' he said, 'same time tomorrow.'

They spent the rest of the day improving the camp and cleaning their weapons.

The next morning, at 0400 hours they again moved into position just outside the village and at 0500 hours started the search. The response was the exact opposite of the previous day. They were sullen and uncooperative. One man drew a knife and tried to stab one of the young marines with Rhodes. Rhodes used the butt of his rifle to knock the knife away and then dropped the man to the ground with a butt stroke to the side of his head. They found some EOKA leaflets in the house and next door, under a baby's bed, two pistols and twenty rounds of ammunition. In some of the other houses were some banners in various stages of being completed. One which had been finished said 'British Pigs Get Out'. The police had been summoned by radio through 45 Commando HQ and took six of the village men into custody, including one with a badly swollen face. The marines were delighted with their success and later in the day Major Todd returned from HQ with a bottle of beer for each one of them.

Over the next week there were several incidents on the island. In one, shots were fired at an army lorry, wounding the driver. The AW Troop were being very active, with night ambushes and village searching. They were also searching wells and caves. Rhodes had five marines with him and were searching the steep hillside above a small village when they found a cave that had been sealed with rocks. They cleared the entrance and found some bags of chemical fertiliser, not a usual method to fertilise the ground by the very poor farmers. The 2 cwt bags were handed over to the local police, who decided that it was intended to be used to make a crude explosive mixture.

On another occasion the AW Troop was used to break up a demonstration outside a police station. They were stoned by the hostile crowd, but the sight of nearly fifty Royal Marines advancing on them with fixed bayonets persuaded them to quietly go home.

It came as no surprise to Rhodes when Major Todd announced they were staying until early November. Letters were getting to them and their replies were being flown out from Nicosia. Julie was fine, as was Michael. She saw Matron at least once a week and met up with Gail Browning quite often at the Naval Wives' Club. Rhodes was attached to a police station near the village of Lapidos and had six marines with him, all national servicemen.

At the police post all the policemen were Turkish, as seemed to be the custom on the northern side of the island. One night they had a telephone call to say that two prisoners, suspected EOKA terrorists, had escaped from Kyrenia Prison. Rhodes put a roadblock up outside the police station, as Kyrenia was only fifteen miles away down the coast road. They kept it manned for the next twenty-four hours but there was no sign of the prisoners.

Later that week the police were informed that some anti-British banners were hanging across the streets in Lapidos. Rhodes took his six marines with him and they marched up the road to the village. As they neared the village they came under attack from a hail of stones and small rocks.

'Fix your bayonets,' Rhodes ordered, 'and for fuck's sake don't fire unless you are fired at.'

They raced into the village in extended line. Seeing that the marines were not retreating but advancing, the villagers ran for their houses locking the doors. The marines grabbed two of the younger men who were reluctant to move and arrested them. The banners were then torn down. One read, 'We are not afraid of commandos'. One of the young marines said, 'I think they may be now.' The patrol then returned to the police station with the banners and their prisoners. One of the marines turned to Rhodes and said, 'We did okay, didn't we, Corps?'

'Yes,' said Rhodes, 'you did just fine, I'm proud of you.'

The AW Troop did several large village searches with the rest of 45 Commando and at the end of one day-long search the CO of 45 Commando presented Major Todd with a red lanyard for every member of the AW Troop, saying, 'You are now full members of 45.'

As their time in Cyprus drew to a close, Rhodes thought of the first time he had visited the island. It was, of course, to assist the population after the earthquake. How things had changed in such a short time. He remembered the village of Paphos, where they had rescued the old woman who had been buried under the rubble of the church. If he went back there now on his own they would most likely kill him.

The AW Troop had changed its camp location three times.

They had all been in the north of the island. Their final camp was further east. There had been some intelligence to suggest that arms were being smuggled in from the sea, and that had decided their final location. At night half of the troop would move down to selected sites and split into groups of two or three, they could then cover a mile of coastline.

On one such evening, Rhodes and two marines were in position watching a small inlet. About 0100 hours, a green light flashed from out at sea. It was answered by a red light flashing from the beach about a hundred yards from the marines' position. The marines watched as the boat approached the beach. It anchored about fifty yards out. Four men waded out to the vessel and started to bring some boxes ashore. Rhodes and his men quietly moved down towards them. They got within yards of the water's edge when there was a shout from Rhodes's left and a shot was fired in their direction. Rhodes fired one round in the air over the top of the boat, but two more shots were fired at the marines. These were wild and missed the marines by yards. Rhodes instructed his men to fire five rounds at the cabin area of the boat, the crew promptly jumped over the side, being at anchor they could not escape. The marines were now at the water's edge and grabbed two of the men who were cowering prostrate on the sand. With one of his men covering the two prisoners, Rhodes fired at the swimmers. Two decided to come ashore while the others swam out of sight around the entrance to the cove. The marines now had four prisoners, but then a moan came from their right and a fifth man was now in the marines' custody. This one with a bullet wound in his thigh.

The marines gave the injured man first aid and found that two of their prisoners were boys of no more than fifteen, with the others in their twenties. Out of the darkness they heard a call of, 'AW Troop,' as Major Todd and ten marines identified themselves and came scrambling down the slope onto the beach. Rhodes quickly explained what had happened and the major sent four marines to search the area to the right and four to the left. The major was euphoric.

'Well done, you lads, this is a great result. As soon as it is daylight we will see what we have got.'

He then sent instructions to bring the rest of the troop to assist them and got a signal off to 45 Headquarters. By dawn the beach and the surrounding area was swarming with marines and the fishing village a mile away was being carefully searched. The four boxes that had been brought ashore were opened and a small printing press was found in one while the other three contained ink and paper as well as khaki shirts and trousers. But the biggest prize was on the boat, three boxes containing twenty rifles and four Sten guns with about a thousand rounds of ammunition. The marines searching along the shoreline found a body floating in the sea. He had been shot in the head. He turned out to be the brother of one of the men they had captured on the beach.

The CO of 45 Commando saw Rhodes and his two marines later that evening in the AW camp. He shook hands with all three of them.

'So you are Rhodes,' he said. 'One of my troop commanders has mentioned you, I think you know him, Captain David Pope?'

'Yes, sir,' said Rhodes. 'He was my section officer in Malaya, we had some exciting times together.'

'So I've heard,' said the CO. 'You do seem to attract a fair share of that.'

The other two marines were on cloud nine. Few national servicemen would be able to look back on a day like this and they would remember it with pride for the rest of their lives. The next day the AW Troop took part in a large sweep of the coastline to the north and south of the successful arms find. The attitude of the Cypriots was in the main hostile, but in some places they were greeted with smiles. EOKA was obviously not universally popular. At the weekend the AW Troop were withdrawn from the scene and taken to the docks where the *Reggio* had arrived to take them back to Malta. The CO of 45 Commando was there to see them off. He spoke to them all on the jetty, thanking them for their hard work and congratulating them on their success. Captain Pope was with him and Rhodes and he managed a quiet chat together before the *Reggio* sailed.

Chajn Tuffieha and an Old Friend

Four days later they entered Grand Harbour. It was 2000 hours before Rhodes could get ashore, but there on the jetty with several other wives were Julie and his son Michael.

Later on that evening after Rhodes had showered and had a meal they both got ready for bed. Michael was by now fast asleep.

Julie said, 'I've got a little surprise for you, I won't be a minute.'

She went into the bathroom; when she came out Rhodes gave a gasp. She had put on a black bra and panties with black stockings and a suspender belt. Rhodes grabbed her and smothered her in kisses. He then led her to the bed. The black bra was the first item of clothing to go, quickly followed by the panties. Rhodes lay naked on the bed and Julie was giving his rampant member a close examination.

'Peter,' she said, 'you could break rocks with that, but not just now, I have other plans.'

Rhodes was busy working his way down Julie's body. He kissed the soft white flesh above the tops of the black stockings and then, as her legs parted, he moved his body forward and thrust himself deep into her. Julie gasped and pulled him even closer. Their bodies thrust at each other. A frantic pace overcame them both, and then with a final powerful thrust Rhodes reached his climax closely followed by Julie. They lay there for a few minutes getting their breath back and marshalling their scattered senses. Rhodes was the first to speak.

'If you dress like that again you will send me to an early grave. Mind you, I will have a smile on my face.'

Julie giggled. 'I thought you would like the "night wear". It was just a little welcome home present; I thought you might want a little encouragement to perform.'

Rhodes ran his hands down Julie's back and on to her bottom and pulled her close, nuzzling her neck.

'We have some catching up to do. Have you got your breath back?' he asked.

Julie sighed. 'I thought you would never ask,' she said and pulled him close.

The next day they went to the families' lido at Kalafrana. Michael enjoyed being in the warm water. Julie was wearing a black two-piece bathing costume and sat in the water with Michael on her lap. Rhodes watched them both. He thought to himself how lucky he was. He loved them both to distraction, and could not imagine life without them. It was perfect. On the bus back to Paola an elderly Maltese couple made a great fuss of Michael and kissed his little hands when they left the bus. Julie waved goodbye to them.

'The Maltese are so nice, Peter, and they love children. What better place than here for Michael to start his life?' she said.

On the Monday Rhodes made his way to the *Reggio*. Once aboard the sergeant major told him that Major Todd wanted to see him on the *Meon* at 1000 hours. Rhodes took the opportunity to shine up his belt and shoes and at 0930 made his way across to the ship. The major was in a good mood.

'Good morning, Corporal, had a good weekend?'

'Yes, thank you, sir, we had a great time,' said Rhodes.

The major passed Rhodes a letter. It was headed Senior NCOs' Course Royal Marines Training Centre Chajn Tuffieha. There was a list of ten names, his being second on the list.

Major Todd smiled. 'I take it you are pleased?'

Rhodes nodded. 'I didn't think I was senior enough for this just yet, sir.'

'Rubbish!' said the major. 'You are a King's Badgeman, that's worth two years' seniority and with your record and two gallantry awards, it's overdue.'

Rhodes was informed that the course would start the following Monday and would last two weeks. As he left the *Meon*, Major Todd wished him well and said, 'We are off to Benghazi for two weeks, see you on our return.'

Julie was delighted with his news.

'Pass this course, Peter, and they will promote you to sergeant very quickly. I just know it.'

Rhodes smiled. 'It's not as quick as that in the corps. It's dead men's shoes, but we will see.'

Rhodes reported to Chajn Tuffieha on the Monday as instructed and as he entered the RSM's office a familiar figure rose to meet him. It was Hairy Henry Higgins, now the regimental sergeant major of the training centre. Rhodes was delighted to see his old sergeant major and they greeted each other warmly.

'Don't expect any favours, young Rhodes,' said the RSM.

Rhodes laughed. 'I know you well enough not to expect any.'

Rhodes was then given a copy of the course programme and directed to his accommodation. The course started after lunch and they were told that they would first sit the RMET1. If they passed the education test, they would continue on the course. If not they would return to their units. For the next four hours, with just a fifteen-minute break, they toiled away and then they were finished. That evening after they had dinner, they were called in one at a time to be given the results of their education tests. Rhodes had passed along with eight others. Only one had failed and by 2100 hours the unfortunate was back with his unit.

There was some practical work involved on the course, but mostly it was classroom based with a great deal of map reading and planning of exercises. Each course member was given an objective and they would be required to develop a plan that they would have to present to the rest of the course. Afterwards it would be dissected and the good and bad parts examined.

At the end of the first week they were given leave until 2300 hours on the Sunday. Rhodes and Julie went to a dance at the Hotel Phoenicia on the Saturday night while a friend looked after Michael until they returned. The dancing had not tired Julie too much and when Rhodes made an advance to her in bed he was warmly received. Early on the Sunday evening, Rhodes made his way back to Chajn Tuffieha. Most of the course members had their wives in Malta with them, but nonetheless by 2300 hours all had returned. Week two began with each of them being given a subject to speak on for fifteen minutes. These were not of a military nature, but ranged from chicken farming to the running of an airport. They were given five minutes' preparation time and Rhodes was asked to speak on the role of a village vicar. They all enjoyed the presentations as it was good fun and it made them think on their feet.

The following day they presented plans of attack using sand models and little toy soldiers. There was, of course, a serious side to this. As one of their instructors pointed out, the success or failure of their plan would be measured by counting the number of the poor little buggers that you have to bury, indicating the toy soldiers.

Towards the end of the week their percentage marks began to appear on the notice board. Rhodes was pleased to see he was in the top two or three. The final day of the course was a wash-up on the work they had done over the fortnight. It was a no holds barred session and a few feathers were ruffled. After that they all had their final interviews. Rhodes was second in and he was asked how he thought he had done after which he was told how they thought he had performed. When he came out he was satisfied he had done enough to have passed and when the list was published that afternoon, he was second in a descending order of merit. Before he left Rhodes called in at the RSM's office to say goodbye to Henry Higgins and after a brief chat and a farewell handshake, Rhodes made his way back to Paola.

That night as Rhodes and Julie lay in bed they were deciding how to spend Christmas, which was now only three weeks away. Julie suggested inviting Matron Mary to spend Christmas Day with them. Rhodes agreed and suggested they also invite Henry Higgins as he had no family and would otherwise spend a lonely Christmas.

Julie agreed saying, 'It will be company for Matron and make a nice foursome.'

So it was decided. Rhodes had also thought of asking Sergeant Green, but remembered Green saying that he and his Wren friend had booked a room at a Sliema hotel. With Christmas now arranged, they went into a passionate embrace, which, as it reached fruition, left them breathless but at ease with the world.

Rhodes seemed to spend more time on the *Meon*, the head-quarters' ship, than his own ship, the *Reggio*, so Major Todd told him he would try and get him temporary promotion until a permanent post was offered. As Christmas drew near, plans were already in place for a joint British, French and Italian exercise starting on 6 January, involving landings in Sicily and the Italian mainland near Salerno. Rhodes wondered if he would find his father's grave there, he would certainly look.

Matron Mary wanted to attend Midnight Mass in Paola Church, so she would stay with them over the Christmas period. Henry Higgins had accepted their invitation with surprise and pleasure and would arrive at about 1030 hours on Christmas Day. On Christmas Eve Matron Mary Pendred arrived just as Michael was being bathed. Rhodes and Julie found it strange to call Matron, Mary and were more comfortable calling her Matron Mary. The matron thought this was hilarious, but was quite happy with the arrangement.

At 1145 hours they all made their way to the church. Michael was still asleep, so Rhodes carried him, making sure he was well wrapped up. They shared a pew with the Borg family, who were delighted to see them. The service lasted about an hour and Michael slept through it without making a sound. As they made their way back to the flat, the sky was clear, it was a beautiful night, a bright moon and millions of stars. They all agreed it was a perfect start to Christmas.

The next day, after a lazy breakfast, they opened their presents. Michael had a row of teddy bears, all of different sizes alongside his cot. Matron Mary had been given perfume by Rhodes and a lace shawl by Julie. Rhodes had bought Julie some perfume and some underwear.

Julie had given Rhodes a silver identity bracelet, saying, 'If you can't wear it keep it in your pocket.'

Henry Higgins arrived on time. He had met Matron Mary once when they had been in Malaya and Rhodes and Julie exchanged surprised glances when the two of them were soon chatting like old friends. They all helped prepare the dinner, the men peeling potatoes and shelling peas. Dinner was a great success. The conversation flowed and Rhodes had never seen Henry H so relaxed. Henry nursed Michael while the others washed up and when they had finished they came back into the lounge to find both of them asleep.

Henry left about 2100 hours, the duty driver from RMTC

coming to pick him up. As he left, he thanked them for such a nice day, kissing Julie's and Matron Mary's hand as he left.

When he had gone Matron Mary said, 'Such a charming man and a perfect gentleman, Hal has asked me if we could go out some time, I told him to give me a call next week.'

Julie and Rhodes were delighted and said, 'When did he say his name was Hal?'

Matron Mary laughed. 'Oh, when you were both getting tea.'

Matron stayed the night and left for Imtarfa the next morning.

She thanked them both, saying, 'I'm lucky to have such good friends.'

When they were alone Rhodes kissed Julie, 'That was great, a fine meal with good friends, but fancy, "Hal"!' They both laughed.

Salerno Reunion

The AW Squadron with 40 Commando embarked, sailed for
Sicily on 6 January. The landings took place near Catania, and
considering that it was January the weather was quite good. The
Italians had their own landing ships but despite the language
problem all went well. They spent five days in Sicily, so Rhodes
had the chance to go to the top of Mount Etna. It was impressive,
despite the strong smell of sulphur. Some of the marines called it
the hill of a thousand farts, inaccurate but descriptive.

They moved on the next day to the Italian coast. They now
had some French landing ships with them, with two companies of
French marine commandos aboard. The landings at Salerno
attracted quite a lot of spectators despite the rain and it blowing
half a gale. Each evening they re-embarked to prepare for landing
again the next day. They repeated this over three days, an
improvement each time. Rhodes was conscious that his father
only got one chance to get it right. When the exercises finished
the French ships returned home and the Italians sailed for Naples.
The AW Squadron made for Amalfi and anchored in the small
harbour.

Major Todd asked Rhodes if he was going to the military
cemetery at Salerno to see if he could find his father's grave.
Rhodes said he would like to. The next morning a minibus was
arranged and about ten navy and marine personnel would make
the trip, all for different reasons.

The military cemetery was vast and well cared for. The gate-
keeper was very helpful and showed them the records, all in
alphabetical order, which showed the section and grave number
of the person they sought. Rhodes made his way to his father's
grave, which he found quite easily. As he stood there and looked
at the inscription, he desperately tried to remember what his
father looked like. He knelt by the grave and placed his hand on
the gravestone. He heard a slight noise behind him. It was Major

Todd.

'I can't remember what my father looked like,' Rhodes said.

'Perhaps this will help,' said the major. He thrust a faded photograph into Rhodes's hands. It was a group of about twenty marines. In the centre stood a very young looking second lieutenant. Next to him was a sergeant, it was his father and the second lieutenant was clearly Major Todd.

The major explained to Rhodes that they had landed at Salerno on 9 September 1943. The major said he was slightly wounded in the first hour and taken to an aid station. He rejoined his section the next day to find that Sergeant Rhodes had been killed earlier that morning in an attack on a German machine gun position.

'Your father was a fine man and a very brave one, you have good reason to be proud of him, as no doubt he is of you.'

Rhodes's eyes filled with tears, for the first time he felt the loss of his father after all this time. He looked round and saw that the major was about ten yards away, looking at some other gravestones. Rhodes collected his thoughts. He now felt at ease with himself. He placed his right hand on the top of his father's headstone, said a silent prayer and farewell and walked back to the entrance of the cemetery.

Four days later they were back in Grand Harbour. As Rhodes made his way to Paola and Julie, he regretted not having a camera, as he would then have had a picture of his father's grave. Julie looked wonderful and Michael was growing at a tremendous rate. He kissed them both tenderly; they were his life.

Julie told him that Matron Mary and Hal had been out together twice and Matron thought he was wonderful.

Apparently Matron had said, 'Hal is such a gentle person, all that hair makes him look so fierce, but he is a cultured, sensitive man.'

Rhodes smiled. 'I must admit that's not quite how I see him, but I am delighted they have got on so well.'

Later he told Julie about the visit to his father's grave and about the photograph Major Todd had shown him.

As they lay in bed together that night, Julie said, 'Did you miss me very much?'

Rhodes threw back the covers. He had an enormous hard-on.

Julie gasped, 'Gosh, as much as that?' and dissolved into a fit of giggles.

A Change of Direction

Rhodes spent the next two weeks on the *Reggio*. They had some new beach lights that flashed 'Dah-Dah-Dit-Dah', the letter 'Q' in Morse, which meant 'beach here'. In daylight the use of a yellow flag achieved the same result. One morning he was told to report to Major Todd on the *Meon*.

'Are you a good swimmer, Corporal?' asked the major.

'Yes, sir,' said Rhodes.

'Well then,' said the major, 'I'm sending you on a diving course, with the clearance diving team. We need a couple of shallow water divers in the unit, so take one of our marines with you. The course starts on Monday and lasts three weeks.'

Rhodes selected a regular marine, as opposed to a national service one, to join him on the course. They both had medicals to ascertain their fitness to dive and on the following Monday reported to the fleet clearance diving team at HMS *Phoenicia*.

The chief petty officer in charge hardly made them welcome. He seemed to resent having to deal with Royal Marines. After he had made a couple of phone calls all that changed. For the rest of the day they had lectures on the physical effects of oxygen breathed at certain depths, the first signs of oxygen poisoning. 'Atmospheres Absolute' was explained, as were helium and nitrogen gases. Flow rates and natural buoyancy were explained. At 1700 hours the marines went home quite bemused, but eager to start the practical side of diving.

The next day Rhodes asked the CPO, 'Why the initial hostility?'

The chief smiled. 'Your SBS are brilliant, but the role you blokes are to play is different. I was told I either teach you or the army and I don't want any fucking brown jobs learning our skills.'

They were shown how to get into the rubber diving suits, how to put on the neck ring and how to fasten the rubber hood. They were then given a pair of rubber flippers each, told to get into the water and swim on their backs up and down Sliema Creek. After an hour they suggested they be allowed to come ashore.

The response of the chief was to throw a house brick at them and the advice, 'I'll tell you when to fucking well come out. Keep swimming.'

Just before noon they were allowed to come out of the water. The chief explained to them that when they had their breathing set on they would have sixty minutes of oxygen in their main bottles plus a thirty-minute reserve, so they would need to be prepared for long periods in the water. That afternoon they were allowed to dive in a Salvus suit using oxygen.

The Salvus suit is a good test of a person's suitability to be a diver. The suit is made of canvas and rubber. To put it on, entry is gained by an opening at waist height. The legs are inserted first and then the suit pulled up to the waist. The top half of the suit is then pulled over the head and shoulders. The entry vent is then gathered together and secured in a metal clip, which is tightened by a spanner to make it watertight. You now cannot get out of the suit unless someone undoes the clip. Rhodes felt the first pangs of panic. It was an intense feeling of claustrophobia. He took a few deep breaths and the fear passed. Through his visor he could see that his fellow marine had met and dealt with the same fear. The breathing apparatus was attached, they turned their oxygen on and when they were comfortable they were lowered into twenty feet of water. As their apprehension faded they both began to enjoy the sensation and were disappointed when they were pulled to the surface after about thirty minutes.

The CPO greeted them with a smile when they were released from the suit. 'About five people out of ten fail the course at this point, they can't stand being shut in. Well done,' he said.

The next few days were a mixture of practical and theory. They were told that oxygen can only be used to depths of thirty-three feet, beyond that it gradually poisons the body. The frogman's suit and breathing apparatus are for tactical use, the chief explained. You re-breathe the oxygen after it has been scrubbed through a soda lime container in your breathing apparatus. He went on to say that only a few small bubbles are released to the surface, so your presence can go undetected. They learnt how to recharge their oxygen bottles and how many lead weights they individually needed to achieve to balance their body weight. They spent many hours in the water by day and at night, under very close supervision.

One day they were taken round to Grand Harbour by the diving launch and told to swim up one of the creeks and report on how many submarines they could find on the bottom. Rhodes and James thought it was a wind-up, but to their surprise they found two. One was clearly empty and was in two pieces, the other was intact with all hatches secured. When they reported they had found two, they were told both had been sunk during the wartime bombing, and that the bodies of the crew were still on the intact submarine. It was a war grave.

The next day they went to the diving tank, swam to the bottom, removed their breathing apparatus and came to the surface releasing the air still in their lungs. All these exercises were designed to give them confidence in themselves and their equipment.

At the weekends Julie was convinced the oxygen was affecting their sex life.

'You always seem to have a hard-on,' she said. 'I'm not complaining, in fact I'm flattered, but what happens when you finish the course?'

Julie also had a secret. Matron Mary had confided in her that she and Hal now had a physical relationship.

'I wasn't the Virgin Mary to start with, so Hal has not ruined me,' she had said.

Julie thought this was wonderful and enquired if wedding bells were in the offing.

'If that is what Hal wants, then so do I, but it's not a condition of our relationship,' Matron had said. Julie did not tell Rhodes straight away, she decided to keep it to herself for the time being.

The last week of the course arrived. By this time both marines were confident in their new working environment. There were three night exercises to start off with. The first night they swam underwater the length of Sliema Creek and left proof of visit cards on two destroyers. On the second night they were required to saw through two pieces of metal pipe on the bottom of the creek opposite the jetty and finally, with leaded boots on, walk across the bottom of the creek from one side to the other.

They had two written tests to pass and also a practical that would prove their ability to strip down and reassemble their diving equipment. At the end of the week they were given their diving badges.

The CPO congratulated them, 'Well done, lads, for thick marines you have done pretty well.'

Rhodes and James made their way back to the *Reggio*, where there was an envelope waiting for Rhodes. Inside he found a copy of the group photograph showing his father next to the young Major Todd and a photograph of his father's grave, and a brief note saying, 'I thought you would like these,' and signed by the major. When he got home Julie was most impressed.

'That is really thoughtful,' she said. 'Your major is a great bloke.'

Rhodes agreed.

That weekend they went to the cinema and saw John Wayne in *The High and the Mighty*; Wayne was an airline pilot. Rhodes felt Julie's hand on the top of his leg; there was an immediate reaction.

Julie leaned over and whispered in his ear, 'It's just like an aircraft control column, when we get home you can crash on top of me.'

When they got back to the flat, Julie collected Michael from their neighbours. He was fast asleep and did not wake up even when they changed his nappy. Rhodes looked at his son's little penis.

'Will he have to be circumcised?' he asked.

'Certainly not,' said Julie. 'His foreskin is not tight and I can ease it back when I bathe him.'

Rhodes was pleased the last thing he wanted was for their son to suffer any discomfort.

Later when they went to bed, Julie pretended to be asleep when Rhodes climbed in beside her. His hand slowly moving up the inside of her thigh persuaded her to open her eyes and take an interest in the evening's final entertainment.

As her hand moved slowly over Rhodes fully erect member,

she said, 'Is there something wrong with it, it seems a bit flaccid.'

Rhodes promptly inserted himself, causing Julie to give a little gasp.

After a few energetic minutes of thrust and counter-thrust, ending in a satisfying climax for them both, Julie said, 'So I was wrong,' and gave a delicious little giggle.

Secret Survey

When Rhodes returned to the *Reggio* on the Monday, he was told that he and Marine James were to collect their diving equipment and go over to the *Meon* and report to Major Todd. He told them they were going to Tripoli the next day on the destroyer HMS *Diamond*. A naval officer would accompany them and they were to survey about a mile of beach fifteen miles east of Tripoli. He went on to say it would take about a week and on the Saturday, providing they had finished, a naval aircraft would collect them from Wheelus Field and return them to Halfar. They took all their equipment over to the *Diamond* and were informed that they would sail at 0900 hours the next day. Rhodes had taken the opportunity to thank Major Todd for the photos.

'It was a pleasure to help,' said the major, 'a real pleasure.'

Julie wasn't overjoyed that he would be away again.

'We really miss you, Peter, come back as soon as you can,' she said.

The next morning Rhodes was back on board the *Diamond* by 0800 hours, as was Marine James. The ship sailed at 0900 hours; there was a calm sea and Rhodes was surprised how fast the *Diamond* was. At 1400 hours they were alongside in Tripoli Harbour. As soon as they had offloaded their equipment, HMS *Diamond* sailed out of the harbour; she was going to Gibraltar.

The two marines sat on the jetty and wondered where their naval officer was. Ten minutes later a jeep drove up towing a small trailer. A naval officer was driving.

'You Corporal Rhodes?' he asked.

Rhodes saluted and said he was.

'Get in and put your equipment in the trailer,' they were told.

As soon as they were aboard, the officer drove off at a furious rate. Rhodes, sitting beside him, hung on for dear life. They drove out of Tripoli and along the coast road.

After twenty minutes Rhodes said, 'I thought we were only

going fifteen miles out from Tripoli, sir.'

The officer said, 'There's been a change of plan, we are going to the other side of Benghazi, near Tobruk.'

They stopped at the army base in Benghazi where they topped up with petrol and were given a meal. To Rhodes's surprise the naval officer ate with them. They continued their journey and made camp about four miles west of Tobruk. Rhodes and James erected the tent that was in the trailer. It was a six-man model, so there was plenty of room for the three of them and all of their equipment. Also in the trailer was a good supply of food and water. Whoever had loaded it knew what he was doing.

James made some tea and the officer told them what they were going to be doing over the next few days.

'Forget what you were told we were going to do and when we get back forget what we have done,' said the officer. This posed more questions than it answered, but Rhodes decided to wait for the opportunity for clarity; it certainly was not now.

The next morning after James had cooked breakfast, they made their way to the beach, which was about a hundred yards from the road. The officer said his name was Radcliffe, but they were to call him Mick. Rhodes and James were amazed; this was unheard of. They were then informed he would call them Pete and Joe.

James whispered in Rhodes's ear, 'Perhaps he's queer.'

To their surprise they all got on fine, Mick stuck a white post in the ground. He told them to stay put, walked back to the jeep and drove it back along the road towards Benghazi. Then he returned.

'I have placed another white post in the ground exactly one mile from here,' he said.

He then explained that first they would spread out and walk to the other marker covering the ground between the road and the beach, for the whole mile.

'We are looking for any salt marsh or very soft ground in the area I have described,' he said.

They spread out and walked slowly and carefully towards the distant white marker. About a hundred yards from the marker the ground became quite marshy.

'Shit,' said Mick. 'Go and get the marker, Joe.' And walking another fifty yards back towards their camp, he said, 'Stick it in there.'

Joe complied. They then all walked back to the first marker.

'We need a mile of beach for our purpose,' said Mick, and went on, 'we have lost one hundred and fifty yards. Let's see if we can gain it back this end.'

They took the marker out of the ground and carefully paced out the extra distance. The ground was firm and the marker was replaced. They had their mile of firm ground.

They then took their diving gear down to the beach. Mick showed them a chart of the sea area including the beach.

'I want the sea bottom searched for any rocks or obstructions for the full mile of beach going out one hundred yards to seaward.'

Rhodes suggested that they did a wading depth survey for the whole mile to start with, and then concentrate on the deeper water. Mick agreed and for the rest of the morning all three of them walked the mile of beach at times up to their necks in the sea.

In the afternoon, after a mug of tea, Rhodes and James put their diving gear on and started the survey. By 1600 hours they were getting tired, so Rhodes told Mick that was it for the day; there were no arguments. After a rest James cooked a meal. After they had eaten, Mick showed them the detailed chart he had drawn; it was very professional.

They all slept well and made an early start the next day. The weather was good and there was little surf on the beach. Rhodes insisted they have a two-hour break at lunchtime and then only work a further two hours. Their oxygen bottles needed recharging and the one large bottle on the pump would need replacing the next day. When Rhodes told Mick this he said, 'I'll drive back to Benghazi tomorrow and get a bottle from the hospital there. It's got to be ninety-nine per cent pure, is that right?' Rhodes nodded his agreement.

The next day things went pretty well. Mick returned about 1400 hours with the oxygen and some more supplies. He was surprised to see they were both out diving. At 1530 hours they came ashore; they were clearly tired.

Mick surprised them by saying, 'That's enough for today, lads, you look knackered.'

They had a rest then recharged their bottles for the next day. Afterwards James cooked a meal; Mick had brought back some steak from the army base and it was delicious.

They gave Mick the findings of the day's survey. They had found a cluster of rock at three fathoms, one hundred and ten yards out. Mick marked it on the chart.

'Should not be a problem,' he said. 'But we will take some bearings on them tomorrow.'

They were just over halfway along the mile of coast by now. Rhodes told Mick they needed a day off.

'We all do, Pete. We will finish at noon tomorrow and take three days off.' At noon the next day they drove back to Benghazi and, to Rhodes's and James's surprise, straight to the airfield. Mick left them for about ten minutes.

On his return he said, 'They will fly you to RAF Luqua in about thirty minutes and on Tuesday morning fly you back here leaving Luqua at 0730 hours, have a good time.'

The flight to Malta took about fifty minutes. An RAF driver picked Rhodes and James up at the airfield and dropped them off in Paola Square twenty minutes later. The driver told them he would pick them up at the same place on Tuesday morning at 0630 hours.

Rhodes made his way up Arcade Street to their flat. Julie was not home, so he sat on the doorstep and waited. A woman across the street called out to him.

'Your wife and her friend went into Valletta about an hour ago. Come in and I'll make you a cold drink.'

Rhodes was reluctant to accept but the woman was persistent. Once in the house he was given some chilled orange juice and the woman, whose name was Kath, kept on about how often her husband was away and how lonely she was. She sat opposite Rhodes and treated him to a fair amount of leg. Her skirt was quite short and every time she re-crossed her legs more of her thighs were exposed. She was a pretty girl with dark hair, a little bit older than Julie. She said that they had no children and had been married four years. Her husband was a seaman on a destroyer.

She came over to Rhodes and poured some more orange juice into his glass, her thigh pressed against his arm. Rhodes was by this time acutely aware of how attractive she was. He had to get away. She stood in front of him and started to undo the buttons on her blouse. She had no need for a bra and Rhodes could see her bare breasts.

At that moment he heard Julie's voice outside; she was talking to her friend.

Rhodes got up to leave.

'Thanks for the drink, it was most kind of you, I can hear my wife outside.' The girl did up the buttons on her blouse.

As she showed him out she said, 'If you are lonely any time come over, he's never here.'

When Rhodes got outside, Julie had already gone into their flat. He tapped on the door. Julie opened it and on seeing him threw her arms around him. Once inside, he told her about the girl opposite.

Julie smiled. 'Had a narrow escape, did we? Yes, we all know about Kath. She is a nice girl but her husband is knocking off a Wren and hardly ever comes home.'

Rhodes made a fuss of Michael who was full of beans. He played with him for an hour while Julie cooked a meal. Later that evening Rhodes bathed Michael and then put him to bed; within minutes his son was asleep. Later when he and Julie went to bed, she asked him what they had been doing in Tripoli.

'Oh, the usual thing, charting out possible exercise areas.'

Rhodes had decided, there was no need to bother Julie with the details of where they had been.

As they lay close to one another Julie said, 'What did Kath get up to that scared the pants off you?'

'Oh,' said Rhodes, 'she gave me a flash of the promised land.'

'This,' said Julie, 'is your promised land.' And she slipped off her nightdress.

Rhodes buried his face in Julie's breasts and worked his way down her stomach. Julie sat up and grabbed hold of Rhodes's penis.

'You are mine, and not anyone else's,' she said and she knelt across Rhodes and guided his weapon home. The headboard beat out its familiar rapid tune as the bed sought to keep up with their thrashing bodies. In the morning Julie asked Rhodes if he could remember the girl across the road.

'What girl?' said Rhodes.

With a sense of regret Rhodes left the house just after 0600 hours on the Tuesday morning, but with any luck they would be finished by the weekend. By 0900 hours they were back on the ground at Benghazi. Lieutenant Radcliffe was there to meet them and, after reloading their equipment, they were soon on their way to their beach.

They worked hard for the next three days. At Mick's suggestion they rested up on Friday and at 1600 hours on Sunday finished their survey. They spent Sunday night in the army base at Benghazi and Mick bought them a few beers in the canteen. That night they slept like logs.

On Monday they drove back to Tripoli. The LCT HMS *Rampart* was there and as soon as they had loaded their equipment it prepared to sail. Mick said his goodbyes, shaking them warmly by the hand.

'Don't tell anyone where we have been or what we have been doing. Major Todd will fill in your diving records, so you will have some diving pay to come. All the best,' he said, and he was gone.

At 0800 hours the next day they entered Grand Harbour and tied up alongside the *Reggio*. Rhodes spent the rest of the day with James cleaning all their equipment and recharging the bottles of their diving gear. Major Todd came on board at 1500 hours and sent for Rhodes.

'Enjoy your little trip?' he asked.

'Yes, thank you, sir, hard work but worthwhile I'm sure.'

'No need to say any more,' said the major, 'and by the way I've entered you and James with forty hours' diving time, you will be paid that next month. You and James are on leave now until 0800 hours next Monday.'

As Rhodes made his way to Paola on the bus he worked out his diving pay. At a penny a minute that was five shillings an hour.

Forty hours worked out to ten pounds, a month's rent. He shared the news about his diving pay with Julie and after a welcome home kiss, she was deciding how to spend it.

'I need a new nightdress,' she said.

'Why bother?' said Rhodes. 'It never stays on for more than five minutes.'

Rest and Recreation

During Rhodes's leave they took Michael to the beach at Mellieha Bay. They rigged up a sunshade and their son played happily in the sand. Julie went swimming while Rhodes stayed with Michael. He watched her as she walked out of the water and came towards them. Her figure was superb, fine high breasts, nice legs and a neat firm bottom.

Rhodes took his turn for a swim and, when he came out of the water, two men were standing, talking to Julie. As he came nearer he could hear her voice was angry and Rhodes could see that both of the men had been drinking.

As he reached them Julie said, 'These louts are being disgusting, Peter,' and began to cry.

Before he could stop himself Rhodes launched himself at the two men. The nearest one to Rhodes caught the full force of a swinging right and went down in a heap, the other started to run away, but Rhodes caught him and smacked him straight between the eyes. Rhodes turned and went back to Julie, while the men scurried away to the other end of the beach. Rhodes took Julie in his arms and dried her tears, while Michael still played in the sand, as though nothing had happened.

'Come on, let's go home,' said Rhodes and he started to gather their things together.

As they moved across the sand to the road and the bus stop, a car stopped, a voice called out; it was Gail Browning.

'I saw what happened,' she said. 'Those men have been causing trouble all afternoon, they are soldiers from the tented camp on the hill.'

She insisted that they get into the car. Then she drove up to the camp's guardroom.

'I wish to speak to the duty officer,' she said.

When the duty officer arrived, she said, 'My name is Gail Browning. My husband is the commanding officer of HMS

Phoenicia. Some of your men have been behaving in a disgusting manner to the ladies on the beach, what do you propose to do about it?'

The officer looked shaken. 'What have they done?' he asked.

Julie said, 'When my husband was swimming, they came over to me and said, "If your husband wasn't around we would fuck you to a standstill."'

Within minutes the camp burst into activity and a party of soldiers with a sergeant in charge went down to the beach and rounded up the men there. They were made to walk past Gail Browning's car. Julie picked the two men out. It wasn't hard – they both had swollen faces.

'Those are the men,' she said. 'My husband spoke to them, and then they ran off.'

The men were taken in to the guardroom; a lieutenant colonel had arrived and spoke with Gail Browning.

Out of the hearing of Rhodes, Gail said, 'My friend's husband is a Royal Marine, he is the holder of the DCM for brave conduct in Korea and the MM for gallantry in Malaya. He is on leave and his wife was insulted by your men, it's not good enough, Colonel.'

'Indeed it is not, Mrs Browning, they will be severely dealt with, and by the state of their faces your friend's husband has already started the process.'

The colonel then walked over to where Julie and Rhodes were sitting. 'Please accept my sincere apologies, they will be dealt with severely.' He then saluted Julie and walked away.

Gail Browning drove them home to Paola. She stayed for tea and, as Julie had now recovered her composure, they were able to laugh at the incident.

Gail said, 'I saw Peter do his knight in shining armour bit; it was most impressive.'

Julie looked at Rhodes. 'Yes, he's good at that. It's not the first time he has defended my honour.'

'Perhaps,' said Gail, 'I could borrow him some time.'

'No chance,' said Julie, 'he's mine.'

Later that night when they were in bed, Julie said, 'What does it mean to be fucked to a standstill?'

'This,' said Rhodes and ten minutes later a breathless Julie said, 'Oh, I understand the first bit, but who's at a standstill?'

'I am,' said Rhodes.

About a week later Gail Browning saw Julie at the Naval Wives' Club. She showed Julie a letter from the colonel at the Mellieha Bay camp. There was also an envelope inside addressed to Mrs Rhodes. Both letters said almost the same thing, the two soldiers had been charged with bringing disgrace on the Queen's uniform and had been sentenced to fourteen days' detention. The letter finished with another apology, and was signed J J Williams-Hunt, Lieutenant Colonel.

It was now mid-June and, when Rhodes came home one evening, Julie said, 'I've had a letter from Mum. She wants to come out for a week, is that okay?'

'Of course,' said Rhodes. 'I'll send her a cable. She can come when she wants to.'

Two weeks later they met Mrs Grey at the airport. She couldn't keep her hands off baby Michael. Rhodes managed to get a few days' leave and they took Julie's mum all over the island.

They had lunch in Valletta with Gail Browning. Matron Mary and 'Hal' Higgins came to tea at the weekend. When Rhodes was out of the flat, Mrs Grey asked Julie if she was happy.

Julie smiled. 'Life couldn't be better, Mum. Peter's a fine man and a loving husband and father.'

Mrs Grey gave a sigh. 'I need not have asked, it's written all over your face.'

When they took Mrs Grey to the airport at the end of her stay, Rhodes whispered in her ear, 'Come and see us any time, don't ask, just surprise us.'

Major Todd came over to the *Reggio* one morning. Rhodes and James were diving, checking for a leak in one of *Reggio*'s fuel tanks.

When Rhodes came back on deck and greeted him the major said, 'I've come to the end of my tour and will be going home in two weeks. Thought I would pop over and say goodbye.'

Rhodes was disappointed and it showed in his face. 'We are

going to miss you, sir, it won't ever be quite the same, with you gone.'

Major Todd smiled. 'That's an unusual thing to hear, I must say, but thank you. I'll see you before I go. Incidentally, my relief is a Major Baker. I believe you served under him in Malaya.'

A week later the marines of the AW Squadron had a farewell parade for Major Todd. He shook hands with them all and wished them well. He then introduced Major Baker who spoke for a couple of minutes, then said he would see each of them over the next two weeks. As he was about to leave for the *Meon*, the major saw Rhodes and came over to him.

'Well,' he said, 'Major Todd told me I would recognise some old faces, but I thought you would be in the brigade, not here.'

Rhodes explained that all his attempts to transfer had failed and enquired if the major could assist. Major Baker laughed. 'I don't intend to start in my new post by getting rid of my best men, remember, "A good man is a good man anywhere."'

Rhodes and Julie had a small party on 23 July to celebrate Michael's birthday. As the next day was their wedding anniversary they decided they would combine the two. A few friends from the flats around them, Gail Browning, Matron Mary and Hal Higgins, and the Borgs had called early on in the day. The party was a great success and, before Hal Higgins left with Matron Mary, he told him that their old troop commander was now a major and senior marine officer in the AW Squadron. Hal Higgins gave that strange smile.

'In that case, Peter, your promotion to sergeant is assured, he thinks the sun shines out of your bottie.'

Canal Confrontation

On 26 July 1956, Gamil Nasser, the president of Egypt, national-ised the Suez Canal. The reaction of the British Government was to put intense pressure on the Egyptians and to make plans for a possible invasion of the canal zone. Major Baker called Rhodes over to the *Meon* and to his surprise Mick Radcliffe was there, now a lieutenant commander.

'We have been discussing the survey you and Lieutenant Commander Radcliffe made near Tobruk. This is highly sensitive information and in the light of this you are promoted to acting sergeant as from now.' He went on. 'A revisit in daylight to the area is out of the question; Egypt has friends in Libya, so a night-time recce over two nights should do the trick.' He added, 'The SBS should do this work, but they are busy with the brigade in Cyprus, so you and James can do it with Lieutenant Commander Radcliffe working from a submarine.'

Later that day Rhodes and James met with Mick Radcliffe on the *Reggio*. Radcliffe swore them both to secrecy.

He said, 'What I am going to tell you is top secret. It is one of the several options available should the British Government choose to retake the canal zone by force.'

He then went on to tell them that a large force, consisting of Royal Marine commandos and the parachute regiment would land by sea on their previously surveyed beach. A large number of tanks and trucks would also come ashore with massive supplies of food ammunition and essential materials; an armoured brigade based in Benghazi would join them. The combined force would then cross the Egyptian border east of Tobruk and race along the coast road, first to Alexandria and then on to Port Said.

Radcliffe went on, 'The object of this operation would be to force the Egyptians to reconsider their actions or face an occupa-tion of their country. Another threat was that their power stations and railway network would be destroyed by the RAF and the Fleet

Air Arm.'

As the information sunk in, Rhodes said, 'Christ, is this for real?'

Radcliffe smiled. 'Indeed it is.'

Julie was delighted with his temporary promotion.

'This is great news, Peter, will you be paid extra for this?'

Rhodes explained he would be paid the sergeant's rate of pay for as long as he held the rank. Rhodes then had to tell her he would be away for about a week.

'It's Tripoli again. Having a look at some of the beaches.'

'Hurry back, Peter, life's not the same without you.'

It was Rhodes's first time on a submarine. As they loaded their equipment on to the submarine's deck, the crew helped to take it down inside. They sailed out of Sliema Creek just after dark and when they were five miles or so out of Malta they submerged. The following afternoon at about 1500 hours they were opposite their beach area, but about two miles out.

At 2200 hours Rhodes and James stood on the deck of the submarine as it moved in closer to shore on the surface. At 2230 hours Rhodes and James slipped over the side of the submarine and headed for the beach. On reaching the shore they found their marker where they had placed it. That night they spent three hours and covered about a quarter of a mile at wading depth and then swimming at a depth of two to three fathoms parallel to the beach. They found no new obstructions.

They swam back out to sea and found the submarine about three hundred yards out. Mick Radcliffe was on the submarine's casing and helped them out of the water. Once below they were given a tot of rum and some cocoa. They had become quite chilled despite it being early August. Once they had got out of their dry suits and into something comfortable, they went over Mick Radcliffe's charts and showed him how much they had covered. They then had something to eat, and got their heads down.

The following night they covered at least another four hundred yards, finding the rocky outcrop again. This time it seemed less than two fathoms down. When they returned to the submarine they told Mick Radcliffe. He checked his chart and noted the change. He told them that there was only about a metre between high and low water in the Med; in fact some people thought, wrongly, that there was no tidal influence at all.

The captain of the submarine suggested they put a pellet buoy on two and a half fathoms of cable on a heavy sinker over the rocks. The next night they launched a small rubber dingy with the buoy and sinker in it and Rhodes and James towed it to the rocks before placing it in position. The crew had painted the buoy a dark green colour so it was almost impossible to see it from shore. That night they completed all but two hundred yards of their task. The following night the weather was very rough, so they stayed on the submarine to await an improvement.

By the next day the weather had returned to the balmy conditions of the first two nights. That night they were able to complete their task and in the early hours of the morning they started back for Malta. They entered Sliema Creek at 1100 hours the next day and by 1400 hours they were back on the *Reggio*. Lieutenant Commander Radcliffe told them he would try and get them a couple of days' leave and that evening Rhodes went home to Julie with two days to spend at home.

In bed that night they made love very slowly. Rhodes explored Julie's body, taking great pleasure in her firm breasts and bottom. As his mouth and lips sought her intimate parts, she in turn caressed and kissed him. Finally, he thrust himself deeply into her and they thrashed their bodies to a climax.

'If that's what being on a submarine does for you, transfer to their service. That was awesome,' said Julie.

They had a cup of tea in bed the next morning and Julie was just saved from another encounter by Michael waking up and demanding some attention.

Julie smothered their son with kisses.

'My son has saved me from a terrible fate,' she cried.

When Rhodes returned to the *Reggio* after his leave, he found that the ship was about to go into dry dock to have the fuel tank seam sealed, but it would only be laid up for two days.

Things were beginning to move on the Suez front. 40 Commando and most of 45 Commando had returned to Malta and it was rumoured that 42 Commando was coming out from the UK.

Rhodes made sure all of their diving gear was on top line and they kept two full large bottles of oxygen with their pump and the bottles on their diving sets were also topped up.

Over the next few days a large number of metal ladders were delivered to the *Reggio* and *Striker*. *Reggio* now out of dry dock. She took her landing craft back aboard and the ladders that had arrived were placed in the landing craft. They had been made to fit neatly in the landing ramp space. Each ladder had eight rungs and could accommodate two people climbing abreast.

Two hundred marines from 40 Commando embarked on the *Reggio* and the same number on the *Striker*. They made their way round to Kalafrana Bay and for the rest of the day practised landing the marines onto the jetty there. The landing craft had to keep their bows up against the concrete jetty so that the metal ladders were firmly in place for the marines to climb up and out. They quickly found it easier to keep the landing craft straight by having the engines going very slowly ahead. As the day went on they found that the exit times from the landing craft were getting better and better. By the end of the day all of the problems they had encountered were overcome by good sense and ingenuity. They practised this for the next two days and the brigade commander who watched the final landings was satisfied this method could be used to land the marines on the concrete mole at Alexandria. So another option for the recapture of the Suez Canal was available.

It was now September and Malta was beginning to fill with ships coming out from the UK. Some strange tracked vehicles had suddenly appeared. They were called LVTs, or landing vehicles tracked. They could drive down the ramps of the LSTs or LCTs and 'swim' ashore, their tracks providing motive power.

The *Reggio* and *Striker* embarked them, took them round to Mellieha Bay and launched them. They could do about four or five knots in the water and almost five times that on land. Rhodes watched them come ashore. He thought they were too slow in the water, but of course once they hit the beach they could carry their troops straight inland. He spoke to one of the drivers and had a look over one.

'Are the sides armoured?' he asked.

The driver grinned. 'No, Sarge, we need a crane to drop the armour in the sides and it slows us down, but the front is armoured, which takes care of me.'

There was a conference on the *Meon* the next day. Rhodes was invited and he sat at the back. Major Baker informed everyone of the current situation. The landings near Tobruk were out. King Idris of Libya was refusing to allow his country to be used as a springboard for an attack on a fellow Arab country. The two options still open were a seaborne assault on Alexandria or a seaborne and airborne attack on Port Said. If Port Said were chosen it would be delayed until late October because the parachute regiment had not had any parachute training for over twelve months. That was being put right now in Cyprus, but it would take another month to complete. The meeting broke up with some disappointed faces. Lieutenant Commander Radcliffe came over to Rhodes.

'All your hard work for nothing. But it was worth the effort and it got you another stripe.'

Rhodes laughed and declared, 'I am hoping to hold on to it.'

Julie was asking lots of questions about what was going on.

'Do you think we will really invade Egypt?'

Rhodes gave her a little hug. 'It wouldn't surprise me at all. There is a lot of stuff arriving by the day and it's not for an exercise.'

That night she said, 'Just give me a cuddle, Peter, that's all I want tonight.'

He held her close till she fell asleep.

The next day Rhodes was told the Alexandria option had gone and the assault on Port Said by sea and air was the final decision.

Dawn Assault

Each day saw the arrival of more ships from the UK and with them came a vast mountain of military hardware, which was growing at different locations adjoining Grand Harbour. Planning sessions were taking up huge amounts of time; decisions were being made then changed in a matter of hours. The British Government was under a great deal of pressure not to undertake an assault on Port Said. The only allies they appeared to have were the French and the Israelis. The Americans were giving dire warnings on the consequents of launching a military adventure in the Eastern Mediterranean.

The Russians, who had troubles of their own in Hungary, pledged support for Egypt and increased their military aid in the shape of aircraft, tanks and artillery. The propaganda machine in Egypt was pumping out half-truths and lies, suggesting that if the British attacked Egypt, Russian planes would bomb London. The servicemen arriving in Malta and those already there still had no clear idea of the role they were expected to play.

Several LSTs arrived in Malta carrying tanks and artillery pieces that had been loaded in the wrong order, so the LSTs had to dock 'bow-to' by the Fleet Post Office. They then offloaded all of the vehicles they had carefully loaded on in England and, having been given hastily drawn up beaching plans, re-embarked their loads. Most of the loading was common sense; when the LSTs beached, tanks were to be the first ashore therefore they needed to be last vehicles embarked.

Rhodes and the Beach Unit spent most of their days in Mellieha Bay. 42 Commando had arrived from the UK and, with 40 Commando, spent hours landing from the *Reggio* and *Striker* using the LVTs and LCAs.

45 Commando had returned from Cyprus and were going to be landed by helicopters within an hour of 42 and 40 seizing the beaches. All of the vehicles to be used in the landings had been

painted with a large letter 'H' in white. This was to avoid them being fired on by our own troops and aircraft; the 'H' standing for the name given to the operation, 'Hamilcar'. There was a certain amount of confusion later when the operation was renamed 'Musketeer'; the white 'H's, however, were retained.

The Amphibious Warfare Squadron had now grown to twenty ships, an ageing mixture of LSTs and LCTs. Seven aircraft carriers were also involved; five British and two French. The French were now also committed to the operation. The aircraft carriers *Theseus* and *Ocean* would transport 45 Commando Royal Marines as well as their Whirlwind and Sycamore helicopters. The other carriers had over two hundred aircraft, with which to provide the landing force with close air support.

The French were also providing the only battleship, the *Jean-Bart*. It had fifteen-inch guns which would devastate any Egyptian positions in the landing area. Also in the invasion fleet would be cruisers, destroyers and frigates; a formidable amount of fire-power. The RAF had moved Canberra bombers to Cyprus, but not without problems. The Canberras sit rather low on the ground and to 'bomb' them up, a descending ramp is required. No ramps existed in Cyprus, so the ground crews had to dig them out.

The invasion plans were now almost decided. British para-troops would drop on Gamil Airfield, which was three miles east of Port Said, and prevent Egyptian armour crossing the road bridge from Alexandria. French paratroops would drop on the Port Fuad side of the canal. Royal Marine Commandos would land on the beaches of Port Said and French Marine Commandos would land at Port Fuad.

All of the wives of the servicemen involved in the operation were getting concerned and did not share the enthusiasm of the British press for the adventure. Rhodes tried to make light of the affair by suggesting it would probably be cancelled, but secretly hoping it would go ahead. On one of her visits Matron Mary unfortunately mentioned that Imtarfa Military Hospital and Bighi Naval Hospital were making arrangements to receive large numbers of wounded. This reduced Julie to tears and Matron Mary spent an hour reassuring her. Rhodes felt the benefit of this upset that night when Julie was more passionate than usual.

One morning as Rhodes was watching an LVT trying to re-verse into the tank deck of *Reggio*, a familiar voice greeted him; it was Bob Jones.

The first words Jones said were, 'How the hell did you make sergeant?'

Rhodes assured him he was only acting up.

'You were always good at that,' said Jones.

He then told Rhodes that all the marines from the Rhine Squadron were out in Malta to drive the extra landing craft. He was on the LST *Lofoten*. Later that evening Rhodes took him to see Julie. She was delighted to see him and extracted from him all the news about Jane.

'You will see her next week as she is being detached to the BMH at Imtarfa,' he said.

They told Jones that Matron of their Malaya days was there and now a close friend. Jones made a great fuss of Michael who was revelling in the extra attention. After a meal, Rhodes took Bob down to the bus stop as the *Lofoten* did not allow all night leave and he had to be back on board by midnight.

The following week Jane arrived in Malta. Preparations were now complete as far as the invasion force was concerned and it just required the politicians to say yes or no.

On 28 October the invasion force put to sea. Rhodes had managed to see Julie the night before and had said his farewells. The Beach Unit embarked on the *Anzio* and managed to find room to sleep and store their equipment on the crowded tank deck. The troops involved in the operation had not been fully briefed, one reason being that the landing plan was being changed day by day. However, with the fleet making an impressive sight, as no doubt it was intended to, London still hoped that the news of the fleet may still persuade the Egyptian Government to back down.

On 31 October, the RAF began bombing military targets in Egypt. Canberras from Cyprus and Valiants from Malta started an intense bombardment of airfields, military bases, tank concentrations and gun emplacements.

This provoked international outrage at the United Nations

and a Security Council resolution to cease this aggression was vetoed by Great Britain and France. The invasion force was now thought to be at threat from Egyptian submarines, they had two, and their whereabouts was unclear. The fast mine layer HMS *Manxman* sped up and down the slow-moving LSTs and LCTs; its impressive speed of thirty knots caused a great deal of interest in the watching troops.

Major Baker came and found Rhodes in the tank deck.

'We are on the wrong ship, it seems, we should be on the *Lofoten*,' he said, and added, 'we are to transfer in an LCA that the *Lofoten* is sending across.'

Thirty minutes later the Beach Unit had all its equipment on deck, but the ships could not heave to in these hostile waters so they would have to use the scramble ladder near the stern of the ship. The LCA from the *Lofoten* came alongside and the marines of the Beach Unit formed a chain down the length of the ladder and passed their equipment into the LCA. Major Baker's biggest fear was that one of his men would fall in and be sucked into the ship's propellers, but all went well.

Some of the tank crews watching said to Rhodes, 'You wouldn't catch us doing that, Sarge, that's beyond the call of duty,' and gave him a wave as he went down the ladder.

The landing order was now finally agreed. The Beach Unit would be in the first wave of LCAs, following behind the slower LVTs. They would land with 42 Commando on the right of the Casino Palace Pier, 40 Commando would land on the left. The first role of the Beach Unit would be to secure an exit and bring ashore fourteen Centurion tanks, which would spearhead the marines' advance into Port Said. The remaining eighty tanks would come ashore as soon as the bridgehead was secure.

Rhodes settled in on the *Lofoten* along with the other Beach Unit marines. Bob Jones helped him take his equipment down to the tank deck, where they found some stretchers to sleep on. The tank deck was full of ammunition and little else.

Jones said to Rhodes, 'If this lot goes up, we will be back in Malta sooner than we think.' They both laughed.

Major Baker kept the Beach Unit informed as to what was happening. French aircraft and the Fleet Air Arm were now involved in the air bombardment with Sea Hawks, Sea Venoms and Corsairs now keeping up the attacks on the Egyptians, whose air force had deserted the skies. The general commanding officer, General Stockwell, had been told that the largest calibre naval gun to be used was four point five. This deprived the invasion force of the fire power of the *Jean-Bart*'s fifteen-inch guns and the British and French cruisers' six-inch.

Rhodes said to Major Baker, 'I'm surprised they're still allowing us the use of the four point fives.'

Little did the marines know but the government had wanted to ban any naval bombardment to support the landings. And only a suggestion by a very senior officer that in that case he would return the invasion force to Malta stayed their hand.

Back in Malta Julie listened to all the radio news programmes; it was an anxious time for all the wives. Gail Browning took her into Valletta for lunch to try and take her mind off the drama unfolding in the eastern Mediterranean. Most evenings Jane would visit and sometimes stay the night; both of them were anxious as news bulletins were confusing. Michael was a bundle of energy and growing fast and helped keep Julie fully occupied.

The Americans were putting increasing pressure on the British Government to stop the bombing. On one occasion an American submarine sailed down the centre of the Invasion Fleet, flying a huge 'Stars And Stripes', making sure she was seen as not hostile.

One marine watching said, 'She may not be hostile, but is she friendly?' Most onlookers agreed with that.

The fleet sailed on getting ever closer, now sailing in a zigzag course to avoid any submarine attack. On 4 November Major Baker informed the Beach Unit that the invasion was definitely on and told them that the paras would land on Gamil Airfield at 0530 hours on 5 November and French paratroops on the Port Fuad side of the canal.

Early the next morning the marines waited for news of the airborne assault. When the news came it was mixed; the landing had gone quite well, with few casualties, but the resistance to the paras moving into Port Said was stiff and, had it not been for the close air support of the Fleet Air Arm, the position of the paras would have become untenable. By that evening the airborne troops dug in by the sewage farm just west of Gamil Airfield.

In the final briefing that night Major Baker gave them an up-to-date picture of the beach defences. One question that was on everyone's lips was, 'Were the beaches mined?'

'No intelligence on that,' said Major Baker, and he went on, 'when you run up the beach keep in the tracks of the LVTs.'

Reveille the next day was to be at 0300 hours, embark in the landing craft at 0400 hours, form up in the beaching order and land at 0500 hours.

The next morning there was a fresh wind blowing and the sea was choppy. The marines embarked in their landing craft and moved to their form-up position. The LVTS with the marines aboard rolled down the lowered ramps of the LSTs into the sea. They were now in position four miles off shore; with the LVTs leading in line abreast, the armada of landing craft slowly started their run in towards the distant beaches.

In the beaching plan there was supposed to be at least a hundred yards between the successive waves of landing craft. At two miles from shore eight destroyers had heaved-to, broadside on, to the beach, with sufficient space between each ship for the landing craft to pass through. As they passed through the destroyers they opened fire; the concussion of the guns and the scream of the outgoing shells brought home to the marines the situation they were about to face.

Rhodes stood next to Major Baker and watched as the naval guns blasted the beaches; rows of beach huts were now burning fiercely. Adding to this picture of destruction were the planes of the Fleet Air Arm firing rockets and machine-gunning the beach defences.

It became clear to all the marines that the firing was not all one way; the snap and crack of returned fire began to sweep over the landing craft as they crept nearer the shore.

As the first line of LVTs came within a hundred yards of the beach the naval bombardment ceased. The marines did a final check of their equipment and cocked their weapons, then the first LVTs were ashore and moving up the beach.

The first wave of LCAs grounded and the marines were

storming ashore, performing a role they had practised hundreds of times. Rhodes followed Major Baker up the beach. On reaching the first Egyptian trenches they paused to allow their formation to regroup. Marines of 42 Commando were passing them as they moved to their assault positions. As Rhodes glanced into the first trenches there were no dead Egyptian soldiers there, just a pile of chapattis in one corner and evidence of a recent Egyptian bowel movement in the other. What surprised him most of all was the number of heavy machine guns in place there; if the Egyptians had stood and fired them at the landing craft instead of departing, the marine losses would have been horrific.

The Beach Unit started to get organised; they started to direct the follow-up waves of LCAs to their required beaching areas. Then two LSTs were called in to land the fourteen Centurion tanks, the exit points having been decided. The blazing beach huts to their left suddenly exploded as an Egyptian ammunition lorry parked between them was engulfed in flames. Two marines of 42 Commando had been wounded and were being treated at the Beach Unit's HQ. The tall buildings opposite the beach had been put out of bounds as regards shelling, fire from these buildings had slowed the advance of the marines.

Two sections of marines had entered the buildings and were slowly clearing the opposition floor by floor. The first tanks had moved off the beaches, adding to the noise by the detonation of the charges that removed the waterproofing from their turrets. The marines of 42 and 40 Commando had all reached their designated positions and were preparing to advance to their next objectives, with the tanks leading followed by the LVTs.

Next to come ashore were the marines of 45 Commando who were on their way in on the helicopters from HMS *Theseus* and HMS *Ocean*. They were going to land on the football field near a statue of Ferdinand de Lesseps, the builder of the Suez Canal. They managed to land without any great incident, despite coming under sniper fire.

As 45 moved to its appointed position they were hit by machine gun fire from a Fleet Air Arm aircraft, causing several casualties including the commanding officer. Despite these casualties the marines of 45 Commando regrouped and joined 40 and 42 Commando as they began to advance to their next objectives.

Rhodes watched as his fellow marines began their advance into Port Said. The role of the Beach Unit was now to move round to the Fisherman's Harbour and see that the follow-up LSTs beached in the right order.

To his surprise he saw Sergeant Green of 40 Commando come back up the road and speak to Major Baker. Rhodes was called over.

Major Baker said, 'It would appear that 40 Commando want to borrow you as they are shortly likely to meet up with some French paras on their left flank. You okay about this?' Rhodes was delighted to get into some action and indicated he was happy to assist.

Sergeant Green and Rhodes hurried to catch up with the advance of 40 Commando; the opposing fire was getting heavier and the advance was slowing down. As the marines came up to each road junction and started to cross they were raked by machine gun fire and started to take casualties. The tanks with them gave as much covering fire as they could, but the answer was to clear the houses and flats as they advanced. This was a slow business as each floor had to be cleared and some of the blocks had six or eight floors. Rhodes took over the section of a badly wounded sergeant and he led them through the ground floors of the houses, seeking some cover as they moved further into the streets of Port Said. The marines in the LVTs had advanced the furthest, but they had taken casualties because the sides of the LVTs had not had the armoured plate replaced prior to their being embarked in Malta.

The troop Rhodes was attached to swung left and started an attack on the police barracks and the custom house. Four tanks gave them support and gradually they managed to clear the buildings. At the custom house they called in an air strike, as heavy machine-gun fire was coming from the roof area.

Two Royal Navy planes made two attacking runs each, leaving the roof area devastated. As the marines moved forward the first Egyptians began to surrender. Two marines were left to guard the twenty prisoners, with instructions to shoot the bastards if they gave any trouble. The CO of 40 Commando was aware that he needed to stop any of his troops getting too far ahead of one another, as there was more resistance in some places than others. In spite of this he managed to keep things pretty much under control.

Rhodes felt he was back where he belonged. He knew some of the young marines he was with and some of the more senior marines had heard of him. As they progressed they came under mortar fire from several hundred yards away. A request for an air strike was answered within minutes and the firing stopped as quickly as it started.

The advance was slower now, it was 1400 hours, and the marines had been on the move for almost nine hours. The advance stopped and the marines rested up for thirty minutes while ammunition was brought forward to them. By 1500 hours the marines were on the move again. Information on the progress of 42 and 45 Commandos was non-existent, but the sound of heavy fire coming from their right flank suggested that the other units were keeping up with their advance.

As the marines of Rhodes's section cleared the fourth floor of one building, they burst into a room where a woman and three children were cowering in one corner. In the opposite corner stood a man with a rifle in his hands. One of the young marines went to shoot him, but Rhodes stopped him. Rhodes moved forward and took the rifle from the man who was standing in a puddle of his own urine and threw the rifle out of the window. The man crawled over to his wife and children, giving the marines a look of gratitude.

In another room the marines found ten rifles and a box of ammunition. They removed the bolts from the rifles and threw the ammunition and rifle bolts out of window of the front of the building and the rifles out of the back.

At 1600 hours the marines got to the Basra Bridge and linked up with the French marines. Rhodes was soon in conversation with the French marines and passed on the instructions from his troop commander. The CO of 40 Commando arrived and Rhodes was detailed to accompany him to see the French commander.

The two commanding officers greeted each other warmly, Rhodes translating as instructed. They were soon drinking coffee sitting around the table of office formerly occupied by an Egyptian official.

'And where did you learn to speak such good French?' asked the French commander.

Rhodes explained about his aunt and the influence of Helen Dupré.

The French officer said, 'Helen Dupré was close to you. I can tell by the way you spoke her name.'

Rhodes felt himself blush; the officer laughed, 'As close as that then, my young friend?'

When they left the headquarters three hours later, the CO of 40 Commando told Rhodes to stay with his adopted troop and thanked him for his help. With the light fading fast the marines moved forward almost to the edge of the Sweetwater Canal and dug in as best they could. With all ninety-four tanks ashore, 40 Commando had over twenty to boost their defensive position and as night fell they felt confident they could hold their positions if the Egyptians launched a counter-attack. The marines were issued with some ration packs and made themselves as comfortable as they could. They then took it in turns to eat and make tea in the shelter of the ruins behind them.

Rhodes had twenty marines in his section and one corporal and he had placed them in groups of three across the thirty-yard front assigned to them. As two in each group rested, one would stay awake and alert. At midnight some mortars opened up from the Egyptian positions, but they went well over the marines' heads and landed in the beach area. It then went quiet for the rest of the night. Just before dawn, the troop commander came over to Rhodes and told him that there was a suggestion from General Stockwell's headquarters that a ceasefire had been arranged and no further advances were to be made until further orders were given.

Major Bishop, the troop commander, said, 'I have a feeling this is as far as we are going, someone in London has got cold feet.'

By mid-morning it was apparent that there would be no

further advance made; 40 Commando withdrew and were replaced by the reserve parachute battalion. The marines were only a few hundred yards back from their forward positions, but were in the comparative comfort of the blocks of flats previously occupied by the Suez Canal pilots and their families.

The bonded warehouse had been bombed and the vast quantities of duty free spirit were available to all and sundry. Rhodes's section had been given a crate of Vat 69 whisky; they took four bottles down to the food dump by the beach where a grateful RASC sergeant gave them four extra boxes of rations.

Major Bishop called Rhodes over to him and said, 'We need to talk to the French battalion commander again. We are going to start a proper search of the buildings in our sector for arms and ammunition and we need his help.'

They made their way back to the French position, where a British paratroop officer was trying to communicate with the French and clearly getting very angry.

'These French bastards are just being fucking awkward,' he said.

Major Bishop smiled. 'Perhaps we can help, we fought alongside these men yesterday, and consider them our friends.'

He turned to Rhodes. 'Piss on this fire, Sergeant, and restore the status quo.'

Rhodes did his stuff; the French commander greeted him like an old friend, saying, 'Who is this pompous English arsehole?'

Rhodes explained that the officer was from the parachute regiment and that they were nearly as good as the Royal Marine commandos. Over the next hour Rhodes with Major Bishop's help managed to defuse the situation and with handshakes and salutes left the scene still as allies.

By dusk the marines, with the French marines' help, had searched most of the buildings in their immediate area. They had recovered a vast amount of arms and ammunition. Just before the light failed completely, Rhodes took four bottles of rescued Vat 69 whisky up to the paratroops' position, where he handed them over to the paratroop officer.

'Compliments of our French allies, sir.'

The officer looked at Rhodes then smiled. 'Thanks for your

help, Sergeant, I'll give all my men a tot of this tonight, it's much appreciated.'

Rhodes saluted and went back to his section.

That evening after the marines had eaten, they each had two tots of whisky. Suddenly the door of the room opened and a girl entered. She was wearing black stockings and panties and a black bra. She had blonde hair and looked gorgeous.

A collective gasp went round the room and hands reached out to grab her. A look of pure panic crossed her face and she dived for the door closely followed by the lust-crazed marines.

'It's fucking me!' cried the 'girl' as a hand grasped her panties. 'It's fucking me, you dumb bastards!' cried the voice of Marine Edger.

Later as the marines settled down for the night, Marine Edger now with his confidence restored said, 'Did I really fool you?'

All of the marines shook their heads. Marine Jake Thomas called over to Edger, 'There is a spare space over next to me, mate.'

'Thanks, Jake,' said Edger.

As he settled down next to Thomas, Jake put his arm round him, 'Put those black panties back on, love.' Edger gave a cry and fled the room with the laughter of his fellow marines in his ears.

A sure sign that things were returning to normal was the sight of an MP sergeant at the gate of the food store. He was trying without a great deal of success to confiscate crates of whisky which was the currency for extra rations and suffering the usual insults, such as, 'The fighting must be over if you fuckers have arrived.'

Each day the pile of captured weapons and ammunition grew, a solution had been found as to its disposal. LCTs were being loaded with the captured ordinance and taking it two miles out to sea and dumping it in deep water.

Major Baker had told Rhodes he could stay with 40 Commando as long as they needed him. This suited Rhodes as he still thought the ceasefire might be temporary. This was not the case and it soon became clear that the United Nations were coming in. Rhodes was asked to go on to the French hospital ship, the *Marseilles* as it had some British wounded aboard. There were eight on board, six marines and two paratroops. He helped with their documentation as they were all going to be taken to Gamil Airfield and flown to Cyprus within the next day or so. One of the French nurses was very attractive and made it plain to Rhodes that she liked him. Rhodes resisted the temptation, just. This made him think of Julie. He couldn't get back to her quickly enough.

It soon became crystal clear that the operation was over. The Egyptian population became increasingly unruly. Several mini riots started over the distribution of food and the British troops were becoming fed up with their untenable position.

The withdrawal of the paratroops and the marines of 40 and 45 Commandos had started with the latter returning to Malta and the paratroops leaving for Cyprus. 42 Commando were staying a few more days as were the Beach Unit. Rhodes found himself being used as a link with the French troops still remaining, a role he was quite happy to play. HMS *Forth* was being used as an accommodation ship and the remaining marines were giving up their temporary homes in the canal pilots' flats.

The last night in these flats saw a great deal of men and women's clothing being liberated. Rhodes had 'won' a couple of nice shirts, but left the women's underclothes and wigs to the more adventurous marines, who were unlikely to make the same mistake as Marine Edger.

The final evening of their stay in Egypt saw them polish off the last of their whisky. As Rhodes sat with a group of marines from 42 Commando, one of their sergeants, whom Rhodes had known in Malaya, was giving some of the younger marines the benefit of his vast experience with women.

'There I was,' he said, 'the only decent looking bloke in the bar and this bird sitting opposite me was a cracker. Looking at her I became as hard as a "chocolate frog" and I looked at her with love in my eyes and murder in my trousers. Christ, what a night!'

One of the young marines said, 'Did you shag her, Sergeant?'

The sergeant fixed the young marine with a steely stare. 'No, she turned out to be a fucking bloke!'

Rhodes looked at the sergeant. 'I thought you told me you only found that out in the morning.' The room erupted in laughter.

Two days later the remaining marines left Port Said. As they sailed past de Lesseps statue, they could see perched on his head a Green Beret, a reminder to the Egyptians that the marines had called.

It took five days to reach Grand Harbour. They arrived at midnight, but had to wait outside at anchor until 0900 hours the next morning. When they entered harbour a large crowd had gathered to welcome them home. Rhodes could just make out Julie and little Michael. An hour later he was ashore, and Julie was in his arms, with Michael seeking and gaining his attention.

Rhodes contacted the *Reggio* and the sergeant major told him to report back aboard in five days' time. As they took the bus up to Paola, Rhodes couldn't take his eyes off Julie. She looked stunning. She kissed him and whispered, 'You will have to wait till tonight, love.'

Rhodes smiled at her. 'I can wait; the main thing is I'm home.'

It was quite late when they finally got an excited Michael to bed. Thirty minutes later, after he had gone to sleep, Rhodes and Julie got into bed together. After a prolonged embrace Rhodes covered every inch of Julie's body with kisses; he missed nothing. He finally spread her legs apart and slowly entered her. Julie came alive and responded to his thrusts with enthusiasm. As the pace of their lovemaking grew Julie cried out, 'Now, Peter, now,' and with one final thrust Rhodes exploded inside her.

After a short rest Rhodes took her again, this time more slowly. As they climaxed, Julie bit his ear gently.

'Welcome home, love.'

They both drifted off into a deep sleep until at 0700 hours Michael woke up and got into bed with them.

Malta Respite

Things in Malta were returning to normal. 42 Commando had returned to the UK, 40 and 45 Commandos had now returned to Cyprus, while Jane and Bob had gone back to their bases in Germany.

Rhodes and Julie repeated the Christmas of the previous year, with Matron Mary and Hal Higgins spending Christmas Day with them. On Boxing Day they all went to Matron's flat and were told that she and Hal were planning to marry at Easter. It was a memorable Christmas.

In the New Year it got even better as Mrs Grey took Rhodes at his word and flew out to spend the week with them. Julie's mum saw much more of the island than she had before. With Rhodes busy on the *Reggio*, Gail Browning drove Julie, Michael and Mrs Grey to most of the interesting places. Michael was now old enough to enjoy the spooky catacombs that formed an underground labyrinth at Rabat, as well as the sandy beaches at Pretty Bay. When Mrs Grey flew home she knew that Rhodes and Julie would be home towards the end of June, when his two and a half years would be up.

Rhodes was also giving some thought to his next home posting. Captain David Pope had told Rhodes that his had already been decided and that his next appointment was as adjutant in the Royal Marine Barracks at Eastney.

In late January the *Reggio* sailed to Cyprus and anchored in Kyrenia Harbour, where they spent three weeks. Most of the time they used their landing craft to patrol the coastline, embarking marines from 45 Commando as boarding or landing parties. On a couple of occasions Rhodes went along and met up with Captain Pope again and was offered a chance to join the parade staff at Eastney Barracks when they both returned to the UK. Captain Pope assured Rhodes that he could arrange it and it would confirm his rank of sergeant as well as the chance to do a drill instructor's course.

When Rhodes returned to Malta and told Julie she was delighted and that night fully showed her pleasure with a storming performance in bed. In the morning Rhodes put on a show of pleading for mercy, with Julie suggesting his powers were on the wane. Only Michael demanding some attention saved her from a good seeing-to and, with a smile, she jumped out of bed to get their breakfast.

They still heard from Paul and Helen Dupré. In their latest letter, Helen had said Paul was having a few problems with his heart and had been diagnosed has having angina. In spite of this they were determined to stay in Malaya, Helen stating, 'We think of this as our real home.'

At Easter the wedding took place of Matron Mary and Hal Higgins. It was a great day, with the chapel at BMH Imtarfa packed to capacity. Rhodes saw many of his old friends from his Malaya days, with Major Baker giving the bride away and Captain Pope being the best man. Rhodes was the chief usher. That night the bride and groom sailed for Sicily on the *Star of Malta* for a week's honeymoon. One of the strangest wedding gifts was an electric hair clipper, with the message 'To help you find it'. Mary and Hal roared with laughter, Mary saying, 'I can assure you all, it doesn't need finding.'

The mysterious Lieutenant Commander Radcliffe suddenly reappeared and asked Rhodes if he fancied a few days in a hot place. Knowing that Radcliffe's 'few' days could mean weeks, he asked for more information.

'It's the Persian Gulf, old son.'

Radcliffe went on to say no more than two weeks and flying out and back.

That evening Rhodes told Julie that he might be going away for two weeks. Reluctantly she agreed, knowing that the home-coming was always memorable.

Three days later Lieutenant Commander Radcliffe, Rhodes and Marine James loaded all their diving gear on to a plane at RAF Luqua and three and a half hours later they landed in Cyprus. They spent the night there and at 0700 hours took off for Kuwait, landing there just before midday. Within two hours of landing they were aboard RFA Blue Ranger settling into their new accommodation and wondering what they were doing there.

The next day in a borrowed motor boat they anchored a hundred yards off the beach in a cove a few miles north of Kuwait City. All day they dived into the clear waters and charted rock formations and gradients. The clear water was a contrast to the filthy waters around Kuwait docks, where you could hardly see your hand in front of your face.

Over the next ten days they moved a few miles along the coast and on day twelve completed their survey. As before, Mick had completed a first-class chart of the area. Their light tans had now developed into a really dark hue and Mick told them they would never get into the European Club now.

On the fifteenth day they landed at RAF Luqua and by 1600 hours they had cleaned and stowed their equipment back on the *Reggio*. Lieutenant Commander Radcliffe arranged for them to have five days' leave and at 1700 hours Rhodes was knocking on his flat door.

When Julie opened the door she gave a little cry of joy and surprise.

'You are almost black, where have you been?'

Rhodes laughed. 'I can't say but there was a lot of sand.'

That night Rhodes made love to Julie with complete abandon, leaving her gasping.

'It is you?' she asked. 'Not an African stud?'

Rhodes pulled the sheet back down.

'See, it is me.'

Julie laughed. 'Oh yes, that little white willie is a dead giveaway.'

Towards the end of May, Major Baker sent for Rhodes.

'I'm delighted to confirm your promotion as permanent. Lieutenant Commander Radcliffe has been quite persuasive at the Admiralty and it will appear in Orders in the next couple of days. Well done.'

Rhodes was delighted and so was Julie.

'Special treat tonight,' she said. 'Fish and chips.'

In the first week of June, Rhodes was told that he and his family were flying home on the twenty-fifth, which gave them just under three weeks to make their leaving arrangements. Charlie Borg was sorry they were leaving. Gail Browning told them that she and her husband were going home in August, after extending their posting to three and a half years. The last few weeks were frantic with so many people to say goodbye to. Mary and Hal Higgins were also going home in December and they promised to keep in touch.

Home Again

At 0900 hours Rhodes, Julie and Michael took off from Luqua airfield. Michael was beside himself with excitement and once airborne sat on Rhodes's lap looking out of the window. They landed in Sardinia, then again in Lyon, finally arriving at Blackbush around 1600 hours.

They had decided to spend the night in London at the Union Jack Club, where they were given a family room. After a meal Michael fell fast asleep. The next morning they travelled on to Portsmouth, where Rhodes called in at the barracks and was given a leave chit and his pay.

By lunchtime they were at the cottage in Petersfield and into the welcoming arms of Mrs Grey. For the first week of his leave Rhodes did very little. He went to town on the garden and did a few jobs around the house. In the second week he completely repainted the outside of the cottage with a little help from Michael who 'borrowed' a paint brush and covered his legs and shoes in cream paint.

The following week they went down to Kent and spent the week on the farm. Michael was being hugged and kissed by all and sundry and loved it.

'He's just like his dad,' said Julie.

Mark and Linda still had not produced a child, but they were happy enough. Mark was running the farm and Linda was enjoying teaching French at school, which pleased her parents and Aunt Marie.

His former head teacher asked Rhodes if he would go back to his old school and give a talk on his life in the marines. With some reluctance he agreed. His appearance in uniform with still a very deep tan made him an instant hit with the female pupils and his talk on Malaya, Cyprus and Suez made him instantly popular with the boys. After a prolonged 'Question and Answer' session, which included many about the medals won in Korea and Malaya, the ordeal came to an end. After generous applause he left the stage where an admiring crowd of children surrounded him. He was rescued by the headmaster and taken to the staff room for tea and biscuits. With a feeling of relief he left the school and made his way back to the farm, vowing never to repeat the experience.

When they returned to Petersfield, Julie told her mother of the school talk. Mrs Grey pleaded with Rhodes to repeat the performance at her school. Rhodes had no option but to agree, but that night he told Julie that he was going to revenge himself on her for suggesting it. After his revenge, a contented Julie told him she was writing to every school in Hampshire offering his services.

His talk at Mrs Grey's school was as popular as the one in Kent and Rhodes had to admit he had enjoyed the experience. During his sixty days' leave they went back to Kent again. Rhodes took Julie and Michael to see June. The visit to his surprise was a great success and June was besotted with Michael and it was with some regret that it was time to leave. The leave seemed to go very quickly and then it was time to report back to Eastney Barracks.

Rhodes was made welcome in the sergeants' mess. He had his own room or cabin as it was called. His kit had arrived back from Malta and for the first two days Rhodes was kept busy cleaning and polishing to get it up to barrack standards. On the third day he was told to report to the drafting office. There were two postings for him, both connected, drill instructor's course and parade staff at Eastney, the second on completion of the first.

He was to go to ITCRM for his course starting the following Monday, and it was to last four weeks. Julie was not overjoyed that they would be apart again even for a few weeks, but the thought of at least eighteen months at Eastney placated her.

The journey down to Exeter and then on to Exmouth brought back memories to Rhodes of his recruit days, but at least he didn't have to carry his kit up the hill. He knew two of the other nine sergeants on the course and within hours they were hard at work learning their new skills.

The quartermaster sergeants or 'First Drill', as they were known in the corps, were first class; with the RSM looking on, they went through the complete drill manual in the first week.

They were taught company drill, which Rhodes had never heard of. This involved moving large formations of men on the parade ground. A lot to remember, but to his surprise Rhodes loved every minute of it, even the mistakes.

At times they were given recruit squads to drill under the watchful but helpful eye of their instructor. After two weeks they were given weekend leave and Rhodes hurried back to Petersfield to spend as much time with his family as he could. As they lay in bed that night Julie asked him what the course was all about. Rhodes explained about drill and posture on parade.

As he was talking, she suddenly placed her warm soft hand on his cock, saying, 'Well, that knows how to stand up straight.'

As Rhodes's hands began to get busy over Julie's naked body, she asked in a breathless voice, 'Is there a drill movement for this?'

There was a pause and Rhodes chanted, 'Over two three, in two three, out two three, wiggle two three, thrust two three, tremble two three… ahhhhhhh two three.'

A breathless Julie commented, 'Christ, two three.'

Back at ITCRM the drill instructor's course progressed. They practised some ceremonial drill that would be used perhaps once in a lifetime, Royal funerals, gun carriage and changing guard at coffin vigil. They took it in turns to perform the parade duties of the RSM at morning main parade under the very watchful eye of the RSM, who gave his opinion of their performance in the privacy of the parade office.

As the course came to an end, Rhodes wished it could have gone on for another two weeks. All of the course members were called in one at a time to hear the verdict from the 'First Drills' and the RSM. Rhodes was next to last in. When his name was called, he took a deep breath and marched in. A stern-faced RSM listened as the 'First Drill' read out his assessment. It was fair and surprisingly good. As they finished, the RSM added his comments, after which it was over.

In the mess that evening, the RSM told Rhodes that he would be pleased to have him on his parade staff at any time. As this RSM was the senior one in the corps, Rhodes was delighted. He was then asked if he knew RSM Higgins, Hairy Henry. Rhodes said he did and had been at his wedding and that 'Hal' was a family friend. They all burst out laughing, but it was good-natured and 'Hal' was liked and respected by all the senior staff.

Parade Ground Life

On his return to Eastney, Rhodes was thrust straight into his parade duties. His first drill session was to take fifteen young officers under training and in the RSM's words, 'To shake the young buggers up.' Rhodes did just that.

He stayed in barracks during the week and went home to the cottage and his family at weekends. To his surprise, on his first weekend home, Julie told him she wanted another baby. In bed that night she asked him if he thought he could manage that.

After a passionate ten minutes with an explosive finish, she said, 'That might have done it, very impressive.'

Rhodes smiled in the darkness. 'I'll give it another go in the morning, if you are that keen.'

Three months later Julie confirmed she was pregnant. Her mother was delighted, as was Rhodes.

A brother or sister for Michael; a complete family, thought Rhodes with satisfaction.

Mary and Hal Higgins were now home and he had been posted to the Royal Marine Commando School as RSM. Matron Mary was now going to be Matron at Plymouth Military Hospital. Mark and Linda had finally done the trick and Linda was now four months pregnant and Aunt Marie and Uncle Bill were delighted. Christmas came and went, along with a snowy new year and Julie now obviously starting to show. Michael was into everything and drawing on papers, books and walls, not always being appreciated by Julie or her mother.

In March Rhodes was detached to the naval college at Dartmouth for two months as their drill instructor had broken his leg. He made an instant impression by rewarding the young naval officers with an hour's extra drill each evening for a week. Feeling he was about as popular as smallpox, he was surprised to find that he was much admired. One of the naval instructors told him that an old friend, whose son was there under training, had written home and said, 'Our Royal Marine drill instructor is a real hero, twice decorated for gallantry, and a brilliant bloke, he really gives us some stick, but we love it.'

Rhodes felt flattered. He also taught drill to the Wren officers with no mercy given. Little did he know that in some of the young ladies lockers was his photograph, copied from the staff notice board, in the centre of a lipstick-drawn heart.

Rhodes managed to get home to Petersfield every two weeks. Julie was expecting the baby in August, so they made love slowly and carefully. Michael was curious about his mummy's 'bump' and would spend a few minutes every morning listening to the sounds it made.

The naval college requested Rhodes's tour be extended to cover the passing out parade and this was granted. He drilled the young officers, male and female, to a high standard and on their 'passing out' did themselves and Rhodes great credit.

When it was all over, he was invited to join them and their guests in the Great Hall. He lost count of the number of students who introduced him to their proud parents. It was a moving moment for Rhodes, one he was unlikely to forget.

The next day before the students left, each group presented Rhodes with a photograph of their class with Rhodes in the centre and signed by each of them.

On 14 August, a week after Rhodes had returned to Eastney Barracks, Julie gave birth to a daughter. Rhodes was allowed to see them about an hour after the birth; both were fine.

Julie said, 'We now have a complete family and the shutters are going up.' Rhodes put on a look of disappointment, which prompted Julie to say, 'Only kidding, love.'

After some discussion they decided to call their little girl Helen Mary Rhodes. Julie's mum was delighted as Helen was her second name, and Julie and Rhodes knew it would please Helen and Paul Dupré, as well as Mary and Hal Higgins. The arrival of a sister had not bothered Michael and he took a great deal of interest in the feeding and the nappy changing. What did concern him was she had no 'worm' with which to pee-pee. Rhodes tried to explain the difference between boys and girls.

'Don't bother,' said Julie, 'if he's like you he will soon find out.'

In September there was a Military Tattoo at Eastney Barracks and Rhodes was put in charge of the drill squad. After a lot of hard work, he thought they were very good indeed. The week of the tattoo came and there were four evening performances. Each night they maintained the high standard they had achieved. On the final night Julie and her mother came with the two children. Michael loved it, with the commando assault on the enemy village particularly enthralling him. Despite all the loud bangs and gunfire, he watched and cheered as the marines stormed and captured the enemy position.

When Rhodes marched the drill squad on, Michael shouted out, 'There's my daddy.' The fifteen-minute display went well. The final section when they fixed bayonets on the march and then fired a 'Feu de Joie' brought the large crowd to their feet. The last item in the programme was the Massed Bands of the Royal Marines. The display climaxed with Beating Retreat when all of the participants marched on at the end, filling the arena and receiving rapturous applause.

Rhodes met Julie and her mother in the drill shed afterwards where the participants and their family and friends could have a drink together. The adjutant, Captain David Pope, came over and met Julie; he reminded her that the last time they had met was in BMH Taiping. He made a fuss of Michael and baby Helen. He had a quick word with Rhodes and told him the commandant general of the Royal Marines, who had taken the salute that evening, was most impressed and sent his congratulations to all concerned.

Another face appeared. Much to Rhodes's surprise, Commander Radcliffe greeted Rhodes like an old friend and insisted on being introduced to Julie, Mrs Grey and the two children. Rhodes congratulated him on his promotion.

'Oh that,' said the commander, 'that's to keep my mouth shut. If you get bored, old son, give me a ring at the Admiralty, I'll brighten your day, don't forget.'

He then said his goodbyes and left.

'Who was that?' said Julie. 'I think he is a very dangerous man, charming but sinister.'

Rhodes laughed, 'You could be right, I think he's a spook.'

Barrack life has a certain tedium and as much as Rhodes enjoyed the parade side of marine life, he did at times wish for something more exciting. It was now December and he had been back in the UK for eighteen months and in six months' time he would expect to do another overseas tour. The rules had recently changed on the time spent abroad. If you were married and took your wife with you, it was still two and a half years. But if the tour was unaccompanied, it was only eighteen months. Rhodes did not want to drag his two children from school to school, so it would be best that Julie and the children stayed in Petersfield when he went abroad next. He decided to discuss it with Julie at an opportune time, which was in bed that night, after a passionate encounter. To his surprise Julie thought the idea had merit. Though she would rather be with him and would miss him terribly, it would not be for just that.

After Christmas leave, Captain Pope sent for him and informed Rhodes that he was leaving the post of adjutant in May. He asked Rhodes if he wanted to get back to the commando brigade. Rhodes said he did and after some discussion Captain Pope said he would try to arrange it.

Rhodes was loaned again to the naval college at Dartmouth for March and April, and while he was there he decided to ring Commander Radcliffe at the Admiralty. To his disappointment he was not there. The woman whom he spoke to told him she would tell the commander he had called.

Rhodes got on with his work; the young officers enjoyed the parade side, and worked hard for him. He was surprised to receive a telephone call from the commander at 2200 hours.

'Just got back, old son. Getting bored, are we?'

Rhodes said he was, but in any case he would be posted overseas in May or June.

To his surprise the commander said, 'Yes, that's what David Pope said, I'll be in touch shortly,' then he rang off.

Two days later, the commander rang again.

'It's all fixed, you fly out to Malta on the first of May, temporarily attached to Brigade HQ at St Patrick's Barracks, see you then,' and rang off.

Well, thought Rhodes, that's fucking done it.

Rhodes managed to get home once a fortnight, but he decided to not tell Julie the news until he had finished at Dartmouth; why spoil the weekends!

He completed his duties at Dartmouth on 10 April and returned to Portsmouth. The RSM saw him as soon as he set foot in the barracks and handed him his posting notice.

'I'm sorry to lose you, Sergeant, your efforts have been much appreciated. I wish you the best of luck,' he said and shook Rhodes's hand.

Rhodes started his embarkation leave straight away and when he got to Petersfield he told Julie of his posting. She kissed him. 'It's no surprise Peter, I wish I was going with you but we must think of the children.' Mrs Grey told him not to worry about anything while he was away, everything would be fine.

His leave passed quickly. Julie was dreading his departure and their last night was one of high passion, with an encore just before the alarm went off.

'Saved by the bell,' said Julie, then hugged him to her.

Rhodes said a tender goodbye to them all and took the train into Portsmouth, collected his kit and made his way to London. Rhodes had arranged to meet Captain Pope at Waterloo Station where they had a coffee together and then made their way to Blackbush airfield.

Omani Defence Force

Their RAF plane took off at 1400 hours, had a short stop in Nice to refuel and then on to Malta. They landed at Luqua at 2100 hours. A 15 cwt truck was waiting for them. The marine driver saluted Captain Pope very smartly and loaded their baggage for them. Twenty minutes later he dropped Captain Pope off at the officers' mess in St Patrick's Barracks, then Rhodes at the sergeants' mess. Within the hour Rhodes was fast asleep, and missing Julie and the children already.

Rhodes was up by 0600 hours. He shaved and showered, then dressed in freshly pressed khaki drill and went for breakfast. He reported to the RSM's office at 0815 hours, where he received a friendly greeting and the surprising news that he was not staying in Malta. That was as much as the RSM was prepared to say, except that Rhodes was to report to the intelligence officer at 0900 hours.

When Rhodes presented himself five minutes early, a familiar voice greeted him. It was Commander Radcliffe. Captain Pope was sitting next to him with a satisfied smile on his face.

'Hope you didn't unpack, old boy, 'cause you are not staying here,' were Radcliffe's opening words.

Rhodes laughed. 'Why am I not surprised? My wife said you are charming but dangerous, how right she was.'

Commander Radcliffe smiled. 'Ah, the lovely Julie, you did yourself proud there, it's a good job I'm an officer and a gentleman.'

He took some papers from the desk and handed them to Rhodes. 'Sign at the bottom of the top two forms and then initial the amendments on the other one.'

Rhodes examined the forms, they were referring to the Arab States of Oman, and a six-month attachment to their defence forces.

'Well,' said Radcliffe, 'you said you were getting bored. I don't think you will find the next six months boring.'

He then explained to Rhodes and Captain Pope that they would fly to Cyprus the next day, then on to Oman via Kuwait. They had some equipment to draw from the brigade stores. When this was completed the commander told them to go and change into civilian clothes. He then drove them over to Marsascalla and treated them to lunch at The Hunters' Tower. After a splendid meal and two bottles of wine, they drove carefully back to the marines' barracks.

'I'll say goodbye here, you look after one another, and I'll see you back here in six months' time,' said the commander, and with a wave drove off. Captain Pope and Rhodes looked at one another.

'The last time I did an operation with you I was nearly killed,' said Captain Pope.

'Well,' said Rhodes, 'I was hit twice to your once.'

'Ah,' said Pope, 'but I'm an officer, we feel twice as much pain as ordinary marines.'

The next day they flew to Cyprus. It was uneventful and after refuelling they flew on to Kuwait, where they were to spend the night. Captain Pope took the opportunity to tell Rhodes about their new role. He explained that Royal Marine officers and senior NCOs had been attached to the Sultan of Oman's forces since 1957. Normally they spent two years there, but in their case it was to be six months. He would be taking charge of a company of Oman infantry and Rhodes would be a platoon commander in his company. The current trouble in Oman was caused by the Imam Ghabia and his brother Talib, who, aided by Egyptian money, were trying to overthrow the Sultan by attacking road convoys and raiding villages. Rhodes thought it sounded exciting, but where would they be going after their six months were up.

'Let's survive the six months first,' said Pope. 'We are replacing wounded personnel, as it is.'

Their take-off was delayed by a couple of hours due to an engine fault, so Rhodes took the opportunity to write a letter to Julie telling her some of the news, but not all of it. At last they were on their way and, as the light was beginning to fail, they landed at Oman in a small dust storm. They were driven to the army barracks and shown to their quarters, plain, but clean and cool. Rhodes was surprised to find himself eating in the officers' mess. He was introduced to the colonel, who was a large friendly man and a former Royal Marine major.

'You will fit in here, boy, and you will enjoy the experience,' said the colonel.

They were told later in the evening that they would spend two weeks in the field and a week in barracks, as in the past this had proved to be the most effective use of the colonel's resources.

In the morning Captain Pope was placed in charge of C-Company. Rhodes was to be in command of No. 1 Platoon, which consisted of thirty Omani infantry men.

Rhodes went to see his men straight away and took them on parade. He had three native NCOs to assist him. Language did not seem to be a problem and he was pleased with their appearance and attitude. He inspected their rifles, they were British No. 4s using .303 ammunition. He had three Bren guns as well as a two-inch mortar; all of the weapons were clean and not over-oiled.

The whole company were paraded for Captain Pope. He spoke for ten minutes and when he had finished his company gave him polite applause.

The colonel took the two marines to one side later that day and told them their Green Berets and marine cap badges should not be worn. In their place they were to wear an Arab headdress in barracks, with the Omani crossed sabres and star cap badge, in the field the headdress would be khaki jungle-style hats.

Over the next few days they were shown their area of operations. It was a bleak unfriendly landscape, rock and sand and hills that led up to mountains. When in the field the companies occupied small forts which were easily defended at night. During the day, apart from patrolling the hills, they would man road blocks in 'sangars' (a rock-walled defensive position). The commando brigade had recently been issued with the new rifle, the SLR, or self-loading rifle, and Radcliffe had promised to send half a dozen to the Omani defence force. Captain Pope and Rhodes were considering if this was a good idea, given the attraction these weapons would have to local tribesmen, but they decided not to lose sleep over it, but just wait and see if the weapons ever arrived.

On Monday morning C-Company left for two weeks' deployment. Rhodes was impressed with the attitude of his platoon, they were a cheery bunch, in many ways very much like marines only, of course, a slightly different colour.

As soon as their transport had dropped them off, Captain Pope led them into the hills, with Rhodes's platoon leading, all in single file and well spread out. After an hour they took a ten-minute break. Rhodes was pleased to see that his men did not take more than a mouthful from their water bottles, the water had to last the day. Soon after they resumed their march, a volley of rifle fire struck the ground amongst the leading men of his platoon.

Rhodes shouted, 'Do not fire unless you have a target.'

His men had all gone to ground, crawling to shelter in the rocks around them. Rhodes called up his mortar section and set them up behind a large outcrop of boulders. Captain Pope crawled up alongside him.

'Did you see where the shots came from?'

'No,' said Rhodes, 'I'm waiting for a repeat performance, then we can give them a taste of the two-inch mortar.'

'Good,' said Pope, 'I'll get the other two platoons ready for some fire and movement.'

A few minutes later the tribesmen lost patience and fired again. This time their positions were spotted. Rhodes gave the mortar team the range and told them to fire three HE bombs. The first was short but the next two bombs were close to where the shots had come from.

The mortar bomb is very effective in rocky terrain. As it lands it does not penetrate the hard ground so the shrapnel effect is enhanced as well as hurling rock splinters in all directions. Captain Pope's company moved forward, with two and three platoons moving on the left and right flanks, and Rhodes's platoon taking the centre. No more shots came their way, so they made their way to the top of the hill and rested on the crest. They could find no evidence of the tribesmen; they had even collected up the empty cartridge cases.

One of the other platoon commanders had told Rhodes that

the hill tribes even had their own little munitions factories in some of the villages, with the women doing all the work of course. That night C-Company sheltered in one of the old forts, which in most cases were at least a hundred years old. The nights were bitterly cold in the hills, a complete contrast to the day temperatures. The next day one of the platoons stayed in the fort, while the other two split to search other parts of their area. Rhodes took his platoon down a valley between two hills. They proceeded with care and kept out of the valley bottom because it provided little cover. After an hour they came across the remains of a fire; the site had been used recently as there was still some heat left in the fire's remains.

Rhodes spread his men well out, and they moved up the hill slope towards some caves they could see near the crest. As they crept nearer they could smell the sweet sickly odour of rotting flesh. Whatever it was it was in one of the caves. Rhodes took two of his men to investigate, leaving two corporals to put the men in a defensive posture. They followed the appalling smell into one of the caves. Three bodies lay in front of them, two young men and a woman; their clothing had been removed.

The two men had massive injuries to their heads, one head was almost detached from its body. The woman had been quite young, and judging by the position of her body, with the legs spread wide, she had provided the killers with some 'entertainment' before they had killed her by cutting her throat.

Rhodes called the senior of his two corporals to him, and asked where did he think the dead people had come from.

'Oh, a local village, sir. The tribesmen had decided to teach the villagers a lesson, it is a common occurrence.'

Rhodes had the bodies removed from the cave and, as the ground was so hard, they were laid out side by side, their limbs were straightened to give them some dignity, then they were covered with stones to give the bodies some protection from the packs of wild dogs which roamed these parts.

The platoon then made their way back across the ridge and down almost to the valley floor the other side. It took some time for the smell of death to leave Rhodes's nostrils.

He thought to himself, Terrorists are the same the world over, their weapons are fear and intimidation. Bastards!

When they got back to the fort, Rhodes made his report to Captain Pope. They discussed the incident and looked at the maps to see where the nearest village was. It appeared to be about eight miles away. Captain Pope decided to pay it a visit the next day; with a full company it would be an impressive show of force and they might get some information.

In the morning, after a good breakfast, they set off at 0700 hours, hoping to complete most of the journey before it got too hot. It took them almost four hours to cover the eight miles over the hilly rock-strewn terrain. The village was a poor place, a ramshackle collection of fifteen huts, not many animals, but it had a well, and that fact alone made it an important place. With the aid of the three corporals, they spoke to the village father. He was reluctant to talk to them until the discovery of the three bodies was mentioned. As one of the corporals described to him what they had found, the old man's eyes blazed with anger; he rose abruptly and walked a few paces from them and stood looking into the distance. After a few minutes he returned and sat down. He then spoke to the corporal for five minutes, barely pausing to take breath. As he finished, he turned abruptly and went into his hut.

The excited corporal blurted out what the old man had said, 'The bodies were of his daughter and two sons. The tribesmen had taken them as a punishment to the village for failing to provide them with food. They said they would be back tonight or tomorrow, for food and water.'

Captain Pope indicated they should leave at once; after they had put a mile or so between themselves and the village, they halted. Captain Pope then explained his plan, Rhodes's platoon would wait here until it was dark, and then make their way back to the village, stopping two hundred yards short. If the tribesmen appeared they were to get as close as they could, move two of their three sections to the flanks, then alert the tribesmen by moving forward noisily and let the flanking sections engage the tribesmen as they left the village. Captain Pope with the other two platoons would move back to within two miles of the village and spread a wide ambush in case the tribesmen came back their way.

As soon as it was dark, Rhodes moved his platoon back towards the village. They moved carefully over the rocky ground as silently as possible. A few fires were burning in the village and they could hear the low murmur of conversation, nothing had disturbed the occupants so far. When they were about a hundred yards away, they lay still, their bodies flat against the cold hard ground. After two hours, they were all cold and stiff. Rhodes thought he would give it another hour then move back, if only to exercise their bodies.

Suddenly a dog barked, and this was followed by a yelp. They could tell the villagers were alarmed as their voices were raised in protest. Rhodes moved two of his sections round to the right flank. After two minutes he began to move forward. As his sections moved to within twenty yards of the village a woman screamed. The sound was like a bugle call to charge, and Rhodes and his men swept into the village. Shots were fired at them but his section held their fire until they were amongst them. Rhodes smashed a black-clad figure to the ground with a vicious butt stroke from his rifle; then, as a shot was fired at him, he fired into a kneeling figure. The rest of his men were also engaged.

To his right he could hear his flanking sections getting involved, two Bren guns adding to the rising din. Suddenly, it stopped and went almost quiet apart for the moaning of the wounded.

The villagers lit reed torches and Rhodes was able to make some sense of the situation. Two of his men were wounded and were being given treatment by their colleagues. His flanking section's corporals reported no injuries, but five enemy were killed as they ran from the village.

In the vicinity of the huts two bodies lay, one was the man Rhodes had struck with his rifle, his jaw was smashed but he was alive. The women of the village were hovering around him. His terrified eyes mirrored their intent. Rhodes was about to interfere when he remembered the spread limbs of the woman they had found in the cave. He moved away. There was a rush of bodies and a terrible gurgling scream, which died away as the man's body was hacked to pieces.

As the sky lightened to herald the approach of dawn, Rhodes mustered his men and formed a defensive perimeter. He visited his two wounded men, one had been hit in the arm and could walk, the other had a wound to his leg which had broken the bone. He spoke to every man in his platoon telling them how proud he was of their actions, lots of smiles from them all, and the usual post-action euphoria.

An hour after dawn Captain Pope arrived with the rest of the company. He was delighted with the result of their plans and when he saw the dismembered body, he merely raised an eyebrow. The villagers had gone very quiet and the head man thanked Captain Pope for his help but told the corporal, who was translating, that the tribesmen would take a terrible revenge on the village.

Hill Fort

Captain Pope called his platoon commanders and their NCOs together for an 'O' Group. They discussed the position of the villagers and the threat of retaliation by the tribesmen. They all agreed that if they abandoned the village to their fate, the prospect of other villagers giving them information was zero.

It was then decided by Captain Pope that a small defensive position be established on the hill overlooking the village, manned by a platoon. Rhodes suggested his platoon, as they had struck up some relationship with the villagers and so it was agreed. Supplies were a problem and particularly water. The well in the village would be fine for washing and could be all right for cooking but not for drinking. Over the radio drinking water and food were ordered. They would be delivered to the fort by road with an armed escort within two hours. Captain Pope told Rhodes the other platoons would hand over their food and water, then early the next day they would return with water and rations to last them for a week.

The rest of the company then left taking with them the two wounded soldiers. One of the corporals in Rhodes's platoon explained to the village elder that they would be staying on the hill above the village for at least a week. This brought a big smile to the old man's face and he excitedly explained the news to the rest of his village. Rhodes took his platoon to the top of the hill and drew with his bayonet the outline of their defensive position in the stony soil. With two men standing guard, they spent the next four hours building a perimeter wall three feet high around their position. The women and the children of the village helped by collecting rocks. By the end of the four hours a substantial sangar had been constructed and, being on the top of the hill, they could not be fired upon from above. The triangle shape of their position meant the platoon's three sections each manned a side, with the mortar team in the centre with Rhodes.

It had been quite cloudy during the day, giving them some respite from the hot sun. As night fell the sky cleared and by 2100 hours it was a bright moonlight night. Rhodes set out three sentries, one in front of each section; he changed them every hour. He and his three NCOs, did an hour each inside the sangar to make sure the sentries were changed each hour.

It turned out to be a quiet night. Just before dawn, Rhodes took one section and did a sweep around the village out to a distance of two hundred yards. After they had breakfast, using the last of the food and most of their water to make tea, Rhodes gave the platoon ten minutes' physical exercise. His men were surprisingly uncoordinated, arms raising forwards sideways and upwards was beyond them, but it made them laugh, and that had to be good for morale, in any case their fitness was not in doubt.

For most of the morning Rhodes kept his men busy. One section was sent out to the south to patrol for two hours, one hour out one hour back, one of the other sections did the same to the north. The remaining section improved the sangar walls, making them as solid as possible. Just before noon Captain Pope and the rest of the company arrived with their supplies and the news that the colonel was delighted with their success. The position on the hill was to be manned for at least the next three months. The two sections Rhodes had sent out returned shortly after Captain Pope's arrival, they had nothing to report.

The rest of the week was uneventful. Each day Rhodes had the sangar improved, it now was looking quite formidable and had an air of permanence about it. He had managed to get some white paint sent up with the stores and placed range markers around his position at two, three and four hundred yards, painted white they even showed up in the moonlight. His two-inch mortar team had constructed their own sangar just outside the main one, with aiming marks painted on the sides.

After they had been in the field a week, Rhodes handed his sangar over to one of the other platoons of C-Company, and returned to Captain Pope's position. He was just in time as they were just off to investigate the stopping and looting of two civilian lorries, which had happened about ten miles away.

Two lorries and an armoured car took them to the scene of the latest outrage. They found the two trucks burning by the side of the road. The two drivers were unhurt, though shocked by the experience, so they were taken in the armoured car to their depot in Oman. The lorries' contents were flour and dried fruit, some had been taken but most of it was just burned. Captain Pope lost no time in mounting a pursuit, but the direction the tribesman had taken was towards the mountains, and they had a two-hour start.

It was now 1400 hours, and the two platoons of C-Company found the going difficult over the rocky and steadily rising ground; the terrain was an ambushers' dream. In view of this the progress was cautious and by nightfall there was no evidence of the tribesmen. It was a bitterly cold night and the men huddled together for warmth.

As soon as it was light enough to move, the company made their way further into the mountains. After an hour they stopped and had breakfast. The limit of their pursuit would be midday as they had no rations to support them beyond that day. Shortly before 1100 hours, they came under fire from two or three rifles. No one had been hit, and they continued their advance in a well-spaced extended line. They pushed on until 1300 hours, they would go no further and after a short break they began to retrace their footsteps.

They got back to the road just as the light was beginning to fade and cautiously made their way to their base at the fort. With the fresh supplies there, a substantial meal was prepared, and with full bellies, Captain Pope sat down with Rhodes and the other platoon commander and reviewed the day. They all agreed that the few shots fired at them was a ruse to encourage them to launch an assault on that position. Once they were close enough, the whole party of tribesmen would have engaged them. Later that evening Rhodes and David Pope had a long chat together and shared a mug of tea. They decided this short tour was to be no picnic and the enemy was a disciplined ruthless opponent who deserved some respect.

In the morning, a radio check was made with the hilltop sangar. Nothing to report there. It was a similar story from headquarters. Over the last four days of their two-week stint, the company patrolled in section strength in order to cover as much of their area as possible. When they were relieved on the fifteenth day, their departure for headquarters was delayed as they waited for their sangar platoon to return. Two hours later they were back in their more comfortable barrack surrounds.

The old routine of 'clean your weapons then yourselves' applied and when Rhodes went in for dinner that evening the company and its equipment were shining like a new pin. The colonel was in good form and was delighted with the progress of Pope's company. After dinner he told Captain Pope and Rhodes his game plan.

'Don't let the bastards get away with anything. Always respond. Be as ruthless as they are. Forget the Geneva Convention, it doesn't apply here.'

As they digested his remarks he added, 'You are invited to a bash at the British Embassy in Oman tomorrow night, at least you can have a drink there.'

The next day a large crate arrived for Captain Pope, it contained ten new self-loading rifles, properly known as the FN. There were also a thousand rounds of the 7.62 mm ammunition and twenty spare magazines. There was a note inside from Commander Radcliffe which said, 'A few new toys for you to play with, God bless, Love Mick.'

For the next two hours Captain Pope and Rhodes, having studied the manual Radcliffe had included, stripped and reassembled the rifles until they were comfortable with the new weapons. The rifles weighed about ten pounds and the magazine held twenty rounds and was semi-automatic. The colonel, on seeing their 'new toys', was delighted.

'I take it one is for me?' he said with a smile.

'Of course, Colonel,' said Pope, 'three to each company, we must get them zeroed in.'

That evening they attended the bash at the British Embassy. Rhodes had four letters from Julie to respond to, but was determined to enjoy the evening. They were a surprisingly friendly crowd, not quite what Rhodes had expected. One of the female secretaries came up to him.

'Where did you spring from?' she said.

Rhodes explained his role in Oman, and that he was only there for six months.

'I'll get you another drink,' she said.

As the evening went on Rhodes was conscious of how attractive the girl was. She had already asked him if he was married; he needed to get away from her. David Pope called him over.

'There is a French military adviser here who doesn't speak English, help him out, Peter?'

Rhodes made his apologies to the girl, went over to the French officer and introduced himself. As they conversed in French, the relief on the officer's face was obvious and for the rest of the evening they kept each other company. When it was time to go the girl came over to Rhodes.

'I expect we will meet again, I'm Rita, I understand you are Peter, a gallant Royal Marine who speaks beautiful French.' Her lips brushed Rhodes's cheek.

'Goodbye for now,' she said.

When Rhodes got back to his room he put the evening's events out of his mind and wrote to Julie. He told her some of what had happened to him since his arrival in Oman but not all; he had no wish to upset her unduly. He was so engrossed in his letters he lost track of time and was surprised to see it was 0200 hours, well past his bedtime.

The next morning, they took their new rifles down the range and zeroed them in. Rhodes was pleased with his, it had a good feel to it and it appeared accurate. Rhodes and Captain Pope issued one to each company commander and two for each platoon commander to fight over.

Rhodes had also had a letter from Paul and Helen Dupré. Things were improving in Malaya and terrorist activity was declining. Both were well. Paul's angina was under control, as long as he took things steady. Helen said she would love to see them all again, as they had been such good friends. Rhodes thought of Helen and their nights in Ipoh together. Well, he thought, that was before I became a respectable married man. The rest of their week in camp passed quickly, a couple of visits to the swimming pool and a game of tennis and then they were preparing for their two weeks in the field.

On the Monday, the company deployed to the fort, with Rhodes's section once again spending three days in the sangar overlooking the village. The last section who had occupied it had improved the sanitary arrangements, with a toilet box over a length of drain pipe which led at an angle to a deep crevice in the rocks.

For three weeks now the tribesmen had left the village in peace, but Rhodes thought it would be just a matter of time before they were attacked again. Two nights later, just after sunset one of the villagers came up to the sangar; he was lucky that he was recognised. He told them that his cousin had visited that day, but had refused to stay the night, which was most unusual, as he had always stayed over before. Rhodes sent him back to the village, assuring him all would be well. Then Rhodes, leaving one section to guard the sangar, took the other two sections around the back of the village. They took up their ambush positions and waited. The ground was hard and it was quite chilly, but Rhodes resigned himself to an uncomfortable night.

After they had been there for almost four hours, a slight sound brought them instantly alert. Another noise to their right front and each man in the section eased off the safety catch on his rifle. Suddenly a line of figures seemed to rise out of the ground in front of them. Rhodes shouted, 'Fire,' and a blast of rifle fire tore into the ranks of the tribesmen. The next few minutes seemed like hours as the two forces clashed at close quarters.

Rhodes emptied his twenty-round magazine and then used his rifle as a club as neither side would yield an inch. The two-inch mortar in the sangar fired a parachute flare, lighting up the scene. This gave the advantage to Rhodes's men and they forced the tribesmen to give ground. As the tribesmen started to withdraw the mortar fired three rounds of high explosive into their midst and another parachute flare, then it was all over.

Rhodes mustered his men. He had two killed and four wounded, they stayed where they were until daylight, giving first aid to his wounded. As the first signs of dawn appeared in the sky Rhodes and his men moved forward to see what damage they had inflicted on their attackers. Fifteen bodies lay in front of them and a further four lay some hundred yards away as a result of the mortar rounds. The villagers were coming up the slope towards them, smiling and laughing; this ceased when they saw that two of their protectors were dead. The women were in tears as the two bodies were carried to the sangar wrapped in their groundsheets. Some shouts came from the village as a wounded tribesman was found. Rhodes shut his ears as the man's screams filled the air, then it was over and another life had gone.

By noon Captain Pope was with them and the dead and wounded were on their way back to barracks. Rhodes estimated that they had been attacked by a force of at least forty and there were most likely more wounded amongst those who had escaped. He knew that any tribesman who was wounded got little sympathy from his fellows if he slowed them down, and death was his reward for failing to stay healthy.

The villagers showed their appreciation to Rhodes's men by killing and roasting a goat and presenting it to their saviours. The rest of the week passed quietly and Rhodes was not sorry when he was relieved and rejoined the company back at the fort. The second week passed without any sign of terrorist activity – Captain Pope and Rhodes tended to refer to the tribesmen as terrorists, a habit from their days in Malaya.

Tennis and Temptation

Back in barracks Rhodes was surprised to receive a visit from Rita, the girl he had met at the British Embassy. She told him they were playing tennis at 1900 hours against the military attaché and his wife.

'You do play, don't you?' she asked.

Rhodes said he did and with misgivings accompanied Rita to the embassy in Oman. As Rita drove them the five miles into Oman, Rhodes was very conscious how very attractive she was. Her cream-coloured skirt seemed to have crept up her legs since the journey had started. Her constant chatter was irritating, but it took his mind off her physical presence. On arrival at the British Embassy Rita went to get changed in her room, while Rhodes walked out to the tennis courts and changed in the men's room. The military attaché and his wife were already on the tennis court. Rhodes introduced himself to them and they stood talking until Rita made her appearance. She was wearing the shortest pair of shorts Rhodes had ever seen and a tight sports top which showed off her firm breasts unencumbered by a brassiere. Rhodes heard Jim, the military attaché, say, 'Christ,' and Molly, his wife, give an annoyed snort.

When the game began Rhodes quickly realised this was not a friendly encounter. Rita was a good player and very quick at the net. Rhodes was more of a serve-and-volley man and he and Rita won the first two games to love. The match lasted about an hour, Rita and Rhodes winning two sets to one.

The two women went back into the embassy to shower and change, while Rhodes and Jim showered in the men's changing room. Jim was very pleasant and told Rhodes about life in the embassy, in particular he mentioned Rita.

'She is after a husband, Peter, so watch your step, the fact that you are married means nothing to her, so be careful.'

Rhodes thanked him for the advice. They made general conversation until the girls reappeared, then they all went into the embassy for a drink. At 2200 hours Rhodes made his excuses and said goodbye to Jim and Molly. Rita followed him down to the gates.

'Don't go yet, Peter, we could go to a club in town.'

Rhodes took her hand. 'I'm a very happily married man, with a lovely wife and two gorgeous children. I'm flattered by your interest in me but it won't work.'

He kissed her hand and left. As Rita watched him go she smiled, and said to herself, You won't get away that easily, Peter Rhodes.

The next week Rhodes was dispatched into the hills with his platoon. They took five days' rations and two mules to carry the extra water. The routine for patrolling the foothills of the mountains was now established; an early start and a two-hour rest period between noon and 1400 hours. His platoon was vastly experienced in the mountain conditions. Rhodes took the advice that his section commanders offered and as a result the morale of his men was high.

On the third day, while resting up at noon, they saw a body of men moving towards them, about twenty in number. Rhodes placed his men in a defensive position and awaited the tribesmen's arrival. After thirty minutes nothing had happened. Rhodes took one of his corporals with him and had a good look around the slopes to his rear. He could just see the last of the tribesmen disappearing over the ridge to his rear. For the rest of that day Rhodes retraced his footsteps, without any sign of the tribesmen; it was time to start back anyway. That night Rhodes took great care in deploying his men, having two sentries alert in each of his three sections throughout the night.

Rhodes's platoon rejoined the rest of the company at noon on day six; he told Captain Pope of their sighting; the rest of the company had seen nothing, it was quiet, too quiet. The next morning they heard from the colonel that a convoy of lorries had been ambushed between Muscat and Oman. Leaving one section to guard the village they had promised to protect, the rest of the company spent the next three weeks guarding convoys using the coast road between Muscat and Oman.

Rhodes saw Rita a couple of times. She made it plain to him she was available, but Rhodes resisted her charms, just. A week later he saw her with one of the other company commanders who had only just arrived, strangely enough he felt a pang of jealousy.

The time had gone quickly for Rhodes and Captain Pope. They had just two weeks of their six-month tour left and they were already wondering where they would spend the next twelve months. David Pope was engaged to be married and had been promised he would be back in the UK by Christmas 1960 when the happy event would take place. The sangar on the hill overlooking the small village was now an established and permanently manned post, and as a result the village had doubled in size, its residents comfortable in the safety of the hill fort. A party was given at the barracks to give Rhodes and David Pope a good send-off. It was a happy occasion with lots of laughter and leg pulling; Rita and her new boyfriend were there. She came up to him and gave him a farewell kiss.

'You don't know what you are missing,' she said.

'Oh, but I do,' said Rhodes, 'but it wasn't to be.'

On their last day, Captain Pope formed his company up on parade and said goodbye, shaking hands with every man. Rhodes did the same with his platoon, taking the opportunity to speak to every man, it was a sad day. As they left the barracks for the airport the next day, they drove through the whole garrison who waved them farewell. Rhodes couldn't speak and tears ran down his cheeks. He glanced over to David Pope who was in a worst state than he was.

As the plane took off Rhodes looked down on the small country that had been his home for the last six months, a barren parched land, but the people were the salt of the earth. They landed in Kuwait a few hours later, refuelled and flew on to Cyprus where they spent the night. In the morning, at 1000 hours, they took off for Malta. They broke their journey at Benghazi and dropped off some army personnel. They then flew on to Malta and by 1700 hours were back in St Andrew's Barracks.

Christmas and Another Move

It was now 22 December and Brigade HQ were preparing for Christmas. Rhodes and Captain Pope didn't seem to belong to anyone. Captain Pope had a phone call instructing him and Sergeant Rhodes to attend a meeting in the Hotel Phoenicia at 1000 hours the next day.

Funny place for a meeting, thought Rhodes, wondering who was behind it.

As instructed they made their way to the Hotel Phoenicia. On arrival the receptionist gave them each a room key, they were on different floors. Rhodes went to his room; as he opened the door he smelt a familiar perfume and then a figure rushed into his arms, it was Julie. When he stopped kissing her, they sat on the bed together and Julie told him the full story.

Commander Radcliffe had phoned her at the cottage and asked if she could leave the children with her mother and fly out to Malta for Christmas. He told her he would arrange the flight through the Ministry of Defence. She had agreed of course and her mother was delighted to be left in charge of the children.

'So here I am,' said Julie. 'I had a companion on the flight out, it was David Pope's fiancée, Becky Travers. We got on really well. Mick Radcliffe asked her if they required separate rooms and she said, "Certainly not, we are getting married next year anyway."'

At that moment the phone went. It was David Pope.

'I'm getting a taxi to go up to the barracks to get some extra clothing, do you want to come?'

Rhodes agreed and they raced off to St Andrew's for a change of clothes.

Rhodes managed to keep his hands off Julie until 2200 hours that night. They had dinner with David and Becky and then all of them decided they would have an early night. Julie came out of the bathroom with nothing on.

'Didn't seem much point in putting on a nightdress,' she said.

Rhodes smothered her with kisses. He caressed her body, dwelling over her breasts, then moved to the tops of her legs. As he kissed the inside of her thighs, she spread her legs for him and he slid into her; she gasped as he pushed himself fully home. Slowly they made love, he savoured every movement, then as the pace increased so did their breathing. Then in a sudden rush they came together.

'Well, that was worth the flight out,' said Julie with a giggle. 'And you are so brown, you didn't get that tan in Malta.'

Rhodes explained where they had been for the last six months.

'Never heard of it,' said Julie. 'Come here and explain yourself.'

As she said that she grasped his penis; as usual it stiffened for her.

'Well, that's still nicely disciplined,' she said, sitting astride Rhodes and riding him to a stirring finish.

When the girls flew back to England a week later they all agreed it had been the best Christmas ever. On the last night they had drunk to Mick Radcliffe's health.

'To Mick, wherever he is.'

David Pope and Rhodes returned to St Andrew's Barracks. The next day Commander Radcliffe arrived and took them both out to lunch at the Hunters' Tower.

'Whenever we come here with you we finish up being shot at,' said David Pope.

'How ungrateful,' said the commander. 'And what about my Christmas presents, don't say you didn't enjoy the company of your lovely ladies?'

They both offered their thanks and admitted it had been a wonderful Christmas.

'And all I ask,' said the commander, 'is that you shed, perhaps, a few drops of blood for your country.'

'And where do we shed these few drops?' asked Pope and Rhodes together.

'Kuwait, old things, just for a couple of months, and I'm coming with you,' said the commander.

Two days later they flew to Cyprus and then on to Kuwait. The commander seemed to know everyone of any importance and they were soon in their air-conditioned quarters. The commander explained what he wanted from them over the next couple of months.

'Assume this country is to be attacked by a neighbouring Arab state. Forget Saudi Arabia, that leaves Iran and Iraq. I want you to have a look round and put together a plan of "Defence in Depth", using easily moved UK forces like the Marine Commando Brigade and the Parachute Regiment.'

After a cold drink he went on, 'You both have spent the last six months operating in a very hot country similar to this one. Use that experience to help you develop some ideas. We start tomorrow.'

Over the next few days they covered a lot of ground, getting to know the area over which they would be expected to operate. The deepest they went into Kuwait was about forty miles and they took a look at the Mutla Ridge, which was about four hundred feet above sea level. A good observation post where any Iraqi armoured advance could be seen miles away.

Commander Radcliffe had good intelligence on what resources a defending force would have available, planes, tanks, artillery and anti-tank weapons. The desert itself could be used in terms of trenches and tank traps. The biggest factor would be the surprise element. Rhodes thought any troops brought in should be issued with ten empty sand bags each, once in position they could quickly fill up the sand bags and construct either a single defensive position or pool them together for a section strong point. After a couple of weeks they had drawn up a detailed plan, showing fall back positions from twenty miles from Kuwait to ten miles from the city boundaries. When this was shown to the Kuwait Defence Force they insisted it be referred to as plan 'A' and that a plan 'B' and a plan 'C' also be required.

Commander Radcliffe was not overjoyed at extending his stay and that evening said to Captain Pope and Rhodes, 'I'm off in the morning, I'll leave you to finish off. Plan "A" is the key, plans "B" and "C" will be to accommodate either a larger response force, or a slower build-up.'

Captain Pope nodded his agreement and Commander Radcliffe said his goodbyes to them both and left for the airport.

Over the next two weeks they carried out a final survey of the ground over which an assault would be made. The final plans were presented to the Kuwait garrison commander who merely glanced at the three documents and thanked them for their efforts. As they left his headquarters they wondered if it had all been worth the effort; only time would tell.

Two days later they left for Malta with a stopover in Cyprus. When they finally arrived in Malta they made their way to their respective messes and settled back in to barrack routine. Rhodes answered Julie's letters, thinking to himself, Just under ten months left and I'll be back in the UK.

A Sojourn in Malta

The news from home was reassuring; both children were in good health and bursting with energy. Michael was at school now and taking life very seriously; he insisted in reading the daily newspaper each evening, usually upside down. All was well on the farm, Mark now doing most of the work, with Uncle Bill semi-retired and Aunt Marie doing the books. Bob and Jane were back in the UK, Jane was at Aldershot BMH, while Bob was an instructor at the Amphibious Warfare School at Poole.

Rhodes was sorting out his personal belongings. He had a large number of photos back home in Petersfield, now he had added to his collection a large print of C-Company in Oman and one of his platoon, which was very special to him. He looked at the photograph. It was a formal group with him seated in the centre of the front row with his NCOs either side of him. What made it special was that they were all smiling.

On his leaving Oman he had been presented with a mahogany shield with an Omani cap badge mounted on it. As he handled the mementos he was conscious of how lucky he had been to serve with these men.

The next morning he reported to the RSM's office. He was told to take a few days' leave and report in three days' time. He decided to look up Charlie Borg and his family, so he made his way to Paola. He spent the day there and passed by his old flat. An English woman came out of the door as he was passing and asked if he was looking for someone. Rhodes explained that he had once lived there. She chatted away saying how much she liked the flat and telling him that her husband was in the air force, based at Luqua. Rhodes walked down to Paola Square with her then said his goodbyes.

He made his way to Charlie's house. The Borgs made him very welcome, wanting to know all the news of his family. He told them about his daughter, Helen, and where they were living in England. He left at about 1600 hours and made his way back to the barracks at St Andrew's where he ate in the mess, had a few beers and had an early night.

The next day he went to Valleta and was having a coffee in Kingsway when a hand touched him on the shoulder. He turned round and gazed into the smiling face of Gail Browning. Rhodes stood up and embraced her. He was very aware how attractive she was. She never stopped talking for the next ten minutes; her husband was on the C in C's staff and feeling very important. They decided to have lunch together, Rhodes thinking that he would have to be very careful not to get involved; she was very tempting.

He told her what he had been doing, Oman and Kuwait, all about Julie and the children. She was a good listener. They shared a bottle of wine with their lunch and took a leisurely walk up to the gardens overlooking Grand Harbour. As they stood side by side looking over the battlements, her hip pressed against his leg, he could feel the beginnings of an erection and a wave of heat passed over his groin. He returned the pressure, she turned and faced him and said, 'For the next hour, Peter, we have no responsibilities, except to ourselves; after that nothing has changed in our marriages.'

With that they walked to her car, they drove to Zurrieq and parked in a quiet place on the cliff top overlooking the sea. They moved into the back seat and went into a passionate embrace. Rhodes slid his hand under her dress and slowly worked his way to the soft flesh just above her stocking top. He had developed an enormous erection which was desperate to escape the confines of his trousers. Gail undid the buttons and it sprang out; she gasped and bent forward and took him in her mouth, her tongue teased it to the point of no return and it exploded in her mouth, almost choking her.

As sanity slowly returned to them both Rhodes kissed her and apologised for the brief encounter.

Gail laughed. 'I should have realised you would have had a full tank, that's the first time I've done that, quite an experience.'

They sat talking for the next hour, it was beginning to get dark. Rhodes leaned across and kissed her; she responded, her tongue finding his. Slowly they caressed one another. She removed her panties, giving him full access to her lower body. He had unbuttoned her dress and her breasts were free, his tongue dwelt over her nipples bringing them erect, then he moved down between her legs. As his tongue entered her she started to moan and move her hips back and forth. Rhodes slipped on a condom and pushed his penis into her, lifting her legs up higher to enable him to make a full entry. Slowly he started to move in and out, the movement gained a faster rhythm; he was thrusting deeply into her, she responding by lifting her body to meet him. A final frantic thrust and they climaxed.

As their breathing slowly returned to normal Gail kissed him. 'We both needed that Peter, two old friends giving each other relief.'

She drove him back almost to the barracks; as Rhodes got out he smiled, 'Thanks for the ride.'

Gail burst out laughing. 'Here is my phone number, give me a ring,' and drove off smiling.

The next morning Rhodes made his way into Spinola. He walked into a bar and ordered a Hop Leaf beer. There was a telephone in the corner and with just a slight hesitation, Rhodes walked over and dialled Gail's number. It was answered almost straight away.

'Can you talk?' said Rhodes.

'Yes,' said Gail, 'he's gone to Naples for three days for a NATO meeting. I'll come and pick you up, where are you?'

Ten minutes later she collected him from the bar.

'I'll get some things from the NAAFI then we will go to my sister's house in Mosta and I'll make us a nice lunch.'

The house was on the outskirts of Mosta. It was quite new and very impressive, with a nice roof garden and a splendid view of the famous Mosta Dome.

Gail explained that her sister was a Wren based at Halfar; she and another Wren officer had rented the house for the last six months. Gail often visited and had a key. She told Rhodes that the two women had a relationship, so only one of the bedrooms was in use. The other was furnished but spare. She and her husband spent the occasional weekend there, but Ralph couldn't understand why the two women slept together.

He often said, 'How bloody odd those two are.'

Gail opened the wine and they took the bottle into the bedroom, where both removed their clothes and lay on the bed naked. Gail explored his body.

'You are so brown and your muscles are so firm, and look at that!'

His penis was in its excited state, responding to the attention it was receiving. Rhodes began his own exploration with his hands and mouth soon bringing Gail to an advanced stage of excitement. He moved over on top of her and parted her legs. She guided him into her. Slowly at first, then slightly quicker, he thrust himself fully into her. The tempo increased and the headboard began to knock against the wall. They both were aware of the noise but used the beat to respond to the erotic rhythm. With one final thrust that forced Gail to cry out, Rhodes climaxed with Gail a close second.

As they slowly regained their composure, Gail complained that she had lost the ability to walk. They both laughed and Rhodes got out of bed and refilled their glasses.

'Let's go up on the roof,' said Gail, putting on her bra and panties. Rhodes slipped on his underpants and followed Gail's attractive bottom up the stairs to the roof garden. It was the first week in March. The sky was clear and the sunshine made the roof garden a very pleasant place to sit; warm but not as oppressively hot as it would be in a few months' time. Rhodes and Gail were completely at ease with one another, both knew this was a very temporary affair and Rhodes's true love was Julie. After an hour Gail went down to the kitchen and prepared lunch. Twenty minutes later she called out to Rhodes to help her carry the food to the roof. They sat in the deckchairs and ate their lunch in the bright warm sun; almost perfect, thought Rhodes, almost perfect.

They both fell asleep after lunch. After an hour Rhodes woke up and watched Gail as she slept on, her breasts gently rising and falling. He moved across to her and unclipped her bra. He took one of nipples in his mouth and ran his tongue around it, causing it to harden.

Gail awoke. 'You randy bugger, are you never satisfied?' she said.

Rhodes laughed and picked her up and carried her down into the bedroom. He laid her face down on the bed and slid her panties off, he laid on top of her and inserted himself into her from behind. Gail gave a little moan as he started to move in and out of her. She pushed her bottom back into his stomach taking every part of him in. He thrust harder and harder; then gave a shudder as he came. Afterwards they lay side by side, talking quietly to one another; then they both fell asleep.

'Well, who's been sleeping in my bed?' said a woman's voice.

Another female voice said, 'And look at the size of that.'

Rhodes struggled to regain his composure, his head still spinning from his deep sleep. Gail was laughing.

'Hi, Sis, just been entertaining a friend, hope you don't mind?'

Rhodes was then introduced to the two Wren officers while he held a pillow across his groin area.

He smiled. 'I suppose I should salute, please forgive my lack of manners.'

The two girls laughed. 'You already did,' they said.

The two girls left the room so that Gail and Rhodes could get dressed. When they were ready they went into the dining room where the girl's had made a pot of tea. Rhodes and Gail spent another hour with the two girls. Finally, he thanked them for their hospitality and they left. Gail drove Rhodes back to Spinola. After promising to ring her the next day, Rhodes kissed her and made his way up to the barracks.

Rhodes arrived to a scene of frantic activity. He was told to contact Captain Pope immediately; the commando was under orders to prepare to move. When Rhodes got through to David Pope he was told to pack his kit then report to the Intelligence Office of 45 Commando. Thirty minutes later he did just that. Pope told him they were flying to Aden the next morning as part of the advance party. They were both now posted to 45 Commando, Pope as Y-Troop commander, Rhodes as one of his troop sergeants. As soon as he could, Rhodes phoned Gail to tell her the news.

She told him. 'We had a great time. Let it be our secret. Our marriages are important, so no regrets. Look after yourself, Peter, and God bless.' She then hung up. Rhodes wrote to Julie telling her he was off to Aden and would write a longer letter when he had settled in.

Return to the Red Rock

Early the next morning they were taken to Luqua airfield and by 0800 hours they were on their way. The rest of 45 Commando were going by sea. An aircraft carrier was standing by in Grand Harbour ready to sail as soon as they were aboard. Rhodes slept most of the way to Cyprus. A short stop there to refuel and then they were on their way to Kuwait. The overnight accommodation in Kuwait was basic to say the least, a far cry from the air-conditioned quarters of a few weeks ago. The aircraft took off at 0900 hours, all on board being glad to be on their way again. Just before noon they landed at Aden. Rhodes thought it was just like Oman, the same coloured mountains and hills, and the same intense heat.

The Aden Protectorate was about half the size of France and the Aden Colony about seventy-five square miles. Captain Pope told Rhodes that two troops of the commando were going up to Dhala, about ninety miles from Aden and near the border with the Yemen, where most of the trouble was coming from. They would be going up to Dhala the next day as an advance party for their Troop. 45 Commando's CO was using them because of their experience in Oman.

The next morning at 0630 hours Captain Pope, Rhodes and ten marines left for Dhala in two wide-based 15 cwt vehicles. It took them almost five hours to make the journey, but apart from one wheel change it was uneventful. Dhala was nothing special, a small town, mostly a trading place with a complex mix of nationalities. They went to the small army camp and received a warm welcome. When Captain Pope told them of his and Rhodes tour with Omani forces they were looked on with growing respect.

Over the next week they got to know their area and all was ready for the rest of their troop to join them. The CO of 45 Commando came out to visit and told Captain Pope he would rotate the two troops at Dhala every six weeks. However, he asked if Pope and Rhodes would stay there for three months to pass on their experience of the local conditions. They could hardly refuse and the colonel said he would not forget their generous offer.

Rhodes thought, We don't have any fucking choice.

His activities with Gail in Malta were now just a pleasant memory. He had written to Julie telling her where he was. Strangely he felt little guilt for the adventure with Gail, seeing it as being 'therapeutic' – like taking an aspirin for a headache.

The following week the rest of Y-Troop arrived. Rhodes knew the sergeant major from his days in Malaya and were good friends. The other sergeant had only just been promoted and was somewhat in awe of Rhodes. The marines in Y-Troop were typical, a mixture of youth and experience, but with a much higher level of morale than the average army unit. Captain Pope and Rhodes had worked out a short training programme, both of them giving talks on the local ground conditions and the importance of 'water bottle discipline'. Little did Rhodes know, but his reputation had gone before him and his exploits were much enhanced by the retelling. In fact he was now the only serving marine who held the DCM and the MM. It was even rumoured he could speak five languages including two Cantonese dialects.

The first patrol Y-Troop undertook was a three-day hike through the foothills. Rhodes had a young officer in charge of his half troop; Lieutenant Cooper was his name. David Pope had told Rhodes to let the young officer have full charge unless he was making a complete fuck-up. All went well until they made camp for the night. The troop had split into two, one half on one hill, the other half about four hundred yards away on another hill. As soon as his half troop had settled, Rhodes got them to construct a low sangar about eighteen inches high around their position. Everyone took a turn on watch, including the officer. Lieutenant Cooper thought the sangar was a waste of time and said he would not be standing a watch; he was in charge, not Sergeant Rhodes.

In the morning Rhodes stood the marines to just before dawn. Lieutenant Cooper walked out of the sangar and relieved himself twenty yards away. As his urine steamed in the early light a burst of automatic fire struck the ground in front of him and with a strangled shout he ran back to the sangar and threw himself over the top and to safety.

Rhodes called out, 'Nobody is to fire, watch for their position.'

Another burst struck the sangar and ricocheted overhead.

One marine called out, 'Saw a muzzle flash three hundred yards to our front in the saddle between those two hills.'

Another burst and it was confirmed.

'Well done, lad,' called out Rhodes. 'Corporal Smith, you and the marine on either side of you fire five rounds each, on my command. Stand by, fire.'

As the marines fired the impact of their rounds could be clearly seen. Whoever had fired those shots at Lieutenant Cooper was now long gone. Rhodes told the marines to pick up their spent cartridge cases, explaining that the Yemeni tribesmen would find a use for them otherwise. Lieutenant Cooper had reappeared. Rhodes asked him if he was okay. A somewhat subdued officer confirmed he was, apart from a badly bruised face. They all had breakfast and, after radio contact with Captain Pope, set off to patrol some hills to the north. Lieutenant Cooper asked Rhodes to take a sub-section ahead of the main body. Rhodes agreed and suggested the rest of the half troop kept well spaced out. By 1000 hours it was very hot and Rhodes warned his marines to be careful with their water intake. There would not be a chance to refill until the evening when they would meet up with the rest of Y-Troop.

At noon they had reached the top of a ridge where they could see some small caves. Rhodes thought it a good place to lay up for a couple of hours. He suggested this to Lieutenant Cooper who agreed. The officer then went and threw himself on the ground in the shade of the caves. Rhodes deployed the rest of the half troop in whatever shade they could find, warning them again about conserving their water.

He walked over to where the officer was resting, just in time to see him drinking the last drops of water from his bottle.

'Can I have a word, sir?' said Rhodes.

'What is it now?' said Lieutenant Cooper.

Rhodes knelt down by the side of the officer.

'You are responsible for these men,' said Rhodes, 'and

behaving like a stupid little prick doesn't help. You have finished off all of your water. In two hours' time you will be dehydrated and useless, get a grip.'

With that Rhodes stood up and walked to where the rest of the marines were resting, leaving the officer with his mouth wide open.

By 1500 hours the officer was in a bad way. He began to stagger and fell to the ground. Rhodes had put one of the corporals in the lead and went back to the officer. One of the marines was about to give the lieutenant a mouthful of his precious water.

'You will need all of that for yourself,' said Rhodes. 'Leave him to me.'

Rhodes helped the lieutenant to his feet and gave him enough water from his own precious supply to moisten his mouth.

'We will be back with the rest of the troop in two hours, sir, don't let yourself down.'

The lieutenant nodded, got to his feet and began to walk after the rest of the marines, with Rhodes walking a few yards behind him. Just after 1700 hours they met up with the rest of the troop, who had already constructed a low sangar big enough to provide cover for all of the troop. A fresh supply of water was issued and the troop began to settle down for the night, eating some of their dwindling rations. Rhodes reported to Captain Pope, who nodded in the direction of an exhausted-looking Lieutenant Cooper.

'What happened out there, Sergeant?'

Rhodes smiled. 'Oh, Mr Cooper was completing his education, sir, he will be all right.'

They made their way back to Dhala early the next morning, and by 1100 hours they were back in their compound. As Rhodes gathered the half troop around him, he asked Lieutenant Cooper if he would like to say a few words.

'Yes, thank you, Sergeant. Well done, all of you, we will all learn from our experiences of the last few days. Dismiss the men, Sergeant, please.'

Rhodes added a few words of his own and dismissed the marines.

Lieutenant Cooper said, 'Just a word in your ear, Sergeant Rhodes, don't ever call me a stupid little prick again.' Then with a smile, 'Thanks for the help out there, it was much appreciated.'

As Rhodes watched the officer walk away, he thought to himself, I think he's got the makings of a half-decent sort.

The next couple of months flew by with lots of newsy letters from Julie. She had overheard Michael tell a school friend, 'My dad's a general in the marines.' When Julie got him home she told him not to tell untruths and that Daddy was a sergeant.

Michael had said, 'But he's brave enough to be a general, Mummy.'

Julie said, 'I couldn't argue with that.'

They did another tour in the hills around Dhala, then Y-Troop were withdrawn to Aden, and the dubious pleasures of patrolling the hostile streets of the Crater area. Lieutenant Cooper and Rhodes now got on really well and Cooper was becoming a fine officer. Rhodes knew how far he could go with the lieutenant and didn't overstep the mark. A chance meeting with an officer from the French Embassy gave Rhodes the opportunity to brush up his French. The contact resulted in an invitation to a weekend sailing trip around Aden's coastline. David Pope and Ralph Cooper completed the English crew and with their three French friends had a relaxing weekend. Rhodes wrote to Julie about the boat trip, making sure she knew no women were on board.

The street patrols were as hazardous as patrolling the hills. Rhodes was leading a section of marines when a grenade sailed over a wall and landed in the middle of the marines. They scattered and threw themselves to the ground, the grenade failed to explode and twenty relieved Royal Marines gave thanks to the inefficiency of the Arab bomb makers. A few days later two marines from another troop were badly wounded in a street ambush. One of the wounded marines later died; the first, but sadly not the last, to lose his life in Aden.

A week after the fatal shooting, Y-Troop did a sweep through an area of the Crater district. Some shots were fired at them from an old warehouse. Lieutenant Cooper and Rhodes led an attack on the building and in a savage encounter five Arabs were killed and one marine was slightly wounded. The week ended with another vicious encounter, with a further four Arabs dying. Captain Pope and Rhodes remembered their colonel's advice from their days in Oman, 'Don't let the bastards get away with anything, always respond and be as ruthless as they are.' This was the kind of language the marines understood and it became the watchword of their troop.

Towards the end of September Y-Troop were sent to Dhala for three weeks. There had been two attacks on the outskirts of the town and the people there were getting jumpy. Y-Troop spread themselves out over a mile, guarding the route to Dhala from the mountains. They built a line of sangars two hundred yards apart, six men to a sangar. They called it the Red Line as their unit's lanyard was red. Rhodes was in charge of the extreme right sangar. He and his five marines worked hard each day to improve their small strong point. Each morning at 0900 hours Captain Pope came along and visited them, bringing food, water and the mail.

One morning he called Rhodes to one side. 'Remember the favour we did the colonel when we first went to Dhala? Well, he's letting us go home a month early; we fly home on 3 November.'

After they had been in the Red Line for a week, Rhodes and the sangar to his left came under a sustained attack a few minutes after midnight. The marines were thankful that the work they had put in to strengthen their fortress was now paying off. They were able to return fire from comparative safety and the Arab attackers withdrew after an hour. Over the next two nights they were again attacked, with the same result. When Captain Pope visited the next day with the food and water, Rhodes suggested that as soon as it was dark he should take his men out and wait in ambush a few hundred yards to their front. Captain Pope reluctantly agreed, saying he would tell the marines to their left what they intended to do.

As soon as it was dark, Rhodes led his small force out from the security of the sangar and laid his ambush. It was a very dark night with thick cloud preventing the moonlight being of any assistance. It soon became very cold and a chill wind made life out in the open unpleasant. Rhodes was considering moving his men back to the comparative comfort of the sangar when he heard a noise from directly ahead of them.

For the first time that night a shaft of moonlight broke

through the clouds. About twenty yards from their position were a group of men. Rhodes's small group raised their rifles. He had told them not to fire unless he did. Success or failure was going to be decided by their discipline. When the tribesmen got within eight yards Rhodes quietly and calmly said, 'Fire.' The marines with their SLRs probably got off thirty rounds in total in about four seconds. The effect on the approaching tribesmen was dramatic. They had been closely grouped so as to not lose contact in the dark. This led to eight of the ten men being hit in the first few seconds.

A few rounds came in the marines' direction. One struck a stone in front of Rhodes causing a rock splinter to slice across his cheekbone. Another burst of fire from the marines met with no response and the night went strangely quiet. Rhodes called out each marine's name in his group, thankfully getting a response from each of his men. With great caution Rhodes moved his men forward in extended line to check the condition of the fallen tribesmen. Six were clearly dead, another six were wounded, four seriously, the other two either shot in the arm or leg.

They first collected the weapons of the tribesmen, then moved the wounded back to the sangar. Rhodes got on the radio and asked for two men to come and assist from the sangar to his left. Two marines arrived within minutes calling out, 'Y-Troop, Y-Troop,' and making sure they were not fired at. For the rest of the night the marines did what they could for the seriously wounded men. Rhodes was well aware that if he had still been in Oman, they would not have taken any prisoners, but here it was under a different set of rules.

When morning finally came, two more of the Arabs had died and in response to their radio message Captain Pope arrived with ten marines and two vehicles to take away the dead and wounded. David Pope congratulated Rhodes and his group on their success.

He told Rhodes the slash on his cheekbone would only add to his reputation, saying, 'It's like a duelling scar, very smart.'

A search of the area around the ambush produced an astonishing find, a small machine gun mounted on two wheels, with two fifty-round drum magazines. They all agreed it was of Russian manufacture and had most likely come from Egypt.

Rhodes mentioned to Captain Pope that they had seen them before during the landings at Port Said.

They finally completed their stint at Dhala and moved back to Aden. Rhodes had told Julie that he hoped to be home in time for Christmas. She, in her letters, had said, 'When does not matter, just come home safe.'

The remainder of Rhodes's time in Aden was almost uneventful and at last he and Captain Pope said their goodbyes to Y-Troop.

The colonel saw them both before they left and thanked them for their efforts, saying, 'I would have you back tomorrow if I could.'

Completing the Circle

On 2 November 1960 Rhodes and Captain Pope flew out of Aden and started their journey back to the UK. Two days later a surprised and delighted Julie answered a knock on the door at their Petersfield cottage; Rhodes was home again.

Rhodes lost track of the embraces he gave, Julie (a long one), Mrs Grey (a bit shorter), and the two children, Michael and Helen (lots of wet kisses and a wet face, Michael had a runny nose). Rhodes handed out the presents he had brought home.

Julie touched his face. 'That's a fresh scar, Peter, was it worth it?'

Rhodes smiled but did not reply. That night when they finally got to bed, Rhodes gently kissed and then made love to Julie. They started slowly and built up to a deeply satisfying climax. Julie sighed and kissed his scarred cheekbone and placed her small warm hand on his penis.

'It's gone to sleep,' she said.

'Just a little nap,' said Rhodes. 'It's not as young as it was.'

Julie gave a deep sigh. 'None of us are,' she said and fell asleep in Rhodes's arms.

The next day they went for a long walk in the country. The days were getting shorter and winter was on its way. The deep tan Rhodes had developed over the last eighteen months was a subject of conversation when he and Julie did some shopping in Petersfield.

When they got back to the cottage Mrs Grey said, 'There was a phone call for you from a Commander Radcliffe. He wants you to ring him back, he left a number.'

Julie looked at Rhodes. 'Tell him to bugger off, Peter, you have only just come home.'

Rhodes picked up the phone and dialled the number. A familiar voice said, 'Welcome home, old son, I just spoke to David Pope, he said you enjoyed yourselves. Just thought I would mention your next posting, it's a two-year appointment as a drill instructor at the depot, RM Barracks, Deal.'

Rhodes thanked him for the information. Radcliffe said he would keep in touch, then hung up.

Julie was delighted. 'We will rent a little house, Peter, for the two years near the sea front. The children will love it and it will give them the chance to meet new friends.'

Mrs Grey was not quite so pleased, but could see Julie had made up her mind. The rest of their leave passed quickly. They went to see Aunt Marie and Uncle Bill. Mark and Linda were very happy together but were unlikely to have any children because of a medical problem Linda had. They managed a couple of days down in Plymouth. Mary and Hal Higgins were delighted to see them and they exchanged all their news. In the last week of their leave they went to Deal for a couple of days and found a three bed-roomed house, one street in from the sea front, just a few minutes walk from the barracks.

On the day before he was due to report to the barracks, Rhodes and Julie moved into their furnished house. The children loved it. The landlord was a retired naval officer and very pleased to have them as tenants.

The next day Rhodes reported to the RSM and the commanding officer. He had served with both of them before; the signs for the future were good. He felt the wheel had turned full circle for him, this was where it had all begun.

The RSM told him he would assist one of the other drill instructors for two weeks then he would be given the next squad of recruits as their instructor. Rhodes appreciated the chance to fine tune before he took over his first squad. He enjoyed working with the other instructors and listened to whatever advice they had to offer. The time passed quickly and Rhodes took great pains to have everything spotless for the big day.

The new recruits arrived at East Barracks on the Monday afternoon, suffering the same indignities Rhodes had done almost twelve years earlier. They were given the same instructions to be in their barrack room at 0800 hours to meet their instructor. The recruits had looked at the photos of the drill instructors in the reception block. They had asked one of the corporals which one would be theirs.

He looked at them and smiled. 'The big sergeant with all the medals.'

The next morning at 0750 hours Rhodes marched into East Barracks. He made his way to the reception block and checked his appearance in the large mirror at the bottom of the stairs. As the barrack clock started its preamble to striking the hour, he climbed the stairs to the recruits' room. On the first stroke of the hour Rhodes opened the door and entered. He stood for a few seconds, letting the thirty-six pairs of eyes look him over.

'My name is Sergeant Rhodes and I am your squad instructor. You will obey without question all of the orders I will give you. In return for your full cooperation, I will turn you into Royal Marines, and make your parents and loved ones proud of you. Now, when I say "Move", you will double outside and fall in three ranks. You will do this in absolute silence. Move.'

The recruits did as they were told. As the last one passed him Rhodes smiled. Yes, the wheel had turned full circle.

Epilogue

It was the middle of August 2000. Former RSM Peter Rhodes, DCM, MM, BEM, Royal Marines, stood in the shade next to his hire car. His wife, Julie, was having her hair done in the hotel saloon.

'I'll be about twenty minutes,' she had said thirty minutes ago.

They were in the last few days of their two-week holiday; it was a nostalgic time for them both, a return to Malaysia after almost fifty years.

They had spent the previous week on the mainland, based in Kuala Lumpur, and had visited Taiping, where Julie had worked at the military hospital. Rhodes had been treated there after he had been wounded. A visit to the old A-Troop camp at Tambun had been a great disappointment to Rhodes. The house which had been at the centre of their small camp was in a desperate state and was in an advanced condition of decay, it being overwhelmed by the advancing vegetation.

What had not changed was the looming, sinister row of gunongs. They were like massive sentries guarding the past, present and the future. Their limestone mass opposite the former home of the marines had always been there and always would be.

A visit to the military cemetery at Batu Gajah had been of importance to both Julie and Rhodes. As they looked at the graves of the Royal Marines who lay in peace there; Rhodes could still put a face to their names. After giving each marine a quiet greeting they moved over to the European cemetery. They soon found the graves they were looking for. Helen and Paul Dupré were buried next to one another, although Paul had died two years before Helen. Rhodes and Julie could not contain their sorrow and, clinging to one another, they wept.

As Rhodes waited for his wife he thought of their other friends. Julie's mother had died five years earlier and lay next to her husband in Petersfield churchyard. Uncle Bill and Aunt

Marie had passed on, Mark and Linda still had the farm but they had installed a manager to run it. June seemed to have disappeared, they could find no trace of her in Chatham, perhaps that was how she wanted it.

David Pope had reached the top in the corps, retiring as Lieutenant General Sir David Pope, MC, DSO, CBE, Commandant General Royal Marines.

After leaving the marines Rhodes had been persuaded to work at the Ministry of Defence with Rear Admiral Michael Radcliffe, CBE, Royal Navy. The fifteen years he had served here had given him a very nice pension to supplement the one from the Royal Marines.

Hal and Mary Higgins were living in Herne Bay in contented retirement and Rhodes and Julie saw them at least twice a year. David Pope always sent an invitation to them all to attend the last night of the Mountbatten concerts at the Albert Hall. They sat in General Pope's private box, Rhodes and Julie, Hal and Mary, Admiral Radcliffe and his latest girlfriend, and David and Becky Pope. After being enthralled by the magnificent Massed Bands of the Royal Marines, they all went to dinner together.

Bob and Jane Jones had also kept in touch. Bob had left the marines after twelve years and joined the Essex Police, while Jane had worked at the Colchester Military Hospital. Bob had retired with the rank of chief inspector, so everyone had done well. Each Christmas they received a card from Gail and Ralph Browning who had retired to Malta and were living in a house overlooking St Paul's Bay.

Rhodes and Julie's children, Michael and Helen, were doing well. Helen was a schoolteacher in Chichester. She was married to a doctor and had two children. Michael had followed his father into the Royal Marines and was a colour sergeant on the staff of the commandant general at Whale Island in Portsmouth. He was married to Susan, who was a civil servant, and they had two children, both boys, one about to finish his training in the Royal Marines, the other waiting to join.

Rhodes looked at his watch, and then at the entrance to their hotel. They were staying at the Casuarina Beach Hotel on the Batu Ferringhi road in Penang, not far from where Sandy Croft leave centre had been. A school now stood on that site and some of the original buildings were still in use. Julie suddenly appeared, looking as attractive as ever. As she reached the car she smiled.

'Getting a bit pissed off, were we?'

Rhodes protested he was not and they got into the car.

As they drove along the road with air-conditioning going full blast, Rhodes reflected on the value of friends like Mick Radcliffe. When they had met last in February at the Albert Hall, Rhodes had mentioned they were flying out to Malaysia in August.

'What airline are you using?' had asked Radcliffe.

'Oh, Malaysian,' had said Rhodes.

'Oh, I know one of the directors,' Radcliffe had added.

Rhodes thought no more of it, but when they checked in at Heathrow the smiling clerk told them they had been upgraded to business class outward and return.

'Compliments of the board,' she had said.

'And where are we going today?' said Julie.

Rhodes smiled. 'It's a surprise.'

'Well,' said Julie, 'this must be a first. Your surprises usually take place in the bedroom.'

As they drove through the streets of Penang, they noticed that all the traffic lights had dispensed with the amber, they went straight from red to green, and green to red.

They arrived at Penang Hill and Rhodes parked his car in a shady spot. A smiling Malay boy took his one Ringet parking fee.

As they walked together up the road, Julie looked at Rhodes and said, 'They say it's ten degrees cooler at the top.'

Fifty years disappeared in a flash.

'You are very lovely,' croaked Rhodes.

Julie laughed, her eyes sparkling. 'And so are you.'

And together they walked hand in hand to the waiting cable car.

Lightning Source UK Ltd.
Milton Keynes UK
UKOW04f2051180915

258903UK00001B/1/P

9 781844 260300